Relationship Material

Rachel Spangler

RELATIONSHIP MATERIAL
© 2025 BY RACHEL SPANGLER

THIS TRADE PAPERBACK ORIGINAL IS PUBLISHED BY
BIGGER TABLE BOOKS, FREDONIA, NY 14063

SUBSTANTIVE EDIT: LYNDA SANDOVAL
COPY EDIT: AVERY BROOKS
COVER DESIGN: ANN MCMAN
AUTHOR PHOTO: ANNA BURKE
TYPESETTING: SUSAN SPANGLER
FIRST PRINTING: JUNE 2025

ISBN: 979-8-9991392-0-7

For Susie, who continues to help me chisel masterpieces from blocks of marble. This, like so many other things, is all your fault.

One

"What a week." Robin Walker crashed onto a chair at the first open table she came to. Tossing her head back, she stared at the high, tin ceiling of her favorite local queer bar before sighing heavily. "Am I right?"

"Such a week," her colleague Tegan agreed, tousling Robin's dark curls a bit before sagging next to her.

"Week?" Gillian asked. "What a year."

Tegan bumped their boss's shoulder with her own. "It's only the middle of April."

"I wasn't talking about the calendar," Gillian said drolly, without hiding the hint of affection in her tone.

Robin sat up to see their ever-elegant leader gracefully take the seat across from her and cross one leg over the other. "You seem to be holding up, G-Money, but the first round's on me."

"I'm going to let that happen." Gillian smiled. "I'm not sure I can get out of this chair again without collapsing, or at least groaning."

"You're in a sapphic bar," Robin said. "No one here minds women groaning."

Gillian rolled her eyes. "I'll take a martini."

Robin sat forward and smirked. "Your wish is my command, but first, tell me you like it extra dirty."

"Dry," Gillian deadpanned.

"Like her wit and humor," Tegan added.

"You two are in rare form tonight." Gillian glanced around. "Where's Brooke when I need her?"

"Damn fine question," Tegan said. "We need someone to restore balance."

"Balance?" Robin snorted playfully. "You're looking for someone to kiss you senseless."

Tegan shrugged. "I can hold space for both things at once."

"Spoken like a therapist who's about to get her full license." Robin gave her a little salute.

"Oh good, another transition." Gillian shook her head.

"If it's anything like the last one, I'm here for it." Robin waggled her eyebrows.

Brooke seemed to materialize out of the crowd, and clasping her hands on Tegan's shoulders from behind, she dropped a kiss atop her head. Tegan's eyes lit up. She hopped out of her seat and practically into Brooke's arms.

Tegan cupped her girlfriend's face in her hands and whispered, "I missed you."

"Same. So much."

Gillian shook her head. "They were apart for like, twelve hours, right?"

She shrugged. "Time, like all the best things in life, is relative."

"Not true. That martini you promised me is not relative, and it better become one of the best things in my life soon."

"Gotcha, Gilly Bean." She glanced quickly at Brooke and Tegan, who were totally absorbed in each other. "You two want the usual?"

They didn't respond, didn't even seem to know they'd been spoken to.

She and Gillian sat there for a long couple of seconds before her boss pushed back from the table. "Come on. Let's give them a minute and get ourselves bitter drinks to offset all their sugary sweetness."

"Good plan."

Robin threaded her way through the after-work press of people. The vibe, a little relaxed with a dash of cruising at the periphery, happened to be her personal favorite, and she tapped her toes to the Whitney Houston dance beat being played at a reasonable volume while she waited for the bartender to bring their drinks.

Turning her head to the side, she caught Gillian watching her with the slightest quirk of a smile. "Yes?"

Gillian shook her head. "You're so cool all the time."

"Thank you. Also, why would I not be?"

Gillian lifted one shoulder in a half-hearted shrug.

"Come on." Robin wrapped an arm around her waist. "What's got you out of sorts?"

"Nothing. These are my normal sorts. They're perfectly in their regular place."

Robin waited patiently, silently, creating space even in the increasingly crowded bar.

Gillian broke first by glancing back at their table where Tegan and Brooke sat, hands and heads together. "They're like that all the time."

"Fucking adorable?"

Gillian laughed. "Yes."

"And?"

"I should be used to it by now. It's been, like, six months. Intellectually I know they're head-over-heels in love, and yet there are still these moments when I see my best friend practically stick her tongue down my supervisee's throat, and it's a little hard to process."

"That's super fair, G-Major." Robin gave her a little squeeze. "I think that's why I like to see it. Love against all the odds, and from Brooke of all people. Boggles the mind and fills the heart."

Gillian searched her expression, as though she might be joking, or at least exaggerating. Robin got the reaction frequently, and she stood comfortably under inspection. "It doesn't weird you out even a little that our entire dynamic's turned upside down?"

"Oh yeah, it's weird and wild, which is my jam, but it doesn't have to be yours." Robin nodded back to their friends and colleagues as Brooke kissed Tegan quickly on the cheek. "I really dig watching them together."

3

"Because you have voyeuristic tendencies."

"Aw, thanks for affirming my kink, Boo, but in this case, I meant that at work we see so many people fighting to get it right, struggling, grappling, falling down, and missing the mark."

"We're therapists. It's the job."

"And I dig that, too, every step of the journey, but some parts are better than others, and love's the best. It's freaking beautiful when people get it right, and those two,"— Robin nodded again to Brooke and Tegan—"they got it right. Right for them, right for each other, right for the balance of the world and the cosmos. I get what you mean, though. The sappy stage isn't right for you at the moment, even though plenty of women would love a shot at that with you. It's not right for me either. Not now, or probably ever, which is okay, too."

Gillian arched her eyebrows.

"What?"

"Ever? You're going to wax poetic about love being right for the entire universe, then say, 'None for me, thanks?'"

"I've got nothing but love. Love for them, love for you, love for my job, love for the beautiful sapphic population of Buffalo, as a whole, and several specific individuals, in particular."

Gillian laughed. "So not a 'not for me' on love so much as a 'not for me' on monogamy."

Robin let her eyes wander around the room. "I have so much love to give. I could give some love to the bartender with her black tank top." She tossed a few bills on the bar as their drinks arrived. "I could give love to the soccer team sitting in the corner over there. I could give love to the cutie at the end of the bar with a hungry edge in her eyes."

"So you've already done an inventory of everyone here?"

"A love inventory, boss."

Gillian rolled her eyes with more playfulness.

"I've got love for you, too." She went up onto her tiptoes, fully intending to smooch her cheek, but Gillian stopped her

4

with a palm on her forehead. "I'm good, thanks. Grab the drinks."

They both took a glass in each hand and carefully waded back to the table.

"Okay, break it up, you two." Gillian set a martini in front of Brooke and kept one for herself. "Brooke, if you're going to run off back to college when the mood strikes you, the least you can do is tell us what you're learning."

"Or teaching," Robin amended as she passed a strawberry daiquiri to Tegan. "You're molding young, impressionable minds other than Tegan's, right?"

"As long as it's only their minds." Tegan sipped her daiquiri, then stuck out her artificially red tongue at Robin.

"Don't tempt me with a good time."

"For the love of God, right the ship, Brookesy," Gillian pleaded.

"Yeah, I'm with you on this one. I'm not sure I'm molding any minds but my own this semester. I'm teaching the intro classes, of course, and because I'm a glutton for punishment, I'm taking a seminar in restorative justice practices."

"Oh yeah, that sounds cool." Robin sipped her cider. "Can't wait for you to come back and bring the new tools with you. Hey, you are coming back, right?"

Gillian covered her ears. "If the answer is 'no,' please don't tell me yet."

Brooke laughed. "I've got four more weeks of this semester, Tegan has six more weeks of supervision, then we'll both take some time to sit, breathe, and talk about the future. I promise you'll be the first people to know how we plan to proceed."

"I'm going to pretend you just said, 'Of course I'm coming back. Who wouldn't return to such awesome colleagues and the best boss ever.' Okay?" Robin asked as she dribbled a couple drops of hard cider down the front of her black T-shirt.

"Oh, that part's true without a doubt." Brooke raised a glass to Gillian. "I do like teaching in so many ways, but working with Maura is … a lot. She's not in my business daily,

5

but she's the department chair, and she runs her faculty meetings much the same way she runs her research."

Gillian grimaced, and Robin got the sense this was about to become an inside conversation. The two of them had a long history of shared memories and acquaintances, and while she occasionally summoned some genuine interest for things like Brooke's boss, Friday night, after a long week at work, was not one of those times. As her mind drifted, so did her gaze.

The bar wasn't slammed yet, and Robin preferred it that way. She had a tendency to overload on high energy, as though too much of her own natural frequency could short out her system. She favored chill vibes she could turn up or down at will, so she tended to try to make a genuine connection early in the evening. Thankfully, interesting people were an abundant resource.

She didn't have a type, at least not physically. She loved stories. She loved quirks. She loved mischievous smiles and a twinkle in the eye. Genuine goodwill and generalized affection soaked her senses as she scanned the faces, and sometimes the bodies, of the people around her. She wasn't on a hunt so much as an exploration, a chance to see, to connect, to learn and experience. Even existing authentically in that mindset upped her pulse a bit.

Everything buzzed with untapped energy, from the woman behind her, who smelled like vanilla, to the young butch collecting darts from a pin-pocked board on the wall, to the couple making eyes at each other across a nearby booth.

"We're allowed to change a few things. No need to repeat the floor mattress performance this time around." Tegan's voice pulled Robin back, reminding her that sometimes she didn't have to eavesdrop on anyone else to hear the most interesting conversation in the room.

She raised her eyebrows. "Mattress performance?"

"Of course that brought you back to us," Gillian scoffed. "We were talking about the fascinating decisions of where these two are going to shack up tonight."

6

"Tegan's place still holds a sort of bohemian charm," Brooke offered.

"But she's basically living with you," Robin finished. "Everyone knows you're going to move in together as soon as T-Cup here has her full license."

Tegan nearly choked on her drink. "We haven't talked about it yet."

"Well, maybe try it out for a week. See how it goes," she said, not sure what the big deal was. Anyone could see these two were going all the way to white dresses and picket fences. Why pretend either of them were made for downtown lofts and carrying toothbrushes in their purses as they slipped back and forth? Not that Robin saw a problem in the latter. In fact... "And while you're at it, how about you let me get a key to your loft sometime? If you're not using the floor mattress, maybe she's lonely, and my place being all the way over on the west side isn't always convenient to work."

Gillian shook her head. "Not convenient to our office, or not convenient to taking women home from the bar?"

Robin leaned back in her chair, dark eyes wandering over to a woman walking past before turning back to them without the slightest inclination to deny the charge. "There might be multiple factors involved."

They all laughed.

"What?" She grinned, liking the idea more and more by the minute. "You have to admit, Tegan bagged the biggest prize of them all, and the trajectory has been epic ever since. All I'm saying is, if your location was enough to get our sweetly steadfast Brooke to follow you home from the bar, maybe it's got some magic to it."

Brooke wrapped an arm around Tegan and pulled her a little closer. "I will not deny the presence of magic from the moment we met, but I can say for certain it had nothing to do with the proximity of her apartment."

Gillian made a noise that sounded like the cross between a snort and gag. "If you weren't the happiest I have ever seen you, I might have to choke Tegan with my bare hands for turning my best friend into such a sap."

Brooke smiled and shrugged. "So happy, Gilly."

"Wait," Robin cut in, not wanting to go all the way back to gushing when she still had an offer on the table. "Solely Tegan magic to seal the deal?"

Brooke glanced at Tegan, who sipped her drink as if trying to hide her smile. "One hundred percent Tegan magic."

"Damn," Robin mumbled, only half-hearing them as the person who'd stepped through the door stood steady and sexy, backlit by the fading sun. Tall, with dark hair, and the jaw of a Greek sculpture in marble, Brooke's mention of magic floated through her mind as she tried to remember they were talking about Tegan and not whatever divine creature had graced them with such a dynamic presence. "Super unfortunate."

She must've continued to stare, her brain trying to catalog qualities, like the way rugged hiking pants hung from slim hips, or the cocky hook of one thumb hitched through an empty belt loop, or the hollow of a throat constricting under the open buttons of an olive-green Henley. The newcomer lifted aviator sunglasses from the bridge of a slightly upturned nose, revealing eyes bright and brimming with light.

Tegan snapped her fingers in front of Robin's glazed-over gaze. "Why unfortunate?"

"Because the most stunning human I've ever seen just walked into the bar."

They all turned in unison, and a smile of brilliant recognition spread across the most alluring lips in Robin's recollection. The expression wasn't just all-encompassing, it was chest-kicking, heartbreakingly beautiful, but before she could even process her reaction, much less what inspired it, Gillian and Brooke vaulted from their chairs simultaneously.

"Sawyer!"

Two

Sawyer Stroud-Barton's heart swelled all the way into their throat as Gillian and Brooke practically climbed over tables to get across the bar. In an instant they were enveloped in a crushing group hug. Sawyer sagged into the embrace, soaking up the press of bodies long missed. How had they kept themself from remembering the sensations of letting loved ones hold you up and hold you together? If this feeling didn't eclipse all the other emotions associated with a homecoming, it at least offered a healthy dose of balance.

Sawyer wrapped one arm around Gillian and the other around Brooke, then squeezed tightly. "Man, it seems like y'all might've missed me or something."

Brooke stepped back, tears shimmering in blue eyes. "So much."

Gillian took a different approach and jabbed an index finger sharply into Sawyer's ribs.

"Ouch. What's that for?"

"Two years."

"No."

"Yes." Gillian gave them a little shove. "It's too long."

Sawyer surveyed her, noting little change in Gillian. The woman hardly seemed to have aged from the day they'd literally bumped into each other on campus more than ten years ago, Gilly carrying a stack of books, Sawyer carrying a large mushroom and pepperoni pizza.

Brooke, on the other hand, looked somehow younger than when they'd last been together.

What did they see staring back at them?

9

"What?" Gillian pressed. "No witty comeback?"

Sawyer shook their head. "None witty enough to justify my grave lapse in time and friendship. It has been entirely too long."

"You're here now." Brooke rested a hand on their shoulder, then seemed to notice a difference. Sliding her palm only slightly lower, she arched an eyebrow as the corner of her lips twitched up. Of course Brooke would be quietly affirming without making a fuss.

Sawyer lifted a finger to their lips for a second. A busy bar on a first night home wasn't the time or the place to get too serious. With these two around, there'd be ample opportunity for deeper conversations.

Time.

Sawyer had lost track of it, burned it, tried to store it up, and fought against it for so long they could barely remember seeing it as an abundant sort of luxury. "Buy me a drink?"

"A drink? I'm so happy, I'd buy you anything." Brooke beamed. "How about a pony? You want a pony?"

"I'd love a pony, and I actually have a story to tell you about that."

Gillian laughed. "Of course you do. Let's start with drinks and fries, then stories, and we'll maybe work around to ponies."

"Glad to see you're still the best at working a plan." Sawyer grinned. "I'd love to kick back and catch up a bit before I collapse from the jet lag."

"I'll go place the order. Let Brooke make introductions, but don't divulge the good stuff until I get back." Gillian headed for the bar.

Brooke gave their arm a little tug. "I know a couple of people who are going to be excited to meet you."

"Does my reputation precede me?"

"Always. You're so perfectly you."

"As are you."

"I might surprise you." A smile quirked her lips as they neared the table. "Sawyer, meet my girlfriend, Tegan Cooper."

10

"Hi, Tegan—wait, what?"

Brooke shook her head and laughed as Sawyer did a double take at the beautiful, and obviously younger, woman grinning vibrantly.

"Did she say 'girlfriend'?"

Tegan nodded. "For about six months, and I'm so glad to finally meet you."

They shook Tegan's hand and turned back to Brooke. "Six months? I can't—I mean, good for you. How did you leave the office long enough to get out of your own way?"

"Oh, the office played a major role," another woman said, and when Sawyer turned to see her, they didn't know how they could've possibly missed such a stunning creature until this moment. "I'm Robin Walker."

"Please tell me you're not Gillian's girlfriend." The words were out before they realized they'd even had such a thought, much less delivered it aloud, with an almost desperate edge.

Robin threw back her head and laughed, black, wavy hair shimmering in the neon light and sending a shiver of something darker through Sawyer. "Absolutely not, but please, please, please repeat that when she gets back over here, so we can all watch the blood drain from her face."

Sawyer laughed along, enjoying the mischief glinting in her dark eyes. "I like you already."

"I knew you would." Robin sat back down. "I've heard so much about you over the years."

"Years?" They sat down. "A part of me still can't believe it's been that long, but apparently a lot happened while I was away."

"Yes, and we actually met Robin before you left," Brooke explained. "She was our supervisee at the time."

"I'm 100 percent sure I'd remember if we'd met." Sawyer leaned forward and stopped short of adding that they might not have left at all without getting to know her a little better first.

"You refused to visit the office, and we weren't parading people under our professional obligation out to bars with

11

known ruffians," Brooke said, then with a quick glance at Tegan added, "yet."

"Wait." Sawyer held up a hand. "You're all therapists?"

"Yes." Gillian returned with drinks, then nodded to Tegan. "She's still pre-licensed."

"And you two"—they worried their lower lip and ran a few calculations before turning to Brooke—"have been together six months?"

Brooke nodded slowly.

"Oh, there's a story here, isn't there?"

"Bingo," Robin said with perhaps too much glee. "Wait until you hear how it happened. Absolute gloriousness."

Sawyer turned toward her fully. "Tell me every single detail."

"Well, they met right here. Neither one of them knew who the other one was until the morning after they'd already—"

"Okay, okay," Brooke cut back in. "Not *all* the details, please."

"Agreed," Gillian said.

"The point is, you all work together in Gilly's office?" Sawyer asked.

"Well ..." Tegan drew out the word with a bit of side-eye toward Brooke. "One of us needed a little professional distance."

"Because of the things you're not letting Robin tell me?"

Robin pulled a business card from her pocket and slipped it across the table. "Call me. I'll talk."

"Hey now!" Brooke said.

Tegan laughed and kissed exactly the spot on Brooke's cheek where her complexion had begun to burn. "Let Robin do it sometime when you're not around."

"She's an unreliable narrator," Brooke protested.

Robin grinned. "Creative license."

Sawyer shook their head. "Surely you're not a therapist, though."

"I am." Robin tapped her finger on the business card.

"I call bullshit. You're over here stirring pots and gossiping and telling people's stories with flair. Is that even allowed?"

"The concept of 'allowed' has gotten a little loose in your absence, a fact Robin revels in," Gillian responded dryly.

"Come on, Gilly, it's not that dire." Robin patted her boss's hand before turning back to Sawyer. "I'm a therapist, not *their* therapist."

"I see," Sawyer said, still harboring some doubts.

"I'm serious." Robin pushed. "I'm the fun one."

Sawyer pursed their lips. "Fun therapist? Isn't that an oxymoron?"

Everyone else around the table objected at once, and Sawyer chuckled. "I just wanted to make sure I still had what it takes to get you all riled up. News flash, I do."

"I'd expect nothing less, but you can tease us all later," Gillian said. "Tell us where you've been. The last I heard was a postcard from Norway."

"I got one from Iceland," Brooke added.

Sawyer grinned as a few memories surfaced of midnight sun and lupine and glaciers. "When I left here, I only intended to take some time in Canada, up through the French provinces, but once I wandered into St. John's, it's a hop, skip, and a jump toward the edge of the Nordic countries. Then I ended up in Germany for a bit, and you know how it goes. I got laid up over a long winter on the Rhine."

"I do not know how that goes at all," Gillian said.

"Come with me next time. I'll teach you."

"No." Brooke cut back in. "No talking about next time. You just got here … from Germany?"

"Germany was last winter, and I did intend to come back from there. I was even en route, back the way I'd come, when I met a woman in Reykjavik who studies geothermal activity."

"Of course you did," Gillian said, but she couldn't hide a smile, and Sawyer realized how much they'd missed watching her try.

13

"You know how I love to learn new things, so I spent a couple months exploring volcanoes and geysers."

"So freaking cool," Robin muttered with a hint of awe.

Sawyer turned to see a glint of something adventurous in her eyes. "Do you travel?"

"Not as much as I'd like."

"Still more than the rest of us," Tegan said. "She went scuba diving a few months ago."

"Nice." Sawyer lifted their glass in salute. "I'm open water certified. You should see the water in Silfra, Iceland, where the tectonic plates meet."

Robin's chest rose and fell a little quicker, drawing Sawyer's eyes and attention for a second.

"Did you cross the northern lights off your bucket list?" Brooke pulled them back.

"Oh Brookesy, you have no idea."

"Tell us."

Sawyer practically melted under the memory. "It's what sent me back east, and, well, also north. The first time I saw the aurora dance, I don't know, something in me fell into a trance. I chased it all the way to the Arctic. Ended up in Lapland."

"Finland?" Gillian asked. "Buffalo winters weren't cold enough for you?"

They laughed, but it died a bit on their lips. "It's weird. Part of the time warp, I guess. You go for the long nights, and then one day there's no day at all. I sort of disappeared into a different kind of existence. You forget things in the dark, or maybe your mind opens different doors. Things that used to seem important. You can't see yourself the same way, except by firelight."

Sawyer realized everyone was staring at them, expectant, or maybe concerned, and they sat up a little straighter. "Anyway. By March the sun rose all the way, and the people I'd been working with all winter went their separate ways. One day I sort of looked up and said, 'I wonder what Gilly and Brookesy are doing right now.'"

"So, you just started back toward Buffalo?" Tegan asked as if she found the whole thing mystifying.

"I did. You have to understand, sometimes these two have the same pull as the aurora borealis."

Tegan looked at Brooke in a way that made Sawyer's chest ache. "Oh, I get it."

Robin laughed. "I'm not sure I'm all the way there, but it's pretty cool that you still feel the pull toward home after all you've seen and done."

"Home." Sawyer grimaced. "It's a very complicated concept for me. I guess it's more of a feeling than a place."

Robin leaned forward, resting her elbows on the table and her chin in her hands as she seemingly gave Sawyer every ounce of her attention. "Do you feel it right now?"

Sawyer took a second to look around the bar, then back at the women around the table as they searched their feelings. There was something warm and comfortable, something familiar, and also, something below the surface they weren't quite ready to dredge up yet. Still, when their eyes landed back on Robin's darker ones, a hint of electricity caused the hair on the back of their neck to stand on end.

"I'm not sure if 'home' is the most apt description, but I do get the sense I'm meant to be here."

Sawyer fully sank onto Gillian's couch, and their muscles virtually melted into the cushions. "Do you ever get so physically tired you feel like you might sob if your brain would shut off long enough to let you?"

Gillian smiled down at them, a mix of sweetness and concern. "We've had a big night. It's okay to shut it down."

They yawned. "I'm not great at shutting it down."

"How can I help?" Gillian eased back toward the armchair on the other side of the coffee table.

15

"Don't you dare." Sawyer laughed. "If you assume the therapy position, I will go back to Iceland right now."

Gillian rolled her eyes. "Where would you rather I sit?"

"On my lap."

Gilly snorted softly and sat next to them instead. "You've got an answer for everything."

"You love that about me." Sawyer lay back and kicked their legs across Gillian's lap. "And you missed that about me."

"You have no idea."

"I still have endless questions about what the hell happened when I was away, but for right now, how did you not have a coronary when Brooke slept with your supervisee?"

Gillian closed her eyes and let her head fall, strands of copper hair fanning across the back of the couch, reminding Sawyer of a sunset. "Not sure."

"Was it as epic as Robin suggested?"

"Even her hyperbole is probably an understatement, and in many ways, we're still living it."

"And how are you adjusting to your new reality?"

Gillian shrugged, grimaced, and rolled her eyes all at once in quite the trifecta of body language overwhelm.

"That good, huh? I have some leftover Zoloft in my bag if you want me to share."

"I can get my own Zoloft, thank you very much, plus that stuff isn't nearly strong enough to make sense of our Brooke having a one-night stand turned ethics crisis, turned torrid affair, turned enduring age-gap romance."

"Fair dues." Even Sawyer's mind spun a bit. "That might call for some ketamine?"

Gillian's eyes went wide. "You have ketamine in your bag?"

"No, but I know a guy."

She shook her head. "You're all going to be the death of me."

"Nah, you'll whip us into shape eventually. You're too strong to be broken. Honestly, I've sort of missed having that kind of order and standards in my life."

16

"I'm not sure mine are quite what they used to be."

"None of us are kids anymore."

"Really? You still seem wildly youthful, gallivanting across the globe."

Sawyer shrugged and closed their eyes. "I thought of you every time I felt like I might be losing my grip on who I am."

Gillian gave their leg a little squeeze. "Did it help?"

"Come here." Sawyer extended their arm and waited for Gillian to curl up beside them. When had they touched a woman without the expectation of anything more than open affection? "Even the thought of you has meaning for me, Gilly Bean, but this is better."

"Yeah?" It was Gillian's turn to yawn. "I thought of you, too, you know?"

"When Brooke fell in love?"

"Yes. I wondered how it would've been different if I'd had you to talk to, or if she'd had you to talk to because she couldn't talk to me, and I couldn't talk to her the way either of us talk to you."

"You don't talk to Robin?"

"Oh, Robin." Gillian chuckled. "She's a whirlwind, keeps us all on our toes."

"Tell me more," they asked sleepily, not having to fight to stay casual, but also not shying from the warmth of being close and comfortable with someone again. How many nights had the two of them spent like this over the years? How long had it been since they'd felt quite so content?

"I don't think either of us is going to stay awake long enough, and besides, Robin is a personality best experienced live."

"I can't wait, so long as she hasn't usurped my position as your favorite instigator."

"Never." Gillian closed her eyes again and snuggled closer, resting her cheek more fully on Sawyer's chest. "You're irreplaceable, and for what it's worth, I'm really happy you're back."

"Even if I end up only adding to the chaos?"

"I've no doubt you will. Want to go to work with me on Monday? You'll fit right in."

"Nice try. What if, instead of going to the therapy place, I stay on your couch and eat all your food?"

"What if we get some sleep and talk about it later?"

"Winning," Sawyer mumbled.

"And we can also talk about your top surgery whenever you're ready," Gillian said in the same tone and register as someone might mention the weather.

The corners of Sawyer's mouth curled up. "Deal."

Three

"Hey T-Ball." Robin practically bounced on her toes as Tegan came into the office on Monday morning. "Was your weekend off the hook?"

"Pretty good, but why do I get the sense it wasn't as fun as yours? What'd you do after the rest of us left the bar?"

"Not much. Played a few games of darts, then called it a night."

"Alone?"

"Yep."

"Seriously? No sexy fun times?" Tegan eyed her suspiciously. "In that case, mine was better than yours."

Robin raised her hand above her head, and Tegan slapped it with her own as Gillian walked in.

"Oh God, are we high-fiving at 9:00 on a Monday morning? Is this my life now?"

"We're reliving Tegan's weekend exploits."

"Sweet Jesus," Gillian mumbled and moved directly to the coffee maker.

"It's not as salacious as it sounds," Tegan said. "Besides, Brooke was with you and Sawyer all day on Saturday. Maybe you had the most fun this weekend."

Gillian smiled. "Yeah, there's that."

Robin suffered a slight pang of something approaching envy. It seemed like some old group dynamics that predated her might be reasserting themselves. That wouldn't normally be a big deal if the person who'd sparked them wasn't as utterly intriguing as Sawyer. "I bet you two are happy to have your buddy back. Did you spend all day catching up?"

19

"I'm not sure I'd call it catching up. We mostly hung out and talked about old times or inside jokes." Gillian's expression turned wistful. "Do you have friends you can go ages without seeing, and then ten minutes after they walk back in, you're twenty-five again, and nothing has changed even if everything has?"

Robin's chest tightened, and she nodded even though she wasn't sure she had anything exactly like that in her life.

"Twenty-five," Tegan echoed. "That's it. Sawyer's turned you both back into the people you were when you met."

"Oh my God," Robin whimpered. "Teegs, we're older than them now. We're the adults in the room."

"Lord help us all," Tegan said. "I like it, though. Brooke's happy."

"Brooke's been happy for months, in case you hadn't noticed." Robin nudged her.

"Thank you. It just feels like this puzzle piece had been missing, and now it's sliding back into place."

Gillian nodded. "I don't normally subscribe to illusions about other people offering wholeness, or completing anything, but even I admit I'm feeling more balanced over the past few days."

Again, something inside Robin pinged, and she finally gave voice to it. "Okay, I'm going to need more."

Tegan's eyebrows went up. "More?"

She shrugged. "I don't know why, but like, we were just settling into being a quad, the three of us and Brooke, and now there's this new person who isn't new to all of us, and ..."

Both women stared at her as if waiting for more, but Robin couldn't figure out what she was feeling, much less give it voice. "Sorry, maybe I'm bored and fishing for entertainment."

Gillian grinned. "Sawyer is entertaining."

"Invite them to Take-Out Tuesdays tomorrow," Robin suggested, though as soon as the words left her mouth, she recognized it wasn't a great idea. Sandwiching a non-therapist into their tradition of inhaling food together between clients wasn't exactly the ideal setup for quality interaction.

"They won't come to the office," Gillian said flatly, "but I did promise to cook a big meal Wednesday."

"Italian feast night?" Tegan asked hopefully.

"Yes, and you know I can't make a moderate amount of sauce. Why don't we make it an everyone's-invited dinner?"

"Sauce and a chance to get to know Sawyer?" Tegan smiled. "Sounds perfect."

"Thanks, Gilly." Robin wasn't sure she'd go all the way to "perfect," but couldn't tell why. She had no claim to anything more, and yet something niggled in the back of her mind every time she got a break between clients all day. At one point she got so lost in thought she didn't even hear Tegan approach until she was all the way inside the door to her office.

"Hey you," Tegan whispered.

Robin started a bit, then laughed. "Why are you sneaking up on me all creepy?"

"I knocked," Tegan said without a hint of defensiveness as she made herself comfortable on Robin's couch. "Is the haze you're in today tiredness, introspection, or something more?"

She paused to give the question its due. "I'm not tired."

Tegan waited.

Robin shifted slightly as she tried to pay better attention to the recesses of her mind, but instead of finding answers, she brought forth another question. "Is it weird for you to see Brooke with Sawyer?"

"Weird how?"

"You've been such a huge part of her life for almost a year now. You shook her, and shaped her, and you've built this all-consuming thing together. Then suddenly there's another person who knows her in ways you couldn't possibly, and it's huge, too."

Tegan's expression softened into something sympathetic. "I hadn't thought of it that way, but I think that's a pertinent thing to consider, for both of us."

"I don't have the same stakes as you, though."

"I'm not sure I'd agree." Tegan proceeded carefully. "Sawyer's a friend to both Brooke and Gillian. They aren't a

21

lover, or a partner, or even an ex, so their relationship doesn't really intersect with me and Brooke's dynamic, but they do have a very similar dynamic to the one we have as a cohort of friends."

Robin saw where this was headed. It wasn't as though she hadn't been aware over the years how she'd taken up a position in the group that Sawyer had once occupied. They'd even talked openly about Robin being the wild one, the fun one, the instigator, and the comic relief in Sawyer's absence. "I'm not afraid of being replaced."

Tegan gave one quick nod. "Good, because you're the definition of irreplaceable."

The affirmation loosened something in her chest she hadn't been fully aware of until it began to dissipate. "I'm not worried about getting cut out or anything. I swear I'm not some insecure—"

"Of course not," Tegan said quickly. "You're the most confidently grounded human I've ever met."

"I'm just so freaking curious, you know?"

"Sure."

"Friday night, I tried to act all chill and politely interested, but like, as Brooke and Gillian were falling back into people they used to be, I was falling forward into the person sitting across from me, right then and there."

"Oh." Tegan sat up a little straighter. "You felt something … a spark?"

"Don't go writing me a romance, Tegan," she said quickly. "I'm glad you got yours, but I don't mean to imply fatedness or anything."

"Okay, tell me more."

"I'm not sure I know more, other than I've wondered about Sawyer for years. I've heard so many stories and asides and comparisons. I guess after a while you begin to form an idea in your head, and then it's as if a character from a book hopped off the page. Maybe I wasn't prepared for them to be real, or maybe I wasn't prepared for them to be more dynamic in real life than they've been in my imagination."

"But they are?"

Robin lifted a shoulder, trying to seem casual even though her heart gave her a little kick in the ribs at the memory of Sawyer, sexy and backlit in the doorway. "I mean, you were there."

Tegan laughed. "Indeed. It's not hard to see how Sawyer bowled over stoic and steady women like Brooke and Gillian. They have charisma for days."

"Weeks," Robin corrected. "Normally, I'd absolutely know what to do in that situation."

"They would've spent the weekend at your apartment instead of Gillian's."

"I wouldn't say that exactly—"

"You didn't. I said it for you, which makes it okay instead of boastful."

"You're a good egg, but really, I think I'm just trying, or hoping, to get a handle on who this person is, not as a character or some ghost from a friend's past, or some entity I know without having met. Hell, even that sounds silly and vague."

"Not at all." Tegan stood and smiled down at her. "You're interested in something, and you're doing what you do, figuring it out. I get it. I think you're after the same thing you always are."

"Yeah, what's that?"

Tegan dropped a hand atop Robin's head and gave her hair a little tousle. "Something real."

"G-Money!" Robin called as soon as she pushed open Gillian's front door without knocking. "If that sauce tastes half as good as it smells, I'm going to have to kiss you on the mouth."

"If you do, you're fired," Gillian called back from somewhere around the corner, and a low, smooth laugh welled up to meet them both.

"I like a woman who makes an entrance." Sawyer sat up and glanced between them both, short chestnut hair slightly mussed and a gray, long-sleeve T-shirt featuring a llama in a stocking cap slipping off slender shoulders.

"And I can appreciate a person who's on the couch in pajamas at 7:00 on a weeknight." Robin kicked off her shoes and dropped a bottle of sparkling lemonade on the counter. "Are you turning in early, or just getting your day started at vampire o'clock?"

"Vampire o'clock?" Sawyer snorted. "I like that, especially coming from the woman dressed in all black."

"Hey, if you can't beat 'em, join 'em." Robin shed her leather motorcycle jacket and tossed it over the back of an armchair.

"Robin's our resident night owl," Gillian explained. "I think she runs on coffee, and not the blood of her conquests, though I can't say for sure. I'm more concerned to see her riding jacket but no helmet."

Robin came over and gave her boss a sidearm hug. "Thanks, Mom, but it's too cold for the bike, hence the coat sans headgear."

Sawyer sat up a little straighter. "You drive a motorcycle?"

"I've got a Triumph for when the weather's nice."

"And in Buffalo, that's what? Three glorious months in the summer?"

"Four if I get lucky." She grinned and tried not to care too much that Sawyer seemed appropriately impressed. "And I usually do get lucky when I'm riding."

"I don't doubt it." Sawyer gave her a nod of appreciation.

"Hello," Brooke called as she and Tegan stepped through the door. "It smells amazing in here, Gillian."

"Well, don't offer to kiss her," Sawyer said. "Robin's already been threatened with termination if she does."

Tegan laughed. "If she needs to kiss anyone, it won't be the boss."

24

"New rule." Gillian pushed off her chair and lifted one finger in emphasis. "No one kisses anyone until I've had at least two glasses of wine."

"Then let's get you started, because I like to keep my options open." Sawyer hopped off the couch and wandered over to the open kitchen-dining-room combo. Moving with an easy sort of familiarity that clearly came from more than a few days of shared space, they snagged glasses from the cabinet and a bottle opener from a drawer. Robin watched with a kind of natural curiosity. She'd been to Gillian's downtown loft plenty of times, but not often enough to know where she kept various utensils or feel comfortable grabbing them.

Without asking, Sawyer poured two glasses of wine, handing them to Brooke and Gillian, before turning to Robin and Tegan. "And what will the newest members of the team be drinking?"

"The nonalcoholic version for me," Tegan said.

"Same." Robin pointed to the bottle she'd brought. "Fizzy lemonade."

Sawyer picked up the bottle and turned it around to look at the ingredients, then shrugged. "Do you mind if I play a bit?"

"I'm game for anything," Robin replied at the same time Tegan said, "I have an early client tomorrow."

"I see how you ended up with Brooke." Sawyer grinned at Tegan, then turned to Robin. "And why Gillian might fire you."

Sawyer set to work quickly, confidently. Moving between the fridge and counter, they snagged a few strawberries, some ice, and a bit of lavender from Gillian's centerpiece. Robin was hypnotized again as Sawyer crushed, mixed, and shook everything together before straining the concoction into highball glasses.

Tegan took the first one and sipped. "Wow. That tastes like … summer."

Robin accepted hers and arched an eyebrow. "Is this about to blow my mind?"

25

Sawyer shrugged, but the quirk of smugness in their lips suggested they knew the answer.

Robin sipped tentatively, but the first brush of flavor across her tongue melted moderation, and she took a bigger swig. Sweet and sour and soothing with a hint of something slightly floral without becoming sticky. She eyed Sawyer with a mix of suspicion and interest. "Where did you learn this magic? Are you a professional mocktail mixologist?"

"Not hardly."

"You'd make a great one," Tegan said. "I'd love this recipe."

"There's no recipe," Sawyer said. "I made the most of a moment."

Tegan lifted the glass as if trying to inspect it more closely. "What all did you add to the lemonade?"

"I saw the ingredients, but not the proportions," Brooke said.

"Doesn't matter." Sawyer waved them off. "You can't recapture it exactly, and even if you make it the same way again, it would taste different in a different room, a different glass, with different people. Let that moment provide its own inspiration."

Tegan glanced at Brooke and Gillian as if not sure whether they were being teased, but Gillian only sighed.

"I make the sauce the same way every time, but each batch does turn out a little different."

"Because you're a little different, Gilly," Sawyer explained, "though not too much. You're more like magnetic north, slight variations in a constant pull. Like the wine, same varietals, same notes, different vintage. If I'd been making a drink for you, my inspiration would've produced something else entirely."

"So then, what was your inspiration for this one?" Tegan asked as she cradled her one-moment-out-of-millions mocktail close to her chest.

Sawyer bit their lip, and for a second, Robin thought they might withhold the answer, but after a pause just long enough for anticipation, they said, "Robin can't ride her motorcycle until it warms up. Perhaps a part of me sought to summon a warming trend in the form of a little wishful drinking."

Robin's chest tightened, and if not for the others watching, she might've cracked her cool right then and there.

It had been a long time since someone else had been the smooth one in a conversation where she was concerned, but Sawyer had suave for days. Still, it took a second, and another swallow of the drink before she raised her glass in toast. "Here's to an early summer."

"So, you were a sleigh driver?" Brooke asked, her voice filled with wonder, and Robin couldn't fault her.

Sawyer had been regaling them with stories of life under the northern lights, and each one sounded more magical than its predecessor.

"So, like horses?" Tegan asked.

"Sometimes. And I wouldn't call it a driver so much as a guide. When I'd take out the big wagon, I'd have to keep the horses in check, but when we used the reindeer—"

"What?" Gillian held up a hand. "Did you say 'reindeer'? Like Santa?"

"I mean, there's always a chance of running into him once you enter the Arctic Circle." Sawyer winked at her playfully and shoveled another bite of spaghetti into their mouth. "But seriously, they all know the way. I mostly kept the whole train of tourists moving. We'd do several runs a night, because night was almost all the time."

"I can't believe that's a real job." Robin sopped up an extra bit of sauce with a hunk of garlic bread and dripped a bit down the front of her shirt.

"You got a little bit there." Sawyer pointed to her chest, then seemed to think better of it, and pulled their eyes back up. "I mean, on you."

"It's kind of her trademark move," Gillian explained.

"Yes, some of us travel to exciting places, some of us simply wear the foods of many cultures down the front of all our clothes."

"Nice. Italian is super fetching on you."

"It's the hot new accessory of the season." Robin played it off. "Can we go back to how one even becomes a reindeer wagon-train driver? Is there a certification? A special permit?"

"Nah, just the right place at the right time, and a willingness to try new things."

"I have a willingness to try new things, but it seems like you'd have to possess certain skills to lead animals through the Arctic."

Sawyer shook their head. "The people are more complex than the animals."

"Now, *that* I understand."

"Something the two of you have in common," Brooke offered. "You're both endlessly capable of entrancing anything with a pulse."

"Says the woman who's good at everything," Sawyer shot back.

"No, this is different." Brooke leaned forward.

"Of course it is. I can't juggle." Sawyer nudged Robin. "Can you juggle?"

"Not even a little bit."

"Wait." Tegan turned to her girlfriend. "You can juggle?"

"Yes." She waved off the aside. "But you two get people to bend to your will without them ever realizing it wasn't their idea."

"People and animals," Gillian corrected. "Do you think the reindeer follow everyone around, or just Sawyer?"

"Everyone with carrots in their pockets," Sawyer said.

"Or maybe they thought you were happy to see them," Robin said, and Sawyer snickered.

"And you're one to talk, Robin. Remember when we were all in the park for your adult kickball tournament?" Tegan said, then turned to Sawyer. "A squirrel came right up to her in the middle of the game and tugged on her pant leg."

She rolled her eyes. "He didn't tug, just kind of scratched at me because I was eating sunflower seeds."

"I'm more interested in the fact that you were playing adult kickball."

"She gets teams of people to follow her into all sorts of escapades," Gillian said. "The kickball is a tame example."

"Really?" The playful turn in Sawyer's tone caused a little shiver of pleasure in Robin. "Please tell me about the less tame options."

She shook her head. "It's nothing major. I'm always trying to get these three to do perfectly reasonable things with me, but they refuse on completely fabricated concerns about safety or some other nonsense."

"Aren't they the worst? It's always"—Sawyer held up their fingers to make air quotes—"'safety,' or 'illegal,' or 'ethics crisis.'"

"Brooke got a little lax on that last one," Robin teased, "but yes, all I've wanted to do for, like, weeks now is go whitewater rafting in Zoar Valley, and—"

"That's a fantastic idea," Sawyer cut in quickly. "What day did y'all decide on?"

"They won't go!" Robin practically shouted, then turned to her friends. "See, Sawyer gets it."

"Their unqualified agreement is never an endorsement about the safety of any activity," Gillian said.

"Come on, Ivy League." Sawyer jumped right to Robin's aid. "I'm sure they have life jackets and helmets."

"Not helping." Brooke took Gillian's side. "The fact that you need those things only proves the risk of bodily harm."

Robin piled on excitedly. "Cars have seat belts, but you still drive them."

"Because they're useful."

"And adventures are fun. All work and no play will make you dull girls," Sawyer added. "I've been away too long. I get the sense poor Robin here has been swimming upstream all by herself."

"I really have." Robin sighed. "Sometimes Tegan votes with me for fun, but only with movies and sporting events, never heart-thumping adventure."

Sawyer looked to Tegan as if she might defend herself, but she merely lifted one shoulder noncommittally. "I'm all full up on heart-thumping right now. The last year carried plenty of drama and high-stakes rewards without introducing the risk of physical injury on top of it all."

"Aw, honey," Brooke teased, "you say the most romantic things."

"See." Robin sat back. "They're a team, three against one."

"Three against two," Sawyer corrected, meeting Robin's eyes with mock seriousness. "I stand with you."

Robin's heart fluttered and her stomach flipped a bit, or maybe that was something slightly lower, because with Sawyer so close and seemingly pledging something important, it wasn't hard to get her mental and emotional wires crossed.

"Hey now." Tegan piped up. "No need to draw lines in the sand. What if this isn't time for a battle cry at all, but rather an opportunity for everyone to get their needs met?"

Sawyer snorted softly. "My God, you really are a therapist."

"She's a pretty good one," Robin admitted begrudgingly, then nodded to Tegan. "I'm listening."

"You've been lacking a thrill buddy. Sawyer's just back from far-flung adventures and might be easily bored with the rest of us, but we really want them to hang around for a while." She turned to include Gillian and Brooke. "Right?"

"Absolutely," Brooke said at the same time Gillian said, "Very much."

"Then, let these two go do their wild stunts and borderline dangerous stuff together. Then we all get to hear the heart-thumping stories and live vicariously when we all meet up for dinner or drinks in some safe location."

30

Robin nodded slowly, even though her mind spun at all the implications of the proposal. Not only would she have someone to go rafting with, that someone would be amazing, exciting, interesting as hell, and pretty damn sexy to imagine dripping wet. She almost said as much to Tegan, but Brooke beat her to the punch by blurting out, "I love you so much."

"And I like you quite a bit." Gillian tipped her wine glass in mock salute. "I have great taste in employees."

"I'm grading papers for the next few days solid." Brooke turned to include Robin and Sawyer. "Having the two of you tell me wild tales of your Western New York exploits at the end of the week sounds like the perfect respite."

"You're going to need it after the end-of-semester faculty mixer Saturday evening," Tegan added. It might've been another uninteresting work aside if not for the way Sawyer's body stiffened beside her.

"Faculty mixer?" they asked, as if straining to sound casual.

"Yes." Brooke's business-polite smile ratcheted up Robin's concern even further. "I mentioned that since I needed a little professional distance while Tegan finishes her year of supervision, I've been teaching."

Sawyer nodded slowly, as some of the blood drained from their already fair complexion. "Right, I think I might've been too jet-lagged to do the math last weekend. Teaching in the illustrious program from which you graduated?"

Brooke sipped her wine, then nodded stoically.

"Did Maura make you an offer you couldn't refuse?"

"More like, she offered something meaningful in a moment of need." Brooke was using her centering voice, and it might've worked wonders in another room, but this crew had too much experience to accept such easy comfort.

Still, Robin also had plenty of practice sitting with other people's discomfort. She did so without issue all day, but she wasn't at work now, and she didn't feel even the slightest inclination to remain neutral. Instead, she blurted out, "She's coming back to our practice."

31

"We're still working out details," Brooke continued evenly.

"But we all know she can't live without us long term," Robin tried again to insert some levity without fully understanding why.

Sawyer's once mischievous gaze remained cloudy. "I'm sure you're a great professor, Brookesy. You're great at everything you do. Hey, does your girlfriend know you can play the harmonica?"

"I've heard." Tegan grinned at Brooke, whose eyes hadn't left Sawyer, and Robin wondered what sort of unspoken negotiation was happening between them.

Brooke reached for their hand. "It's just a job."

"Nah." Sawyer forced a tight smile but didn't meet her halfway. "Send my regards to the boss."

"I'd rather not be the bearer of that news." Brooke seemed to choose her words carefully. "But you know I'll toe any line you need me to."

The sincerity, or maybe something deeper, finally cracked through Sawyer's haze. "You don't need to. I'll crash one of her prestigious symposiums soon enough."

"I'd be happy to join you," Brooke said.

"Me too," Gillian quickly offered.

"It'll be like old times," Sawyer said. "But it's not going to happen this weekend."

Brooke and Gillian exchanged a quick look that everyone clearly saw, but while Robin's chest tightened, Sawyer merely laughed. "Don't go diagnosing me telepathically. I'm not dodging. I'd go with you Saturday, but I already have plans."

"Oh yeah?" Gillian pushed. "Hot date?"

"Absolutely."

Robin's stomach clenched at the announcement, but the bottom seemed to drop out as Sawyer turned and flashed them the most brilliant smile. "Robin and I are going whitewater rafting."

Four

Sawyer tried to inconspicuously wipe their chin to make sure they weren't drooling. The sight of Robin walking down the trail in a skintight wet suit had an almost Pavlovian effect, and damn if they weren't salivating at the way her hips rolled as she stepped over rocks and logs in the dappled sunshine of a springtime forest. What had Tegan called it? Something about heart thumping? Sawyer wasn't sure this was exactly what she'd had in mind, but their pulse did beat faster than usual, and they hadn't even reached the river yet.

"Okay, folks." Their young guide was ripped and enthusiastic as he clapped his hands together. "We have two choices of routes today. First is a fun little run through some Class I and II rapids. You get amazing views and mild thrills with very little risk of going in the drink. The second option is a longer trip with mostly Class II rapids and a hot shot through some Class IIIs. There's a good chance of getting wet on this one. What are we choosing? Class II or III?"

Several people around them began to discuss their options, but Robin and Sawyer merely glanced at each other before saying "three" in unison.

It had been months since Sawyer'd fallen into such an easy camaraderie with someone they found so attractive, though the sense of adventure radiating off this woman definitely added to her sexiness. Maybe you couldn't separate the two.

The two of them ended up in a large blue raft with a single guide and two dude bros from Buffalo State, who were polite enough and educated enough to ask about pronouns, but once they stepped their first foot into the Cattaraugus Creek, they were clearly too amped up to notice anyone else. To be fair, Sawyer wasn't the least bit interested in them either. Between the sight of Robin looking so hot and the frigid water threatening to fill their neoprene boots, they were already in sensory overload by the time they pushed off the rocky bank.

"You can sit your butts on the side of the raft with your paddle over the side, and then you wedge your front foot under this thwart." He pointed to the overhang of what Sawyer might've called a bench. "Use your other foot to brace yourself."

It wasn't the most complex or complete set of instructions ever, but no one in the group seemed to have trouble mimicking his position. Robin and Sawyer sat to either side of the boat's bow, and the Buffalo boys took the middle with their guide in the back to steer, before pushing off without much ceremony.

The current caught hold of the raft quickly, and the passengers had to paddle only to keep themselves on the right trajectory. Still, it was the most physical activity Sawyer'd had for weeks, and their muscles creaked a bit in resistance. A quick glance at Robin suggested she had no such issues. Her biceps strained against the constraints of her wet suit while she engaged her calves and thighs to lean further over the edge and dig deeper.

The sound of rushing water intensified ahead, and their guide called out, "Easy Class I rapids. Just stay the course."

Robin turned to grin at Sawyer, helmet covering her hair and paddle poised as the first waves hit. The glint of mischief in her dark eyes caused a surge of electricity to spark, and they paddled a little harder as things got bumpy.

"It's like a bouncy castle," Robin called.

"I haven't been in one of those in a while."

"Sad." Robin laughed.

They rocked back and forth slightly as the water pushed them over the river's gentle hills and valleys, but all in all, the rough patch ended before it had a chance to get going.

The guide seemed to read their minds as the surface smoothed out again. "Don't worry, that's just a taste to let you get your bearings. Class II rapids are going to be the same concept on a bigger scale."

"When do we hit those?" Buffalo Bro Number One asked.

"We're going to come around a big bend, and then we'll hit them on the next straightaway."

Robin snorted softly enough that only Sawyer seemed to notice.

They arched their eyebrows.

"Straightaway." Robin smirked. "It sounds like a bug repellent, but for straight people."

Sawyer snickered. "There've been times when I would've paid good money for that."

"Every single time I go to a bar."

Sawyer gave her a once-over. Her dangerous curves and full lips would appeal to people all up and down several sexuality spectrums. "Thankfully, less of a problem for me these days."

Robin gave them the same kind of slow appraisal. "I don't know if I should say 'lucky you,' or 'lucky me.'"

Sawyer's breath caught at the blatant statement. They were used to delivering lines like that, not receiving them.

Still, the situation at hand warranted their attention as they cleared the gentle curve and caught first sight of the rapids. These were indeed bigger and louder, white-capped peaks with the dips churning a deep greenish-brown.

"Paddle to the right," the guide called, and Sawyer wasn't sure if the interruption annoyed or relieved them. "Line up so we're headed right down the middle."

Sawyer did a quick scan of the sloping banks to each side, mentally calculating possible escape routes, but it didn't take much to figure their best chance was to stay in the raft. An assessment confirmed when they tipped forward and the first slap of freezing water hit them in the face.

"Fuck." They gasped at the same time Robin whooped in celebration.

Sawyer tried to keep their bearings, paddling the water as they crashed down, and then managing to catch air only as they rose again, the bow of the boat lifting slightly out of the river before dropping with another emphatic splash.

"Left, left, left," their guide called, and Sawyer did their best to push the raft back toward the middle, but it still surprised them when it actually worked.

"Dig, dig," Robin called, her voice full of amusement. "One more!"

They hit the last set of waves squarely, and for a second, it felt like they might somersault, but maybe that was merely Sawyer's stomach, because as they slid back into smooth water and checked their surroundings, everyone seemed a bit wetter, but no worse for wear.

"Yes!" Robin cheered. "More, more!"

She looked radiant and wild with drops of the river's remnants dripping from her nose and thick eyelashes.

"Way to push there, adventure buddy." She lifted her hand for Sawyer, who slapped it. "Crushing it."

"Me? I'm just keeping up. You look like you're high on adrenaline."

"Totally jonesing for that buzz."

"I don't think therapists are supposed to say stuff like that."

"All-natural, baby. Who needs drugs when I have adrenaline, dopamine, endorphins, the whole slew?" Robin shook her head and knocked on her own helmet. "If I don't need one of these, am I even living?"

"It does suit you."

"Besides," Robin lifted her paddle again, "I'm *a* therapist. I'm not *your* therapist. Big difference."

Sawyer frowned at the distinction and didn't want to explore why. Glancing away from Robin, they scanned their surroundings, increasingly steep rock walls into thick vegetation budding with new life. It was as if spring had sprung above them, while here at ground level, hints of winter hadn't

36

quite released the river from its chilly grasp. Sawyer felt suspended, adrift between the two.

"I've never been out here before," Robin said offhandedly.

Sawyer turned to see her inspecting the same surroundings that had held their attention seconds ago, only Robin didn't look lost or drifting at all. Her eyes held a spark of wonder and purpose, while the quirk of her beautiful lips suggested she might even see possibilities no one else had considered. Then she turned and leveled the same expression at them. "It's beautiful."

Sawyer nodded slowly, but they could no longer see the river, the cliffs, or the trees beyond the woman, so close and so consuming. "Stunning, really."

Sawyer had grown used to raising their voice to be heard, either over the rush of the river or the din of their own pulse. This time, though, they heard both in equally increasing measure.

Their crew had run through several rough sections, working together when the flow got fast, or steep, or bounced them about, then taking breaks between them to catch their breath and get their safety gear tightened up before going again.

Sawyer found the paddling got easier and more intuitive with each attempt, and they enjoyed the building sense of mastery with conquering a challenge. Robin, on the other hand, seemed anything but chill. Every time she was pushed around or nearly washed overboard, she only laughed louder.

The woman was fearless, often hanging out of the boat farther than the bigger guys behind her. At one point she seemed to be holding on only by the tips of her toes as she kept them from crashing over a small boulder, grinning broadly the entire time. More than once Sawyer caught themself watching

Robin instead of the river, a dangerous but appealing habit as the din ahead grew into a roar.

Turning to their guide for confirmation, Sawyer called, "Big one up ahead?"

He nodded and raised his voice to be heard over the churning water. "The biggest. A solid Class III."

"Let's go," Robin shouted into the canyon surrounding them.

"We've got hazards here," their guide explained. "We'll have to choose our path and stick to it. Everyone needs to do their part."

"Lay it on me." Robin grinned with a little bob and weave of her shoulders, like a boxer psyching up to face an opponent, and Sawyer couldn't resist soaking up some of her excitement.

"We have to stay to the right for about the first third of the run, then after a big dip, there's going to be a rock formation jutting out from the side and we have to clear it by a few feet, or we'll get sucked in and hit the side," he explained. "The rapids on their own aren't much bigger than anything we've already faced, but the hazard raises the skill level."

"Bring it on." Robin cheered over the rising sound of waves approaching.

"Hell yeah." One of the Buffalo Boys egged her on. "This woman is wild."

Sawyer couldn't disagree.

"If I say 'bump,' everyone duck inside the boat and hold on." Their guide had to shout now. "If you go in the drink, keep your toes and your nose above water, point your feet downstream, and float. Don't fight the flow. Ride it out."

Sawyer found that information rather sparse and delivered entirely too late for their liking, but at least they understood the sentiment. They had plenty of experience not fighting the flow.

Robin reached over and knocked roughly atop their helmet, smiling brightly. "You ready for this?"

"Hell yes." Sawyer wasn't entirely sure what they'd agreed to, but in that moment, amped up and under the passion of that gaze, anything this woman asked of them would've been answered in the affirmative.

From there, everything felt a bit like bedlam.

They must've been working in tandem, because the boat slid right into the chute they'd aimed for, but the next step was hard to see with the spray of water in Sawyer's face. Even an hour in, the shock of cold still stung, but they didn't dare stop paddling, knowing there was some sort of big rock ahead. Adventure was one thing, but slapping into a boulder like some cartoon coyote didn't sound appealing.

"Paddle," their guide yelled as they took a wicked dip, and Sawyer squinted through the splash.

"Whoo!" Robin shouted gleefully as they careened over another rise.

"Left, left, left," the guide yelled.

Sawyer turned their head to see the people on the other side of the raft scramble against the stream. Robin dug in hard, laughing almost manically as she arched her full body into the fight, but even with her valiant effort combined with one dude bro and one professionally trained guide, Sawyer could tell they were going to miss the rocks only by inches instead of feet.

Sure enough, they barely cleared the biggest hazard and immediately tipped down what felt like a fire hose over a waterslide.

"Bump! Bump!" the guide called, and Sawyer heeded the warning, ducking hard to the inside of the raft and grabbing hold of the safety handle.

Robin, on the other hand, continued paddling with all her might until the second they struck the steep wall of rock.

The impact reverberated through the raft like a rubber ball bouncing with malicious force.

Robin wobbled, rocked, and rolled as the boat spun around. Now their guide was to the front, and Sawyer grasped for the woman falling off the back.

They caught hold of an errant strap on her life jacket, and the hold proved insufficient for anything other than pulling themself upright. Robin continued to tip backward until the bends of her knees buckled across the edge of the raft.

Only now she wasn't the only one at risk, as Sawyer found themself in the exact opposite position that their guide had prescribed.

Standing upright with no foothold and facing backward, they had a great view of the splash Robin made when she broke the surface. It would've been nice if everything had happened in slow motion like it does in the movies, but it took only an instant for Sawyer to be thrown completely overboard, and seemingly less to be completely submerged.

Cold water hit with offensive force, and for what felt like too damn long. They couldn't even remember to breathe, much less get their toes up, but some sort of survival instinct must've taken hold as they rolled onto their back. The life jacket kept them afloat as Sawyer skimmed the surface, unable to hear anything but the rush of water, or maybe that was their own pulse, until off to one side they picked up the sound of … giggling?

They rolled their eyes between blinking away water, and despite their precarious position, the corners of Sawyer's mouth quirked up. How could they not with Robin laughing somewhere amid the chaos. Their heart rate stabilized, and breathing came a bit easier, too. Soon, even the water slowed, and a hand caught hold of their arm.

"Got ya." Robin pulled them toward a patch of rocky shore.

Sitting a bit more upright, Sawyer realized they'd floated to the side of the main channel and could stand.

They took a second to shake water from their ears and wipe their eyes before turning to the woman beside them. She stood dripping wet, one hand on her paddle and the other on her hip as full lips curled with a hint of pride. "You're welcome."

"For what?"

"Rescuing you."

"You're the one who knocked me overboard."

Robin looked more smug than before. "You're welcome for that, too."

"I think you mean 'sorry.'" Sawyer managed to sound only slightly more incredulous than amused.

She shook her head. "I don't. I mean 'you're welcome.'"

"Why?"

"Because"—Robin pursed her lips playfully—"is any activity really worth doing if you don't get a little wet while you're at it?"

Five

"God, that was fun!" Robin still buzzed with excitement after they reached the parking lot where they could return their gear and head home. A part of her wanted to turn back toward the river and go again, but with the sight of Sawyer leaning up against a split-rail fence still dripping wet and deliciously disheveled, she found plenty of reasons to draw her forward as well.

Sawyer had unzipped the top of their wet suit and peeled it down to their waist, revealing a navy-blue rash guard that clung, damp and delightfully close enough to showcase the outline of collarbones, pecs, the slight indent of a slender waist, and the subtle curve of hips. They must've noticed Robin's blatant appraisal, because Sawyer smiled, a slow, languid sort of expression as if they had all the time in the world and a few good ideas about how they should spend it.

Robin warmed despite the cold air. She was used to both looking and being looked at, but something about Sawyer's gaze felt different, like they weren't just asking, that somehow, they already knew the answers.

"You're wild," Sawyer finally said, without judgment or amusement, a mere statement of fact.

"I heard you are, too."

"Oh?" Sawyer raised their eyebrows and pushed away from the fence. "Then you've got an advantage. I've heard virtually nothing about you, but you seem to have some preconceived notions about me."

"A sketch, really, along with a whole lot of curiosity."

Sawyer ran their hand through a floppy mop of chestnut hair, shaking out a few more drops of the river's remnants. "Well, I can tell you already the information you may've received from my best friends seems a bit relative now."

"How so?" Robin reached for the Velcro fastener at the back of her neck, but her fingers fumbled around the collar.

Sawyer stepped closer and, with a gentle hand on her shoulder, turned Robin around. Then freeing the strap, they pulled the zipper down slowly, all the way to the small of her back before saying, "What constitutes 'wild' differs greatly depending on who's delivering the descriptor. Brooke and Gillian would assess my wildness in relation to their own, making it momentous by comparison. But you …"

Robin held her breath, feeling Sawyer against newly exposed skin.

Sawyer sighed. "I think you'll find me relatively tame when presented within the context of your own adrenaline seeking."

Robin turned around. The two of them were the same height, and even of similar builds, but for some reason, Sawyer felt bigger. "Are you worried you'll suffer by comparison?"

Sawyer laughed lightly. "No. I'm usually the wildest one in most company, but there's always something compelling in meeting my match."

"A match, huh?" She shook her head. "I think people misread you."

"Oh?" Amusement sparked in Sawyer's gray eyes. "You've decided that in a few hours?"

"Yes."

"Well, don't hold back. Lay the diagnosis on me."

Robin shook her head. "Not a diagnosis, only a feeling that what people read as wild is actually an engaging kind of chill."

"'Chill'?"

"Yeah. You're down for whatever. You're not a 'no' person. You're not a five-year plan person. You're not a pro vs. con list person. When an opportunity presents itself, you accept, you engage all the things. You roll with them, you chase things if you have to, but you don't let anything pass you by. You act before you think because you know without thinking. I bet a lot of people probably read that as wild because it's so wildly different from how they move through the world."

Sawyer's lips parted, and their chest rose slightly as if they'd drawn their breath a little deeper than usual.

"And you don't seem to fluster easily," Robin added, "even about things that would rattle our mutual friends."

Sawyer smiled again, but this time the expression seemed more wistful. "You were onto something right up until that point, or maybe I find different things flustering, but either way, I think you're giving me a compliment, and I don't make a habit of turning down praise from beautiful women."

Robin rolled her eyes playfully. "Chill *and* smooth."

"Guilty as charged." Sawyer hooked their thumbs in the open wet suit and peeled it off.

Robin felt as if Sawyer had backed away, at least conversationally if not physically. There was clearly something, or multiple somethings, worth asking about there, but there was no clock ticking or ax hanging over their heads. She enjoyed having the time to explore at a leisurely pace, and as her eyes danced a deliberate trail over Sawyer's form stepping out of its strict confines, she could think of plenty of things she'd also like to take her time doing with this human.

She was still watching them as she tried to wriggle free from her own wet suit, but as she drew her leg out of the tight neoprene, she lost her balance slightly. Her foot snagged on the cuff, and she managed to hop a couple of times before tipping forward.

She squeezed her eyes tightly shut, bracing for the impact that always came with biting the dust. Instead of hitting the dirt, however, she collided with the warm, steady softness of another body.

"Whoa." Sawyer's strong arms wrapped around Robin and pulled her close. "Easy there, Ace."

Robin sank into the embrace automatically and opened her eyes to see Sawyer staring down at her. Those perfect lips turned up slightly, and light irises gave way to rapidly expanding pupils.

"Good catch." Robin made no move to pull away.

Sawyer's breath grew shallow, a subtle rise and fall of the chest Robin still pressed against. "You need help getting out of your wet clothes?"

"Need? No." She smiled. "Want? That's a much longer list."

Sawyer made a low hum of amusement, or maybe assent, and eased a little closer, only the space of a shared breath separating them. "Sounds about right."

Robin's lids grew heavy, and her line of sight dropped to focus on the mouth so close to her own. Anticipation tingled her senses. Still, Sawyer hesitated. Robin gave every single signal she was ready to be kissed, and she'd been kissed enough to know when someone else wanted the same, yet no kiss came. The tension went from exquisite to excruciating. Finally, she whispered, "If you're looking for consent, I can offer it physically, verbally, and enthusiastically."

Sawyer smiled broadly, even as they stepped back. The two reactions were so discordant, Robin's head spun.

Sawyer continued to hold her up, but at arm's length. She'd been sure she was about to be kissed and felt relatively certain about her ability to predict such things. Still, as Sawyer finally let their hands fall from her shoulders, the heat that had simmered between them seconds ago faded to a dull kind of warmth.

"Shall we head back?" Sawyer asked, as if nothing out of the ordinary had happened. It took entirely too long for Robin to realize they meant "back to Buffalo" and not "back to what they'd been doing in each other's embrace."

Still, she nodded. "Yeah, sure. I'm good to go."

The drive back to the city took about an hour, and while Robin sensed a bit of cooling down from where they'd been in the parking lot, Sawyer hadn't exactly pulled away as they told stories and jokes the whole way.

"So, that's why I had been smelling squid everywhere I went. It wasn't the town, it was me. I smelled like squid for days!"

Robin laughed. "I don't even know what squid smells like."

"Not good." Sawyer leaned back in the passenger seat, arm resting out the open window, head angled slightly toward Robin. They painted a perfect picture of relaxed happiness in the spring sun.

"How long were you in Spain?"

"That time or total?"

"Either."

"That trip was only about a month, but over the years, I've probably spent six or seven months there, all told. How about you?"

"Zero months."

"You've never been?" They sounded surprised, and for some reason, Robin felt as if the lapse was a little shocking, though she'd never given it any thought before. "*¿Por qué no?*"

"Maybe because my Spanish is *no bueno*."

"That's why you must go. Like many of the best things in life, total immersion is the way."

She could think of several things she'd like to immerse herself in right now, and world languages weren't in the top five.

"So, do you speak French?"

"No."

"*Vraiment?*" Sawyer raised their eyebrows. "Not even *voulez-vous coucher avec moi?*"

Robin laughed. "Well, maybe I picked up a few phrases that seeped into pop culture, but I can't say that I've ever needed to use that particular phrase in any language other than English."

"I'm sorry to hear it. I've found it tremendously helpful in Quebec, France, and one very interesting, long weekend in New Orleans."

Robin shook her head. "Maybe I should practice then."

"I could help," Sawyer offered, their smile turning a little coy. "French lessons tailored to very specific situations would be on-brand for me."

Robin's body warmed slightly as her mind filled in the blanks of what types of situations those lessons might entail.

"I'm surprised you didn't take either French or Spanish in high school, though," Sawyer mused. "You seem like one of those college prep kind of kids."

"I always wandered along to the beat of my own drum," Robin explained as she took the exit toward downtown Buffalo. "I did two years of sign language."

"What a great choice. You let your hands do the talking."

She laughed. "My reasoning exactly."

"I get you."

She glanced over at them, enjoying the disheveled look of their wind-dried hair, all tousled and sexy.

"What?"

"I suspect you do probably get me better than most people I meet."

"What makes you think so?"

"A vague sense, a good judge of character, and the fact that we're both a mess from falling into the same river right now."

"One of us dove, one of us got toppled in, but even that's a kind of bond, I suppose, the unity of people prone to going overboard one way or another." They glanced down at their damp board shorts and the bunched-up towel on the car seat. "I think I'm about to track our shared mess into Gillian's swanky apartment."

Robin pretended to grimace. "Good luck with that."

"How long do you think the fact that she missed me tremendously will keep me safe from her natural obsession with creating order?"

"As the primary pusher of that particular button in your absence, I don't care to hazard a guess." Robin bit her lip as if she maybe shouldn't say the next part, but restraint wasn't exactly her strong suit, at least not in social situations. "If you want to play it safe, you could come back to my place and shower there."

Sawyer pursed their lips as if giving the idea its due or maybe trying to hold in their cocky grin. "It'd be the only responsible thing to do, not to wear out my welcome and respect house rules."

"Right? You're a guest at Gillian's, and she won't be home to show you what towels you can use when you're really dirty."

Sawyer leaned conspiratorially close. "Are we really dirty?"

Robin gave them a deliberate once-over as she drove right past Gillian's. "I'd say mid-level … but the night is young."

Sawyer nodded. "It's not even dark, really. I have no curfew. What about you?"

"We're supposed to meet the others for drinks after Brooke's faculty thing."

Sawyer grimaced, and this time it didn't look pretend. "I forgot about that. Ugh."

Robin's heart beat a little faster at the reaction. It wasn't that she didn't want to hang out with her friends so much as that if Sawyer didn't want to, it might bode well for them making other plans together. "We could cancel."

"You have the power to shut down a faculty mixer?"

Robin laughed. "No, but we could not meet the others for drinks. I'm notoriously flaky. They won't think anything of it. I mean, they won't think anything of it socially. If I missed a work thing, Gillian's head might spin all the way around."

"Right." Sawyer's chuckle sounded more subdued than it had all day. "'Cause Gillian is a born girlboss. I keep forgetting."

"Forgetting Gillian's a boss?" Robin turned into a slightly run-down residential neighborhood. "That's some top-tier selective amnesia."

"No, I mean it's weird that she's your boss, or that you're a therapist at all. Every time I start to wrap my head around it, you say something inappropriate or dunk me into some Class III rapids."

"I'm a wealth of new experiences."

"But also a therapist." Sawyer rubbed their hands over their face as Robin slowed in front of a large Victorian home that had clearly been divided into several apartments.

"*And* also a therapist." She killed the engine and turned to look at them more fully, noting their complexion had lost a hint of its natural hue. "You okay?"

"Yeah. Thinking."

She waited. She had plenty of practice, but apparently Sawyer had their own skills for introspection, closing their eyes and drawing a slow, steady breath. Robin's chest constricted as she felt them slipping away even while still very much within arm's reach. When Sawyer's eyes fluttered open again, they were distant and unfocused. Robin pushed down the urge to groan. Instead, she nodded toward the house. "Care to step inside my office and tell me about it?"

Sawyer's jaw twitched, and they looked fully away. "Actually, no. I'd better go."

"Go?" She couldn't make the simple word compute.

"Yeah. I remembered there's something I need to deal with."

"Right now?"

"Sorry."

Robin sighed. "It's cool."

"Really, I do have a thing. It's complicated, but I really am sorry."

As she restarted the car, she repeated, "Totally cool, no apologies. They aren't really my jam. We're good."

People could change their minds. People could remember things they forgot. People could get triggered or whatever the hell just happened. She dealt with it all the time ... at work.

Only she hadn't expected Sawyer to be work.

Six

"Serious question." Brooke paused outside the university ballroom, and Sawyer's shoulders tightened one more notch. They wouldn't have thought it possible to ratchet up the tension any higher than when they'd left Robin a couple of hours ago, but the fact that it had spoke volumes about why they had to be here.

Still, Sawyer turned and forced their gaze to meet Brooke's directly. "Yes?"

Brooke reached out and straightened the knot of Sawyer's tie, probably more for effect than need. "Did you have a four-piece suit in your duffle bag?"

"What?"

Brooke cracked a smile. "I saw your luggage at Gilly's. It's like a backpack and a rucksack. Then a week later you crash this party looking like James Bond. I'm wondering if you carried a dress coat and silk vest across Iceland and Finland and other far-flung places."

Some of the tension melted as they slipped their hands into their pockets and struck a dapper little pose. "Of course, Darling. I'm a bon vivant, not a hobo."

Brooke's grin widened. "Oh, there you are."

"And here you are."

"Always," Brooke said with gravity, but instead of bringing the mood down, it bolstered Sawyer, who extended an elbow.

"Shall we?"

Brooke looped an arm through theirs with a decisive nod, and they stepped inside.

On the surface, it wasn't unlike any number of rooms Sawyer usually glided through with ease. They were completely comfortable in crowds of wealthy, powerful, or brilliant people, spaces often filled with strangers destined to become friends. Maybe that was the problem here ... too few strangers.

"Can I get you a glass of wine?" Brooke asked with a subtle tug toward the open bar.

"No." They rolled out their neck. "It's never wise to dull one's senses around Maura."

As if sensing their cue, several people in the middle of the room parted, and the hair on the back of Sawyer's neck stood on end.

An elegant woman a few yards away paused, as if sensing a similar sort of electricity, and turned slowly toward them. She wore a slim-fitting, gray suit coat over a crisp white Oxford, a matching pencil skirt, and heels high enough to not to be seen as sensible. Sawyer had to give a slight nod of appreciation. Their mother knew how to project an image, and this one spoke to professional sophistication laced with command. Her eyes, however, suggested anything but detached composure as they widened in recognition, then shock, then something else. Relief? Surely nothing so trite. Whatever the emotion, it passed quickly, or at least got covered by a slow smile tugging at thin, tight lips.

They moved toward each other, in some absurd metaphor of magnetism. Meeting in the middle of the room, there was an awkward collision, not quite a hug, a brush of bodies, the press of cheeks, the suggestion of a kiss that didn't quite connect.

"Sawyer."

"Mother."

Maura stepped back, a hand on their shoulder, the quick flick of eyes in a summary inspection. "You look ... well?"

They nodded, noting the way her blonde hair had yet to show a hint of gray. "And you look perfectly coiffed as usual."

"Thank you."

Sawyer wasn't sure either statement had been a compliment, but they weren't prone to overanalyzing.

"I'm glad you're home, and safe."

They lifted one shoulder, trying not to let their mind land for too long on words one might take issue with, like 'glad,' 'home,' or 'safe.' "It's good to be back in Buffalo."

"A brief visit, or a prodigal sort of homecoming?"

Sawyer forced a smile. "Only time will tell."

"Of course." Maura traced the lines of Sawyer's face with her inscrutable gaze. "Shall I prepare your room at my apartment?"

Sawyer let out a little laugh at the idea, then caught themselves. "No. Thank you. I haven't worn out my welcome at Gillian's yet."

A twitch at Maura's jaw suggested the news landed a bit like a barb, but she covered well enough. "How wonderful to reconnect with your friends. So, you've already settled in?"

"I'm not sure 'settled' is ever an apt description for me, but I'm working on reconnecting."

"I see you've worked through the process in order of importance." Maura's smile contained a saccharine sort of practice, as she seemingly registered Brooke's presence for the first time. "Thank you for making sure she found her way back to me."

"They"—Brooke emphasized gently—"actually surprised me by showing up tonight. Completely of their own volition."

Maura chuckled lightly. "Sounds like our Sawyer, only ever doing anything of their own volition."

Sawyer's shoulders relaxed slightly at the ease with which their mother noted the correction. "I've been back only long enough to overcome my jet lag. You're receiving the freshly washed and fully refreshed version of me."

"I'm glad you're here. I've missed having you around, and found myself eagerly awaiting even your sporadic communication, though I imagine I've missed a myriad of details along the way." Maura reached out as if she intended to touch Sawyer's face, maybe cup their cheek.

53

Both the move and her tone were so tender, Sawyer froze. Their mother seemed to read the confusion and changed course to merely give their arm a little squeeze through their suit coat.

"We've all got a lot of catching up to do," Brooke offered generously. "I, for one, can't wait to hear more about their exploits in Iceland."

"Indeed." Maura's smile softened. "I received a postcard of a volcano with very little description to offer context. She likes to keep us guessing."

Sawyer noticed the pronoun slip seemed to come with a hint of annoyance this time. "The eruption I saw wasn't like in the movies. It was slow, and a bit misleading from the road, because it flowed with a deceptive calm, but as I got closer, the heat was so intense it softened the soles of my boots."

"I hope you didn't get close enough to be in danger."

Sawyer grinned. "It's always a fuzzy line with me."

"They," Brooke cut back in, "have the most inherent sense of adventure of any human I've ever met."

"True." Maura sighed. "She was a pusher even as a little girl."

This time Sawyer did wince. A pronoun was one thing, but the word "girl" grated like sandpaper on sensitive skin. Unfortunately, Maura seemed to catch the outward sign of discomfort. She was too good at her job to miss such a tell.

"I apologize," she said in her professional tone. "I'll admit I did let myself believe you'd work your way through this particular phase in your long absence."

"Phase?" Sawyer arched an eyebrow. "Oh, my gender fluidity? I'm surprised you haven't consulted your trusty copy of the DSM-5 on that. Do you still keep one next to your bed?"

"I do, actually. I consult it regularly as I wonder where you are in the world and if you've found something there that's offered respite from the persistent dysphoria you've often claimed despite your inability to fit the diagnosis consistently." Maura said the words evenly enough, so much so that Sawyer felt more patronized than cared for. "I'm relieved your wit hasn't dulled amid your travels or your struggles, though even I'll admit your current aesthetic suits you."

"Thank you?"

"You're welcome. Truly, it is both a joy and a relief to have you appear so unexpectedly, looking healthy and vibrant. Whatever changes you've made internally seem to have left you sturdier than when you left."

Sawyer nodded while they took a deep breath and released it slowly. "Your professional assessment is spot-on, though I doubt anyone in this room would be surprised to hear it. My gender dysphoria has largely abated since my top surgery a year ago."

Something swift flickered over Maura's expression as her eyes dipped to Sawyer's chest and then back to their eyes, revealing something sad, dark, and maybe sympathetic. For a second, Sawyer felt a sting of hurt, not on their own behalf, but radiating from their mother, reminding them that this woman had a fluid nature of her own to contend with.

Then it was gone. Maura forced a placid smile, a trick of her trade, devoid of any personal revelation. "Then I'm also glad you found a course of treatment that works for you, even if it varied from the one I would've prescribed."

"It has," Sawyer confirmed.

"I suppose it's also a comfort to know your oppositional defiance doesn't include all medical care, only the maternal kind."

"Sawyer?" A man in a boxy sport coat ducked into their line of view. "Oh wow, it is you. Sawyer Stroud-Barton. Man, I haven't seen you around here in years."

They forced themself to take him in with more than a quick glance, noting his ruddy complexion and bulbous nose. Once those details registered, others clicked into place, as if a dam had been breached. His wine glass, the noise around them, the milling bodies in business attire, Sawyer's senses had focused so keenly on their mother, they'd lost track of the larger situation.

"You probably don't remember me," the man continued with a hint of chagrin.

"Of course I remember you, Dr. Alexander. You gave the most wonderful lecture on eye movement desensitization and reprocessing when I was about fifteen."

His smile blossomed, and his chest puffed up a little. "I can't believe you remember. You must've been to hundreds of lectures on a multitude of diverse topics."

"Yes, but yours had slides with photos of pregnant primates. I had never seen a chimpanzee giving birth before. It left quite an impression."

"An old trick I learned, include something a bit salacious to keep my students from drifting off."

"Sawyer enjoys little so much as the salacious," Maura cut back in. "It's good to be reminded some things stay consistent across the decades."

"I've always admired how much Sawyer's amazing core qualities remain constant amid their ebb and flow," Brooke offered with a slight brush of her fingers against the back of their hand.

"Hmm." Maura seemed to give the matter a passing thought. "I've always thought their inconsistency was evidence of a more fundamental internal push and pull."

"Of course you have." Sawyer laughed in a humorless way that at least kept them from clenching their jaw. "And as my mother is wont to remind us all, the way you label something affects how you experience it."

"She's right, you know?" Dr. Alexander beamed at his colleague with admiration.

"So I've heard." Sawyer took a step back, sensing their cue to make a break for the door. "Which is probably why I shouldn't monopolize her attention all evening. She's got an adoring public to face."

"Don't go on my account. I'd love to hear what you've been up to lately," he said quickly, then turning to Maura as if looking for backup added, "You haven't mentioned their exploits in a while."

56

She stiffened slightly and played it off with a wave of her hand. "I'm always so focused on work when we speak, but perhaps now that Sawyer's back in town and popping in around campus, she, excuse me, they, will deign to come by the office and regale us all with tales of the adventures that kept them away for so long."

He laughed again. "Maybe you should give the lectures this time. Wouldn't you attend that one, Brooke?"

She smiled at Sawyer broadly. "Whenever Sawyer speaks, I will gladly listen."

Sawyer fought the urge to look at their mother again to see if she'd caught the contrast. Very little got past Maura in a personal or professional capacity, but Sawyer knew better than to hope she'd make any meaning of the awareness. They'd given up on things like hope in that arena several years ago. Still, they'd accomplished what they'd come to do. "I'm sure you'll all see and hear plenty of me in the next few weeks."

"Weeks?" Maura nodded slowly, and some of the tension seemed to slip from her shoulders. "Lovely to hear."

It was a good note to end on, and Sawyer had experienced enough to know those didn't come around often, not for either of them. They stepped forward, catching the scent of their mother's signature Dior perfume, then pressing their cheek to hers and offering a one-armed embrace, whispered, "I'll be in touch."

"Good."

It was just a word, but it said enough. Sawyer turned for the door without having to wonder if Brooke would follow.

"Hey." Brooke caught their sleeve with a gentle tug.

Sawyer startled and spun around. "Shit."

"It's okay. You're okay." Brooke said the words in a tone that made it abundantly clear she was placating them, but also in a way that made Sawyer believe her. Damn her unshakable skill.

"Yeah." They ran a hand through their hair and glanced around. They'd been so hypervigilant during the conversation with their mom, they must've just shut off when they left. "Brookesy?"

"Yes?"

"Did I run?"

Brooke shook her head, her smile a little sad. "You walked quickly, but not until you did what you needed to do."

"Yeah." They sighed. "It could've been worse."

"With Maura? Undoubtedly."

"I told her."

Brooke nodded. "You told her so much. Which parts have meaning for you?"

"Don't do that." Their jaw tightened. "Don't fucking counsel me right now. I don't need to be managed."

Brooke laughed. "As if I'd be dumb enough to try. You are wholly ungovernable."

"Yeah." This time when they said the word, a smile tugged at their lips. "I really am."

"One of the many things I love about you."

"She knows I'm here." Sawyer looked around to get a stronger sense of where "here" was, somewhere near the middle of campus in the low glow of a lamppost on a chilly night in spring.

"She does." Brooke folded her arms across her chest and gently rubbed the thin sleeves of her little black dress.

Sawyer slipped out of their suit coat and draped it over her shoulders without asking. Then they smoothed the front of their own dress shirt. "She knows about the top surgery, too."

"Indeed." Brooke waited, watching, no doubt cataloging a myriad of emotions flickering across Sawyer's face.

"It's fine. I'm okay. I ... did you catch her response? She's glad I found a course of treatment that works, even if it varied from the one she would've prescribed? Who says shit like that?"

"Your mother. She has a real talent for conveying complex emotions with a brutally concise bite." Brooke reached out and loosened Sawyer's tie gently. "And I'm sorry for that."

"Meh." They shrugged. "Maybe she's right. Maybe my, what did she call it, 'oppositional defiance'? Feck me, can't believe I'd blocked that phrase."

"Hey." She gave the tie a little jerk. "She's not right."

"She's brilliant. Did you see the way those people look at her? Tell me she hasn't earned it."

Brooke opened her mouth, then closed it again.

"I know." Sawyer's shoulders sagged.

"She is brilliant," Brooke conceded. "She's undoubtedly one of the most impressive minds in our field, which makes it utterly galling that she thinks it appropriate to diagnose her own child. It's not okay. It's never been okay."

Sawyer waved her off. They didn't need to have this discussion again. "It's okay. Enough for tonight. It's over."

Brooke looked at them like she disagreed with their last statement, but instead of arguing, she played along. "Sure. Let's get you home."

"Not home. Out."

Brooke's smile spread. "If you're game, so am I. Want a ride to the bar?"

"Nope. I need more."

"More?" Brooke laughed. "Didn't you go whitewater rafting today?"

"Yes, and I agree that's enough bodily harm for one afternoon. Your friend is crazy by the way—hey, that's an idea."

"Really? Care to share it with me?"

"Let's call Gilly and your girl and crazy-sexy-cool Robin. I bet she's a blast at karaoke."

"No," Brooke said flatly.

"She's not?"

"I mean, she probably is. I wouldn't know because I don't do karaoke, and neither does Gilly."

"Gilly doesn't do karaoke because the rest of us don't stand a chance with you in the room. I know for a fact you've got a beautiful voice."

"Aw, thank you, and it's still a no. It has nothing to do with vocal talent, and everything to do with public humiliation."

Sawyer snickered. "I don't think that would stop Robin."

"We don't make plans based on where Robin sets her boundaries."

This time Sawyer cackled outright. The more Brooke protested, the more they wanted to push forward. They did a bit of mental gymnastics to keep their mother's voice from echoing "oppositional" through their brain. "How do you feel about private performances?"

Brooke eyed them suspiciously. "Seems like a trick question."

"I know you don't mind singing for me. What about Tegan? Have you sung to her yet?"

Her cheeks flushed a shade of pink visible even in the dim light. "Maybe she's heard me in the car, or the … around the house."

"Sure, let's pretend you weren't about to say 'shower.'" Sawyer started walking again, a more purposeful and familiar path through the quad this time.

Brooke kept up, because of course she did. "You know that even if you convince me, Gillian will never stand for a karaoke bar."

"Who said anything about a bar, Babe?" Sawyer grinned back at her. "Summon the crew. Tell them to BYOB."

"Summon them to where and what?"

"The hottest private showroom in town."

"Why does that make it sound like a strip club?"

"Only if you want it to be. You're so fond of boundaries, set them for us." Sawyer came to the back door of the music building, then pulled a set of keys and a pocketknife from their slacks. "The stage is yours, or it will be as soon as I jimmy this lock."

Brooke snatched the keys. "No picking locks at my place of employment."

"Why? I've done it before. You've been with me. Come on, it'll be like old times. Don't you want to—"

"Hey." Brooke cupped their face in her hands before saying, "I'm not arguing. I'm just saying it doesn't have to be exactly like old times because I've got a key card now."

Sawyer stood there for a second, soaking up the casual tenderness in Brooke's touch as a slow smile spread. "So, what you're saying is, I'm not breaking and entering, you are?"

Brooke pressed her forehead to Sawyer's quickly, then stepped back and snagged a faculty ID from her purse. "No one's breaking. We're all entering."

Sawyer snickered as Brooke swiped her card and the door latch clicked open. "Sounds like my kind of party."

Seven

"Which room?" Robin wasn't sure why they were whispering. She remained relatively certain Brooke wouldn't invite this group to some place they shouldn't be, but the quiet desolation of an academic building after eight o'clock on a Saturday night still gave "off-limits" vibes.

Gillian and Tegan seemed to agree as they tiptoed along behind her without turning on any lights.

"I don't know the number, but I'm getting a sense of déjà vu," Gillian said softly. "Turn right at the end of the hall."

They did as instructed, with only the light of Tegan's phone to illuminate the way, until she stopped abruptly. "Wait, what's that?"

They all paused at the sound of music, soft and clear, up ahead. Gillian's smile quirked wistfully. "Sawyer."

Robin's heart beat faster, and her hand tightened around the bottle of champagne chilling her fingers.

Brooke had been uncharacteristically vague in the message she'd sent Tegan saying to meet her on campus and bring their drink of choice. Of course, she'd wondered, or even hoped, Sawyer would join them, too, but given the way they'd left things earlier, she wasn't sure what to make of her own emotions on the subject. Now, though, with all the hypotheticals of their reunion gone, her confusion slipped in line behind the thrill of anticipation. Still, not even her prolific and creative imagination could've prepared her for what she found when she followed the sound to its source.

Pushing open a rather ordinary classroom door, they found Sawyer sitting at a baby grand piano. They were shrouded in the warm glow of a single light above them, wearing black slacks and a starched, white dress shirt open at the collar. A pang of something hot and sharp shot through Robin's chest and down into her stomach. She stood in the doorway for entirely too long, staring without breathing as her brain worked overtime to take in every detail of Sawyer's hands running languidly over the keys, or their bare feet pressing pedals. She'd never seen anything as sexy as this human, slightly undone, and pressing all the right buttons. Maybe nothing this sexy had ever existed before. Her mouth went dry as every bit of wetness in her body headed south, and her limbs went a little numb from the lack of oxygen. Her fingers started to slip from around the bottle of bubbly. Mercifully, Tegan chose that moment to place one hand on her back.

"Down girl," Tegan said under her breath as she slipped past her and eased the champagne from Robin's weakened grasp. "Breathe."

She tried to shake off the lapse, but the deep inhale she had to force into her lungs probably gave her away. "I'm chill."

Or at least she had been working to approximate chill until Sawyer noticed their presence and turned with a sultry smile.

"What are you doing in here?" Gillian asked, her voice grating on Robin's raw nerve endings.

"Sawyer's idea." Brooke materialized out of nowhere, or had she been there the whole time?

"Shocking." Gillian stepped around Robin to greet them, giving Sawyer a one-armed side-hug while they continued to play a light, lilting melody.

"I suppose I should've seen this coming. You've been home a couple of weeks. It's about time for the breaking and entering to begin."

Sawyer grinned up at her. "I'm not breaking, just entering."

"That's what she said," Robin interjected without thinking.

Gillian rolled her eyes, but Sawyer snorted softly. "You going to stand in the doorway, or come grace us with your chaotic energy?"

Robin shrugged as if that wasn't the most enticing invite she'd received in a while. "I suppose I could hang for a bit."

"Generous of you." Sawyer seemed completely at ease conversing and tinkering with the keys at the same time. They turned to Gillian. "I would've chosen somewhere with a bigger stage and audience, but Brooke said you wouldn't want to go to a karaoke bar."

"Correct," Gillian confirmed. "Everything about that sounds heinous."

Sawyer exchanged a knowing glance with Brooke. "Agree to disagree, but out of an abundance of respect for your boundaries, I secured a more private venue for your performances this evening."

"Aw," Tegan said at the same time Gillian grumbled, "Hell no."

Sawyer laughed. "You all previously set the limit at physical harm. I met your standard of care."

"What about emotional harm?" Gillian shot back. "Can't we add an addendum forbidding activities that risk any kind of harm?"

"Sorry." Sawyer shook their head. "I already saw my mother tonight, so the 'first, do no harm' ship has sailed."

Gillian grimaced and immediately dropped her argument. "I'm glad you called."

Every ounce of Robin's natural curiosity came forward and clashed with her limited sense of decorum. There was clearly something big and heavy there, but Sawyer wasn't offering details, and no one else seemed to find it appropriate to ask. Then again, maybe they all knew, and it set her teeth on edge to be the only one in the room who wasn't acquainted with Sawyer's demons.

Still, Sawyer didn't seem to be battling any unseen enemies at the moment, as they stroked the keys with a grace and command that showcased talented hands. Robin's breath grew shallow.

"So, we're, like, what?" Tegan asked. "Having a personal cabaret or something?"

"Or something, yes." Sawyer nodded and picked up the tempo of their melody. "And your girl is about to get us started."

"Seriously, you're going to let her go first?" Gillian pushed back again. "You can't set the bar that high for the evening."

"Okay, Boo Bear!" Sawyer played the opening notes of a processional. "Take the stage from her, Boss Woman."

"Not a chance." Gillian fell into one of the student desks scattered throughout the room, crossing one leg over the other and folding her arms over her chest. Then her pressed lips gave a little upward twitch. "But you're right. I'm the boss, and while I work to dismantle hierarchies at the office, I don't mind reinforcing them on a Saturday night."

Sawyer laughed. "Get after it, girl."

Gillian's expression took on a hint of mischief. "Tegan, you're up first."

"Me?" Tegan feigned shock. "Why?"

"Given how your first few days in the office went, we never got into playful 'new girl' hazing."

"I would've thought the trauma more than paid my dues," Tegan argued.

Sawyer leaned toward Robin, who still stood to the side of the piano. "I'm still very eager to hear this story."

"It's not even one story," Robin confirmed conspiratorially. "It's like a whole book."

"Glorious." Sawyer shook a few strands of hair from their face, and Robin fought the urge to run her fingers through the lush, thick mop. "Maybe you'll lay it on me next time we go thrill seeking?"

Robin pulled on all her professional training to keep her eyebrows from shooting up at the mention of a next time. "Sure. I'm down for whatever."

Sawyer grinned. "I like that about you."

Robin fought the urge to say she liked literally everything about Sawyer right now. "Mutual."

"Tegan goes first, or no one goes." Gillian cut back in.

"Damn." Sawyer laughed. "She got bossier while I was gone. What do you say, Teegs? Consent?"

Tegan's cheeks flushed pink, but she nodded. "Do you know any Taylor Swift?"

Sawyer threw back their head and laughed. "As if I haven't wooed many a woman with this one."

Tegan's eyes lit up as Sawyer segued perfectly into the opening strains of "Lover."

"Oh Lord." Tegan shuddered, then locked eyes with Brooke, who beamed right back at her. "Okay, it's like a trust fall. I can do it."

"Wait, you need a microphone." Robin glanced around quickly before remembering the bottle of champagne. She passed it to Tegan, who immediately committed to the bit. Gripping the neck, she sang right into the cork top, though her eyes rarely flicked away from Brooke as she crooned about leaving Christmas lights up until January and making a place of their own.

She could sing. Not, like, Taylor Swift-level sing, but she could more than carry the tune, and everyone giggled or gave a hoot of approval as the silliness and joy of finding this out about a friend mingled with the fun of the number itself.

Sawyer swayed along as they played with feeling. Robin marveled at how quickly and easily it had all come together. How could this human just summon them and orchestrate a performance, beautiful, vulnerable, dreamy, like some maestro of music and artistic musing. Even Gillian in all her grumbling had found a way to play along as she sat in the front row and rocked back and forth as Tegan used the song to swear to be overdramatic and true.

Suddenly it didn't quite feel like a silly game, but rather a solemn vow.

Robin eased into the chair next to her boss, and the two of them exchanged a little smile. Tegan didn't seem to notice, as she and Brooke had slipped into their own world again. As Tegan sang about always being this close, Robin leaned over and whispered, "Ten bucks says they move in together next month."

Gillian shook her head, copper hair brushing across her shoulders. "A fool's bet. Some people are too magnetic to resist."

The sentiment hit Robin in the chest and caused her to turn back toward Sawyer, only to find them watching her as they played the final notes of the song with a flourish.

Everyone burst into applause, but she wasn't looking at Tegan anymore or musing on her magnetism so much as feeling her own internal pull to the person playing the piano.

"Well done," Gillian congratulated with only a hint of grudging. "I should've known you'd set the bar high."

Brooke wrapped her arms around Tegan and kissed her soundly.

Robin reached out and snagged the bottle from her friend's hand so she could return the embrace more fully.

"Hey," Sawyer called, "you can sing into an empty bottle as much as a corked one."

"God, I appreciate the way you think." Robin set about unwrapping the top. "Besides, T-Bird earned a drink after that stellar rendition."

"Yes, she did," Brooke called. "Pop that cork."

"Pretty sure you've already popped her cork," Robin said, causing Sawyer to snicker and everyone else to roll their eyes, but she did manage to open the bubbly with minimal spillover. Then she passed the bottle to Tegan.

"We didn't bring any cups." Tegan flushed and stared at the bottle longingly.

"Meh." Robin waved her off. "You and Brookesy swap spit on the regular."

Brooke shook her head. "You always say the most romantic things."

"And I'm not regularly swapping spit with anyone," Gillian added.

"No, but I did see you accidentally drink from Tegan's oat milk latte last week, so you swapped with her, and by extension that means that you and Brooke have—"

"Stop." Gillian held up a hand. "You could've said, 'we don't mind sharing drinks among friends,' but if you say 'spit' one more time …"

"Got it!" Robin laughed. "What about you, Sawyer? Do you mind a little transfer of bodily fluids between friends?"

Sawyer lifted one shoulder and grinned. "I'm not really a drinker, but I'd be open to other methods under the right circumstances."

Robin's breath caught, and her mind rushed back to the image of those lips so close to her own. She wanted to blurt "me too," or lean in to demonstrate her willingness, but as quickly as she flashed back to their near kiss, she summoned the memory of Sawyer shutting down and pulling away. She felt the pull as much as the push, and torn between the two, she settled for a simpler test of physical contact. Raising her hand, she grinned. "High five."

Sawyer didn't even hesitate. Rising up, they slapped Robin's palm with authority.

"Brooke," Gillian pleaded behind them, "I can't take two of them in the same room."

"Yes." Sawyer turned their attention back to the room at large. "Brookesy, save us from ourselves. Take that bottle from your boo and bring that sultry voice of yours to the stage."

"What can I possibly sing to meet the incredibly high bar Tegan set?"

Sawyer smiled and began to play. It took a few seconds, but when Brooke recognized the melody, her smile spread, and looking at Sawyer with so much love and affection, she mouthed, "Perfect."

Then, with a deep breath and a beautifully clear voice, she launched into the opening lines of "Can't Help Falling in Love."

Gillian hadn't sung anything, but after several incredibly moving performances, she declared the need to lighten the mood, and Sawyer obliged by cuing up "Don't Go Breaking My Heart" for Brooke and Tegan to do as a duet. They all laughed and cheered and took turns passing the bottle-turned-microphone, either to drink from or sing into. Robin took a dance solo, then grabbed Gillian's hand and got her to dance along. She was softening. They all were. It had been so long since any of them had allowed themselves to be silly, a fact Gillian gave voice to when the song ended.

"I'm out of practice."

"With what?" Tegan asked. "Dancing? Laughing? Generalized shenanigans?"

"Yes," Gillian answered emphatically.

"Then it's a good thing I've returned to whip you back into shape." Sawyer stopped playing for the first time since they'd walked into the room, and scooting over on the piano bench, patted the spot they'd vacated. "Come on, Gilly, what's it going to take to get you to sing for us?"

Tegan passed her the bottle/mic, and Gillian took a healthy swig, then seemed to think for a moment before laughing. "Nope, still not loose enough yet. I'm afraid we might kill this bottle long before we kill my sense of decorum."

"No fun," Robin said.

"You haven't taken a turn yet," Brooke observed. "Maybe you need to do a number to get Gillian loosened up."

"I've spent years of my life trying to get Gilly Bean to let down her hair without much success."

"Not true," Gillian shot back. "You've gotten me to go ax-throwing, and to laser tag, and to a midnight showing of *The Rocky Horror Picture Show*."

"Seriously?" Sawyer laughed. "Mad props. I don't know if I should be impressed or jealous that you did those things with anyone but me."

"You were gone a long time." Gillian rested her head on Sawyer's shoulder. "Robin had to fill the void."

"That's what she said," Robin said quickly, and this time got a little chuckle from even Tegan, before she continued. "But I am absolutely feeling jealous of the fact that you breezed back in and now you have these three singing and dancing in your personal cabaret."

Sawyer waved her off. "They secretly want to cut loose. You just have to know which buttons to push for social lubricant, which, incidentally, is *also* what she said."

Robin cackled. "Teach me your ways."

Sawyer met her gaze and held it for a second longer than usual, as if searching or taking stock, but the intensity behind gray eyes faded in a blink, replaced by amusement. "With your talents for mischief and my insights for leading stoic women astray, I'm not sure the universe could handle our combined powers."

"We could not." Gillian gave Sawyer a gentle shove and turned to Robin. "Don't even think about ganging up on us."

"I would never," Robin said with mock solemnity, then winked at Sawyer.

Brooke laughed. "Quick, pick another song, Gilly, before they start plotting mutiny."

"No," Sawyer said. "I'll pick the songs."

"I don't consent," Gillian shot back quickly.

"You will though," Sawyer pushed. "I'll pick something so enticing you won't even realize it wasn't your idea in the first place."

Gillian rolled her eyes. "I bet that's what you say to all the girls."

"Yes, but I've had no complaints."

"Good God." Gillian turned to Brooke. "Rescue me."

Brooke pursed her lips as if pondering her options. "I'm not inclined to extract you from the situation completely. However, I may offer a reprieve, as I need to run to the restroom, and I'll make Sawyer promise not to start up again before I get back."

"Deal," Sawyer said.

"I'll go with you," Tegan offered.

"Then Robin has to go, too," Gillian said. "I can't have you two disappearing and letting the chaos twins gang up on me."

"Fair." Tegan grabbed Robin's arm and tugged her toward the door.

She let herself be led into the dark hallway, with only a slight wistful glance back at Sawyer. It would've been fun for them to tag team the boss, but she did have a question that had been biding its time in the back of her mind, and a few minutes away from Sawyer might help her to process it a little more clearly.

Brooke led them to a bathroom and entered one of the stalls, with Tegan taking the one beside her. Robin eyed herself in the mirror. She'd detangled her hair from the trauma it'd suffered in the river earlier that day, then immediately mussed it up again in a more stylized sort of disheveled. She hadn't worn any makeup other than a little mascara, but her tight, black V-neck made her eyes seem even darker in the low light. It wasn't a bad look for her, and if they'd gone to the bar as originally planned, more than a few women would've taken notice by now.

Had Sawyer?

"Hey," Tegan called from inside her stall, "how was whitewater rafting?"

"Amazing," she said. "We did end up in the river at one point, but choices were made."

"I love how you say that in passive voice, like they weren't made by you."

She smiled. "You know how it goes. There are decisions you make deliberately, and ones that present themselves to you in a flash of inspiration."

"I love your inspirations … and Sawyer's too, apparently. This is so fun."

"Maybe you should let people like us set the itinerary more often."

71

"Don't sign on that dotted line," Brooke warned.

Robin glanced at her reflection again and enjoyed the mischievous curl of her own lips as she imagined what she and Sawyer could get up to if given half the chance. Still, that's all it was, imagination. She'd been given some pretty good indicators of where Sawyer's mind might go, but despite her usual ability to read people pretty quickly, she still had concerns about what'd happened earlier, or at least what she thought had happened, as her understanding remained cloudy.

"About that," she started as Tegan exited the stall and met her by the sinks. "Earlier, um, Sawyer and I were having a great time, and then, I don't know, maybe it ran its course, but Brooke, you know them better than I do, you know?"

"As well as anyone can know Sawyer," Brooke confirmed.

"So, like, are they shy, or, I don't know, old-fashioned?"

Brooke laughed lightly. "Old-fashioned?"

Robin tried again. "Like, with women. Are they reserved, or do they like to take things slow?"

This time Brooke's laugh wasn't restrained at all. It echoed off the tile walls and floor. It shook Brooke's shoulders as she exited the stall and rattled across Robin's nerves.

Brooke stepped to the sink and started washing her hands, still trying to catch her breath from what she'd clearly read as a joke, but when Tegan placed a hand gently on her arm, she glanced up first toward her girlfriend, then, reading her expression, looked toward Robin. Her entire demeanor shifted, but she managed to say only, "Oh."

Robin cringed. Her friends were too good at their jobs and too good as friends to misread the situation.

"They're just back in town," Tegan offered kindly. "I'm sure re-entry is overwhelming."

"Of course." Robin waved her off.

"And there's a lot of relationships in play," she continued in a soothing tone. "Sawyer's staying with your boss, and best friends with Brooke. There's a ton of history, and you're a colleague."

"Yeah, yeah." She forced a little laugh of her own. It wasn't as if she hadn't known all those things. She just hadn't cared, at least not enough to worry. She didn't often worry about other people's reactions. She also knew Brooke and Gillian well enough to trust them to handle any genuine emotion, and it seemed odd that Sawyer wouldn't feel the same way. "I might've misread the situation earlier."

Brooke's expression softened even further. "I doubt it, but maybe there are multiple situations at play. You're very good at reading the ones you have access to."

"Ah, I get it." She didn't, not really, but she at least understood the sentiment, and she recognized the way they'd learned to talk to each other about things they couldn't talk to each other about. Brooke knew things about Sawyer, and she wouldn't betray that trust, even in a safe space with people who she might usually confide in. Robin adored her for that, even if she couldn't control a subtle hint of jealousy that Brooke knew both her and Sawyer in ways they hadn't been allowed to know each other.

Still, a boundary was a boundary, and she respected that enough not to push. Sawyer'd said they had something to do tonight, and given their playful attitude over the last hour, maybe they'd done it. Maybe Robin hadn't misread anything. At least Brooke had confirmed that Sawyer wasn't generally opposed to letting a good time lead where it may, and maybe Robin hadn't misstepped at all so much as bumped into a broader context. There was only one way to find out. She squared her shoulders, lifted her chin, and grinned. "Shall we get back in there?"

Eight

"I'm proud of you, you know?" Gillian bumped Sawyer's shoulder with her own. Just a little move, a little affirmation, but given the source, it meant a lot. Gilly wasn't the kind to initiate physical affection or blow smoke, and that knowledge both warmed Sawyer's stomach and made it tighten.

"It was nothing." They shrugged, not wanting to make too much of anything, even though they were self-aware enough to realize that summoning their friends for a command performance was, in some way, a celebration or an avoidance, depending on who you asked, but they hadn't asked.

"It's something," Gillian pushed gently, "but you don't have to dwell on it now."

"What, I don't need to narrate my trauma before it sticks?"

Gillian gave them a wry smile. "Are we labeling the evening as traumatic?"

Sawyer played a little trill on the piano. "Walked right into that one."

"I'm off the clock." Gillian placed her hands on the keys and tested a few gently. "I was never on the clock with you."

"But you're too damn smart." They'd always liked that about her. Gillian understood things other people didn't. She didn't flaunt it, but she didn't shy from her IQ either, a rare mix in Sawyer's world. "When you were in school, I loved how much you admired my mother without being taken in by her. Some people are afraid of her, some of them don't recognize her brilliance, and some go all-out sycophant."

"Accurate." Gillian tentatively tapped out the opening notes to "Heart and Soul." "Glad to know I didn't fall into the latter category in your estimation."

"You could never be a bootlicker, Gilly Bean."

"Gee thanks. You say the sweetest things."

Sawyer picked up the chords to Gillian's melody, matching her deliberate pace. "I think I was drawn to you because I knew you would always form your own opinions."

"Now that's a compliment worth giving." Gillian picked up the tempo slightly. "What changed? Or should I say, which one of us changed?"

"Maybe neither of us did. Maybe that's the problem." Sawyer layered in chords on top of Gillian's carefully pecked-out notes. "Maybe we were always going to be these people, but, for a moment, we were still finding that out at the same time."

"I'm still finding that out all the time," Gillian mused.

"I like that about you, too. Always on the journey."

"Something we have in common."

Sawyer smiled. They'd never thought of it that way, maybe because it hadn't felt that way when they'd left. "Once you started your own practice and then Brooke joined, all the talk about school, and movies, and women faded. It didn't feel like you were searching anymore. It felt like I was still fooling around, and you'd already found out. I knew it was just a matter of time …"

"Until what?"

"Until you and Brookesy got your shit together enough to see me the way that she does."

Gillian's breath caught, and she stopped playing. Sawyer didn't turn to face her, but they felt the intensity of her gaze. They didn't want to see the emotions in those green eyes. Hurt, shock, pity, concern, it didn't matter. They'd imagined it all a million times already, so they merely whispered, "It's okay."

"It is most certainly not okay," Gillian shot back.

"Thought you were off the clock."

"I very much am." Gillian gave them a little shove as if to prove their point. "I would never speak to a client the way I'm about to speak to you. Of all the fucked up, unfair, and completely unfounded things to pin on me, Sawyer. After everything we went through, everything we did, all the nights you led Brooke and me into God-knows-where, all the sunrises we watched, you actually thought—"

"I didn't say it was logical."

"And that makes it better? Two years. You disappeared for two years, because you didn't trust me enough?"

"Because I didn't trust *me* enough," they corrected as a door down the hall closed. "Hey, quick, is Robin seeing anyone?"

Gillian opened her mouth and stared at them, cheeks flushing almost as red as her hair. "Are you serious right now? That's your segue?"

Sawyer laughed lightly. "It's not a bad one."

Footsteps grew closer in the hallway, and Gillian blinked some of the fire out of her eyes. "This conversation is not over."

"It'll never be over between us, Gilly." Sawyer grinned. "We have our whole lives to figure it out, okay?"

She didn't look at all convinced, but some of the tension left her shoulders. "You're maddening."

"And you love me."

Gillian sighed. "So much."

"Now, answer my other question."

"No." She pursed her lips.

Sawyer laughed again. "Good, I didn't want you to tell me anyway. I'm more of a fuck around and find out kind of person."

Gillian finally cracked a smile. "See, we're the same people we used to be. You still like to push buttons."

"And you still let me."

"Let you what?" Brooke asked as she came back into the room, followed by Tegan and Robin.

"Gillian lets me test her boundaries."

"She always has," Brooke said wistfully. "Are you about to cross a line with your next song choice?"

"Absolutely." Sawyer sat a little straighter. "And I'm going to pull on inside information to do it."

"Don't you dare," Gillian warned, but not with any of the ferocity that had burned in her a moment ago.

Sawyer grinned at her wickedly as they brought their hands to the keys and played the iconic opening to "Hit Me Baby One More Time."

Tegan and Robin exchanged a confused look, but Brooke laughed so hard she doubled over.

Sawyer played it again, and Gillian started to shake her head. "I haven't had nearly enough champagne."

Sawyer didn't stop though, and Brooke piled on. "You have to. It's Britney, bitch."

Gillian rolled her eyes.

Robin jumped in. "Are you a closet Britney Spears fanatic?"

"No," Tegan said, then asked, "Wait? Really?"

"It's not happening," Gillian protested, then undercut herself by asking, "Can you even play this song on the piano?"

"Watch me." Sawyer took off into the opening verse, but still Gillian had her heels dug in. They turned to Robin, who was already bopping along, eyes sparkling with mischief and mirth. "Come on, thrill buddy. Help her out."

It didn't take any more nudging for Robin to spring into action. She grabbed Gillian's hand and hauled her to her feet singing, "Oh baby, baby."

Gillian cringed. "The only thing worse than me singing it would be you singing it to me."

"Let's do it together," Robin encouraged. Then, before getting a response to her offer, she grabbed the now nearly empty bottle and crooned about how her loneliness was killing her.

Gillian rolled her eyes, but as the chorus rolled around, she caved. Sawyer had never doubted for a second. Gillian was 100 percent boss at her core, but no one wanted to be in control all

77

the time. Sawyer continued to play as Robin and Gillian began to vamp it up, and Tegan and Brooke lost their damn minds, but the performance itself wasn't nearly as appealing as the moment Gillian surrendered to her silly side.

Sawyer's chest swelled with pride at the fact that they still had the ability to soften those sharp edges. They didn't want to break a boundary so much as bend it. Again, their mind flashed to their mother's comments about their oppositional nature, but this time, they didn't let the comment stick around long enough to sting.

Gillian was their friend, and she hadn't turned into someone else, at least not the someone else Sawyer's mother had tried to train her to be. No, Gillian hadn't fallen under Maura's spell. She'd fallen under Sawyer's, and there was a certain satisfaction to that.

Still, as Robin leaned in and shook out her dark, shimmering hair on the bridge of a pop anthem, Sawyer couldn't deny that she'd played her own role in bringing this side of the boss forward. Sawyer hadn't done it all on their own. Robin had provided the right kind of peer pressure and offered up her own unwillingness to take herself too seriously as the example for Gillian to follow. And she had followed. Gillian hadn't been able to remember her own "no" with Robin happily dancing along to "yes."

The two of them actually made a great team. They played off each other, moving to the beat, improvising moves, playfully spinning and taking turns with the "microphone" or singing backup for each other.

The song was in its final chorus, and Gillian was clearly flagging, but Robin seemed to move in the opposite direction. Ready to crescendo, she hopped up to sit on the piano and spreading her arms wide open, she encouraged everyone to sing along on the last refrain. Brooke and Tegan needed little prodding, and even Sawyer managed to lend their voice. How Robin heard them among the cacophony of laughter and music was beyond Sawyer, but she clearly did, turning first her head and then her whole body toward the sound.

Her eyes sparked as she rolled onto her stomach and then onto her hands and knees, as if there was no one else in the room but them. They locked eyes, and the muscles in Robin's arms flexed. Sawyer's gaze ran along her lithe form. The sight of her, close and unabashedly sexy, caused their fingers to fumble.

It was only a little slip, one discordant note, but Robin noticed. Her eyes flicked to Sawyer's hands, then up again as her smile slipped from playful to almost predatory, like a cat about to pounce.

Sawyer finished the song with a little shiver of pleasure. They were used to being the one on the hunt, but with Robin staring down at them, they couldn't do anything other than relish the prospect of being this woman's prey.

"Oh my God, it's after eleven o'clock." Brooke emphasized her point by not quite stifling a yawn.

Sawyer laughed, and Robin joined them. It was clear where the battle lines would fall on this one. Two of them were just getting started, and Sawyer was glad to be one half of that equation.

Gillian came to Brooke's defense. "Go ahead, and yuck it up, you two, but we're not all vampires."

Sawyer grinned at Robin. "Are you a vampire?"

Robin lifted one shoulder noncommittally. "You won't know until you invite me inside."

Sawyer blew out a low whistle. "Fuck being undead, are you sure you're a therapist?"

"She is," Gillian said emphatically. "I can vouch for that, but the jury's still out on the whole sleeps-in-a-coffin thing."

"Who said anything about sleep?" Robin shot back.

"Me." Tegan snuggled up next to Brooke. "I'm ready to get this one to bed."

"*Et tu*, Tegan?" Sawyer acted betrayed. "You can't side with the old ladies. Aren't you, like, nineteen years old?"

"Oh God." Brooke covered her face with her hands. "I'm an 'old lady' and you're a teenager."

Tegan laughed. "I'm thirty, and you're a sexy old lady."

"So when you said 'bed' you didn't mean 'sleep.' Right?" Robin drew out the last word.

Tegan bit her lip. "I meant sleep … *eventually*."

"Well, in that case." Robin lifted her hand in the air. "High five."

Tegan slapped her palm while Brooke shook her head.

Sawyer marveled yet again at how the dynamic had changed in their absence and all the ways it hadn't. Or maybe "change" wasn't the right word, because Brooke and Gillian hadn't become different people so much as expanded.

Maybe that's why it hadn't felt weird to have Tegan and Robin slip so effortlessly into their circle as well. Sawyer had slipped easily back into a more secure sense of self tonight. These women helped them feel comfortable and competent in ways that should've been harder to summon so soon after their mother inspected them like some sort of confusing lab experiment.

They'd spent the last two years learning to live life out from under the microscope, and in doing so, Sawyer developed skills for shaking things off their back. The others in the room might've called them "coping mechanisms," and their mother would've probably labeled them "numbing behaviors." Maybe in the past they even had been, but looking around at these women, the numbness had worn off. "Okay, I'm fine to call it a night, too, after one last song. Who wants it?"

Sawyer turned to Brooke, who seemed the obvious choice, but Gillian cut them off. "Not Brooke. She's too good, and now we know Tegan is too."

"You want the stage, G-Money?" Robin asked.

"Not a chance," she shot back. "You haven't taken a solo yet, and I think that's incredibly unlike you."

"Nah." Robin laughed, swinging her legs from her perch atop the piano. "You know me. I rarely have trouble finding a partner to make sweet music with."

Sawyer chuckled. "I think we have a winner. What's your poison, Chaos Vampire?"

Robin rolled on her side and hit Sawyer with a deep dark stare. "Can you do 'Edge of Glory' by Lady Gaga?"

They nodded. "I like the way you think."

"I like the way you play."

"I like that you're not too shy to say so." Sawyer struck up the opening chords.

Robin's eyes scanned them up and down deliberately, her lips parting as if she might say something else, something more. Instead, she sang the opening line of the song, something about not having any reason they should be alone tonight.

Sawyer knew the tune well enough, but no matter how many times a person had bopped along to a pop song, the lyrics never quite hit the way they did when this woman stretched, lush and languid, across the front of a piano and pointed the words right at them. Suddenly, Robin wasn't the only one on the edge of glory.

So much for numbing behavior or needing to thaw anyone else. Sawyer was downright sweltering, soaking up the heat radiating off Robin. Somewhere inside, they were dimly aware that if they'd made different choices hours ago, they might've already quenched the thirst rising in them now, but where was the fun in winning the game before it'd gotten a chance to really get played?

They wouldn't have missed this for anything, not with Robin singing, over and over again, about being on the edge with them. In theory, there were three other people in the room who could've been included in the phrase, but surely none of them felt it hit their core the same way. No, Sawyer had been on the edge for so long. They lived there, but rarely had they had such enticing company.

"Ta da!" Robin hopped off the piano and took a bow to wild applause. "Forget you bitches who can actually sing. I know how to put on a show."

"Nailed it," Tegan called, wrapping her in a hug. "What a number to end on."

"End on?" Robin laughed. "The night is young for me. I might not get to stay here, but I don't have to go home."

"You do you, friend," Brooke said, catching Tegan around the waist and pulling her back.

"But Tegan's going to do you?" Sawyer finished.

Robin cackled. "My God, you're perfect."

Sawyer rose and took a bow as well. "It's nice to be recognized for my many talents."

"I won't affirm the innuendo about our best friend." Gillian dropped a hand on Sawyer's head and gave their hair a little ruffle. "But you are damn good, both on the piano and at drawing people out."

"Just you, Boo." Sawyer batted their eyelashes at her. "Sure you don't want to go out with Robin?"

"Very much certain about my 'no' on that one," Gillian said. "I'm going to walk back across campus, collect my car, and not pass go or collect $200 as I head straight home."

"Fair," Sawyer said grudgingly. "You earned that, and to show my appreciation, I'll come with and keep crashing on your couch."

"What a generous offer." Gillian laughed as they all headed out, killing the lights and closing the doors behind them as they went.

They made it all the way down the silent hallway and to the outside door before Sawyer noticed the cold on their toes. "Shit, I forgot my shoes."

"Seriously?" Gillian shook her head. "I have never once forgotten to wear shoes in a public space."

Sawyer shrugged. "I'm not good at being restrained."

"I never thought of shoes as restraints so much as protections," Brooke mused, "but we can go back."

82

"Nah, I'll run back. Gilly, why don't you pull up the car, and I'll meet you at the curb, you know, like you're my limo driver?"

"How is that the least weird thing you've asked of me tonight?" Gillian shook her head. "Are you sure you won't lose your way in the dark?"

"I am never sure of that, but I'll take my chances."

"I'll go with them," Robin said casually enough that no one argued, but Tegan did share a quick look, first with Robin and then with Brooke. What was it with therapists being able to talk with their eyes? Whatever the message or question, it seemed willing to wait, or at least to take a back seat to Brooke's hand on her own as Tegan trailed her out the door.

Robin started down the hallway, and Sawyer gave only a passing thought to what the two of them could find to do in the dark before following along.

As soon as they were back in the piano studio, Sawyer located their shoes right where they'd kicked them off. They hurriedly retrieved the socks they'd stuffed inside and pulled everything back on, but Robin didn't seem to be in any rush, another thing to admire about her. Sawyer watched her wander in a slow circle of moonlight coming through a window. She then picked up the empty champagne bottle they'd also forgotten, and grinned. "Should we take this out and recycle it, or should we leave it for some unsuspecting piano professor to wonder what they missed come Monday morning?"

Sawyer pointed to the piano. "Place it on the altar, an offering to the gods of mischief."

Robin did so with great reverence, pausing to genuflect and back away slowly.

"Well done." Sawyer moved closer to stand next to her and admire the scene of the crime. "I think this is the most fun I've ever had sneaking around this campus."

"Have you done it often?" Robin asked without turning to look at them.

"Over the years? Too many times to count."

"So, is this the thing you had to do earlier?"

83

Sawyer turned toward her. "Honestly, it wasn't the thing I was thinking of at the moment, but yeah, I think I did need this more than I cared to admit, maybe even more than the other thing, though this followed logically from that."

Robin smiled. "I'm familiar with the concept if not the details."

"I bet." Sawyer inclined their head toward the door. "Shall we adjourn?"

"On to the next adventure." Robin led the way out into the hall once again.

The quiet felt more eerie with just the two of them, and Sawyer fought the urge to fill it. There wasn't any need. They'd had a great night after surviving the precipitating event with their mother. Sawyer found themself and their people again, and this woman had come along for the ride. What's more, Robin had never argued or brought her own insecurities along. She'd never sought to steal the spotlight, but she hadn't shied away when it'd landed on her. She'd been all in, and she'd been sexy as hell along the way. It didn't hurt that she'd sent all the right cues straight to Sawyer without ever exuding even a hint of neediness. Robin made it clear she was right there, so perfectly present. Take her or leave her.

Was Sawyer really about to leave?

There were plenty of logical reasons. Robin was part of their friend group, which could make things awkward. Robin worked with Gillian, which muddled the relationship. They'd likely see each other often, even if things went badly. Still, as their eyes adjusted to the dim light, Robin's silhouette showed more than enough to suggest things between them would not go badly, at least from a physical standpoint. Did it even need to be anything more than that? It never had before, and Sawyer had broken through stronger personal boundaries for significantly less.

No, the only reason seriously standing in their way with Robin was Maura. She would have a field day with Sawyer being attracted to a therapist. No doubt she'd see it as some transference bullshit, but even speculating on that internally pissed them right off. They'd been attracted to Robin the moment they saw her. They were hot for her while she'd held court in a crowded bar. They were hot for her even when she'd hauled them out of a river. They were hot for her while she'd danced and sung atop a piano. None of those were things Maura ever did, and even trying to picture them made Sawyer laugh.

Robin turned toward them as she reached the door to outside. "Did the voices in your head tell you a funny joke?"

They snorted softly. "Actually, yes."

"Anything you care to share with the class?"

Sawyer shook their head slowly. "I'm not sure I would."

"That's fine." Robin placed her hand on the door, clearly intending to push it open, but Sawyer covered it with their own, stopping her short.

The two of them stared at each other for a second before Robin said, "Whatever it is, you don't owe me an explanation."

The tension slipped from Sawyer's shoulders as they slipped their fingers between Robin's and eased her hand off the door. "Good. Explanations are not my strong suit. Neither is logic when I'm standing so close to such an alluring woman."

Robin's smile spread slowly. "I'm glad you finally noticed."

"Oh, I've noticed, frequently and with great fervor." Sawyer drew her close. "I've just been trying to logic myself out of kissing you."

"Then I'm glad you're terrible at it."

"Me too." Sawyer pulled her close, wrapping their free hand around the flawless curve of her waist, and pausing briefly to relish the rush of confirming how well they fit together. "The thing is, there are some pretty solid reasons in the con column, and only one in the pro, but it's outweighing all the others."

Robin paused, her shallow breath causing her chest to rise and fall against Sawyer's. "What's that?"

"I really want to."

85

Robin ran her fingers up the lapel of Sawyer's suit coat before taking hold and tugging them forward until their lips almost touched. Then, looking Sawyer straight in the eye, she said, "The wanting is enough for me."

It was the sexiest consent ever granted, and the last wisp of restraint snapped inside of Sawyer.

The kiss started off exquisite and only got better from there. Sawyer's mouth had barely brushed against Robin's before she leaned in, equal and open. She tasted like champagne and smelled like eucalyptus, but she felt like heaven, body pressed hot and firm against Sawyer. Their head spun, dizzy with a thrill eclipsing anything they'd experienced amid the rapids.

Had something inside them known it would be this good? Was this what the warning whispers were about? The intuition that said, once they started, they would not be inclined to stop? As Robin's hand snaked up over their shoulders and around their neck, it hardly seemed worthwhile to think about the end amid such a beautiful beginning.

They pressed forward in every way until Robin stumbled back slightly. Sawyer released her hand so they could brace for impact against the wall behind them. Robin gasped on impact, but instead of pulling away, she met them, arching her hips forward, and used her newly unoccupied fingers to take hold of their belt.

Sawyer's tongue ran a slow sweep along Robin's lips, and she opened them. Every sensation expanded as hot breath mingled with sweetness. Their vision tinged red behind closed lids, and Sawyer groaned slightly. Even the hint of what this woman held inside made them hungry for more, and with the wall to her back, Sawyer's hands had freedom to roam down her sides, over the curve of her ass, to the strength of her upper thigh.

They hadn't meant to go this fast, they hadn't meant for any of this to escalate at all, but once you land in the driver's seat of a Ferrari, you don't cruise along at thirty-five miles an hour.

The two of them might've careened completely off the track together if not for the sudden blast of headlights flashing bright white through the door beside them. For a second, the glare of the high beams seemed only to accentuate the racing metaphor revving through Sawyer's brain, but when Robin lifted a hand to block the onslaught of light, the interruption made sense. Gillian had arrived, as Sawyer had asked her to before the whole world went sideways. They'd been a different person back then.

Still, the realization must've seeped into Robin's lusty haze as well, because she eased out from under Sawyer and shook her dark hair. "That went exceptionally well."

Sawyer chuckled, but the sound came out breathless.

"Still going home with Gillian tonight?"

Sawyer opened their mouth, fully intending to say something along the lines of "no fucking way," but that thought collided with the realization that they'd have to tell Gillian where they intended to go instead. The thought managed to cool the heat burning off their brain cells enough that they managed to spit out only, "Fuck."

Robin's laugh echoed off the walls of the deserted hallway and rattled Sawyer's spine. "It's okay. Go sleep on her couch and think of me."

"Are you some sort of sadist?"

"I've been called worse, but like I said, the wanting is enough for me."

Sawyer eyed her skeptically, but even backlit in the bright light of reality, it was abundantly clear Robin wasn't playing coy. "Still? Always?"

She leaned forward and kissed them quickly, then shook her head. "For now."

Nine

"Great work today, Shay," Robin said with genuine affection as she beamed at her long-time client and her new streak of neon-pink hair. "And the new dye is poppin'."

Shay returned her smile, albeit shyly. "Thanks. I think you could do the same thing, but you'd probably have to bleach it first because yours is so dark. Or, do you color it?"

Robin shook her head. "This is all me."

"It works." Shay pushed off her usual spot on the floor, and Robin followed. "I'm going to ponder what you said about positive self-talk this week."

"I know you will. You always give it your best. Be gentle on yourself when you're practicing new skills. Like anything else, there's a learning curve. Nobody's great at everything they try right off the bat."

"I feel like you are."

"Not at all." Robin laughed as she opened the door to her office, remembering singing down at Sawyer from atop the piano. "I've learned to talk a big game, and sometimes doing so gives me the confidence to feel more awesome, which, in turn, actually does help me be more awesome."

"Like the opposite of a downward spiral."

"Exactly. You're going to do great." Robin walked with her down the hallway to the front door, though as she waved goodbye, she couldn't help remembering Sawyer's hand on hers in a similar spot Saturday night. Speaking of upward spirals … things had certainly spun out of her control quickly, but control might be overrated, because she couldn't summon any complaints, even with the gift of hindsight. On the contrary, in these quiet moments between sessions, she found herself reminiscing, which produced more of a craving than anything else.

She turned, shaking her head so forcefully she nearly bumped into Tegan, who came out of the waiting room carrying a few boxes of La Nova pizzas.

"Sorry T-Bear, I'm bouncing around here. You having a party without me?"

Tegan arched an eyebrow as if waiting for a punchline before finally saying, "It's Take-Out Tuesday."

"Seriously?" Robin didn't even try to hide her surprise. "Damn, how did I forget?"

"I don't know. Wasn't that Shay heading out? She's always your Tuesday pregame."

"Right." The fact that even Tegan knew that detail made it even weirder that Robin had forgotten, another indicator of how far her mind kept tumbling down the slippery slope back to Sawyer anytime she stepped into a hallway. Any hallway. It didn't matter if it was day or night, work or the gym, alone or with a colleague. The press of Sawyer's body had left more of a mark than simply its exquisite physical imprint.

"You okay?" Tegan's voice cut through the echo of ragged breath in her ears.

Her hazy vision refocused on her friend's concerned expression, and Robin worried the arousal-laced confusion must be written all over her face. "Yeah, good, great, hungry."

Tegan watched her a few seconds longer, and this time Robin warmed under the inspection.

She wasn't embarrassed about what'd happened. On the contrary, the heat burning her cheeks stemmed from something utterly discordant to shame, and under normal circumstances, she wouldn't mind saying as much to Tegan. The two of them had certainly talked about more than a stolen kiss or two over the last year, but this felt different.

For starters, Tegan rarely knew the other party in the tales of Robin's varied escapades, but this time it didn't feel exclusively like her story to tell. Not that a kiss qualified as disclosure. Robin kissed people all the time. Sometimes platonically, more often not. Sometimes things went further, sometimes they didn't, and in neither case did it mean much after the moment. Maybe that's why she hadn't mentioned the kiss with Sawyer. The memory didn't feel connected to its moment in time yet, or maybe it didn't feel like its moment had concluded. She'd all but told Sawyer she enjoyed the anticipation that came from playing the game. Didn't that imply more to come?

"Hey," Tegan tried again, "where'd you go?"

"Chasing squirrels through my brain."

"Sounds legit." Tegan scooted past her, waving the pizzas right under her nose. "Why don't you chase these masterpieces down to the conference room?"

Her stomach rumbled. "Good call."

Gillian met them as soon as they walked through the door. "Three pizzas for three people? Good call, indeed."

"We might need to come back for seconds between clients. I'm here until 9:00 tonight."

"Same." Gillian sighed as she sank into her usual chair.

"One more for me tonight," Robin said, "but I haven't been this grateful for a cancellation in months."

"You all right?" Gillian opened boxes and sorted the pizzas toward their obvious owners, starting with spinach and feta for herself. Pepperoni and mushroom for Tegan. Buffalo chicken and blue cheese for Robin.

"Yeah, just a little distracted lately."

"Maybe it's Saturday night catching up to you."

"What do you mean? Nothing happened on Saturday," Robin said, then caught the defensiveness in her tone, not to mention the lie. "I mean, things happened, obviously, but what specifically are you referring to?"

Gillian and Tegan exchanged a confused look.

Robin tried again. "You mean, like, the piano thing?"

"Good God, what else did you get up to after we all went home?"

90

"Not much." Robin snagged a piece of pizza so quickly a long string of gooey cheese trailed across the arm of her long-sleeve shirt, but she still shoveled an inordinately large bite into her mouth to keep from saying anything else stupid or patently untrue. Why was she pretending like nothing had happened? Something *had* happened, and obviously it meant something, or she would've tucked it away by now instead of inhaling pizza, which was entirely too hot to be consumed safely. Also, why did she still have it in her mouth, burning her tongue all to shit?

She huffed and waved a hand in front of her face as she tried to do Lamaze-style breathing around the molten cheese lava.

"Spit it out," Gillian said.

"No." Robin breathed fire through her nostrils, or at least that's what it felt like. "Good. I'm good."

The others stared at her as if clearly not buying it until she swallowed, and Tegan pushed a cup of ice water in her direction.

"Do you really enjoy pizza enough to scald yourself?" Gillian asked as she stared at the slice she'd pulled onto her plate.

Robin shrugged and tried to act like her esophagus wasn't still smoking. "It tastes great."

"It'll still taste great in three minutes," Tegan said, not unkindly.

"I'm not good at waiting," Robin admitted, and suddenly that felt like a stone-cold fact.

"Impatience and masochism seem to have several shades of gray between them," Gillian said.

"For sure, but like, don't you two think some things are worth getting burned for?"

"No," Gillian answered quickly.

Tegan seemed to think about it a little more. "Are we still talking about food, because my answer might be different if this has become metaphorical?"

91

"Of course it would," Gillian said, but she turned to Robin. "Literal or figurative burning?"

Robin tried to laugh it off, but the sound came out more like a cough. "All of the above."

"Food, no, people, sometimes," Tegan answered.

"Still going to go with 'no' on both." Gillian held her ground. "But I suppose you could make a stronger argument for impatience with people."

"Oh, I'd think people would have the stronger argument for patience," Tegan said.

"Professionally speaking." Gillian went into her most logic-problem dissection tone. "But it's situational. Giving people patience will change the tenor of interaction. Humans have so many variables. Patience with pizza doesn't fundamentally change anything other than the temperature, which I suppose may affect some textures, but not taste. All the ingredients will remain the same, which is why you suggested we might come back here in two hours and get take two of basically the same meal."

Tegan nodded pensively. "I see what you mean, but if we spend two hours away from a person out in the world, a hundred things could change in that time. They might have multiple interactions, mood changes, different thoughts, feelings. They might get tired, or bored …"

"They could have a physical altercation or get their heart broken, or have a breakthrough." Gillian continued her thought exercise. "Patience with pizza builds anticipation. Patience with a person might, in fact, alter that person in unlimited ways."

Robin's heart beat faster. Is that what she'd done with Sawyer? Allowed for too many variables? What if everything had changed between Saturday and now, and what if another myriad of changes occurred between now and whenever they saw each other again? She didn't want that.

The realization made the lava in her stomach turn cold.

Had she missed a chance?

She'd never wondered that about a prospective partner before.

She took another bite of her pizza without tasting it as she tried to decipher the foreign emotion building in her chest. More wistful than fear, but heavier than curiosity. She sat still, save for her chewing, and tried to take an emotional inventory of a sensation that hovered out of reach. Something like disappointment, but not quite as resolved, and with a tinge of urgency. Like regret, but with the urge to run, not away, but toward.

She didn't do regret. Regret required unmet expectations and looking back. She kept her options open and her eyes on the future. Except, had she let herself set some sort of expectation for a future encounter with Sawyer? Surely, they'd see each other again. She supposed that constituted an expectation, which led her right back to anticipation.

"Shit," she muttered.

Tegan and Gillian turned back to her.

"Sorry. Still a little scalded from earlier." She hadn't meant to make such a true statement, but her friends seemed to connect the sentiment to the pizza and not the scorching kiss they still didn't know about.

"Shocking," Gillian deadpanned. "Your actions had consequences."

Tegan chuckled. "A new concept for you, Robin?"

She grinned despite a sinking suspicion it might be. "I've faced consequences before, and I've always found them worth the risk I took to earn them in the first place."

"Your trademark 'yes' vibe." Gillian nodded.

Tegan smiled. "I've always liked that about you."

Robin took a deep breath, letting a new sensation settle through her. "Me too."

93

Robin knocked on the door in front of her. She'd been here plenty of times, but never when she knew Gillian wasn't home. Still, she knocked again. Not that anyone on the other side would have had enough time to answer, and yet all the talk about patience versus impatience had started her down this path, and all those variables Gillian had detailed rattled through her brain, even after her last session of the day. Robin didn't want to give them any more time to take root until she put her finger on the pulse pounding through her veins.

Sawyer opened the door.

Robin stared at them, noting little had changed except for their attire. Gone was the formal wear, traded for joggers and a lightweight green sweater. The hair was the same mop of chestnut waves, and the eyes the same glacial gray, the same strong jaw, the same quirk of playful lips that managed to be both alluring and a little maddening.

"Angst?" Robin asked without preamble.

"I beg your pardon."

"Is this angst I'm feeling?"

Sawyer slipped their hands into their pockets and leaned a shoulder against the doorjamb. "It's nice to see you, too."

"It feels angsty, but that can't be right. There's something vague and unspecified and a little almost, panicky, but like, in a sweet way, or maybe bittersweet. No." She wrote that off quickly. "It's more forward-looking, but also a little anxious and at the same time exciting."

"Do I need to be here for this conversation?"

Robin stared at them a little longer, trying to give voice to the sensation building inside her, but if it had been hard to think earlier, it was nearly impossible to form coherent ideas with her gaze drawn to the hollow at the base of Sawyer's throat. "I don't really do angst."

"Maybe you're trying something new. There's a first time for everything." Sawyer's mouth twitched as if trying to hide their amusement. "I'd be honored to be your first."

It would've annoyed Robin more if she didn't also see the absurdity of it all. "You think you're worthy of taking my angstinity?"

"Angstinity?" Sawyer finally cracked a smile. "Wow, sounds like a tall order. I promise to be gentle."

She sighed. "Gentle isn't usually my style either."

"Now you're talking." Sawyer stepped back, opening the door wider. "Care to come in and tell me more?"

She wasn't sure doing so offered the wisest choice, but taking the risk helped her feel more secure than standing suspended in this liminal space. "Sure."

Gillian's apartment was dimmer than usual, low lights, no candles, nothing cooking on the stove, but Sawyer's closeness exuded its own kind of warmth.

"So, that kiss …" Robin started, then trailed off.

"Top tier," Sawyer confirmed.

"Right?"

"I've thought about calling you a couple times," Sawyer admitted, sitting down on one end of the couch where they clearly slept.

Robin took the armchair facing them at an angle. "I've thought about doing a lot more than calling."

"So, what's holding us back?" Sawyer asked calmly enough.

Robin shook her head. "Friends?"

"They're all adults, and so are we." Sawyer waved that off. "Though the requirements for adulting are not always my strong suit. I'm not great at long-term, if that's what you're—"

"It's not." Robin cut off that concern quickly. "I'm a solid, short-term prospect, long weekend tops."

Sawyer smiled. "Refreshing to meet someone who's openly setting the bar lower than me on that front."

"For clarity, where's your bar?" Robin remained completely cool conversationally, even as her internal temp began to rise.

"I've been known to do something seasonal, but I think I'm a bit like the weather. As it starts to change, I get the urge to roam."

"Cool." Robin laughed lightly and crossed one leg over the other. "It's Buffalo. The weather changes here even faster than I do."

Sawyer smiled at her, eyes drifting down to the place where her jeans stretched tight over her hips. "Sounds like we're on the same page."

"Low stakes, high attraction, nobody gets hurt."

"What about angst?" Sawyer asked, leaning forward.

"Sure." Robin shrugged. "I mean, why not? Just like a craving to satisfy."

"Craving," Sawyer agreed. "The wanting you mentioned Saturday … I'm there. That kiss was so much, and yet …"

"Left you wanting more?" Robin bit her lip to keep herself from putting words into their mouth.

"So much more." Sawyer stood and extended their hand.

Robin didn't make them wait. There'd already been too much delayed gratification for her liking. She was more than ready to give in to her favorite impulses. Taking Sawyer's hand, she allowed herself to be pulled into their arms. With a deep breath, she surrendered every thought that had addled her brain for the last three days, and let their bodies take over.

The kiss picked up right where the last one had broken off. Sawyer's mouth was everything she remembered, immediately opening, urging, tongue sweeping across her own, not testing, taking.

Strong hands on her hips steered Robin back around toward the couch, and her own fingers found their way under their shirt. This was the ease she'd ached for, the flawless movement of two bodies that knew all along what their brains had tried to deny.

Sawyer's mouth was magic. No, that made it sound sappy. Sawyer's mouth was skilled. Or maybe it was both, because this person seemed to have everything working for them at once, which only made Robin want to see what else they could do. Working her hands up under their shirt, she scraped her nails across their abs on the way toward removing the barrier.

Sawyer paused long enough to whisper, "I had top surgery a little over a year ago."

"Congratulations." Robin shoved the sweater up over their head and tossed it to the floor, revealing a tight white undershirt stretched across lightly muscled pecs. "Any restrictions?"

Sawyer shook their head. "None, just wanted to warn you."

"Warn me, or excite me?"

Sawyer quirked an eyebrow. "You got a scar kink or something?"

"Nope. An authenticity kink, though. I'm very much eager to see the body you fought and bled to inhabit."

"Fuck," Sawyer whispered, "that does make it sound sexy."

Robin had been about to say something back, she was sure of it, but she couldn't remember what as Sawyer's mouth took hers once more. She hadn't even known there was another gear available to them, but they'd unlocked it, only this time Sawyer wasn't content to stay there as they nipped at her lower lip and down along her jaw, tangling their fingers in the hair at the base of Robin's neck and tugging insistently enough only to expose her neck before sucking along her pulse point. Could they feel it throbbing for them to the same beat pounding through Robin's ears?

It took everything she had not to lose every thread of coherent thought as their amazing mouth skimmed over her shirt and nipped at one hard nipple through the thin cotton. Then, hands were underneath, and there was nothing to be beneath anymore as Sawyer tugged off the top and flicked open her bra. Cupping both breasts, they squeezed gently, eliciting a moan.

Sawyer walked her back until her knees buckled across the edge of the couch. Robin caught hold of the front of their undershirt, pulling until they fell on top of her.

"Yes," she hissed as the weight of Sawyer's body pinned her down, applying all the right kinds of pressure. They were a mess of hands and limbs and mouths for a minute, grinding into each other like a couple of horny teenagers. Robin ran her hands down Sawyer's back, wrenching fruitlessly at the tank top before rasping, "Take it off."

Sawyer straddled her hips and rose up enough to yank the offending garment completely off, then quickly tried to duck down to cover her once more. Robin stopped them with a firm hand to the center of their chest.

"Wait," she practically panted.

Sawyer froze as anyone who understood consent would, but the frantic edge to their gaze showed that doing so took a sizable toll.

"I want to see you for a second." Robin did her best to soothe their nerves amid her own aching arousal at the sight of Sawyer straddling her, long and lean and so perfectly androgynous. Strong shoulders and sculpted pecs outlined by a faint scar dipped into flat abs and a V-shaped torso before flaring again into the soft curve of feminine hips.

She ran her hands down the line her eyes had traced, using her nails enough to leave a trail. "Do you have sensation?"

Sawyer nodded. "Yes. Tactile and erotic."

Robin's mouth watered at the implications of those words. Sitting up, she grabbed two handfuls of ass and used them as leverage to pull their bodies together, until her tongue painted a hot path across their chest.

Sawyer sank their hands into her hair and held her close as she circled around one nipple before giving it a little nip, eliciting a gasp. Encouraged by the reaction, she repeated the process on the other side, and this time Sawyer grasped at the back of her head, fist tightening deliciously. God, how she wanted to learn to play this body like the fine instrument it was. Sliding one hand into the waistband of those sweatpants, she then worked it around to the front, and lower. She never let up with her mouth as she worked her way down through wet curls. Sawyer pulsed for her, hard and slick, jerking forward in confirmation.

"Fuck," they growled through clenched teeth, which was entirely too restrained for Robin's liking. Greedy, thirsty, hungry, she wanted Sawyer unrestrained, undone, all over her.

Increasing her pressure and speed at the same time, she rocked forward, pressing into Sawyer in every way their position would allow.

"Easy," Sawyer warned. "I'm already close."

"Good," she mumbled and sucked harder against taut skin. "I want you to come on top of me."

Sawyer sucked in a sharp breath and pitched forward.

Robin fell back onto the couch, breaking contact with their upper body, but enjoying increased access lower as Sawyer hovered over her on all fours.

She took a second to adjust to the view, forearms flexing at either side of her head, back arched, hips pushing forward into her hand, the picture of a person about to tip over the edge. Sawyer's expression tightened, and their eyes squeezed as every muscle above Robin seized at once.

She kept her relentless pace as they shivered and then shook, head lolling from side to side as Sawyer silently surrendered. They were magnificent to watch, a stunning contrast between control and convulsion, every part of them etched in perfection, until one arm gave out and they collapsed half on top of her, half into the crook of Gillian's designer couch.

Robin chuckled and kissed their temple.

"What's funny?"

She sank her hand into their thick waves of hair and mussed them up further. "Gillian would die."

Sawyer smiled against her shoulder. "She'll be home soon."

Robin glanced at the clock under the television. "Probably about thirty minutes."

"It's a good thing you like to go fast, then, because thirty minutes is all I need … the first time." Sawyer surged up, then

99

slid along Robin's body, pausing only to kiss her stomach before going all the way down the couch and taking Robin's pants and underwear with them. She gasped when Sawyer hooked her legs over their shoulders and stared down at her for a hot, hungry second. Then, lowering their head, they put that magic mouth to its best possible use.

Robin clutched for any hold, the couch cushion, a throw pillow, Sawyer's shoulders. The river rapids they'd tackled over the weekend couldn't even compare to the current of desire threatening to wash her away now. Sawyer spent only a few teasing passes to get her used to the direct stimulation before settling into a skilled rhythm, drawing her forward and easing her upward. Their assessment of Robin liking to go fast turned out to be an understatement on every level as she careened toward a climax. Either she was already completely revved from the perfection of taking Sawyer, or they were imminently talented.

Or both.

As Sawyer sucked a little more insistently, Robin's hips lifted off the couch, and her vision spun.

Both.

It was definitely both.

"Yes," she called out as she bucked again.

Sawyer hooked an arm around one of her thighs for leverage and worked another one upward to cup her breast. The added stimulation caused sparks of pleasure to radiate from every place Sawyer touched. Robin was so close, and delayed gratification could go straight to hell. She wanted Sawyer, all of them, all over her, right now, and they did more than oblige, they excelled.

The orgasm hit like a Mack Truck, full speed, full force, and she yelled, not even a word, but a raw sort of satisfaction as her hips writhed under Sawyer's perfection. Sawyer met her every rise and sank into her every fall, hands and mouth working together to pull every last ounce of decadence from their collision, until Robin couldn't catch the breath she needed to go on.

She collapsed into the couch and used what little strength she had left to push weakly at Sawyer's forehead. She couldn't have really stopped them if she wanted to, and she wasn't at all sure she did, but mercifully they eased back with one last, slow kiss to the core they'd just shaken.

Sitting back on their knees, Sawyer stared down at her, looking rather satisfied with themself. "I'd ask if you want to go again, but I think we're on the clock for a very awkward interruption."

"Come here," Robin said with her first full breath in a while.

Sawyer complied immediately, a glorious trait in a lover.

Robin wrapped her languid body around them and nipped at their shoulder, then earlobe, before whispering, relishing the mingled scent of sex and sandalwood, "Not but ... *and*."

Sawyer tensed slightly.

"We are about to get walked in on, *and* I definitely want to go again," she clarified.

Sawyer's muscles relaxed, and Robin took that as a sign to go on. "What are you doing tomorrow?"

"Dinner at Brooke's."

"Oh, right. What about after that?"

"I get the feeling I'm about to have plans with you."

"If you want to do something."

Sawyer eased back to look into her eyes. "I want to do a lot of somethings to you, but what about your long weekend policy?"

Robin kissed them quickly, enjoying the taste of herself on those amazing lips. "Tuesday seems like a great day to start a weekend."

Ten

"I like what you've done with the place, Brookesy."
Sawyer pulled out a chair and relaxed into the old familiarity of
watching their friend.

"Thanks. I hadn't realized how much I've done around
here until I thought about the last time you saw it."

"Yeah. You became a homeowner like four months before
I headed out." They pointed to the living room. "I helped you
paint those walls."

Brooke smiled as she stirred something that smelled
amazing. "You kept dripping paint down the side of the can
and driving Gillian nuts."

They laughed.

"Who's driving me nuts?" Gillian came around the corner,
wearing athletic pants and a Cornell sweatshirt.

"Me, Ivy League," Sawyer said. "Glad you slipped out of
those work clothes, though. I like this Sporty Spice version of
you."

"Me too," Brooke said.

"Me three." Tegan joined them, also having changed out of
her client-facing attire, but from the little extra room in the
sweatpants and well-worn Buff State T-shirt, Sawyer suspected
she'd actually slipped into some of Brooke's clothes.

"Rough week?" Sawyer asked no one in particular.

"Not really." Tegan kissed Brooke on the cheek quickly,
then, without asking, started pulling things from the cabinet,
making it clear she was used to cooking with her girlfriend.
"I'm actually in a good groove lately."

102

"Knock on wood," Gillian ordered, "but, yeah, I'm good, too."

They turned to Brooke, who tried to stifle a yawn before saying, "I'm in the end-of-semester crush. Final projects came in yesterday, and I'm facilitating study groups for exams all next week."

"But then you're done," Gillian said encouragingly. "Almost there."

Brooke opened her mouth to respond, only to be cut off by a knock on the door, but before anyone could answer, Robin let herself in. "Hello, hello, sexy humans."

Sawyer's stomach tightened at the sight of her. She wore all black, from her motorcycle boots to casual canvas pants with a drawstring perched precariously across her killer hips, showcasing the slightest sliver of her midriff beneath the hem of her T-shirt. The real kicker, though, was the leather jacket, clearly meant for both function and fashion.

"Uh-oh," Tegan grinned. "Is it bike season?"

Robin tossed a black helmet trimmed in polished silver onto the end of the couch and let her eyes run hungrily over Sawyer for several long seconds before turning to include the others. "Yup. I broke the seal on the summer."

"It's going to be a chilly ride home after dark," Brooke said.

"I always find a way to keep warm," Robin replied, tongue firmly planted in cheek, and Sawyer fought the urge to confirm they already felt warmer by proxy.

Robin shed her jacket, revealing how thin that T-shirt really was, thin enough to make it clear she wore a tank top rather than a bra underneath. Sawyer had to set their jaw to keep from drooling at the faint outline of the nipples they'd recently had between their teeth.

The arousal overtook them so quickly they actually got lightheaded. It had been too long since they'd had great sex, or at least that's how Sawyer had justified things last night after Gillian had gone to bed. They'd lain awake for way too long, remembering the feel of Robin's body or the feel of her eyes on

Sawyer's body. Her unabashed hunger had awakened something similar inside of them, then only managed to whet that appetite with the quick confirmation of what an amazing combination they could be together.

"Hey, Spacey." Brooke waved a hand in front of Sawyer's glazed vision.

They blinked a few times. "Sorry, what?"

"I asked what you've been up to this week."

"Oh, you know, the usual. Stuff and such." They grinned up at her, knowing the vagueness wouldn't fly.

"Which is taking up more of your time and energy, would you say, the 'stuff' or the 'such'?"

They laughed. "I've got some irons in the fire online."

"What does that mean?" Tegan asked.

"They won't ever say explicitly, but we have theories." Gillian motioned back and forth between herself and Brooke.

They'd played this game before, but it never failed to amuse Sawyer. "Lay 'em on me."

"Ghostwriting," Gillian offered.

"Modeling," Brooke jumped in.

"Personal shopper." Gillian kept going.

"Travel advisor."

"Poker player."

"Stunt coordinator."

"Money launderer."

"Espionage."

Sawyer laughed as the guesses grew more and more outrageous. Still, they kept their body language neutral and relaxed until Robin leaned a little closer, looked them dead in the eye, and said, "OnlyFans."

They cracked. Only a tiny twitch of their jaw, but in a room full of therapists, it was enough. They all pounced at once.

"Oh my God."

"That's it, isn't it?"

"Wow."

Then Gillian turned on Robin. "How'd you guess?"

She lifted a shoulder casually, but her quirk of a smile spoke to inside information if anyone cared to notice it. Thankfully, they were mostly still focused on Sawyer.

"It's not exactly like that, but there's significant overlap," they explained. "I have a following ... on some app accounts."

"Where are these accounts?" A hint of incredulity crept into Gillian's voice. "You don't even have social media ... or do you? Because if you have secret social media where we could've tracked your whereabouts for the last two years and you didn't tell us, I may choke you with my bare hands."

"After a couple drinks, I might be into a little light choking."

"That's it." Gillian lunged across the table and caught them by the scruff of their T-shirt, but Sawyer merely laughed harder.

"God, I love it when the mental health professional chooses violence."

Gillian released them, shaking her head.

"Seriously, Gilly Bean," Sawyer elaborated, "I have a few outlets where I do videos or posts, not porn. People follow along for all sorts of content from tips for traveling while trans or genderqueer, or info on loopholes for overstaying visas or working without them. Some of them are interested in nomadic life, others want nonbinary affirmation, or to see people like us thriving as the sexy beasts we are. Some of them feel trapped in a myriad of ways and want to see someone who's free."

Brooke placed a hand on her chest. "I really love that for you. I hate that you didn't share it with us, but I love that you're putting that kind of good out into the world."

Gillian didn't release her anger immediately, giving them a hard stare as she took a long, deliberate sip of ice water.

"It's not all empathy and affirmation, though," Sawyer said, not wanting to give anyone any ideas. "A lot of people follow me solely for the feet pics."

Gillian coughed and sputtered her water.

Robin cackled.

Brooke went back to stirring the food. "There it is."

"What?" Sawyer laughed. "Multiple things can be true at once. I affirm and titillate simultaneously."

"Fair." Tegan cut in. "It's 100 percent possible to be putting good, binary-breaking content into the world while also having pretty feet. No shame in that game."

"Thank you," Sawyer said. "I like this woman."

"I'm here for kink and kindness, too," Robin added, as if there had been any room for doubt on that front.

Sawyer grinned at her, but the hint of skin she was showing across her waist made it impossible for them to offer any clever or articulate reply. Still, the glint in Robin's dark eyes made it clear she got the message.

Tegan must've missed it though as she continued. "Speaking of holding multiple identities, I'm not going to see clients next Thursday or Friday. Brooke and I are going away for a long weekend to celebrate the end of the semester."

Sawyer only vaguely processed the work talk, their attention still on the woman giving off all the right vibes across the room.

Robin, however, seemed to register the sidenote with more interest, as one expressive eyebrow shot up. "Oh wow, is this time for the big talk?"

Tegan and Brooke exchanged a quick look before Brooke announced, "Dinner's ready. I've got a tarragon cream sauce for the salmon. Who wants it served on the side, and who wants it on their fillet?"

They all stared at her for a second before Gillian said, "Yeah, that wasn't a suspicious redirect at all."

Brooke sighed. "No pressure or anything, though, right?"

Robin laughed. "We're invested."

"And we're taking our time to do things right," Tegan said gently as she plated the food. "I've submitted my hours and my exam score, jumped through all hoops, and am now just waiting on the Office of the Professions."

"Oh my God, the licensure cock-block is killing me," Robin groaned.

"Ew." Brooke wrinkled her nose. "No cock to be blocked here. Only time and space for deliberate conversation and connection. I promise you'll all know what we decide as soon as we do."

Gillian rolled her eyes playfully. "Sure we will."

"Spoiler alert," Robin stage-whispered. "They're going to decide to move in together."

Sawyer was the only one who didn't seem overly invested in this drama, maybe because they hadn't been around long enough, or maybe because they found ruminations on domestic bliss rather dull. "You do you, Boos. I'm going to go wash my hands so I can dig into this amazing meal."

Robin looked torn for a half-second before saying, "Good call. I'll go with."

Sawyer's pulse kicked up a notch as they headed down the hall. The two of them made it all the way to the guest bathroom without saying a word, but as they washed their hands side by side in the double vanity, Sawyer made the mistake of locking eyes with Robin via the mirror.

By some electromagnetic force of mutual agreement, they slammed into each other. Hands, mouths, bodies, everything collided, and they were in full-frontal make-out mode. Sawyer didn't even have the time to ponder how this woman could go from zero to sixty in point two seconds, but they definitely appreciated her ability to do so. Robin's hands were under their shirt, while Sawyer had sunk both of theirs into her thick, black locks. She smelled like eucalyptus and leather, and she tasted like raw desire, hot and wet.

Sawyer's head spun in the most intoxicating way, and they may've begun ripping clothes off right there if not for the discordant burst of laughter from the other room.

Robin must've heard it too, because she jerked away suddenly.

"Fuck," Sawyer whispered.

"My thoughts exactly." Robin grinned. "My place, tonight, if we can manage not to combust over dinner."

"Seems like a tall order."

She nodded solemnly and bit her lower lip, a job Sawyer desperately wanted for themself. "We could just tell them and leave."

Their shoulders sagged. "If we tell them, there's no way we'll be able to leave. Imagine the interrogation you gave Tegan times a million."

Robin gave a little growl. "Talk about a buzzkill."

"I thought you were the one who enjoyed the anticipation."

"That was before I knew what I was missing."

"How about right after dinner, you tell them you're going to take me for a ride?"

Robin's smile turned almost wicked. "Explicit, but I like it."

"I meant 'a ride on your motorcycle,' but I want to consent in advance to the other kind of ride, too."

Robin's eyes dropped to their mouth again, and Sawyer had a tinge of fear-laced arousal at the prospect of neither of them being able to wait that long before Gillian called, "Did you two get lost?"

"Just plotting mad high jinks and an overthrow of polite society," Robin called back.

"God, you're quick."

Robin headed for the door. "It's easier to respond when I'm 100 percent telling the truth."

Sawyer snorted softly as they followed her back toward the kitchen. "I really like the way you think."

"You feel so fucking good. I'm going to get you all the way naked this time."

Robin's words rattled off of Sawyer's frayed senses. They'd used up every ounce of their restraint not to take this woman over the table at dinner, or slip a hand into the waistband of her pants on the way back to her place. Having her perfect ass between their thighs while the engine rumbled beneath them was a type of torture that should be addressed by the Geneva Conventions. Only the prospect of careening to their death before Sawyer ever got to be fully inside Robin kept them from reaching for more until they stumbled up the stairs to Robin's apartment.

The door had barely slammed shut before they were on each other, kissing, groping, ripping at clothes. Robin's jacket hit the floor first. Sawyer stepped over it and yanked their own shirt over their head. "Your turn."

Robin's dark eyes were all pupil and need as they raked over Sawyer's bare torso. Still, she managed to strip out of her own thin T-shirt and tank top at the same time, the hard set of pink nipples further evidence of her own desire. Then they were all over each other again, skin to skin, shared breath and heat.

"Do you know how hard it was not to touch you over dinner?" Robin asked.

"Yes," Sawyer groaned, "as hard as I am for you right now."

Robin didn't take their word for it, and Sawyer appreciated that about her as fingers slipped into their waistband. They helped the exploration along by opening the button and fly. They both gasped as Robin skimmed over the evidence she'd sought. "Oh yeah, exactly that hard."

Sawyer kissed her again. Their tongues danced for dominance. It had been ages since they'd been with anyone who possessed the kind of femme-top energy Robin brought to every interaction, or maybe they'd never been with anyone quite like her. She had an appeal all her own, and Sawyer certainly had no inclination to complain, not with the way she stroked them as if trying to stoke an already flickering fire.

Still, they weren't ever one to totally yield control, and Robin wasn't the only one who'd had to contend with her own imagination for the last several hours. Most of Sawyer's fantasies had involved this woman on her back, so they pulled away again, long enough to glance around the room for any semblance of a flat surface. They had the wherewithal not to use the hardwood floors, which left the entryway out. "Bed? Couch? Or countertop?"

Robin laughed and pulled them forward with one finger hooked through a belt loop and several other fingers someplace way more effective.

The two of them passed through an open door to a bedroom, or rather, a room with a bed, because Sawyer didn't look at the décor any further.

They kicked off their shoes and shimmied out of their jeans before cupping Robin's ass with both hands and grinding into her. They were about to lift her onto the bed when Robin short-circuited their decision-making faculties by grabbing a pillow, dropping it to the floor, and then sinking gracefully to her knees.

Sawyer's mouth went dry at the sight of her glancing up at them through heavy lids and thick lashes. She leaned forward, placing a slow, hot kiss across the front of Sawyer's boxers so they could feel the heat of her breath through the cotton. Then, pulling them down, she did the same thing without the barrier this time.

So much for having ideas of their own. Sawyer couldn't even remember them now. They couldn't remember anything before this woman. They watched, transfixed, as Robin wet her lips with her tongue and just kept going. If the sight were the most erotic thing they'd ever seen, they couldn't even begin to process the feel of that mouth. Sawyer groaned and tilted their hips forward to meet her more fully.

Robin glanced up at them again. "This okay?"

They nodded, unable to say it was so much better than okay.

"Show me," Robin whispered.

Sawyer stifled an impulse to tell her she'd managed to figure things out pretty well on her own so far. They were horny, not stupid, so they hooked one finger under Robin's chin and guided her head closer. She didn't need much encouraging.

110

From the moment Robin's lips made contact, it was all Sawyer could do to stay upright. They snaked their hand along the line of her jaw and into her hair, more for stability than direction, but Robin increased her pressure all the same.

Sawyer widened their stance for both balance and to offer better access as they soaked up every conflicting sensation, the brashness of standing naked in front of this amazing creature, the clash of cool air and liquid warmth, the sight of Robin exerting absolute control from such a position of supposed submission.

"You are a goddess," Sawyer groaned as their vision blurred. They'd promised themself they'd go slower this time, to savor, to play, to sink into the experience, but they hadn't counted on Robin having plans of her own. Who were they to stand in her way? A fool if they didn't surrender to her every wish, and judging from how she worked them over with purpose and precision, she clearly wanted to wreck them.

She was about to get her wish, as Sawyer's thighs began to shake. They gritted their teeth against oblivion, to no avail. They were going to tip over the edge any second, and they were dimly aware they might tip all the way over literally, too. Reaching out, they grasped for any support and caught hold of the corner of the footboard. Only, in doing so, they pressed further into Robin, who caught them with one arm around their waist and another around one leg. She used the slight adjustment to hold them both tightly in place as Sawyer's hips jerked involuntarily.

The orgasm rocked through them with unexpected force, and they had to lock their elbow and knees to keep from buckling. "Yes. Robin. Fuck. Yes."

They held themself upright by sheer force and the exquisite desperation to make this feeling last as long as possible. Once again, Robin seemed to share the impulse. She continued her unrelenting magic until their muscles and lungs threatened to give out at the same time.

Sawyer swayed, pulling her up and back weakly. "Holy shit, woman, I'm going to crash."

Robin laughed as if she weren't out of breath at all, but how could that be possible?

"You're a maniac."

"Guilty." Robin stood and eased them toward the bed. "You gave me a manic edge all night."

"And you couldn't make it the extra two steps to the mattress?"

"Bed sex is a bit basic bitch for me."

Sawyer shook their head and flopped onto their back atop the comforter. "Good to know where you draw those lines."

"My bed, my boundaries." Robin crawled over the top of them and grinned down. "Though I have to admit, seeing you sprawled out doesn't make it seem nearly as boring as the last time I was here, about fourteen hours ago."

They couldn't disagree with her on all fours over them, breasts swaying slightly out of reach of their parched lips. "You know what they say. It's not the tool. It's how you use it."

Robin's grin turned mischievous again. "Come on, then. Show me how to use it."

Eleven

"Thanks for stopping by." Robin handed the young woman one of the little swag bags Gillian had put together for this weekend's mental health fair. Normally she didn't love standing behind a folding table on a Saturday morning, but today she didn't mind for several reasons. First, they were at Central Rock Gym in Buffalo, a cavernous space covered from floor to super-high ceiling with climbing walls, belays, and artificial boulders, all teeming with strong and limber bodies in motion. Second, Brooke and Tegan were with her, making conversation and occasionally jokes as they all did their best to bring up the therapy side of this larger whole-health event. Third, and she almost hated to admit this part, the work, the company, and the eye candy all combined to take her mind off Sawyer for a few minutes, which had become a rare occurrence outside of the office.

"I'm surprised you're not climbing," Tegan said when they got a lull in traffic at their booth.

"I'm on the clock," Robin replied casually enough, even though she also feared her arms might not hold up on the tall walls given the soreness in her biceps, or her triceps, or her thighs … or anything. Every part of her body managed to be slightly sore after four nights of sex that had yet to lose its intensity.

"Working hours have never stopped you before," Brooke said. "I don't mind holding down the fort. This is infinitely more interesting than grading finals."

"I'm good." And she was also happy, sated, and exhausted. She'd driven Sawyer back to Gillian's around two o'clock this

113

morning and then had to be up at eight to set up their display about mental and physical health. Not that she was complaining. She'd gleefully make all the same choices again. She could've called for a night off. Sawyer made it clear they could take a break whenever she wanted, only she'd yet to want one.

The thought caused her stomach to tighten slightly, the same way it did anytime she remembered they'd agreed to a long weekend, and four nights together was already pushing those limits. Still, as they'd said goodbye in the wee hours of the morning, they'd made plans to meet up again this evening.

She'd told herself it only made sense. Saturday was definitely the weekend. Sunday too. No one could argue her logic, and if one were thinking of long weekends, shouldn't they wrap around to Monday as well? There was no need to examine anything too closely until they hit the week mark, but that's exactly what she was doing, thinking, pondering, counting down. When they were together, she lived beautifully in the present, taking each perfect moment at full speed, but in those moments when they let go of each other, she found herself either reminiscing or looking ahead. She didn't know what should concern her more, the fact that they'd gone this long without dulling the hunger, or the idea that she kept making excuses to buy them more time.

"I've never been in here before." Tegan pulled her back into a moment she hadn't made any conscious desire to leave in the first place. "I did a ropes course in college, though. That was fun."

"I've done several workshops here with the LGBTQ youth group. Total mind-body connection between the athleticism, balance, and problem-solving. You don't wear any safety apparatus on the bouldering wall." Robin pointed to the massive structure roughly fifteen feet tall occupying the entire center of the room. "Which is why the pads are thicker there, but they have auto belays to protect you on the climbing walls."

Tegan followed her line of sight all the way up the outer walls, at least forty feet high.

"Honey." Brooke's tone held a mix of adoration and apprehension. "If you're getting ideas, may I please put in a vote for the option with safety gear over the one where you risk a free fall of any size?"

Tegan kissed her on the cheek. "You don't mind working the table?"

"Not if it keeps me off the walls." Brooke looked pointedly at Robin. "And you go help protect the face and limbs I'm very fond of."

"Your girl's good with her hands. Got it." Robin lifted her hand. "High five for scoring the total package."

Brooke shook her head and laughed. "Go."

Tegan walked across the gym to two open spots, side by side. "One for each of us."

"I thought I'd show you how the auto belay works." Robin tugged on the rope to demonstrate its resistance, and the way it locked when tugged hard. "You'll get a jerk if you slip, but you won't fall. Stay calm. Let yourself stop swaying. You can hang there for a second before it starts to lower you down, or you can reach for the wall again, give it some slack, and it'll let you keep climbing."

"What's this 'you' business?" Tegan asked nearly incredulously. "You can't send me up this monster by myself. You're my chief instigator and cheerleader."

Robin rolled her head side to side, testing her shoulder muscles, not at all sure this was a good idea, but she'd, just seconds ago, explained the mind-body connection of climbing, and she did need to get out of her own brain. "Okay, fine. You know I can't be outdone in the adventure department."

"That's the spirit. How do I get hooked up?"

Robin unhooked a harness from its spot on the wall, and after checking a few buckles, held it out toward Tegan. "You're going to step into this, with one leg in each of the smaller holes and the bigger strap around your waist. Surely, you've worn something similar before."

Tegan's cheeks colored immediately, giving Robin all the answers she needed.

"High five."

Tegan, unlike the person she'd probably used such an apparatus with, gladly obliged, slapping her hand with enthusiasm. Then she stepped into the harness and took inventory of the various straps while Robin did the same with her own.

"From here, it's self-explanatory." Robin took hold of the grips on the wall. "As you climb, the rope will adjust, taking up the slack. Staying closer to the wall gives you better control."

Tegan began tentatively, but as her arms and legs flexed, she found her footing. Robin had little concern about her fitness.

"What about you?" Tegan asked when they were only a few feet off the ground. "Have you worn something similar recently?"

Now it was Robin's turn to warm under a friend's question. "Honestly, it's been at least a few weeks since I've stepped into anything quite like this."

She kept her eyes on the next handhold, one after another, steadfastly refusing to add that she and Sawyer hadn't come up for air long enough to reach for any toys. Not that she hadn't given the prospect considerable fantasizing. They'd simply been too busy with hands and mouths and other amazing body parts. The thought brought up their looming deadline again, and Robin tried not to start a list of everything she wanted to do between now and Monday night.

"So, Sawyer's not into penetration?"

Her hand slipped as the bluntness of the question and every implication behind it hit her at once. She might've fallen completely without the belay kicking into action with a jerk. She hung there by her harness for a second, dangling by one arm and the rope, and trying to make her brain work again before engaging her muscles.

"You okay?" Tegan asked innocently, as though she hadn't caused the lapse.

"Uh, yeah." Robin grabbed for the wall with her other hand and engaged her legs again.

"Good." Tegan resumed climbing nonchalantly. "So back to my question. I've been wondering about how the boundaries around Sawyer's nonbinary identity meshed with the way you clearly want to be inside them in all the ways."

Robin sighed and pulled herself level with Tegan. "That obvious, huh?"

Tegan laughed. "From the first moment your eyes landed on them."

"Do Gilly and Brooke know?"

"Not yet. And, honestly, I didn't know for sure until you wrecked yourself there, but while everyone else was watching Sawyer on Wednesday, I was looking at you."

"Aw, that's the sweetest thing anyone's said about me in a long time, Boo."

Tegan rolled her eyes. "I doubt it, but Gillian and Brooke know both of you, so their attention is divided. I'm just yours, and you were so there for me last year through everything. I want to do the same for you."

Robin's chest tightened and her arms ached, but she kept climbing, if only to get further from that sentiment. "It's not the same thing, Teegs."

"Why not?"

"Because you were falling in love."

"Where are you falling ... other than off climbing walls?"

"We're mostly falling into bed, and onto couches, and my kitchen table, and one time, kind of the floor."

Tegan blew out a little whistle. "I mean, good for you, but what's the plan?"

"No plan. Again, you're projecting your stuff onto me, and I'm honored, because you're a good person."

"You're a good person, too."

"Thank you, but I'm not a romantic. I'm having fun with someone whose company I enjoy almost as much as their body. That's all."

"Fair enough. Do you expect your arrangement to continue indefinitely?"

"No." She shook her head a little forcefully and had to pull her body closer to the wall to steady herself. "Not either of our styles. We're thinking a long weekend."

"Oh, I thought you two had already been fooling around for, like, a week. You seemed precariously close last Saturday night."

She hadn't thought of it that way. Had their clock started ticking the first time they'd kissed? If so, they were already at their expiration date. "No."

Tegan stared at her as if waiting for more, but Robin couldn't seem to process the vehemence of her reaction. She could only manage to mutter, "We didn't start on Saturday."

"Okay …" Tegan drew out the word so that it sounded like both an affirmation and a question.

Robin pulled herself up a little higher. "It's fine. It's not a big deal. We're both adults."

"Of course."

"We can handle our decisions."

"Undoubtedly."

She didn't know why she was getting defensive. Tegan wasn't pushing. She never would, and Robin knew that, which meant the pressure building inside her came from herself. Still, she couldn't dismiss the urge to offer justifications. "We're not doing anything wrong, and we don't need to have big discussions or talk about our feelings or other people's concerns. We're our own people."

"Amazing, smart, intuitive people," Tegan agreed. "And you're right, it's no one's business but your own. I want to make sure you know, I'm here for you. No judgment, no split loyalty."

"Except to Brooke."

"There's no conflict of interest there. No one's breaking any rules or even slipping into gray areas this time around. And yes, Brooke will have thoughts when she finds out, and she's going to put it together eventually, as will Gillian."

"G-Money will have so many thoughts if she finds out."

"When," Tegan corrected. "She's going to notice. She already mentioned that Sawyer came in after midnight on Thursday. She hadn't put it together who they were with, though."

Robin climbed faster now. She'd spent all her worry counting down the time limit they'd set for themselves. She hadn't given any mental energy to calculating the variable of when others might find out.

Pushing up harder with her legs, she reached for the next handhold, only to find there wasn't a grip so much as a ledge. Glancing up beyond her arm's length, she realized she was looking at the steel beams of the ceiling. She dropped her chin to check between her body and the wall, and her vision swam as her depth perception adjusted to being several stories up.

"Shit. How'd we get this far off solid ground?"

Tegan chuckled softly. "Is that a literal question or a metaphorical one?"

She clung a little tighter and rested her forehead on her arm, not at all certain anymore. Had she let things get away from her? Had she climbed too high, too fast?

"Hey," Tegan whispered, and Robin finally turned to her, anchoring herself to the security in those steady hazel eyes every bit as much as she did to her safety harness. "You got this."

The first crack in her shell of self-assuredness rattled through her, releasing a sliver of vulnerability. "What if it turns out that we don't even know what this is?"

Tegan smiled broadly at her. "Doesn't matter. I don't have to understand anything to believe that you, of all people, are completely equipped to handle anything."

Her loud thoughts quieted down a bit, and she took a deep breath to draw the feeling deeper into her body.

"And you can trust your people, too," Tegan added. "Whatever you do, whatever you need from us, we're here and we'll follow your lead."

"You think Gilly will follow my lead?"

"Yes," Tegan said seriously, then with a little grimace added, "eventually."

"Fair enough."

"One more important question though," Tegan said.

"Ask away."

"If one were to follow your lead and get someplace they didn't fully intend to be, like, say, several stories in the air, how would one go about getting down?"

Robin wanted to laugh. She wanted it to be funny, but it wasn't because she actually did know the answer to the question, though if it also happened to be metaphorical, she didn't much care for it.

Still, she'd gotten herself, and now someone else, stuck. The least she could do would be to get them both out unharmed.

Taking a deep breath, she tucked her knees and arched her back, ready to demonstrate. "We're going to have to push away from the safety of the wall, let go, and fall."

Robin groaned and tried to roll onto her side to face Sawyer, but between the soreness from climbing and the total wrecking she'd received, she lacked both the strength and the coordination to do so.

"You okay over there?" Sawyer asked from their own puddle of satisfaction and pillows.

"Maybe." She sank deeper into the mattress. "I will be, probably."

Sawyer made a sleepy little sound of amusement, and Robin tucked it away in her memory without really meaning to. She couldn't help it. Her defenses were always a little low in this kind of freshly fucked haze. Still, she managed to keep her mind from wandering too far. There was no need for a future or past in perfect moments like these.

As if to prove the point, Sawyer propped themself on one elbow to look down at her. "How about now?"

She smiled up at them in the mix of moonlight and streetlamp streaming through her window. "A little better."

Sawyer leaned over and kissed her, slow, thorough, all sticky and thick with the mingled scents of their bodies. "How about now?"

She paused to relish the return of blood flow to her brain … and other body parts, then sighed happily. "Better."

"Agreed." Sawyer sat up a little more. "Always better after kissing you."

She smiled and added that to the mental file she shouldn't be compiling.

Sawyer didn't seem to have the same problem, as they ran a few fingers through her hair. "Can I take a shower before I head back to Gillian's?"

"Of course."

"Care to join me? It's only fair that the person who got dirty with me should also get clean with me."

"Not sure it works that way." Robin finally rolled onto her side. "If I get in a shower with you, I'm pretty sure we'll get dirty all over again."

"Not sure I see the problem there." Sawyer stretched, arms above their head, body lean and long. "In case you haven't noticed, I enjoy getting dirty with you."

Her pulse began to beat its low drum in her ears once more, but so did the echo of Tegan's warning. "If you give me a few minutes, I might be up for another round, but it's already after midnight. How much do you want to risk explaining to Gillian why you were out late again?"

"Okay, showering alone it is." They eased out of bed gingerly, and Robin enjoyed the view of them padding around her room stark naked. She'd done her best to kiss, lick, and taste every inch of that amazingly androgynous form over the last five nights together, and yet her mouth continued to water at the sight of them.

She stayed put for a few minutes, not trusting herself with so few barriers between them, but after she heard the toilet flush and the shower start, she wrestled herself first to sitting, then to standing. Grabbing a mix of random clothing from the floor, she ended up in pajama pants and the shirt she'd worn to work yesterday before she wandered into the bathroom.

"Change your mind?" Sawyer asked from behind the translucent curtain.

"Only a little." Robin hopped up so she sat on the corner of the vanity. "The libido is willing, but the body is weak."

"There's nothing weak about your body." Sawyer worked the shampoo into their hair. "I feel completely certain that after a few short hours of sleep you'll be ready to go again."

She warmed under the truth of the assessment. "Guilty. What about you?"

"I'd love a repeat after a few hours and a healthy dose of carbo-loading. Gillian said something about going to Syracuse all day. She's leaving early and won't be home until late. Want to grab brunch?"

The words took a second to compute. There were so many things to make sense of, not the least of which Sawyer had asked them to go out, just the two of them, which sparked a mix of complex emotions she didn't have a second to process before the realization of why Gillian was going to her hometown collided with the word "brunch." "Oh shit, is tomorrow, er, today now, Mother's Day?"

Sawyer stilled completely, letting the water hit their body and the suds roll off unimpeded.

"It is, isn't it?" Robin asked, though she already knew the answer. "Shit. I completely forgot. I'm having lunch with my mom and grandma."

"I'm sorry," Sawyer said with a rare air of solemnity.

"No worries. I adore my mom and grandma." She'd genuinely been looking forward to the outing for a few weeks, right up until the point Sawyer'd breezed into her life and taken over her brain. "Normally, I'd say they were the best entertainment in town, but now that they're up against present company, I'm sad I can't be in two places at once."

"Really?" Sawyer turned off the water and slid the curtain open, as if wanting to see her face. "You get along with your family?"

"Sure. Why?"

"I don't know." They shook the excess water from their hair. "I mean, you're easy to get along with, but so am I… Never mind. I guess it's hard enough for me to think of you as a therapist. I never really considered you having a mom."

Robin laughed lightly. "I guess it's weird to think of the person on their knees in front of you as part of a larger family, but my mom's a kick-ass special education advocate, total feminist vibes. And my grandma is retired now, but she was a financial guru. She's a first-generation American from Laos, so picture this little Asian grandma, but stuffed into power suits with shoulder pads. Now she plays cards with her old coworkers and makes egg rolls that are so much better than you get in restaurants and …" Her voice trailed off as she processed the almost stricken expression on Sawyer's face, before they grabbed a towel and covered it under the guise of drying off. "Anyway, we always do a girls' brunch on Mother's Day. There will be mimosas for sure, but I'm driving, so I won't get lit. I could swing by afterward and pick you up."

Sawyer stepped out of the shower, apparently focused on the task of rubbing every single droplet from their body. "Or maybe text me, in case I get up to something else."

"Deal. Tegan doesn't go home for the holidays," she offered without any pressure, but she got the sense Sawyer might not need to be alone tomorrow. "I'm sure she'd love company if you're bored."

"Hmm." Sawyer's little hum couldn't have been more noncommittal, or maybe they had something else on their mind. "Can you hand me my pants?"

She reached over and snagged the jeans from the side of the counter and tossed them to Sawyer, who managed to catch them without looking up. They pulled them on roughly and tried to scoot past her toward the door, but Robin wrapped her legs around their waist and pulled them close.

Sawyer finally looked up, eyes a darker shade of gray under magnificent lashes, and Robin's breath caught. "You okay?"

A muscle in their jaw flexed as they nodded. "You kind of fried me, and now I'm figuring out plans for tomorrow. I'll get there when I'm more rested."

The answer was vague, but not quite wrong. Robin placed a hand on their chest, circling a fingernail around one nipple before dipping lower to run it along their scar. "You know we're doing this thing, or multiple things to each other, but I can talk, too. We're friends of friends, and I got the sense maybe things were tense with your mom."

"Understatement." Sawyer extracted themself and took a step back before heading into the bedroom.

Robin hopped down and followed, watching as they snagged their shirt off the floor and slipped it on. She reached for them from behind, but this time when her hand slid across their stomach, Sawyer's whole body tensed, and not in a good way.

"You don't have to tell me," she tried again, "but I want you to know that even if I'm not into the whole relationship rigmarole, I'm down for conversation, friends with benefits for a bit, or being humans with each other. I'm a good listener, and—"

"Thanks." Sawyer cut her off quickly. "I appreciate the effort, really, but I've got enough therapists in my life already."

She winced, grateful Sawyer still had their back to her. They didn't like letting people see when their barbs actually landed. It didn't happen often, but despite Sawyer's little dig about her job, she hadn't been in work mode when she'd made the offer. She genuinely wanted to be there for this person, and had let her guard down a bit in order to do so.

Lesson learned.

"Sure. Good to know the boundaries." She eased back both physically and emotionally.

Sawyer turned around, the faint shadow of regret shading their features. "Robin, I like what we have here."

She nodded.

"You're amazing."

Robin smiled faintly. "I get that a lot."

"I believe you." Sawyer softened, reached for her hand, and pulled her close. "I have some stuff, and I'm well aware, like, so ridiculously aware you can't possibly imagine, but I want us to be this for a few more days."

She kissed them quickly, releasing some of the sting she'd held onto. "I can handle this for a few more days."

"Good." Sawyer kissed her again, this time a little deeper, but not unrestrained enough to lead to more. A good kiss, and a goodbye kiss all at once.

"Let me get dressed, and I'll drive you back to Gillian's."

Sawyer broke the contact between them once more. "Nah, I'm going to catch an Uber."

She froze mid-reach for her shoes. She'd driven them home every other night, and while she'd yet to admit as much, she'd come to enjoy the quiet closeness as a sort of wind-down. This disruption confirmed the distance between them was more than physical again. Still, it wasn't her place to push her needs onto anyone else. She did her best to sound chill as she struggled between comfort and consent. "Really, I don't mind."

Sawyer backed toward the door. "I know, but I do."

Robin opened her mouth, not sure yet if she intended to question or comment, but she never got the chance.

Sawyer simply turned to go, calling, "Get some sleep."

She stood there, listening to the sounds of their feet on the stairs until the front door closed somewhere beneath her. Even then she stayed still in the silence, absolutely unsure what feeling the abrupt departure inspired, but whatever it was, she knew for sure she didn't care for it much.

Twelve

Sawyer shifted from one foot to another on the front step of a sleek apartment building in North Buffalo. They didn't have to ring the buzzer. They could still turn around and walk away. No one would ever know. Hell, even if they did ring the buzzer, they didn't have to stay. They could drop off the peace offering they'd bought and then go. They could go anywhere at any time. They weren't trapped. They would never let themself be trapped.

With those happy thoughts, they pressed the button they'd been staring at for entirely too long.

"Yes?" The voice came through the tinny little speaker, distorting its richness, but not the tone of mild annoyance. "I didn't order anything."

Sawyer rolled their eyes. "Well, I got you something anyway."

Their mother didn't respond, at least not verbally, but the door latch clicked open.

Sawyer took the stairs instead of the elevator, grateful for a few extra seconds, but the third floor wasn't nearly high enough to burn off the nervous energy they hated themself a bit for still possessing.

Maura waited in the doorway to her apartment. "To what do I owe this rare and unannounced visit?"

Sawyer held out a bouquet of lilies. "Happy Mother's Day."

The gesture seemed to catch her off guard for a second, her cheeks coloring with pleasure or perhaps embarrassment. Maura never did care much for commercialized displays of sentimentality, so Sawyer held out the more acceptable form of recognition. "I also brought bagels."

Maura nodded in approval. "Thank you."

"Sure. I could leave them with you if you're working," they offered without daring to hope for such ease.

"No. Come in." She opened the door wider. "I'm listening to a podcast and doing the *Times* crossword puzzle."

Sawyer shed their coat, then slipped off their shoes and set them neatly on the rack near the door. "Sounds like a nice blend of stimulating and relaxing."

"Join me." Maura led the way into the kitchen and took the grocery bag from them.

The words were delivered gently enough, though they didn't leave much space for dispute. They took a seat at the glass-top table and watched their mother move about the kitchen. She sliced the bagels and placed them in a gleaming silver toaster oven, then began pulling dishes from glossy white cabinets.

Everything was clean, sleek, polished, like the woman who lived there. Sawyer didn't feel much of anything at the observation. It wasn't surprising, nor nostalgic. Maura had moved here long after they'd left, and even during their childhood, she'd always been on the hunt for a newer build, a better location, more amenities. Perhaps that's where they'd inherited their lack of sentimentality around where they lived or how long anything lasted.

"What?" Maura asked.

"I didn't say anything."

"No, but you smiled. It's not an expression I see often. I'm curious."

They bit back the urge to say they smiled a lot, so if she found the expression rare, it said more about her than them. Instead, they released a breath and said, "I like your new place, and I like how you don't let yourself get too attached to the old ones. You keep finding something that suits you best in the moment."

Maura seemed to turn the idea over in her mind while spreading cream cheese on her bagel. "What meaning do you attach to the trait?"

They sighed slightly. "I don't know. Maybe I got some of my wanderlust from you. Mine just came out less restrained."

Her expression remained impassive. "Perhaps your lack of attachment to neutral stimuli, but your tendency to follow paths aimlessly comes from your father."

Sawyer nodded, pulling on every emotional tool they possessed not to take that bait. Of course a man they barely knew would take the blame in their mother's mind. She couldn't possibly have any part in passing down a trait she found disconcerting.

"Speaking of lodging"—Maura set a bagel down for each of them, along with a plate of lox and a small bowl of olives— "are you still staying at Gillian's?"

"I am, though it's been a few weeks now. I should probably move along."

Maura stilled, mid-reach for the salmon. "'Move along' as in find a new place to stay, or leave town again altogether?"

They hadn't given the question much thought, so they paused to search their own feelings, getting only a slight satisfaction from making her wait. Their baser impulse suggested it might be enjoyable to test her reaction to various options, but as soon as the idea sparked, it vanished. That was exactly what she expected them to do, test, push, needle. There'd be no long-term satisfaction in playing the game. "I may stick around. I've got good friends here, connections, and there are worse places than Buffalo to spend a summer."

Maura nodded as if she found the list reasonable, then tentatively said, "I've got a guest room closet full of your clothes."

It wasn't quite an offer, and Sawyer noted that the room full of their own things was still labeled for guests, but they didn't want to stay here under any circumstances, so they added it to the long list of things to let slide.

"I'll go through them sometime, see if anything still fits."

Maura's eyes flickered toward their chest, a little slip in her carefully cultivated neutrality. "I suppose some of it may not any longer, though your tastes have often covered a wide range of styles."

What a polite way of saying they'd always been fluid without actually addressing the trait she found so hard to study. "How's the research going these days?"

Maura's expression brightened, and Sawyer was struck by how beautiful she'd be if she let a hint of the genuine affection she held for her work extend to other areas of her life. "Wonderful. I have two stellar graduate assistants this year. We're working on incorporating new theories on epigenetics into what we already know about family systems."

"So, the ways people with the same genes may express inherited traumas differently based on nongenetic factors?"

"And how symptoms of trauma are passed down through generations, impacting functionality, and value systems—even down to how they eat or communicate."

"Fascinating."

"Truly. I've stepped back from almost all my teaching now to focus on the field of study, and my private practice has trimmed down to clients who intersect with the research."

"How do you know who will intersect?"

"In theory, everyone intersects, but I find people with sibling rivalry particularly fertile ground for exploration."

They wondered if the clients felt the same way about their traumas, or if they even knew Maura found them akin to lab mice any time they mentioned their siblings.

"Is that why you hired Brooke to cover more classes?"

Their mother sat back slightly. "In all honesty, I tried to hire Gillian and ended up with Brooke instead."

"An even trade."

"Intellectually, yes, though Brooke is more prone to choosing emotional attachment over professional efficiency."

Sawyer flashed back to Gillian snapping, "I would never speak to a client the way I'm about to speak to you."

"You don't agree with the assessment?"

"No, but I can see where you would read the difference in them."

"Also, Brooke appears to be rather taken with her young colleague."

"Tegan?" Sawyer laughed. "I'm not sure she thinks of her as her 'young colleague' anymore, but yes, I believe they're very much in love."

Maura wrinkled her nose slightly, as though she found the idea mildly distasteful.

"You don't believe in love?"

"I wouldn't say that. Love is a complex emotion with endless possible expressions, and I've personally experienced enough of them to understand the force it creates between humans, along with other intangibles like loyalty, purpose, and a sense of belonging."

"All good things."

"Very much so. The research is clear that deep, meaningful connections are some of the most positive indicators for healthy development."

"But?"

"*And*," Maura corrected, her tone turning professorial. "There are also chemical factors at play during early iterations of 'in love' that stimulate arousal responses and produce infatuation, which I find beneath the stature of a practitioner of Brooke's caliber."

Sawyer sat forward a bit, interested despite their discomfort. "Like dopamine or endorphins are driving the bus?"

"Among other things. Those chemicals can function almost with addictive qualities, and, quite frankly, I see areas where they've softened Brooke, perhaps influencing her boundaries or assessments."

"Of Tegan?" Sawyer laughed. "You think Brooke Metcalf got hopped up on happy lust chemicals and crashed her life into a hot young coworker?"

"Now you're dealing in hyperbole, whereas I merely made an observation on how her judgment has shifted with the introduction of new stimuli. I don't even have an opinion on how recent developments play out in her personal life, nor do I particularly care."

"You care about her professional standards."

"When they affect the standards of the students in my program, and the field in which I practice, I expect that a certain level of intellectual rigor be maintained early on to set the tenor of our collective expectations."

"Oh." Sawyer connected a few dots. "She's teaching the intro class, and she's not playing the role of gatekeeper to your liking? No, that totally tracks."

A flash of frustration clouded Maura's face from tight lips to furrowed brow, and this time she didn't dismiss it quite so quickly. "You're editorializing and perhaps projecting a bit of your own defensiveness."

Sawyer laughed again, but the knot in their chest at the comment made the sound come out a little strangled. "Let me guess. You think I'm defending Brooke's softness for her students because she bears a similarly lax judgment about me."

"No." Maura defended quickly, "I meant only that sometimes the qualities a person is drawn to in her as a friend—"

"People like me."

"Or a therapist," she continued without acknowledging their interruption, "may impede neutrality when it comes to assessing their capabilities or weaknesses with a clear head."

Sawyer rolled their eyes, almost certain which of their own supposed weaknesses Brooke might be on the hook for overlooking.

"And in turn"—Maura's tone held an edge of open patronizing now—"she does people a disservice by putting off the type of intervention that, while unpleasant, may lead to effective changes in how they perceive themselves."

Sawyer's face flamed. "Like their gender identity."

"I didn't say that."

"But you've been thinking it, right? Ever since Brooke corrected your pronouns at work last weekend. Ever since you found out about my surgery."

"That's unfair. I've never begrudged anyone a diagnosis of gender dysphoria, nor have I strayed from accepted treatment recommendations for people presenting with a consistent and documented desire to live as the opposite sex."

"Right. If I wanted to be a man, preferably the strong, stable kind in a suit with a steady job and perhaps a truck or a hunting dog—"

"Sawyer." Maura pushed back from the table. "I don't know how to speak to you when you get like this."

"You don't know how to speak to me period, Mother. And that drives you up a wall, because you want clear answers with well-defined limits and easily quantifiable results, but I'm not looking to be analyzed or diagnosed or treated."

Maura raised her hands. "Fine. If that's what you need to believe on this part of your journey, I'll do my best to meet you where you are, but do you really want me to ignore facts that are plainly obvious to anyone with eyes or ears or basic reasoning skills?"

They sighed, exasperated. "Honestly, I do, but since you don't seem capable, why don't you lay those insights on me so we can wrap up this little therapy session you're running before the hour is up, and you can move on to your next client."

Maura pursed her lips and shook her head. "Fine, have it your way."

"No." They threw out their arms, spreading wide to show openness even as they braced internally. "Lay it on me, Dr. Stroud."

Her eyes turned a little sad as the fire slipped away, but her voice remained steady in its professional register. "I find it interesting for someone who eschews mental healthcare with such vehemence to continually surround themself with mental health practitioners, relying on them to house you, keep you company, manage your emotions, and stand guard beside you when speaking to your mother in social settings."

132

Sawyer thought they'd been ready. This wasn't the first time they'd had similar conversations, but this felt like a fresh blow, partially because they couldn't deny the charge. They had, in fact, clung to a group of therapists in every single way their mother suggested, and she didn't even know about Robin.

They rose from their chair, looking everywhere but directly at her. "Okay, well, good session."

"Sawyer, please don't run. Your inability to remain present in situations that challenge you feeds the type of inconsistency that's plagued your relationships since late adolescence. Perhaps if—"

"No. You've given me plenty to reflect on, including a personality trait to wonder whether you handed down by nature or nurture." They blew out a heavy breath and headed for the door.

"What's that?"

Sawyer slipped on their shoes. "Fifty minutes together is our max."

Then they walked out, grateful for the chance to land the final blow.

It wouldn't matter to their mother, but then again, very few things did, perhaps another thing they shared.

As they hit the street, they reached into their pocket for their phone, intending to call for an Uber, but when they glanced at the screen, they couldn't see through the haze over their vision. Instead, they did the next best thing and powered it down completely.

"I'll be at work until about six," Gillian said as she sat across from Sawyer, slipping on her olive-green pumps to match her slacks and the fashionably loose, silk blouse. So perfectly put together even before eight o'clock in the morning. "I'll pick up something for dinner on the way home."

"You don't have to. I can cook."

Gillian eyed them with a hint of concern. Something she'd done last night as well, when she'd arrived home to find them already crashed out on the couch with all the lights off at seven-thirty. They'd tried to tell her they were tired, but clearly their mother's assessments about hanging out with therapists weren't completely off base. They'd known, even at the time, that the charges wouldn't be easy to defend. Not while sleeping on Gillian's couch and eating her food. Not after dragging Brooke into emotional meetings. Not after collecting a group of four therapists into a makeshift karaoke bar to keep themself from going under after their first clash with Maura.

"Four," they muttered, running a hand over their bed head. How the fuck did they even *know* four practicing therapists, and why had they thought it would be okay to sleep with one of them? They rolled over, groaning slightly. They knew why, at least on the surface, but Maura had undercut even their own obvious attraction for Robin.

"Ready to talk about it yet?" Gillian asked calmly.

"No." They sat up and pulled their shit together as best they could. "I mean, I don't need to talk about anything. I just … I don't know. Mother's Day, right?"

Gillian nodded, her eyes full of sympathy as if anything made sense.

"But I'm fine. And I want you to know, I'm going to start apartment hunting today."

"Not necessary." Gillian rose gracefully and stared down at them. "I very much prefer having you where I can keep an eye on your antics rather than gadding about the Nordic countries."

They believed her enough to smile slightly, but the statement didn't exactly conflict with Maura's assessment that they might be subconsciously using their friends as some sort of stand-in therapist/mother figures. The thought made their stomachache. "Thank you, seriously, but we both need our own space."

"As long as said space is close by and allows for consistent social contact."

"You know me"—they yawned and stretched—"all about the social contact, and I know you, all about the healthy boundaries."

Gillian nodded as if she found the answer satisfactory. "There's no rush. Make sure you take the time to find the right fit."

They gave her a mock salute. "Will do, and I'll also make dinner."

She nodded. "I'll allow it."

"Good talk, boss."

She rolled her eyes, but her smile remained in place the whole time she headed out the door.

Sawyer flopped back onto the couch. They couldn't keep this up much longer. Not the crashing on people's couches, not the dodging friends' genuine concerns, not the letting their mother undercut every meaningful relationship in their life. Yes, Brooke and Gillian were therapists, but they hadn't been when they'd all met and become friends. They'd bonded deeply over shared mischief and late nights and coming out and chasing women. Okay, maybe Sawyer had done more chasing than the other two, but they'd totally been there for all the antics. It would absolutely devastate Brooke and Gillian for Sawyer to throw all that love, affection, trust, and history away, simply because they'd ended up in the same field as their mother.

They pulled a throw pillow over their face and screamed into it.

Why did they let Maura do this to them?

Robin.

She's why the blow had landed so hard.

They'd kissed her for the first time on a whiplash kind of night, and everything had spiraled out of control from there. They'd craved that woman the way an addict ached for another hit, and while they knew enough about addiction to understand the analogy might not be fully appropriate, that's how it'd felt with Robin. They wanted her against all logic and judgment and reason. They'd known subconsciously from the very first kiss that Maura would have a field day with their connection, and they just hadn't been able to stop themself.

"I teed that one right up for you, Dr. Freud," Sawyer grumbled aloud.

Night after night they'd fallen into her arms and her bed and her body, and never once had the hunger been fully sated. It felt wild and out of control and reckless, all things they generally enjoyed, but they hadn't ever let themself slow down long enough to wonder why they'd let this woman consume them.

Was that why they'd reacted so forcefully to Robin's offer to talk two nights ago? At the time, they'd written their abrupt departure off as a reaction to the reminder of Mother's Day, but somewhere in their psyche, had they drawn the connection between Mother's Day and Robin's offer of emotional labor?

"Fuck." They yelled again into the pillow. This was insane, and they had only themself to blame for letting their mother tie them in knots … again.

A knock at the door interrupted the shame spiral, and they hopped up, eager for any distraction, even though it was probably a delivery person, or maybe Gillian had forgotten her keys, or—Robin.

She stood there, dressed head to toe in black once again, the purse of her amazing lips and the hitch of her killer hips making it hard for Sawyer's brain to process anything except how devastatingly sexy she was. The only thing that kept them from reaching for her was that the usual smolder in her dark eyes had been replaced with a dangerous kind of fire.

"Okay, well, you're not dead," Robin finally said, "so fuck you."

They took a step back from the kind of warning even an idiot would heed.

"I wanted to make sure I got a good read on the situation before I tipped all the way into livid."

"Robin," they started, then didn't know where to go.

"What?"

"I don't know," they admitted.

She shook her head. "So, you aren't going to offer some explanation?"

"If I had one, I would."

"How about you start with the phrase, 'I ghosted you because ...' or actually, maybe not. I guess that's how ghosting works, there's no explanation. I mean, I think that's how it works, but for reasons I thought were obvious, I've never had it happen to me before."

Sawyer believed her deeply. What kind of moron would have an open invite from someone like Robin and just leave it on the table without response? Only that's exactly what they'd done last night. It had seemed like the right idea at the time. To just quit, to power down their phone and brain, and detach from their body, but now, unable to ignore the dark smudges under Robin's eyes, they felt something entirely different.

"And the thing is," Robin steamrolled forward, "we could've been cool. If you wanted a night off or to never sleep with me again, I would've been fine. I'm not some stage-five clinger. I'm the one who put the long-weekend limit on us in the first place. And yeah, I'd spent much of my day thinking of ways I would enjoy rocking out the rest of our time together, but I don't ever expect someone to feel the same way I do."

"No." They fought the urge to imagine all the ways they would've found to entertain themself and each other over the next few days.

"'No' what?"

"I did want that. It had nothing to do with you."

"It had a lot to do with me, if I'm the one spending the evening alone with my text messages sitting on 'read.'"

They sighed. They hadn't meant for that, or any of this, but when they'd opened their phone for a whole thirty seconds last night, there'd been messages from Robin, and they knew that if they gave them their due, their resolve would crumble.

There was no easy excuse that didn't insult her intelligence, and it wasn't exactly like they could explain honestly. How did one begin to craft a text to say, "My mom accused me of hiding from some legit mental disorder by filling my life with therapists, and I worry she might be right. Now I'm afraid there's some weird Freudian shit I don't want to bring to bed with you." Instead, they said, "It doesn't make sense."

"Something we agree on." Robin still seethed even though the words themselves were calm. "And for the record, I don't need anything to make sense. Making sense is overrated. I didn't even ask for an explanation. You could've said, 'I'm out for tonight,' or 'peace out forever.' Either would've been enough."

They didn't want that. They'd never wanted that, but as evening turned into night and the wanting had started to ache, they'd used it as further proof of why they couldn't afford to get attached or trust their own judgment where this woman was concerned. Anyone they wanted as bad as Robin had to be dangerous. "It's not that simple."

"No, it literally is. Basic courtesy and communication are not complicated." Robin refused to let them off the hook. "You pull out your phone and type, 'I'm tapped out.' Then I respond, 'It's been a blast. See you the next time Gilly makes sauce,' or some shit like that. Because we are going to see each other. We share friends, and, honestly, I had fun with you before we ended up in bed together. I would've liked for us to be friendly."

"Come on, we are friendly."

"Except you stood me up last night and then didn't answer my texts, which feels shitty at worst and juvenile at best, and neither of those things seem like qualities I look for in a friend."

"Fair," Sawyer granted. "I didn't mean to make things weird."

"Well, you did." Robin shot back. "Even if we pull up short on whatever we were doing together, we're going to see each other. I thought you were on board with being adults, but now I feel stupid and awkward, and I don't do either of those emotions on a regular basis. I've worked so hard to build a life where no one else could make me feel less than, and I crushed that goal. The way I felt last night is so far off-brand for the person I've become, I didn't even know what to do. I actually worried maybe something happened to you, and I couldn't even call Gillian to check because I'm hiding things from my best friends to protect the peace for you and me, which now feels extra dumb because you were here the whole time, not giving me anywhere near the same consideration."

Their stomach twisted at the validity of that argument. Robin had been amazing on every level, and they'd repaid her with disrespect. Still, they didn't have a lot of practice at being called out by good people, so even when recognizing the truth, they didn't know how to respond. "I never meant to stress you out or make you feel bad or weird."

"What emotions did you want to make me feel?"

"I don't know. Nothing, I guess."

"Thanks, nothing's a great start." Sarcasm dripped from her voice. "And under your plan, what did you think would happen the next time we saw each other?"

They shifted awkwardly. "I didn't think anything about a next time. I didn't think anything at all, really."

"Seriously? Did you black out or something?"

They shook their head. "No ... not exactly."

Robin stared at them suspiciously. "What's that mean?"

"I just sort of ran. It's a thing I do, run and shut down, it happens. You can ask Brooke or Gillian."

She laughed harshly. "Not a chance. I'm not going to ask my friend or my boss to explain my fuck buddy's behavior. I'm talking to you because I'm a grown-ass woman, and given the very adult fun we've had together, I expected you to be a grown-up, too. It's a low bar."

"Yeah," they agreed, and yet they managed to trip over the hurdle a lot. Hadn't that been their mother's parting shot as well, stay and talk this out? "I'm sorry. I don't have a lot of practice with healthy relationships, or communication, or anything really."

Robin shook her head. "Then I'm sorry, too, but you already made it abundantly clear you don't want my support in that area, and you have plenty of therapists in your life already. Maybe you should talk to one of them, because I'm not going to sit around waiting for you to figure it out ever again."

And with that, it was apparently Robin's turn to walk away.

Thirteen

Robin stormed through the main door to the office, still seething. Her vision remained red around the edges as she ripped off her leather jacket, thrashing a bit as the arms turned inside out and caught on a series of silver bracelets. Grumbling, she shook it out, or maybe she simply shook, because the adrenaline still surged through her at the memory of Sawyer standing in the doorway looking all sleepy and sexy and very much not incapacitated.

"Well, good morning to you, too," someone said, and she nearly jumped out of her damn skin. She didn't know why she was surprised. She'd gone to Gillian's knowing she'd already be at work, but the presence of other humans in the office, or even the world, seemed mildly offensive, yet there stood all three of her colleagues.

Her face flamed at the wave of vulnerability that surged through her as Gilly, Brooke, and Tegan all stared at her as if waiting for some greeting or explanation. She didn't have one. Not one she could give in good faith, or even something approaching sanity at the moment. Instead, she gritted her teeth and mumbled something approximating, "Morning."

Then she half-staggered off down the hall, feeling her way down to the first door on the right and into her own professional cocoon.

"What an idiot." She flopped into her overstuffed armchair. She'd never let a lover make her feel weak and stupid before. Not since high school had anyone else had this kind of effect on her sense of self, and she didn't want to be this person now. She'd built a whole slew of rules and protective

141

mechanisms and emotional best practices so she would never become the kind of person who lost her heart or depended on someone else to hold her together.

And yet, every one of those tools had failed her when she'd left an amazing lunch with people she loved dearly to hook up with someone she barely knew, only to have her texts go unanswered. Disappointment hit first, followed by a few hours of sexual frustration, and then as she sat at home all night waiting to hear from Sawyer, the worry set in.

When she'd finally convinced herself she was within her realm of rights and responsibility to go check on them, she'd totally lost her cool. The sight of them fine and barely even sheepish caused a myriad of unfamiliar emotions, from relief to resentment, to rip through her, and she poured all of them out under the umbrella of anger, while Sawyer barely managed to offer weak apologies with zero explanations.

She covered her face with her hands. She knew better than this. She practiced better than this, day in and day out. If it had been anyone else, she would've been content with the knowledge that very few people ever had real understanding of why they behaved the way they did when elevated, at least not logically. But she also knew people generally engaged with the things they cared about, which was why she'd showed up at Gillian's this morning, acting a fool. She cared about Sawyer so much she'd exploded, while Sawyer had stayed aloof and gorgeous and stoic. If that didn't showcase the inequity in their base levels of feeling toward each other, she didn't know what would. A horror that she'd held at bay seeped in through her rage.

A knock at the door caused her to set her jaw at what would undoubtedly come next. "Yes?"

Tegan peeked her head inside. "Can I join you?"

She tried to steady herself. She'd already bitten one head off this morning. She didn't need to take down an innocent bystander as well. "Did you draw the short straw?"

Tegan smiled and eased farther into the office. "Hardly. We all wanted to come in and check on you, so we arm wrestled for the honor, and I won."

It was the perfect image to break through the last of Robin's walls. "I made a mistake."

"Okay." Tegan eased onto the couch opposite her and pulled her legs up crisscrossed. Then resting her elbows on her knees, she gave Robin her full attention. "I'm ready. Lay it on me."

She shook her head as embarrassment constricted her throat. She didn't want to sound the way she would definitely sound if she told this story, but she clearly couldn't hold everything in without starting to resemble a loose cannon. "Sawyer ghosted me, and I called them on it and lost my temper, and they stood there mumbling something about being complicated while I made a fool of myself."

Tegan nodded. "Thank you for trusting me with that. It must've been disorienting and vulnerable and maddening, and a slew of other things. Quick clarifying question, would you like me to respond as your friend or as a mental health colleague right now?"

Robin thought for a second, because she probably needed both given how she'd behaved, but she wasn't in a place to hear anything calm or sensible yet. "Can we do friend first?"

"Absolutely," Tegan said with seriousness. "How fucking dare they? What kind of total douchebag ghosts anyone, but especially you. I mean, have they seen you? You're ridiculously hot and fun. You ooze sex appeal, and you offer no strings, great conversation, and impeccable taste. Also, from what I hear from several people we know in common, you're epically skilled in bed."

Robin shrugged. It wasn't the kind of thing one could say about oneself, but she'd never had any complaints.

"Does Sawyer have a concussion, or are they seriously the dumbest person in Buffalo? Every sapphic I know would gladly crawl the length of the city to have a chance to tap that." Tegan gestured to the whole of Robin. "I mean, look at you over there giving them that kind of access to virtual perfection, and they couldn't even return a text? That is the most basic, infantile, bullshit, asshole, immature move."

"That's what I said!" Robin finally laughed. "With a good deal of force."

"Good for you!" Tegan continued. "Totally warranted. Asshole moves deserve calling out. Like, 'fucking communicate, Sawyer.' You have other options, Robin. You do not need to sit around waiting for someone who doesn't know enough to recognize the best deal in all of Western New York. If Sawyer doesn't have the brains to snatch up every ounce of time you offer them, someone else will."

"This is a very good pep talk, Teegs." She enjoyed it immensely, and her anger ebbed a bit.

"Thank you." Tegan nodded. "I mean every word."

"All true. I'm a freakin' catch, and I do have other options, lots of them," Robin agreed, only the realization made her stomach clench, and she drew her knees to her chest, tightening into a self-protective ball. "So, why did I lose my shit over them?"

Tegan's expression softened, but she offered no easy explanations.

"I mean, we had amazing sex, and when we did talk, the conversation was solidly above average, but that doesn't justify going off. So they stood me up? Rude, and if I'm being honest, disappointing. I'd looked forward to more of the same, but why storm over and make it a whole thing?"

"I don't know," Tegan said. "I'm tossing out ideas, but it sounds like maybe Sawyer hurt your feelings."

She scoffed. "I'm not the type of person to catch feelings."

Tegan shifted slightly on the couch, opening her mouth before seeming to catch herself. "Do you want me to call them an asshole again?"

Robin shook her head. That fire had burned itself out. "No, it's fine. I know you're dying to slip into therapist mode. Go ahead."

"Emotional outbursts seem off-brand for you, but you do have big feelings. You just mostly reserve them for nonromantic situations, like thrill seeking or mischief making or advocating for others. Honestly, by those standards, you feel things more fully than anyone else I know."

"Maybe," she conceded, "but those are good emotions, or at least righteous sorts of indignation. What I'm feeling now … I don't want these kinds of emotions. I hate them."

"Can you name them?"

"Anger."

"There's the easy one."

She tightened her jaw. "I swear to all things holy, if you tell me that anger is an iceberg emotion, or ask me what's floating beneath the surface—"

Tegan laughed. "I didn't, but you self-owned there, friend."

"Son of a bitch."

Tegan waited.

"I already copped to disappointment, which leads me back to pissed off, because you can't be disappointed if you don't have expectations, which means I let myself expect things from Sawyer, which brings me to embarrassment."

"You think it's embarrassing to expect basic communication from people?"

"No, but I think I expected more, more than we communicated, more than I let myself admit, and now I feel stupid for wanting something I didn't ask for and clearly wasn't about to get."

"And this morning?" Tegan prodded.

"Oh, right back to anger. I burned white hot and lit them up. I made them feel the brunt of my embarrassment, and maybe some sadness, because they didn't seem to care all that much, but I couldn't stop myself from hitting them with both barrels, which made me feel helpless, or at least out of control around them. Even when I started to worry what I was doing was wrong, I kept going. God, have you ever felt that way?"

Tegan laughed outright now. "Short answer, yes."

145

"What's the longer answer?"

"Buddy, I did things I was very not proud of when Brooke and I were actively trying not to fall in love, things that still make me cringe when I think about how badly I handled them, and I think Brooke would say the same."

"I don't believe it, not out of either of you. You two are both unfailingly good."

"You are, too. You're one of the best humans to ever exist, and for what it's worth, deep down, I think Sawyer is probably good, too, but relationships are complicated. So are emotions and communication."

"I know all those things, but Sawyer and I aren't in a relationship. It's more of a situationship."

Tegan's expression turned sympathetic. "I didn't say it was a healthy relationship, but the two of you aren't strangers. You share a social circle. You're going to see each other again."

"Probably. Eventually."

Tegan grimaced.

"Sooner rather than later?"

"It's up to you," Tegan said, then added, "Brooke and Gillian are in the main office making plans for a group dinner on Thursday before we head out for our weekend away."

Robin groaned. "Why?"

Tegan shifted slightly again. "The official answer is to celebrate the end of Brooke's semester."

"What's the unofficial answer?"

"They're worried about Sawyer."

Robin's stomach lurched, and she tightened her hold on her knees.

"It's not your fault," Tegan said softly.

"What's not my fault? What did I miss?"

"You didn't miss anything. You can't know something someone doesn't tell you."

Robin stared at her, trying to wait her out instead of replaying the way Sawyer had stammered and shrunk under her earlier barrage.

"Gillian came home to find Sawyer kind of a low-key mess last night, and she thinks they might've gone to see their mother yesterday."

Robin sighed. "Damn it. The mom is bad, right?"

"I don't know the story, and it's not your job to anticipate someone else's trauma or how they'll react to it."

"What else?"

Tegan hesitated again, and this time Robin didn't have the patience. She started to rise. "If you don't tell me, Brooke will."

"Okay." She lurched forward. "So, Sawyer has a history of running or shutting down. Apparently, they kind of disappear, and Brooke and Gillian are worried about it happening again."

Robin's brain ignited again. "Oh God."

"Robin," Tegan warned.

She hopped off the couch. "Do you think … if they were standing on a ledge, and I—"

"What?" Tegan caught her by the wrist. "Told the truth? Set healthy boundaries? Let them know their actions affect other people?"

Robin started to pull away, but Tegan stood and wrapped her into a hug.

She fought the comfort. She didn't want it, maybe she didn't even deserve it, but Tegan didn't let go, holding her tightly until the tension in her muscles melted.

She couldn't go off again. She couldn't be that person she hated being earlier. She needed to breathe. She needed to think. She needed to remember who she was.

Tegan stepped back, but kept a hand clasped on each of her shoulders. "No matter what you said or what you did, Sawyer makes their own decisions."

She nodded and took another shaky breath. "I'd hate to make things worse, though, if they're struggling or ready to bolt, and I should've—"

Tegan gave her a little shake. "You told them your truth, and we both know that anyone you can lose by being honest with was never yours to hold in the first place."

147

The truth of it made her lungs ache. "So, what do I do now?"

"Just be you, friend," Tegan stressed. "I meant what I said earlier. You're amazing. You're genuine and authentic and so perfectly passionate. Don't dim any of that light. Any person who cannot take you at your fullness isn't your people."

It had been three days since what Robin had come to think of as the best pep talk ever, and she'd gotten a little stronger in her resolve with each client she affirmed or meal she shared with friends or hours of sleep she caught up on.

She hadn't heard from Sawyer, but she hadn't expected to. If they couldn't be bothered to text her back after four nights of earth-shaking sex, she really didn't have any faith in them to open the lines of communication after a complete dressing down. She was self-aware enough to understand she hadn't exactly left them a great path forward, and with the added insight that they had a tendency to shut down or run when overwhelmed, well, she still wasn't exactly proud of the approach she'd taken.

Still, Tegan had been right, as usual. Robin couldn't know or manage emotions or patterns she hadn't been let in on. As far as she could tell, the only real option she had left was to model the type of behavior she wanted going forward. Or at least that's what she told herself as she sat across from Sawyer at dinner and tried to remember how to breathe.

"Anchor Bar or Duff's?" Tegan grilled them on Buffalo debates.

"Anchor Bar," Sawyer said without hesitation.

"Sahlen's or Wardynski's hot dogs?"

"Sahlen's."

"Paula's Donuts or Mayer Bros?"

Sawyer shook their head. "Can't compare. Different genres, different seasons."

"Correct," Gillian said over the rim of her wineglass, before tossing out one of her own. "Best sports team?"

"Bills, Bandits, Bisons, Sabres, in that order."

"Beauts?" Robin finally jumped in. "Queen City Roller Derby?"

Sawyer grinned. "Are the women still wrecking shit? Well then, I put every women's sports team ahead of the boys based on pure enjoyment of the viewing experience."

She nodded, finding the answer satisfactory.

"What about you?" Sawyer asked tentatively. "What's your Nickel City jam?"

"This is home. I love it all."

"Favorite park?" Sawyer asked.

"Broderick Park."

"A river rat, I like it. What about your favorite tourist trap?"

Robin ran through a few options in her mind. She felt relatively certain her friends had concocted the game to remind Sawyer of everything to love about sticking close to home for a bit. "Maid of the Mist at Niagara Falls."

"Good choice," Sawyer said, and a little lull fell in the conversation.

Finally, Gillian said, "Seriously, is no one going to make a joke about Robin choosing a drenching activity at the wettest place on earth?"

Brooke about snorted white wine up her nose, and Tegan guffawed.

Sawyer's cheeks turned a delightful shade of pink. "I honestly hadn't considered it, but I think the joke lands way better from you than it would from me."

Gillian tipped her glass. "And on that note, I think I'm done for the evening."

"I don't see how anyone can top that." Brooke pushed back from the table.

"I don't know." Robin grinned. "I suspect a few of us have some experience topping, but few of us stand a chance when G-Money enters the club, so I'll tap out, too."

Tegan rose as well. "I'm going to let this one go as well, because the sooner you all head out, the sooner I'm alone with my beautiful girlfriend for four whole days."

"Hint taken." Sawyer stretched back, showing a hint of midriff that about made Robin's lower body liquify, and she had to look away in order to find her own feet.

"You've got the keys to both of our places?" Brooke asked Sawyer.

They patted a hand on their right pocket, "Tegan's apartment," then their left side, "and your lovely house."

"Good. I texted you directions about the plants, but they won't wilt over the weekend. Mostly bring in the mail and don't let the place look deserted."

"Got it, Mom." Sawyer gave her a hug. "No wild parties, no wild girls, stay out of the alcohol cabinet, brush my teeth, and in case of emergencies, call 911."

Brooke gave them a little shove. "Same rules apply at Tegan's."

"They do not." Tegan laughed. "Except 911. The rest is totally up to you. Have fun."

They all headed for the door and had nearly made a clean break when Tegan called Gillian back, presumably under the guise of work talk, but Robin had her suspicion she merely intended to give Robin a chance to say a few words to Sawyer, and she might've been offended by that if she hadn't been waiting for the chance all night.

Stepping out on the front porch, she closed the door and wheeled on them.

Sawyer took a step back, appearing to brace for impact.

"Relax," Robin said calmly. "You and me, we're cool."

Sawyer's gray eyes narrowed suspiciously.

"I'm serious," Robin continued easily. "Those women in there love you a lot, and I love them. I refuse to have a custody battle over our friends, so we're both going to stick around and act like grown-ups."

Sawyer nodded slowly. "I'm sorry I wasn't great at that last weekend. You had a right to be angry."

"We both made choices, and we can make new ones now."

"What if I continue to make bad ones?"

"Then I'll murder you." Robin stared at them for a second, then cracked a smile. "I'm kidding. People make mistakes."

"I make more than my share. I didn't want to hurt you, Robin. I have a lot of issues."

"I'm not going to argue. Everybody has issues."

"Even you?"

"Well, not me. I'm perfect."

"Obviously." Sawyer's grin returned. "I suppose the exception only proves the rule, and you truly are exceptional, Robin. The last thing I ever wanted to do was make you feel otherwise. I swear what happened was 100 percent about me. I shouldn't have let it spill over onto you."

"Apology accepted."

"Seriously? No need to rebut or analyze or pick me apart?"

She shrugged. "If you'd said that a week ago, I would've accepted then, too."

"Another exceptional quality in my world." Sawyer's brow furrowed slightly. "I want to say it won't happen again, but I don't trust myself that much. Someone recently made me suspect I can't trust my own taste or judgment in friendship, but if I could, I would've liked for us to be friends."

"It's not too late." Robin nudged their foot with her own. "And that person sounds like an asshole."

"She's brilliant."

"The two aren't mutually exclusive. It's totally possible to be a genius and a real bag of dicks at the same time."

"That's a really good point." Sawyer laughed, but the sound trailed off. "Shit, why didn't I remember that?"

"I don't know. Maybe you don't have enough therapists in your life after all."

Sawyer winced, but this time they didn't look away. "Would you even want to be friends with someone who apparently collects mental health professionals without letting any of their wisdom sink in?"

"Sure," Robin agreed, and not just for their sake. "I suppose one of us is bound to rub off on you eventually … that's what she said."

"Well played." Sawyer lifted their hand, and Robin slapped it but then didn't let go.

Holding onto those amazing fingers, she ran her thumb over the soft palm. "You and me, we're not going to go back to what we were doing, okay?"

Sawyer swallowed and nodded. "Fair."

"I'm not sure 'fair' is the right word. I didn't like the way you made me feel Sunday night or Monday morning, and I don't want to go back there, but I do want us to figure out what's on the other side for us."

"Why?" Sawyer asked softly.

"Gillian and Brooke love you, and that's good enough reason for me to want you to stay."

"What about you? Do you want me to stay?"

She released their hand. "There's only one way to find out."

Fourteen

Sawyer was pushing things.

Robin had set a boundary, and they wanted to respect her right to do so, but they also wanted to see where exactly the lines around their tentative friendship lay, and after three days of either sitting alone in Brooke's house or pacing around Tegan's studio apartment, they were bored enough to take their chances.

Their mother would likely say their oppositional defiance compelled them to snag Brooke's car keys and head out with little more than a vague plan, but their mother had also gotten them into this new limbo with Robin in the first place.

Well, maybe she wasn't totally responsible for Sawyer's actions, but she'd certainly sown the seeds of doubt until they'd grown into a clusterfuck. So what if she'd noticed a thing about Sawyer's social circle? She could've kept her mouth shut.

They shook their head as they fired up the Honda Civic and headed west, and then said, "No, she can't."

Sawyer didn't even mind talking aloud to themself. They needed to hear their own voice to drown out Maura's, because the woman seemed incapable of restraining herself from sharing every clever observation that popped into her brain. And, to be fair, pointing out that Sawyer's peer group contained a lot of therapists was a pretty astute observation to make in the midst of their usual argument.

"It's totally possible to be a genius and a real bag of dicks at the same time."

The echo of Robin's words came back as loudly as their mother's. Also, an apt reflection, and what a way with words.

Sawyer turned down Ferry Street and wound their way toward a place they should've let themself go the moment they'd left Maura on Mother's Day. What would've happened if—

They shook their head. What-ifs could drive a person mad, and they'd spent too many years trying to guess or anticipate various scenarios where Maura came into play. It had never once worked out well, and this last attempt to walk a line had cost them at least one amazing night with Robin, if not more. All they could do now was try to salvage something from the wreckage.

"We're cool," Robin had said, and Sawyer believed her, but that didn't keep them from experiencing a hint of anxiety as they pulled to a stop in front of her big Victorian. They left the engine running and bounded up the stairs. Nervous energy coursed through them as they rapped on an apartment door.

They waited, not nearly long enough, and knocked again. Apparently, if they were making a mistake, they wanted to make it very quickly.

"Keep your pants on," Robin called from inside, then a bit softer, grumbled, "Pants, pants, where are mine? There."

Sawyer's nervousness lessened at the mental image of Robin rummaging through laundry baskets or piles looking for clothes to throw on. They were trying to hide a bit of a smile when she finally pulled open the door.

"What the hell?" Robin laughed. "I thought Brooke told you to call 911 in case of emergencies. Why are you banging on my door like the place is on fire?"

"I left the car running."

"A car you stole?"

They laughed. "Brooke's car."

"You left Brooke's car running in my neighborhood?" She jammed her feet into a pair of sneakers, slammed the door, and jogged down the stairs, leaving Sawyer to catch up.

Sure enough, by the time they hit the porch, there was a group of teenage boys looking longingly at the Civic.

"Nice try, punks." Robin laughed as she hopped in the passenger seat. "If you're going to steal something, you gotta be quick about it."

"Robin!" a woman chided from next door.

"Sorry," she called, then turned back to the gaggle of adolescents. "Stealing is wrong, kids, unless it's from 'the man.' And remember, rich people taste like chicken … probably."

Sawyer cackled as they threw the car in reverse.

"What?" Robin asked innocently. "Someone has to raise up these children in the ways of the Lord."

"I agree. I just can't believe I let someone convince me of some transference nonsense where you're concerned, because you are definitely not a therapist."

"But I am. Those are life lessons I'm imparting, Butthead."

"Butthead? You talk to your clients that way?"

"Some of them, but it doesn't matter because I'm not *your* therapist."

"Right, right, so you keep saying."

They drove north for a few minutes before Robin finally sighed. "What's up?"

"The thing is …" They kept their eyes on the road, not sure how to explain their thought process. "I've sat around for days now thinking about standing you up last week and feeling terrible."

"Meh." She waved them off. "I'm over it."

"I got that the other night, with you being all zen, and it left me kind of jealous, and honestly angry."

"At me?"

"No. At me, mostly, but then also at the thing that set me off in the first place."

"The weird transference nonsense we aren't talking about because you have other therapists in your life?"

They scrunched up their face at the memory of the comment. "Shit, I've been pinning all my frustration on a

Mother's Day conversation when I actually got kind of pissy the night before I ghosted you, didn't I?"

"Little bit."

They pulled onto the Grand Island Bridge. "For what it's worth, same trigger for both events."

"How very efficient of you," Robin deadpanned.

"Right? Like stubbing my toe on the same ottoman, over and over again, rather than moving it. Not smart, but at least I don't go around crashing into everything all the time. I'm actually chill in general, which might be a counter-performative assertion given where I'm taking you."

"Oh, you had a plan? I sort of read this as a coercive kidnapping situation."

"And you jumped right in the car? I didn't even have to offer you candy."

Robin looked them up and down as if they were some kind of treat before saying, "I have a 'yes' vibe. It's kind of my thing."

"I usually do, too," Sawyer admitted, "which is another reason I've been kicking myself. What happened last week didn't sit well with me. Even though you moved on, I've been slowly stewing—also out of character by the way, so I thought I might not be well-served by sulking alone. Maybe you had the right idea on Monday."

Now it was Robin's turn to make a face. "Not my finest moment either."

"No, but you burned hot and fast like a forest fire to my flame flickering in the dark, which made me suspect you could give me lessons."

"Fire lessons? Aw, Boo, did someone tell you about my long history of arson?"

They snorted as they turned toward Niagara Falls. "As if I couldn't smell smoke around you from day one, but no, I meant rage lessons."

"Rage? Not my specialty, unless Republicans are about to attack trans kids or my bodily autonomy."

"Or some douche canoe ghosts you?"

156

She feigned shock. "Who would ever dare do something so egregious?"

Sawyer pulled into a parking lot and killed the engine before turning to face her. "Someone who isn't nearly as adept at arson as you."

"I'm not at all sure where this is heading, but I'm very much liking the dark, chaotic energy you've got about you." Robin held their gaze for a moment longer, seeming to search, or maybe soak them in. "What do you have in mind? Never mind, doesn't matter. I'm in."

Sawyer smiled slowly, then inclined their head toward the little store in front of them with a sign that simply read, "Rage Room."

"Pull!" Sawyer called.

Robin tossed a plate in the air, and Sawyer swung an aluminum bat, turning it into a thousand ceramic shards.

They both laughed almost maniacally, and Sawyer felt Robin's mania nearly as deeply as their own. The sound was surprisingly resonant for someone with such a small frame, but it seemingly came from her belly and shook its way out as she grabbed another plate from the box.

This time, Sawyer called their shot, pointing the bat toward an imaginary center field, like a bash-and-break Babe Ruth.

Robin played along, pushing up the sleeves of her oversized jumpsuit and going into an exaggerated pitching motion even though she stood off to the side rather than in front of Sawyer, for safety reasons. She threw the plate, spinning it into the air, and they sprang into motion as it peaked, timing its arrival in the strike zone with big-league precision. They obliterated the entire thing in one crushing blow, then made a big show of dropping their bat and taking a jog around the imaginary bases within the confines of the small room.

Robin did a slow clap, then whistled through her teeth. "Hall-of-Fame-caliber launch angle there, Slugger."

"Slugger?" Sawyer struck a cocky pose. "I like it."

"Suits you," Robin agreed, "or at least it does tonight. Playful, brash, swaggering."

"Ah, you're saying I'm back in the swing of things, so to speak?"

"Until you made that terrible pun, yes."

"Good." Sawyer lifted their safety goggles and surveyed the damage. Several boxes worth of plates and glass bottles littered the ground in pieces. They'd lost track of how many add-ons they'd bought over the last hour, but a battered VCR and an ancient ink-jet printer smashed to smithereens by Robin's sledgehammer suggested they'd gotten the most of their money and time. The ache in Sawyer's shoulders now came from fatigue instead of tension, and even their thoughts flowed more freely. "With shit like this, who needs therapy?"

"Everyone," Robin said casually enough. "Like, almost every human needs therapy, but in lieu of that, this method of stress relief is pretty cathartic."

"I'll take it." Sawyer unzipped the front of their thick, protective jumpsuit. "I wish I'd done this last Sunday."

Robin placed a hand on their shoulder. "You did it now. This is a great start to our friendship era. I'm glad you kidnapped me."

"Again, you got in the car before I had the chance to, but I've decided I'm not going to make a habit of arguing with you."

"I like this policy. What else are you going to agree with me on?"

They thought for a few seconds. "I think we agree on a lot about Buffalo."

"To Ted's?" Robin asked.

"To Ted's!"

Within half an hour, they sat across from each other in a vinyl-covered booth at Ted's, each the proud new owner of a charbroiled Sahlen's hot dog and a loganberry soda, while they'd gone halfsies on an order of fries and a chocolate milkshake.

Sawyer didn't even try to seem chill about this meal. They'd been back in Buffalo for over three weeks, and the fact that they hadn't been to Ted's yet now felt like the second biggest mistake they'd made since returning. Thankfully, this oversight was much easier to rectify. They bit into the perfection of a Sahlen's hot dog, closed their eyes, and moaned. Savoring every detail from the crisp char to the hot, juicy flavor, they didn't even care what they must look like to Robin, having a near-religious experience with the most phallic of foods.

"Damn," she whispered, "if I'd known all I needed to make you emit a noise like that was buy a four-dollar hot dog, things may've gone very differently between us."

"No one ever accused me of being hard to get."

Robin chuckled. "Something we have in common."

"I bet a lot of people see you as way out of their league," Sawyer said around another bite.

Robin sipped the milkshake. "I've never thought of myself that way. I'm kind of the person who jumps in headfirst."

"Better sorry than safe?"

She smiled. "Pretty much. I have terrible FOMO."

"Same," Sawyer agreed. "A lot of people have asked me over the years if all my running is *from* something, or *toward* something, and I think it's probably both."

Robin nodded but didn't push, and Sawyer liked her even more for it.

"Everything I do, and every place I wander, follows logically from what came before, at least for me. I can trace it all back in my head, even if it doesn't make sense for anyone else."

"If it matters to you, it doesn't have to make sense to anyone else," Robin said quickly. "Other people don't make sense to me most of the time."

"They don't?" The sentiment surprised Sawyer.

"Not always. Honestly, not often."

"But you're good with people. I mean, even though I've seen no evidence, I hear you're a therapist."

Her lips twitched up, and Sawyer enjoyed being the one to spark such a sardonic smile. "Wow, progress. Yes, I am a therapist, and certainly I work with people who possess a deep ability to know all things, so I see why you might be confused."

"You do hang out with people who know a lot about people."

Robin popped a fry into her mouth. "Of course, Gillian is brilliant. I mean, the way her brain works boggles my mind, and Brooke has her spidey-sense style of intuition. Sometimes I think she's clairvoyant. Then Tegan came around, and she sees people so clearly and deeply, she unraveled a woman who'd always seemed impenetrably put-together to me."

Sawyer nodded and snagged a few fries of their own, not inclined to argue with her on any of those assessments.

"And I love them," Robin went on. "Like, I wake up every day grateful to have hit the jackpot in career and colleagues, but we approach the same work fundamentally differently."

"Say more."

Robin eyed them, a little wary. "Dangerous territory. I feel like there's some unspoken limit on how many times a person can say 'therapist' in your presence before you turn into a pumpkin."

"Valid concern." Sawyer resisted the urge to say they'd heard that word more times than any normal person could fathom, and instead lifted up their hot dog playfully. "But this delicacy acts as an anchor. I'm incapable of slipping away when worshiping at the temple of Ted's."

"Well, in that case ..." Robin took another strong pull of loganberry. "I very often don't understand why people act the way they do or make the choices they make or even value the things they value. I find people wildly unpredictable and illogical, and I think they regularly work against their own best interests."

"Wow, tell me how you really feel."

"I'm serious. Humans are absolute chaos creatures to me, and I love them for it. Of course, I believe we can excavate emotions and learn and grow, that's a great part of the gig, but I suspect what makes me most effective at my job is the deeply held belief that I don't need to understand jack about a person to be absolutely in awe of them, or to adore them, or to believe they're capable of great things."

Sawyer's chest tightened, and they grasped the hot dog a little tighter in one hand and the seat of the booth with the other. Maybe Robin had been right, at least partly, because, while they didn't fear turning into a pumpkin, they did have the sudden urge to back away. They'd promised they wouldn't, though, and while they'd broken the same vow to plenty of women over the years, this time they didn't want to. Forcing their lungs and lips to work in tandem, they managed to say, "Very different approach."

Okay, so not the most eloquent reply, but it was the difference they clung to. The philosophy Robin had so beautifully espoused could not have been more diametrically opposed to ideals they'd grown up fending off. Their mother could never approve of anything she didn't fully understand.

Robin shrugged as if she hadn't just shaken their foundation, and in doing so, caused a drop of mustard to drip from the end of her hot dog onto her shirt. "What can I say? I like the messy parts of people, and I revel in the fact that I may never know someone fully, but it works for me. I meet people right where they're at, and I generally accept them exactly how they are. Then we work on leveling up from there."

"Sounds difficult." Sawyer's words still sounded a little choked out, but if Robin noticed, she didn't seem to care.

"Not really. I think I have the best job in the world. I get to meet the coolest people and work with the best colleagues, and spend all day, every day, helping people see how amazing they already are. Have you ever heard the sculpting philosophy about finding an elephant in a block of marble?"

Sawyer shook their head. "Weird turn."

"I'm going to botch the quote, but it goes something like a sculpture student asked the teacher what they intended to make out of a big block of marble, and the teacher explained that they weren't going to make anything, they were going to find an elephant that's already inside. The teacher explained they start with the block as is and gently chip away every bit that isn't a part of the end masterpiece."

Sawyer sat back and slowly let the story sink in, before softly saying, "Seems like a pretty big leap of faith for a starting assumption. What if there isn't a masterpiece?"

Robin reached across the table as though she might touch them. Their whole body tightened in anticipation of even a gentle brush against raw nerve endings, but at the last second, Robin's hand veered toward the fries instead. Sawyer breathed a subtle sigh of relief and regret, then finally dared to meet her dark eyes, and the second they did, Robin said, "Everyone's got a masterpiece inside. That's never the issue, ever."

"What's the issue?"

"Not everyone has the courage or the fortitude to find theirs."

Fifteen

Robin stepped out into the early evening light, trading the confines and hushed tones of the office for the blaring, glaring cacophony of downtown Buffalo after business hours. She flipped down her sunglasses and basked for a moment in the warmth of the outdoors, then took two steps, swinging a black motorcycle helmet by the chin strap before she heard the unmistakable whistle that always precedes a catcall.

Tensing immediately, she gave zero thought to flight before her fight instinct took hold and she wheeled, ready to bite the head off whatever jackass had something inappropriate perched on their lips.

"Easy there, Hot Stuff."

She registered the familiar voice first, and then the soothing rumble of a laugh before her eyes fell on Sawyer leaning up against the building a few feet away. They were lax, long, and languid, their back against the bricks and their feet crossed at a rakish tilt out to the front.

The fire she'd felt a moment before didn't dissipate so much as flicker into deeper parts of her body. "Are you stalking me?"

"I'm sure I wouldn't be the first, but I actually happen to know several women who work here. What makes you think I'm waiting for you?"

"'Cause the other ones are too classy to pick up loiterers on their way home from work."

Sawyer grinned and pushed off the wall, ambling close enough for her to inhale the scent of sandalwood. "I do enjoy a woman with loose standards."

"You could've come inside."

The muscles in their shoulder constricted, rippling under the collar of their thin, black sweater, and for a second, Robin wondered what trigger she'd tripped, but the cocky demeanor returned quickly. "And miss the chance to howl at you like the Big Bad Wolf?"

"Now that you mention it, I've been known to stray off the path and into the darker parts of the woods."

"Plus, you look so delectable in red, Robin." Sawyer's eyes dipped to take in her form-fitting crimson pants, then they gave her an absolutely wolfish grin, inspiring a sudden fantasy of them running those canine teeth along her neck.

"It does seem unseasonably warm." She enjoyed the new kind of heat spreading through her. "It would be a shame to waste the first true hints of summer."

"And I have," Sawyer said with mock solemnity. "I spent all afternoon looking at apartments and wishing for a true friend to come rescue me and take me out for a nice ice-cream dinner."

"A true friend, huh?"

"A kindred soul," Sawyer agreed. "Though I'm not sure I have any suited to the task."

"No?" Robin played along. "Not Brooke or Gillian?"

"Alas, Brooke doesn't eat ice cream before Memorial Day, and Gillian always eats her vegetables first."

"Those are the rules. Tough luck."

"If only I had a new friend who cared less about the rules."

"Or didn't care about them at all," Robin offered with a little shrug.

Sawyer pressed their lips together as if thinking hard. "Hey, is Tegan still inside? She seems fun."

Robin finally laughed. "You ass."

"What? Tegan's not fun?" They tried to play innocent but couldn't quite hold in a smile, and Robin liked them all the more for being the first to break.

"No, she totally is, but everyone knows if you're looking for a rule breaker who wants to eat ice cream for dinner in this office, or even in this town, I'm the obvious choice."

"That tracks, but you seem awfully cool to let a bum like me on the back of your bike. I might bring down your average."

Robin lifted her sunglasses atop her head and let herself scan them without pretense. Their dark jeans hung off their hips as if they'd been designed for them, and the thin sweater hinted at the line of their pecs underneath, or maybe that was her own memory of a body that could still make her mouth water. The way Sawyer jammed their hands into their pockets and straightened their shoulders as if certain they held up under inspection only confirmed they knew exactly where her mind had wandered. Who could blame her for having a bit of a confidence kink. She finally started walking toward her motorcycle. "I always carry an extra helmet with me."

"I bet you have many occasions to use it." Sawyer followed along. "How could the queers of Buffalo ever resist?"

She opened the saddlebag over the seat and tossed the spare to them. "I don't know that many of them ever really try."

Sawyer pulled the helmet over their head and snugged the chin strap. "Now I feel bad I had to work for it."

Robin laughed and swung her leg over, then scooted forward enough for them to do the same. "Yeah, you really had a struggle there. It must be so hard on you, what with being such a gorgeous, educated, white child of privilege, to have to show up and mention your desire to eat ice cream to get all your wishes for the evening granted."

Sawyer climbed on and molded their body tightly to hers before leaning close enough for her to feel their breath behind her ear as they whispered, "What makes you think ice cream is the extent of my wishes for the evening?"

This time, the heat building in her wasn't anywhere near her face. Lifting up quickly, she kick-started the bike in an attempt to think about anything other than the time they'd lost.

She'd thought they'd have two more nights together. She'd made a list in her mind, and that upset her almost as much as the realization she was sitting here in a glorious moment thinking about ones that had never existed anywhere outside her imagination. She'd never been the kind of woman who'd indulged in regret or even suffered the urge to look back, but when Sawyer's inner thighs slid along the outside of hers, she had to rev the engine beneath them to drown out the sound of "what-if?"

The evening was a particular kind of glorious, mild, light-blue skies, a gentle breeze carrying the hint of something floral, the kind of night you can't count on in May this far north. You could certainly hope, but you're still a little surprised when it falls into your lap.

Maybe that's how Robin felt about seeing Sawyer again, too. She'd replayed their conversations last weekend over in her mind more than she was generally wont to do.

She hadn't intended for a hot dog and milkshake to turn into a seminar about her professional philosophies, but something in Sawyer's demeanor, or maybe their need to question concepts like inherent worth, made Robin wonder if they'd needed it, and that thought still felt discordant with the way Sawyer moved through the world. They already seemed so perfect in so many ways, but the more she got to know them, the more she realized parts of them were still encased in protective layers. More than once over the last few days, Robin had caught herself wondering what she might find if the two of them started chipping away at the block of marble together.

It was one thing to be attracted to someone. She also had plenty of people in her life she found interesting or engaging, and, of course, she had deep loyalty and affection for her tightest circle of friends. She had clients and mentees who evoked a sense of protectiveness and emotional responsibility, and so many of her chosen communities came with a strong sense of purpose. There was no singular quality she found appealing in Sawyer that she couldn't also find in her own life, but somehow wrapping them up in one stunning package edged eerily close to relationship material. Thankfully, while she did feel all the things for Sawyer, she didn't feel them in equal proportions, and when jumbled together, most of their finer attributes faded behind sex appeal.

The thought combined with the heat of the body molded to her back, and she picked up speed almost without thinking, causing Sawyer to flatten a hand across her abdomen. Robin couldn't feel the breeze anymore. She couldn't feel the tips of her fingers or toes either, and she couldn't process anything beyond the road or the human holding onto her. Everything outside the white lines could've caught fire and burned to the ground, and she wouldn't have noticed. Perhaps she shouldn't be driving in that condition, but she didn't want to stop.

The exit rose up in the distance, entirely too close and too soon for her tastes, and while she couldn't be sure, she didn't think Sawyer would mind much if she chose to blow past it. Still, the fact that she wanted to keep barreling down the road until she saw clearly if it ended in burning flames or paradise allowed the faintest hint of warning bells to sound over the whine of the engine.

She eased off the throttle and glided onto Hertel Avenue. Sawyer leaned into the turn and her at the same time, and even when the inertia softened, they stayed close until Robin pulled into the packed parking lot of Lake Effect Artisan Ice Cream. Even when she popped the kickstand, they peeled apart slowly. At a standstill, the hold Sawyer'd had on her felt more like a hug than anything else, and Robin couldn't quite remember the last time she'd let herself be held for so long.

"Looks like half of Buffalo had the same idea." Sawyer finally swung onto more solid ground.

It took her a second to process the statement, as her brain lingered on the feel of Sawyer, but she certainly hoped half the city wasn't having the same thoughts. When her eyes adjusted to a wider circle, she noticed the crowd, every picnic table occupied and a gaggle of families milling about. "Oh yeah. Ice cream."

Sawyer didn't even hide their amusement. "Why, Ms. Walker, did something distract you to the point you forgot why you came?"

She shook her head. "What makes you think I came already?"

Sawyer nearly doubled over. "Have I mentioned how much I enjoy your perpetual willingness to up the ante?"

"Enough to use your foot-fetish income to buy me a nutritionally inappropriate dinner?"

"Absolutely." They wandered over to the massive board of Buffalo flavor inspirations. "What's the point of having a completely inappropriate job if you're going to use the money in responsible ways?"

"Exactly." Robin scanned the menu. "And one turn toward the extravagant deserves another. Let's do flights."

"Like wine flights, but with ice cream?"

She nodded.

"Genius."

They discussed their various options to make sure they didn't duplicate, so by the time they found a spot on the curb, they had ten scoops of wildly different flavors spread between them.

"I'm hitting the Big Wayne's Cake Batter," Robin declared.

"Get up in there, girl. I'm going for the Paula's Glazed Donuts one."

"No wrong answer here." She picked up her spoon, but Sawyer stopped her.

"Wait."

"What?"

"Selfie." Sawyer pulled out their phone. "This is too pretty to go undocumented."

She raised her eyebrows. "Are you going to post it to your legions of followers?"

"Unless you refuse consent."

She grinned. "Not something I make a habit of doing."

"Another thing I enjoy about you." Sawyer held up their flight in one hand and their camera in the other, while Robin raised her ice cream as if she intended to lick it. Sawyer snapped the shot and held it out for her inspection.

"Damn, we're sexy bitches."

They laughed. "Couldn't have said it better myself. Let's make all the peasants jealous."

"Do you think Brooke and Gilly are going to internet stalk you now that they know?"

Sawyer shrugged. "Probably not while I'm in town. The foot stuff will be enough to hold them at bay when they have any other way, but I wouldn't be surprised if they overcome their sense of decorum if I disappear for too long again."

"Are you mad at me for figuring it out?" Robin asked. A spoonful of ice cream dripped onto her pretty red pants. "I've worried I shouldn't have blurted it out in front of other people who could use the information to find you in the future."

"Nah." They took a bite of Ice Wine Sherbet and closed their eyes as if savoring, but when they fluttered open again, there was more behind today's shade of gray. "Want to know a secret?"

"Always."

"Sometimes I wouldn't mind being found."

The words hit Robin square in the chest.

"I mean, not by everyone all the time, but the right people in the right moment, which is vague enough to be completely unattainable. I can't ask my friends to telepathically read my mind across continents and oceans."

"Maybe too much to ask," she admitted, "but I don't think anything's too much to long for."

Sawyer gave her a little half-smile. "I like that."

"Do you want someone to find you right now?"

"I think someone has." They leaned their shoulder against her own. "Unless you mean, do I want someone to find us?"

169

"Tegan has," Robin said as casually as she could muster, then hid the remainder of her cringe behind a bite of loganberry.

Sawyer nodded slowly. "I guess I shouldn't be surprised. When you hang out with hyper-observant people, you gotta expect them to notice things. Do you think that means Brooke knows, too, or do we get, like, therapist privilege or something."

"Doesn't work that way with friends, and girlfriends of friends, but I feel like if Brooke knew, one of us would've heard something by now."

"And if Gillian knew, I definitely would've heard something." Sawyer laughed. "Probably not cool of us to have Tegan carry secrets for us."

"But is she?" Robin asked. "I mean she was, for sure, but now we're not doing anything together we wouldn't do in front of them. We're friends with each other and with them. If any of them were the type to eat ice cream for dinner, they could've joined us."

"True." Sawyer drew out the word. "I guess there's no reason not to admit we hang out platonically."

Robin wondered if that statement was completely true. They'd gone out a couple of times without sleeping together, but they hadn't eaten nearly enough ice cream to cool the heat still emanating from her core after the ride over. "Platonic" may've been the letter of the law she'd laid down, but it didn't quite satisfy the spirit.

"What if we sent the selfie to a group chat?"

"Say more."

They chuckled. "You didn't mind when I intended to share it with strangers on the internet. We're eating ice cream, in public, with all our clothes on, like friends do."

The facts were correct, but again, Robin found them discordant to her own feelings. "You know they're going to overthink."

"Insert something about not being responsible for managing other people's thoughts or emotions."

170

She finally laughed. "Point taken, even if the lingo's a bit iffy."

"A lot of things about me are a bit iffy."

She eyed them for a few seconds, not sure she wanted to dispute the assertion or lean into it. Unable to decide, she returned to an earlier question. "Okay, send it."

Sawyer opened a message and added a few contacts, then glanced up with their finger over the "send" button. "Coming out of the closet as friends in three, two, one … we're still firm on the friends rule, right?"

Robin gritted her teeth against the urge to redraw that boundary. "I think that rule's probably for the best, especially if you're about to pull our friends in."

"Got it loud and clear." Sawyer hit send. "New rules, firmly in place."

"Good," Robin said, then for her own emphasis repeated, "good."

What's done was done, and the more people who knew about the rule, the more likely she was to keep it, right? Probably? Things over the last week had been better, mostly. Less drama, more fun, more easy camaraderie and quality company, zero outbursts, and way more ice cream.

She glanced down at the little dish of Peanut Butter Epiphany starting to melt between her hands and did herself no favors by remembering they were out enjoying this perfect evening together only because she had reveled in her status as the group's resident rule breaker in the first place.

Sixteen

The cool breeze along the waterfront stirred Sawyer's hair so it did a tickling little dance along their forehead.

"Are they seriously going to leave our message on 'read' all night?" Robin asked.

Sawyer laughed and turned their face toward the Niagara River to watch the waves swell and dip. "They're backchanneling each other. You know they are."

Robin held up her phone again to reveal the same three dots bouncing from both Gillian and Brooke's numbers. "They must've composed several drafts. Do you think they're actively interrogating Tegan?"

"Surely she's cracked by now." Sawyer strolled along the sidewalk until they reached the place where Broderick Park turned into a breakwater extending out into the river. "Why is this your favorite park?"

Robin sighed and looked past them to the towering structure of the Peace Bridge up ahead, then across its span to the shores of Canada. "I dig the power of the river. It's so fast and almost violent but still soothing. Plus, I like how exposed you are, stuck out here in the middle between two countries, between land and water, standing still while everything speeds by. I guess I enjoy liminal spaces."

Sawyer took a deep breath. "Maybe that's why we hit it off. I live a very liminal sort of life."

"I do enjoy those qualities in humans, as well as landscapes. Static is so boring. I mean, I know I have a job whose name may not be mentioned, but that's the great part of the gig. No two sessions are the same. Even with the same client, they aren't really the same person they were the week before."

Sawyer cast her a little side-eye as they ambled down the raised path barely wide enough for two and only a foot or two above the river on either side. "I can appreciate that in theory if not in practice. I enjoyed the same sort of things about Iceland. Everything's always changing, but people just keep going, totally not fussed. Did you know they have a hot dog stand that's been open every day for eighty years, during holidays and blizzards and volcanic eruptions?"

"That's a level of dedication even Ted's could learn from. I never thought of hot dogs being a real Icelandic sticking point."

"Oh yeah. I mean they also have fermented shark and sheep's head, but the dogs are where it's at."

"Wait. Did you try the shark?"

Sawyer made an exaggerated expression of distaste. "Only once."

Robin laughed. "Enough said."

Or maybe it wasn't, because as the silence fell between them, save for the lapping of the water, Sawyer felt the unfamiliar urge to fill it. They didn't care for the impulse, but they hadn't been able to shake their disquiet since sending the selfie. It shouldn't mean anything. They'd worked through all the logic, and a part of them had even wanted the emotions that came with letting their friends know the two of them enjoyed each other's company. It only made sense, if they were really becoming friends, even without the benefit of the bedroom, that they should be open with the people they both adored.

Only the term "friends" didn't feel completely honest or authentic, not so much wrong as insufficient or incomplete. Sawyer did have fun with Robin, but they also found her attractive and invigorating and insightful and easy to talk to. She always managed to make them think of something in a new or thrilling way. Even here, in a spot where they'd stood plenty of times as a kid, they saw the park differently. Hell, they saw themself differently with her.

Robin loved liminal spaces and liminal people. That hadn't even been a thing Sawyer had thought a person could be attracted to. It wasn't that Sawyer didn't know they had plenty of qualities that appealed to women, their looks, their humor, their adventurous spirit, their charisma. They'd used them all to their advantage over the years, and finding compelling companions had never been a hardship, but they'd always believed those things worked for them in spite of their more transitional qualities, not because of them.

Now, as they stood suspended between two countries with a woman who blurred more than a few boundaries of her own, Sawyer found themself wishing they'd given more thought to their own philosophies on things like human nature. They weren't nearly as adept at the kind of introspection Robin had so easily espoused their last time together. They didn't even share her views that most people were masterpieces ready for revelation, but as they'd pondered the idea off and on for days, they couldn't deny they found the concept appealing. They wanted to believe her, and maybe that's why they still hovered, unsure of how to proceed, and yet unable to back away. Believing in big things carried dangers they didn't easily accept as worth the risk, but wasn't the possibility of getting burned always the appeal of an open flame?

They stole a glance at Robin, her dark hair stirring on the breeze and her beauty in profile stirring something deeper in Sawyer. "Did you know there are geothermal bakeries in Iceland where they bake bread in holes in the ground?"

"What?" Robin stopped walking. "Isn't the ground frozen?"

"In some places, but there are also tons of geysers and volcanoes. They don't call it 'the land of fire and ice' for nothing. You get both."

"Aw, just like us." She bumped their shoulder with her own, then caught hold of their arm to keep them from going off the path.

"Us?" They laughed. "Am I ice to your fire?"

"I mean, you are very chill," Robin said. "It's a little unnerving how cool you can be at times, with your playing piano in your suit and going overboard without mussing your hair."

"First of all, I totally mussed my hair when you knocked me overboard, and second, I took you to a rage room. What could be fierier?"

"I did like the rage side of you, very hot. Maybe you're like Iceland unto yourself, cool on the surface, volcanic underneath."

"I like it." They added the assessment to the long list of things they enjoyed seeing through Robin's eyes. "Steamy, but in a subterranean way."

"Until, bam!" Robin shouted the word. "Smashing plates all over the place."

"I think some folks in your field would have a thing or two to say about that process of frozen to explosion."

"Sure, sure," Robin agreed easily as she traipsed along, "but none of them study geysers, do they? No one ever gets down on volcanoes for processing things in their own way. Go dormant, rumble to life, burn hot and high, flow on down the road, cool off, take a rest."

Sawyer smiled and stared across the waves. They'd never compared their own mood cycle to dramatic landscapes, but as usual, they didn't hate Robin's perspective, and once their mind started down her path, it found a few more things to muse on.

"What do you think?" Robin nudged after another minute of walking.

"That's actually how new land is formed," they said softly.

"What?"

"Volcanoes. They boil over and spill out of themselves to relieve the pent-up pressure, but when the lava cools and stabilizes, there's a new layer on the earth, or if it tumbles into water, it builds a new place altogether. You can stand in a spot never yet touched by humans."

A hint of awe covered Robin's features as she stared at them. "Have you?"

They nodded. "I always kind of liked that. You don't have to go to space to boldly go where no one has gone before. You just have to go to places that are being born or born anew."

"I only thought of volcanoes as being destructive, not the seething, simmering act of becoming." Robin smiled now, too. "Hot, hard, violent, and yet glowing. Damn, I'm enjoying this metaphor more every minute."

"Me too." After a year of working with scientists and tourists and people who built their lives around eruptions, Sawyer hadn't expected to get a new perspective on Nordic life while standing suspended between America and Canada. Then again, they'd started to suspect they shouldn't be surprised by anything where Robin was concerned.

"As long as you don't erupt at individuals, it all sounds pretty awesome to me," she continued. "Is that why you love Iceland so much? Creation and re-creation?"

"There's definitely something elemental in dramatic landscapes that pulls me in. I love the way people in those places go about their business, finding ways to thrive in environments most modern Americans would see as totally unlivable. And not just in Iceland. All over the world. People are bucking the things we accept as wisdom. I don't have a favorite country or place. I don't get attached like that."

Robin turned to look at them. "You don't get attached to places, or you don't get attached to anything?"

Sawyer's brow furrowed.

"Not a therapy question like analyzing your attachment style," Robin quickly added. "I wanted to know on a purely personal level. Not like in a creepy stalker way, like attachment to me personally, but like ... damn, why is this weird?"

Sawyer laughed. "I get you. And in a non-therapy, non-creepy stalker way, I do form attachments, but probably not like other people. I haven't had any long-term romantic relationships as a full-fledged adult."

"Interesting phrasing. Did you have one as a partly fledged adult?"

"I had a two-year crush on one of my best friends in high school that never amounted to more than light petting. Then, during a yearlong study abroad in college, I dated one girl exclusively, but in the end, it turned out our loyalty to each other came mostly from the convenience of being the only two English-speaking sapphics in the program."

"Fascinating."

"Not really. Pretty pedestrian. I suppose my two longest-standing attachments are to Brooke and Gillian."

"Both stellar choices. I like what you said on your first night at Ambush about how they call you back."

"Actually, that's a pretty good example of my attachment tendencies if you want to break it down. I like Buffalo, but there's nothing concrete to make it superior to any other city in the world."

"Except for Ted's."

They grinned and looked out at the expanse of Lake Erie in the orange glow of fading sun. "Of course, Ted's, plus Gillian and Brooke, and even more than them, I'm pulled toward the memory of how I feel with them, secure, inspired, comfortable, cared for."

"Oh, I like that." Robin sounded a little dreamy at the sentiment.

Sawyer couldn't blame her. They'd never quite known they felt that way that fully until they'd said it aloud, but now the idea curled around them like a warm blanket. "I never return to a place, or even another person, so much as I come back to a version of myself this place and these people inspire."

"Is that the person I'm getting to know?" Robin asked softly.

"Maybe, at least at first." They thought for a minute before going on. "That's the person I was the first night, and probably still the night at the piano."

"What about now?"

They turned to face her, taking in the curve of full lips, the way the wind stirred her hair, the way the sunset shimmered in the dark of her eyes. "Maybe now I'm getting to know a new version of me, the person I am with you."

Brooke caught hold of Sawyer's sleeve as they approached the top of a steep incline. "Next time someone suggests hiking, remind me I'm not this kind of queer."

Sawyer laughed. "Sorry, Love, you're the one who chose to date a hot young thing."

Brooke glanced ahead to where Tegan and Robin had crested the high ridge, backs still to them, surveying the view while Brooke and Sawyer surveyed them. Her expression softened and her lips curled. "Think their view is as good as ours?"

Sawyer took in Robin's muscled calves, slender hips, and the perfect ass in between. "Doubt it."

"Come on, stragglers," Gillian called from farther up the trail.

"Who let the Ivy League All-American lead this death march?" Sawyer asked.

"She's the one with the snacks." Brooke started moving again, grumbling something about the insufficiency of her gym membership. Still, as they reached the overlook, no one could deny that if one did, indeed, have to go on a hike, there were worse places than the Niagara Gorge to spend Memorial Day.

The steep rock walls plummeted several stories to their left with expansive views of the river below churning an almost surreal color of turquoise. Eddies gave way to whitewater and whirlpools, while overhead, large birds wafted on the updrafts.

"I can't believe I live in a place that looks like this." Tegan wrapped an arm around Brooke's waist. "Or with a woman who looks like you."

Robin's eyebrows shot up. "Do you live with her?"

Brooke sighed. "Let me catch my breath. Then we'll have that conversation."

"What conversation?" Gillian asked from her spot on a picnic blanket where she'd already taken off her backpack and unloaded a series of containers.

"The one where Brogan finally tells us what they decided last weekend." Robin propped herself up on a nearby rock.

"Brogan?" Tegan sank down at the edge of the red-and-white checkered tablecloth.

"I think it's your celebrity couple name, Brookesy plus Tegan." Sawyer took a spot closer to Robin. "I would've gone with 'Teeksy,' though."

"Better." Robin nodded her approval. "'Teeksy' it is. Assuming you two are about to give in to the lesbian urge to merge, except Brooke is bi … do bi women have an urge to merge?"

Brooke smiled patiently. "I cannot speak for my entire community."

"Props for fluidity." Sawyer lifted a hand for a high five, but Brooke shook her head.

"Glad it's not just me." Robin laughed.

"Good Lord," Gillian pinched the bridge of her nose. "How many ways can this train go off the rails in two minutes? Brooke, Tegan, did you have something you wanted to share with the group?"

Brooke sat next to Tegan and took her hand. "Actually, a few things."

Everyone gave them their full attention. Sawyer didn't feel nearly as invested as the others, but they enjoyed a good dramatic pause as much as anyone. They also liked the way Robin's chest rose and fell with each bated breath.

"Tegan, you want to start us off?" Brooke squeezed her hand.

"Sure." Tegan sat a little straighter. "Brooke has asked me to move in with her, and I was thrilled to say 'yes.'"

Gillian grinned at them, and Robin let out a celebratory whoop. "About damn time."

Brooke blushed slightly. "We know none of you would've minded if we'd made the leap sooner, but given the way we started, it really mattered to me to take the next steps the right way."

"Mattered to both of us," Tegan corrected. "I didn't want guilt or doubt between us either, so we dotted our *i*'s and crossed our *t*'s. Gillian has signed off on all my paperwork, and everything will be sent off this coming week, which means I might need some help moving boxes next weekend."

"Congrats on all counts," Sawyer said. "I missed whatever you all might've had to doubt. I've seen only the amazing aftermath, but it looks like you're on the right track to an outsider."

Brooke rested a hand on their knee. "You could never be an outsider."

They shrugged, not agreeing, but also not wanting to center themself in this conversation. "I'm happy for you, B."

"I'm happy for all of us," Robin said. "We're getting the band back together. Take-Out Tuesdays haven't been the same since you left."

Brooke pressed her lips together and exchanged a quick glance with Gillian. Even Sawyer could read her discomfort, so Robin sure as hell picked up on the shift.

She sat up on her knees. "What is happening right now?"

"Tegan's still in a time of professional transition," Brooke said slowly, then looked to her girlfriend, sighed, and started again. "Sorry, I'm not going to put this on her, it's my decision."

"What decision?" Robin whined.

"She's being excessively noble." Tegan rolled her eyes playfully. "But seeing as how I adore the quality, I've granted my blessing."

"OMG," Robin groaned. "Why won't you say it? Is it bad? Is Mommy moving out of the office forever? Am I going to have two Christmases from now on?"

Gillian shook her head. "She's not coming back to work."

"Yet," Brooke added quickly. "I'm not coming back *yet*. And I'm not the mommy. Gillian is the mommy."

Robin flopped onto the blanket. "I had two mommies. That's why I'm so emotionally stable and have such a healthy sense of self."

Sawyer laughed.

Robin glanced up at them and winked.

"I always thought of myself as the older and more put-together sister, or maybe the cool aunt," Brooke said.

Robin rolled onto her back. "Cool aunts buy you beer. They don't give you abandonment issues."

Sawyer reached out and ran a hand through her mop of dark hair before they even had a chance to think through the move. "It's okay. I'll buy you beer and take you to the best parties."

Robin waggled her eyebrows at them. "Sold."

The two of them stared at each other for a heavy, hot second as Sawyer did a valiant job of refusing to give voice to the other offers on the tip of their tongue.

"Okay," Gillian said awkwardly. "That didn't get weird at all. Brooke, you're going to teach summer school, correct?"

Sawyer tensed. "At the college? Is there a call for intro classes in the summer?"

"One section." Brooke seemed to choose her words carefully. "The biggest part of my responsibilities will center on organizing two major conferences, one in June and one in July. I'm excited to work with a slew of experts on family systems. And of course there's plenty of research opportunities."

"In epigenetics?"

"No."

Sawyer released a breath, then swallowed some of the fear rising in their throat.

"I'm not as interested in those projects, or in working with that particular research team," Brooke continued evenly.

They nodded, appreciating all the unspoken assurances, but their cheeks warmed a little at needing them. "It's okay if you did. The topic's fascinating."

"Indeed, and we'll all benefit from the knowledge at some point, but it's not my area. Honestly, the research side of academia doesn't thrill me. I've found a passion for sheltering people through the early stages of the program though."

"I heard," Sawyer said dryly. "Your boss thinks you've gone soft because you're in love."

Brooke sighed. "I can only imagine I'm a bit of a disappointment to the person who conveyed the message."

Sawyer gave her a mock salute. "Welcome to the club."

Brooke squeezed their knee. "I'm in good company. And if anything, it firms up my resolve to keep an iron in the fire there."

Robin wore a look of curiosity but didn't interrupt, and Sawyer offered up silent thanks. The last thing they wanted to do was explain their long history of letting down Brooke's boss. "Are you sure you'd rather hold the job than steal kisses from your new roommate during work hours?"

"I absolutely would not"—Brooke laughed again—"which is why I need to. Tegan deserves a chance to ease into her new role without me jumping her in the office between clients."

"Again," Robin added, "don't act like it never happened before."

"One time." Tegan and Brooke protested simultaneously, causing both Robin and Sawyer to cackle together.

Gillian shot them a look. "Maybe we shouldn't all work together."

"I had no intention of starting, Gilly Bear," Sawyer said. "I'm trying to find an apartment, so you'll see less of me after work, too."

Gillian shifted on the ground. "After hours doesn't bother me."

"Actually, we wanted to talk to you about that, too." Tegan seemed grateful for a chance to change the subject. "My lease is up next weekend, but it feels a little jinxy to not renew it before we see how cohabitation works out."

"It'll work out fucking awesome," Robin said.

"I think so, too," Brooke added quickly.

"And deep down, I agree," Tegan admitted. "But just as Brooke doesn't want to exert undue pressure by coming back to work, I don't love the idea of her feeling like I'd be homeless if she needs space, so I talked to my landlord, and he said I could commit to another three months."

"Can you afford that?" Robin asked.

"I'll make more money once I'm fully licensed, and Brooke won't let me pay half on the mortgage yet, so I could swing it, but it seems silly to have an empty apartment, so, Sawyer, if you want to sublet for a few months while we figure things out, we could find a price that works for you and gives me a little breathing room in the interim."

They nodded. "Wow, thanks."

"It'll be mostly furnished, but if you didn't like it you wouldn't have to—"

"No. It's not that. I'm sure it's much nicer than what I'm used to."

"It's a glorified studio," Tegan explained.

"Again, not an issue. I've been on Gilly's couch for almost a month. Seriously, this is a very generous offer."

"But?" Robin prodded expectantly.

"I, um …" They closed their mouth. They knew the problem, but they didn't want to say it in their out-loud voice. It was one thing to bolt on people emotionally. Brooke and Gillian's reactions the night they'd returned had made it abundantly clear what kind of toll their long absence had taken, but somehow, dragging Tegan and her precarious finances during a big transition into the equation felt like another level of shitty.

They were about to make an excuse to extract themself when they turned their head and caught Robin's eyes, dark, deep, understanding, and thrilling all at once. Her words from earlier in the week came rushing back, burn hot and high, flow on down the road, cool off, take a rest.

Sawyer widened their circle of vision to include all the people they cared most for in the world, and suddenly the urge to run felt so far away. They knew themself well enough to expect that to change, but what if it didn't happen for a long time?

After running for years, what if they got to cool down and rest in equal measure?

Something stirred inside them, even as Tegan began to backtrack.

"Seriously, we didn't mean to spring it on you. You don't have to decide in the moment, or at all."

"No," they said softly. "I think I do. I think every good decision I've ever made has been on pure impulse."

Gillian grimaced, either at the idea of spontaneous decisions or out of fear of what they'd choose, but Sawyer merely turned to Robin and arched an eyebrow at the last unspoken question.

Robin merely smiled, genuine, vibrant, beautiful, and that was enough.

Sawyer turned back to Tegan. "Yeah, I'd love to stick around for a while."

Seventeen

"Thank you all so much," Tegan gushed as Robin stacked the last box of books into the back of Brooke's Civic and shut the trunk.

"Seriously, easiest move ever." Robin craned her neck to watch Sawyer walking back up the stairs. When she glanced back, Tegan was watching her with concern etched all over her pretty features.

"We're friends now." Robin cut off the question before it could begin.

"Oh." Tegan frowned. "I figured things had gone back to how they were before."

"You mean the sex?" She shook her head.

"Okay … I didn't mean to assume, but you and Sawyer have been acting super chummy the last few weeks."

"You and I are chummy, and I'm not sleeping with you." She laughed. "So, you two haven't … at all since …"

"Teegs, you can say the words. Sawyer and I haven't had sex since they ghosted me." She managed to deliver the line evenly enough even if the sting of that event, and her own reaction to it, still burned enough to remind her why she shouldn't wander back down that path.

"So, not friends with benefits? Just regular friends?"

She shook her head. "Just regular friends. Friendship isn't a subpar category of relationships. Sawyer and I are becoming real friends, like you and me and Gilly, and Brooke … Well, not you and Brooke, but the rest of us."

"The rest of us what?" Brooke came down Tegan's, or rather now Sawyer's, staircase and into the early summer sun, sporting capri pants and a baby-blue T.

"Friends," Robin said ... again.

"Ah." Brooke and Tegan exchanged a look. "So, you and Sawyer aren't having an affair?"

She rolled her eyes. "An affair? Sounds so seedy. No. We hang out. We eat ice cream for dinner and ride my motorcycle and go hiking with you all."

"And whitewater rafting," Tegan added.

"And Sawyer mentioned you went to a concert," Brooke piled on.

"We did. You were invited too. You didn't want to go."

"I did not." Brooke chuckled. "Nor did I want to zipline over Niagara Falls."

"See," Robin said as if she'd proved some kind of point. She didn't want to stand here on the street talking about all the sex she was not having with Sawyer, especially with two friends who were definitely doing it on the regular, but the more they talked about what she and Sawyer were doing, the more Robin missed what they weren't.

"Okay." Brooke raised her hands.

And it was okay, damn it. They were having fun. So what if they could also be having more fun after their little outings. She didn't want to risk a repeat of what'd happened before. If she lost her cool now, it would be way worse than before. Sawyer had just decided to stick around. She could not be the one to muck it up, no matter how often she still had the urge to strip off their T-shirt with her teeth.

"I'm happy my people are happy," Brooke continued. "I care about you both a lot, and when we got the picture of you two together at Lake Effect, it caught me off guard."

"Then you're several steps behind your new roommate." Robin nodded to Tegan. "She'd already given me the full shakedown a week before."

Brooke turned to Tegan, mouth open. "You had?"

"Hey." Tegan gave Robin a playful shove. "I kept your confidence, and this is how you repay me."

"It's a great way to take the heat off me."

"Except now I'm going to tell her everything."

Robin winced. "Not everything. I told you about the first part at work, or at least at work events. That's protected by like, ethics and shit."

"Ethics and shit," Brooke scoffed. "I forgot to put that unit in my course syllabus."

"Not too late to add it now." Robin shook her head, knowing it really was. She'd blurted out too much, and now Brooke would know what Tegan did within a matter of minutes.

Maybe it was for the best. If Tegan really had been protecting them even from Brooke, that had to be a heavy load. And while it had been nice of her to carry, it also felt like unwarranted valor at this point. Robin and Sawyer hadn't so much as kissed in three weeks, which now felt like an eternity. That made them friends much longer than they'd been lovers, but somehow saying as much aloud grated on her nerves in ways she didn't care to examine.

"I'm going back up," she finally said. "You two can feel free to speak about me in my absence."

"Or you can stay and tell me yourself," Brooke offered.

Robin forced a grin and stopped herself from admitting it bothered her a bit not to have anything else worth sharing on the subject. "And ruin the air of mystery I've cultivated? Never!"

Robin paused a few minutes on the stairs to collect herself, take some deep breaths, and count to ten. Once she'd brought her elevation within acceptable levels, she pushed open the apartment door and immediately lost all the calm she'd reclaimed as her eyes fell on Sawyer. Or rather Sawyer's ass as they bent over, rummaging through a toolbox while Gillian stood nearby holding a curtain rod.

She allowed herself to watch Sawyer's thighs and glutes contract under a pair of athletic shorts, their long form nearly folded in half, showcasing a level of flexibility she wished she'd made better use of when she'd had the chance. If only she could be up behind them, hands gripping those taut shoulders, and—

Someone cleared their throat, and Robin jumped guiltily around to see both Brooke and Tegan behind her.

"Sure." Brooke pushed past her. "Just friends."

"You two talked it out already?"

Brooke elbowed her in the ribs as she scooted past. "It's a pretty short story when you walk around looking like that."

Tegan shook her head. "You've got a little drool on your chin."

Sawyer stood up and cast her a smile over their shoulder. "There you are. We need a second opinion. Bath towel curtains … a quirky, smart way to save money, or trashy without a hint of chic?"

"Trashy," Brooke said at the same time Robin said, "Depends on the towels."

"It seems silly to buy window treatments for a place I'm only subletting a couple months, but I got so used to sleeping in the pitch-black last winter, I don't know if regular blinds will be enough now that the days are so long here."

"I find if you get yourself tired out enough, it doesn't matter," Robin said.

"I like the way you think." Sawyer's smile widened. "You have any ideas as to how I might go about that?"

She shrugged. "Maybe a few."

"Should the rest of us leave you to it?" Gillian asked dryly.

"Not at all," Sawyer said, "and I may not have curtains yet, but I stocked my new fridge this morning and placed a pizza order. Should be here any minute."

Tegan objected. "Pizza should be on me. I had way more boxes to move than you."

"Yes, but yours went downstairs, and mine went up," Sawyer said, "and even if they hadn't, you've all fed me for a month now. Let me relish the luxury of having my people in my space."

Gillian threw an arm around their shoulder. "I could get used to that."

Sawyer's color paled ever so slightly, making Robin suspect they were still getting used to the idea of other people counting on them hanging around. She understood the queasiness. She'd worked hard all week not to make too big a deal of the fact that they'd agreed to stay. Robin got the distinct sense it mattered to all of them more than anyone cared to admit, but Sawyer seemed to want to play it cool, and if Robin were being honest, she preferred it that way, too.

Tegan, on the other hand, had no such qualms. "When was the last time you actually had a place of your own?"

Sawyer blew out a heavy breath. "Hard to say. Over the winter I had more of a shared bunking situation, and before that I didn't stay anywhere for more than a couple weeks. I guess I kind of had my own space in Germany after my surgery, but even then, I'd rented a room in a house owned by a nurse, who ended up being kind of my health aide when I didn't recover as quickly as anticipated."

"You had trouble after your surgery?" Brooke eased onto the couch and pulled Tegan down next to her. "What happened?"

"It wasn't a big deal." Sawyer tried to wave her off, but no one else spoke, the downside to being friends with a group of therapists. They were all entirely too comfortable sitting in the silences most mere mortals crumbled under. Robin gave a brief thought to saving them by stepping in, but she honestly wanted to hear the answer, too.

To their credit, Sawyer lasted longer than most people, shifting from side to side and sitting down on the corner of the bed before cracking. "I overestimated my ability to go it alone, physically for sure, and maybe emotionally."

Gillian backed up against the wall as if to brace herself.

189

"It turned out fine," Sawyer said quickly, but it was unclear to Robin if they were trying to soothe the others or remind themself they'd made it through. "You can't lift your arms over your shoulder for a lot of weeks after the operation, or you'll split open the incisions, and it turns out a lot of things in this world are over my shoulders—medicine cabinets, supermarket shelves, seat belts, any shirt that doesn't button in the front. Trying to force it led to pain and bruising, and more blood."

Sawyer paused, and the little muscles in their jaw tightened. "It got kind of claustrophobic being in my body, which was, you know, the whole point of changing my body in the first place. I ended up in a bit of a dark place."

Robin bit the inside of her own cheek to keep from interrupting their discomfort, and the way Brooke had gone completely still suggested she didn't love the recounting either, but she'd had enough practice to bear it.

Gillian, on the other hand, didn't seem to share their penchant for going into work mode. "I could just about strangle you for not telling us."

"What would you have done? Closed your new practice and flown halfway across the world to hold my hand while I oozed blood into surgical drains?"

"Yeah," she said without hesitation, "exactly that."

Sawyer's smile turned a little sad. "I know. I mean, at least I thought you might. You too, Brookesy. And I don't know what would've bothered me more, the idea of the two of you risking everything you'd worked for on my account, or the fear that you'd evaluate your options and decide I wasn't worth it. So, the nurse and I eventually figured it out together and managed to have a little fun after I recovered enough to get creative with positions."

"Oh, for fuck's sake. You slept with your German nurse?" Gillian shook her head, but it broke the tension enough to make the rest of them laugh.

"I missed you, though," Sawyer admitted after another minute. "I wished for you both a lot, and, honestly, if I had it to do over, I'd make different choices."

Brooke frowned. "About including us, or about the surgery itself?"

"About finding a way to bolster my support system. It's still hard to imagine pulling you two into the weird place I was in at the time, and I sure as hell wouldn't have done it here."

"Obviously," Gillian deadpanned. "There are no surgeons in the whole of Buffalo or the larger state of New York."

Sawyer grinned. "None whatsoever. No health professionals at all, really."

Robin's chest loosened at the hint of levity.

Brooke didn't laugh, though. "None far enough from the reach of your mother."

"Bingo." Sawyer tapped their index finger to the tip of their nose. "I desperately needed my voice to be the only voice in the room. That transition or, you know, affirmation, it couldn't feel like my funeral. That's why I didn't change my name. Sawyer's fluid enough, thankfully, but even more so, I didn't have it in me to think of some part of me dying. I needed to construct the process as going through the pain so every part of me would finally get to live. I couldn't let word get back to my mother until I'd cemented that mindset for myself. I wasn't strong enough to risk her acting like she was standing over my coffin when I felt like I was finally breaking out of one."

Gillian had them in her arms in an instant. It was the most crushing hug Robin had ever seen her give anyone, and the intimacy of it was almost too much to watch until the tenderness gave way to a rougher sort of shaking.

"I love you." Gillian stepped back, still holding their shoulders, and glanced at Brooke. "We love you. And if you ever lump us in with your mother again, we won't hesitate to murder you. Do you hear me?"

Sawyer laughed, but this time the sound came out thick. "Yes, ma'am."

"She's right." Brooke rose and joined them. "You can tell us you need safety from that connection, and we'll always protect you. I know I've muddied those waters at work, but I'm really good at setting boundaries and compartmentalizing. We both are."

Sawyer nodded seriously. "Okay. Well, maybe don't compartmentalize completely yet, because I might need your help with something."

"Something surgical or medical?" Brooke asked nervously. "Is everything okay?"

"Neither. I've healed flawlessly." They sent a cocky grin in Robin's direction as if to confirm.

"So freaking flawless." Robin relished the chance to help bring them back into happier places, so she vamped it up a bit, winking at them suggestively. "Ten out of ten, highly recommend German engineering."

Everyone stared at her for a minute before Tegan laughed and Gillian's complexion turned nearly as red as her hair. "How the fuck do you know what their … you know what, never mind."

Brooke turned back to Sawyer. "Let's start with what you need help with first."

Sawyer shook their head, but their tone stayed light. "Apparently, I still have a lot of clothes at my mother's place, and I don't even know what fits anymore, physically or metaphorically."

A buzzer interrupted them, and Sawyer seemed grateful. "That'll be the pizzas."

"Okay," Brooke said calmly. "We've got all night to eat and hatch a plan."

"Well, maybe not all night," Sawyer said playfully. "I might need to go out and find a nice local girl to help me christen my new bed."

Gillian rolled her eyes, but Brooke kept her expression completely neutral. "You're too late. Tegan already picked up a woman at the bar to put that bed through its paces. You're welcome."

"Oh, snap." Sawyer laughed.

Robin's heart started beating normally again at the sound, and she watched them jog down the stairs, fighting the urge to go after them. She'd already revealed more than she probably should have, so she turned back to Brooke. "Well played. Ain't no dirtbaggery like Brooke dirtbaggery, because no one sees it coming. High five."

Instead of slapping her outstretched hand, Brooke shoved her toward the door. "Go with them."

"What? Why? I'm not … we're not—"

"Go," Gillian pointed to the door. "We'll talk about the rest later."

She didn't make a habit out of arguing with the boss or the two people who knew Sawyer best, especially when they agreed with what she really wanted to do in the first place.

She was halfway down the stairs before Sawyer turned around, a stack of La Nova in their arms.

"Hey," they said, then shrugged.

"Hey yourself."

"I'm okay." Sawyer took a few more steps until they were almost level, but Robin didn't step aside to let them pass.

"You're way better than okay, which is why I wanted to tell you, I'm in."

Sawyer arched an eyebrow and stepped forward as if intending to pass her once more, but she caught them with one hand around their upper arm, and for a second, she forgot why, as the biceps rippled under her fingers. When their gray eyes met hers, she remembered she'd wanted more than anything to throw them a line. "Seriously."

They held her gaze. "In for what?"

"Dinner. Misdemeanor theft. Trespassing. Slashing tires. Creating a diversion. Whatever."

As the list went on, the muscles beneath her fingers loosened, and the corners of Sawyer's lips twitched upward. "That's the best offer I've had in a while. What did I do to deserve an evening full of pizza and petty crime?"

"Maybe it just sounds like my kind of party." Robin leaned as close as the boxes between them would allow and ran a hand through their mop of chestnut hair until it curled about their ear and clasped the back of Sawyer's neck. "Or maybe I find the level of vulnerability you showed in there too sexy to resist, what with my authenticity kink and all."

Sawyer took a shuddering breath. "Could go either way, huh?"

She released them slowly. "I guess only time will tell."

Eighteen

Sawyer swung open the door to their mother's apartment building and held it for Brooke, Gillian, and Robin to enter. It was too late to abandon ship, as they'd announced their presence at the buzzer, but at least they weren't alone. They weren't sure whether the presence of the others would make their mother more or less antagonistic, but it definitely helped steady their own emotions.

"Okay, team," Robin said as they entered the elevator, "everyone has their assignments and code names, right?"

"I am not using my code name," Gillian said flatly.

"Why not, Red Ivy?" Robin pushed, "Mama Cougar loves hers."

"I do not," Brooke said emphatically.

"I like mine," Sawyer said, though what they really enjoyed was Robin's ability to keep things light. She'd steadfastly played the role of court jester ever since they'd picked her up this morning, and needling their two more stoic partners featured prominently in her schtick.

"Of course you do. Yours is Golden Eagle." Gillian shook her head. "I think the plan we agreed on holds up without walkie-talkies or aliases."

Sawyer nodded as the doors slid open, but they didn't have time to review anything as Maura was already waiting. "I see you've brought the entire battalion this time."

"Hardly. Tegan's outside in the getaway car," Sawyer said, wishing that were true. They'd left her back at the apartment making pancakes for the aftermath of whatever was about to happen.

Maura inspected Sawyer with a slow, deliberate scan of her icy eyes. "Are the accessories a nod to fashion, or an indication of the choices you've made in the last twelve hours?"

Sawyer sighed and removed their mirrored aviator sunglasses. "I would never dare appear in your presence with anything less than my full faculties."

"Charming." Maura stepped back and held open the door for them.

"Good morning," Brooke and Gillian each said as they passed, but Robin stuck out her hand.

"Hi. I'm Robin Walker."

Maura accepted the introduction. "Dr. Stroud."

Robin didn't seem to mind that she'd been handed the formal title. "Your reputation precedes you, Doc. I quite liked your article last year on patterns of over-functioning in multigenerational family triangulations."

Sawyer didn't even hide their smile as her mother did a double take, undoubtedly reevaluating her initial assessment of Robin, who, true to form, had shown up in low-slung jeans, a black V-neck T-shirt, and silver-buckled motorcycle boots. Together in the back seat on the way over, it had taken an undue amount of restraint to keep from reaching for her, taking hold of the spot where lush, dark waves of hair met the nape of her neck, and kissing her lips until they'd rubbed all the gloss off them. Now, hearing her talk psychological research with the same lightness she'd used to give their friends silly nicknames, Sawyer didn't know if they should be turned on or terrified.

"Do you work in the field?" Maura finally asked.

"No. I work in an office." Robin waited the perfect comedic beat before cracking a smile. "Just kidding. I've actually been in Gillian and Brooke's practice for several years."

"Oh?" Maura paused, and Sawyer watched her recalculate. "You're that Robin. Your reputation also precedes you."

"Mother," Sawyer cut in, not wanting the pleasantries to go on long enough for anyone to dig deeper. "We've come to

196

go through some of those boxes of mine you mentioned I'd left here."

"They're in the guest room." Maura waved them off, attention still focused on Robin. "You didn't come through my program?"

"Nope," Robin said without offering any more information. "Where's the guest room?"

"I'll show you," Sawyer said without actually knowing.

Maura stalled. "Would you like a cup of tea or coffee?"

"I would." Brooke jumped in.

"Me too," Gillian added quickly. "Why don't we help? We had some things we wanted to talk to you about."

Maura pressed her lips together. "Why don't you make an appointment and come by campus sometime?"

"But we're already here now," Brooke said sweetly.

"Besides, it's nothing formal, more like brainstorming possible connections between our practice and your program," Gillian added. "I'm sure it won't take all of us to rummage through Sawyer's old clothes, unless you think they need supervision to review their own possessions."

"I'll supervise." Robin acted as if the idea had just popped into her head. "Offering unsolicited opinions is one of my passions, and I so rarely get to indulge."

Gillian nodded. "Yes, so rare for Robin to share an opinion."

"Don't get your hopes up," Maura said blithely. "My one and only offspring is sensitive about other people's observations."

Robin's mouth fell open in mock surprise. "Is that true, Golden Eagle?"

Sawyer rolled their eyes. "She wouldn't have said so if she didn't have an ample portfolio of evidence to back it up."

"And here I've always found you so easygoing and agreeable. Maybe I'm doing something wrong, or something right, or"—Robin's eyes danced with mischief—"perhaps I've done something so delightfully wrong that it just feels right."

Maura blanched at the brashness of the comment, undoubtedly unused to people talking that way in her presence. Sawyer could've kissed Robin on the mouth right there for doing the unimaginable and making their mother search for a response. Instead, they took the momentary reprieve to send Brooke and Gillian a grateful grimace before bolting down the only hallway off the living area.

True to form, Robin ambled along after them as Sawyer opened doors at random, first finding a bathroom and a linen closet before locating an utterly nondescript bedroom. "This look like a guest room to you?"

Robin peeked in. "Guest room, hospital room, padded room. Boy, your mother has a design style reminiscent of a Soviet-era institution meets purity-movement cult church."

Sawyer laughed as they stepped inside the all-white and concrete space. "If those are the opinions you're bringing to this party, I'm here for it."

"I've got more if you want them. For instance, this floor is as sterile as the woman who probably pays someone else to clean it."

Sawyer grinned and began to pull plastic bins out of a large closet. Thankfully, they'd all been labeled with an actual label maker. Helpful, color-coded tags read, "Sawyer: Tops," or "Sawyer: Bottoms."

Robin giggled. "How very liberal of your mom to sort reminders of your exes into categories based on their preferred sexual roles. Can you find me the box for femme tops? I'd like to start there."

Sawyer shook their head. "Those are hard to come by … or hard to find, easy to come by."

Robin wordlessly lifted a hand.

Sawyer slapped it before grabbing another bin. "Aren't you intimidated?"

"By femme tops?"

"No, by my mother."

"Oh well, hate to break it to you, but your mother is totally a femme top." She paused long enough to let Sawyer make a gagging face before continuing, "But no. Why should I be intimidated?"

"You know her work, right?"

Robin shrugged and started opening things. "Can't get a degree in my field without it."

"Exactly. Most people find her rather formidable, especially people in the psychology arena. There's no denying she knows her stuff."

"Why would I deny anyone else their knowledge?" Robin unceremoniously dumped the first bin onto the bed. "We all know our own stuff, and we get to share it with each other. And speaking of sharing, I will be stealing some of your old clothes today."

"Finders keepers." Sawyer emptied another bin. "Let's start two piles, one for possible matches, and another for the ones that need to die a death of fire."

"Petty theft." Robin pointed to her pile, then to the other. "Arson."

Sawyer smiled, in spite of the lingering tension in their shoulders. They sorted a few pairs of capri pants into the burn pile while pondering Robin's assertion. Over the years, they'd tried capitulating to Maura's desires, pushing back against them, ignoring them, running from her, or working to subvert her entirely. They'd never considered accepting her knowledge of a situation while holding onto their own with equal respect. "You don't think that some people's opinions on a subject are worth more than others?"

Robin tossed a red-and-blue rugby shirt onto the pile for possible keepers. "Sure, in a court of law, in a hospital, when talking about general best practices, or universal standards of not being a total bag of dicks to other people."

They held a pair of jeans up to their hips before deeming them close enough to try on later. "Fair, but like, some people are brilliant and have a knack for nailing things."

"People like your mother?"

They nodded. "I mean, I know some things, but she knows like, all the things, and she's not afraid to cite the specific studies that give credence to her observations, which are always delivered succinctly, dispassionately, and with the brutal precision of God's honest truth."

Robin blew out a breath as she picked up two shirts at once to compare them. "Boy, you sure went through a rugby shirt phase."

"Those were the early reaches of my gender-bending."

"I'm sure Ralph Lauren would love knowing he was your gateway to queer vibes." Robin threw them both into the keeper bin. "But I always think of truth as being infinite. You can't even begin to quantify all the things that could be true for any given person in any given situation. I'm sure Maura has uncovered amazing amounts of truth in her work or life, and so have I, and so have you. We can all agree on a lot of things that are objectively true. Climate change is real, trans women are women, vaccinations save lives, *1989* is Taylor Swift's best work."

"Whoa." Sawyer protested, but Robin held up a hand.

"That's science. We don't need to dispute facts, but we all get to decide what meaning we attach to those things, and we each get to be the expert of our own existence. No one has a monopoly on truth, and no one gets to pin their truth onto someone else's lived experience."

"I like that"—Sawyer pointed to a paisley dress shirt Robin held up—"and I like what you're saying, but I'm not sure it would hold up under scrutiny."

"Anyone who feels compelled to scrutinize someone else's truth probably isn't that secure in their own."

Sawyer let out a bitter little laugh. "No one's ever accused Dr. Maura Stroud of being insecure about what she knows to be true."

"And I have no desire to start"—Robin came around the bed—"because I'm equally secure in what I know."

Sawyer swallowed the urge to say they held no such certainty, but somehow with this woman standing so close, exuding the kind of confidence Sawyer so often appropriated, they wanted to believe her.

Sawyer released a sigh of relief that radiated through their whole body as Robin lifted the final Rubbermaid tub onto the bed. They'd made quick work of everything, and if they continued at this pace, they'd be out the door in minutes.

As Robin lifted the lid to reveal not just clothes, but also photos and personal items, however, that subtle hint of hope evaporated. Sawyer's stomach clenched and the sting of old memories caused them to ease onto the bed.

Robin lifted her eyebrows.

"I'm fine."

"Physically." Robin let her eyes run over them in the way that'd always struck them as resembling a cat about to pounce. "I'd even say 'fine as hell' on that outer shell of yours. What about the inside parts like your brain, or heart?"

They shook their head. "I packed this box."

Robin waited for more explanation, but Sawyer didn't want to talk about the night they ran, or the fights that had sent them spiraling to that point. Honestly, they didn't even remember the details. It hadn't been any one thing so much as the culmination of a thousand little needle pricks, like some weird, disfigured Rorschach of a tattoo they hadn't asked for and still tried not to look at.

Instead, they pawed through the top layer of the bin, shifting things around without actually inspecting much. There were little mementos, a class ring, some handwritten notes, some long-obsolete receipts, a few framed photos.

They lifted one of the latter, trying to anchor themself to better memories.

"Holy shit." Robin peeked over their shoulder. "Is that Gilly playing basketball?"

"Yeah, she's cutthroat, with legs for days." They smiled. "She used to help run practices as a grad student even though she wasn't on the team in any official capacity."

"So very on-brand for her," Robin said. "I hope she still has that uniform, you know, for future sexual role-play."

Sawyer snickered as their jaw muscles loosened.

Robin reached over them and grabbed another frame. This shot featured Brooke on a beach in a swimsuit that would've made Tegan's brain melt, but Robin homed in on a different detail. "Oh God, who let Brooke get a pixie cut?"

"She had one when I met her. I think it might've happened as part of the whole divorce filing/coming out cluster."

"Trauma haircut. We've all been there," Robin mused. "Still a babe, though. You gotta take this bin. Some of these should be proudly displayed in your new place."

"Most of it's probably headed for the arson area."

"Burning photos is sacrilege," Robin said quickly. "We have to remember who we were so we can see how far we've come."

They might've said that some things were best forgotten, or maybe that sometimes they reminded you of how far you hadn't come, or maybe they might've told Robin they worried these things wouldn't create distance so much as pull them back, but Sawyer's jaw had tightened to the point where they couldn't open their mouth to speak.

Robin continued to pick up photos in some reverse sort of timeline of their personal history. In each one, they got younger, prettier ... girlier. Their face and body softer, their hair longer, their clothes more feminine.

Robin grew quiet as they made it back to the time when Sawyer had been on the homecoming court in high school, only it hadn't been Sawyer, not really. It had been some other person, someone people had convinced them they could be if only they hated themself enough to conform.

"Wow," Robin finally said. "This is turning me on."

They nearly doubled over as every muscle in their body constricted. If Robin found that photo attractive ... they squeezed their eyes shut until a hand cupped their cheek softly. The touch singed against raw nerves, and they would've pulled away if they'd had the strength.

"Hey." Robin stroked a gentle line along their cheekbone. Her tone and the tenderness split something open inside Sawyer, causing them to shudder.

"Deep breath," Robin coaxed.

They managed a shallow one.

Robin let her hand slide along their jaw and trail lightly down their neck.

"Again."

They did slightly better this time.

She moved lower, lingering at their throat before dropping to their sternum. Then, extending her index finger, she ran it along their scars through the thin cotton of their T-shirt. "Sawyer."

Their eyes fluttered open at the sound of their name, husky, rich, and laced with heartbreaking compassion.

Robin held up their phone in her other hand. On it, she'd pulled up the photo of the two of them together, beaming, hands full of ice cream, eyes full of mischief and mirth. "The transformation from that picture, to this one, is so fucking sexy I can hardly stand it. I may have to break every rule and rip your clothes off right here in your mother's home, with our friends out there playing human shields."

They sniffed slightly at the horrifying and thrilling image.

"I already thought you were one of the most singularly attractive humans I've ever met, but seeing the person you used to be, seeing what you fought against and whittled away and overcame—that contrast has me so wet right now I might need a towel."

They stared into her eyes waiting for Robin to laugh or at least crack a smile, but she merely held their gaze. She couldn't be serious, but if not, she had the finest poker face Sawyer had ever seen.

"Do you believe me?" Robin asked.

They did, kind of, but they couldn't make it compute, not with the pain still compressing their ribs and the doubt niggling their brain.

Robin reached for their hand, taking it gently in hers, and pressed it flat to her stomach. Then, sliding down, she brushed their fingers inside the waistband of her jeans.

Sawyer's synapses all fired at random, but with their brain on the fritz, their body took over. Slipping lower, they sank two fingers into exactly what Robin had promised they'd find. Closing their eyes this time, they saw only red.

Robin leaned forward into them, pressing her forehead to theirs. "Believe me now?"

They nodded.

"Then, believe all of it. Believe in all of *you*. The growth, the evolution, the work, and the results, your continued saunter down this sexy continuum, every part of it is engaging and arousing to me. You are the masterpiece inside that big block of marble. Look at what you chipped away to reveal all this perfection."

Sawyer bit their bottom lip as a deep part of them tried to protest, but the argument never quite formed, not with the rush of their own blood through their ears to drown out the echoes of the past. Why would they tumble back when they had so much to hold onto here?

Robin's breath fluttered warm across their mouth as their fingers twitched, itching to go deeper.

They may've capitulated to the desire if not for the sound of laughter coming from the other room. Still, even then, Robin didn't pull away so much as ease back, leaving it to Sawyer to break contact, one choice they got to make in the face of so many others they hadn't.

Glancing back at the box on the bed, they took a deep breath. "Almost done."

"With this," Robin agreed, her cheeks more than a little flushed. "Then we'll see where we're at with the rest of it."

They nodded, not wanting to let their mind linger too long on what "the rest of it" might entail.

Robin shuffled past the remaining photos to a pile of clothes below. She quickly tossed a few things into piles, mercifully saving Sawyer from having to make more decisions, but as she lifted a pair of old Converse sneakers from near the bottom of the bin, a tangle of spaghetti straps caught, pulling out a wad of black velvet.

Sawyer watched in mute horror as Robin's skilled fingers made quick work of the knot, and the dress unfolded with a sickening little spring and sway.

"Whew." Robin inspected the little, black A-line number. "That's a bouncy piece of sexiness."

Sawyer swallowed a hint of bile. "It was mine in high school."

Robin shook her head. "No, it wasn't."

"I definitely wore it to homecoming," they said flatly.

Robin kept her tone neutral as she held the dress up to examine the tag more closely. "I test drove a Porsche once, didn't mean it belonged to me. You may've borrowed this, but it was never yours."

They let the words sink in. "I guess I never got around to returning it then. I doubt 5-7-9 will accept an exchange at this point."

Robin's lips twitched up. "Store credits are such a hassle. When I get a piece home before I figure out it's not for me, I usually pass it along to someone who's better suited to it."

Sawyer shrugged, not really wanting to go through that effort either. "Know anyone who'd like a hand-me-down homecoming dress?"

"I thought you'd never ask!"

Sawyer chuckled, rattling some of the ice in their chest loose.

"I'm serious. I never went to homecoming. Would it bother you to see me in it?"

Sawyer eyed the dress again. This time, instead of remembering it against their own body, they pictured it on Robin. It would hug her curves and show off a hint of thigh and her chest … "No. I don't suppose it would bother me … at least not in a bad way."

Robin draped the dress over her arm. "Then we'll call this the first present you ever bought me."

"I didn't know you when I bought it."

"Maybe something inside you knew you would someday." Robin said the words evenly enough, as if the idea weren't overly sentimental or silly. "The same way when you tried it on, you knew it wasn't for you but couldn't explain it yet. Maybe deep down a part of you realized this dress wasn't for the type of person you wanted to be, but it would fit the type of person you wanted to have around when you finally met the person you were becoming."

Sawyer pondered the idea for a moment. It seemed like they should push back. It presumed so much, most of all a level of trust they had a hard time placing in themself and would never have afforded the version of them who'd surrendered so much in the moments Robin gleefully wrote off as almost prophetic.

"Too much?" Robin asked.

"I'm searching for something to fight against," they admitted, "and I'm so used to finding it, but when I scan those memories through your lens, the only thing I can really find to be upset about is that I wish I had actually known you then."

Robin beamed. "Yeah? What would you have done with me?"

"Probably been terrified of you, but I definitely would've wished I could take you to homecoming in that dress."

Robin gave a little twirl. "Not the me who would've been eligible for homecoming. I was a weird, little art-room nerd. You're not the only one who's had a glow-up since high school."

Sawyer stared at her, trying to imagine this woman as being anything other than fully formed awesomeness incarnate. They were just about to say they didn't believe her, or maybe that they still would've liked her, but they never got the chance, as Brooke stuck her head in the door.

"Gillian's doing conversational gymnastics out here. If you don't save her soon, she'll end up supervising seven new clinicians this fall."

Robin's smile spread. "Ooh, fresh meat."

"No." Sawyer laughed. "I don't need anyone else endangering their professional credentials on my account."

"Brooke's got a higher threshold for such shenanigans than she used to." Robin waggled her eyebrows suggestively. "Still, I think we're done for today."

Sawyer glanced around the room before letting their eyes land on Robin. "I agree. Good progress."

Robin grinned for a second, something sweetly unspoken between them before she sprang into action. Within a minute, she had the burn pile crammed neatly into one bin and the keep pile in another. Then she pressed the lid securely back onto the last tub, before saying, "Maybe this one can come with us for whenever we're ready?"

Sawyer nodded, enjoying how neatly everything had been tucked into its new and correct place. They might have even found the whole thing cathartic if not for the looming task of marching it all past their mother.

Brooke and Robin must've done the same mental calculation, as they both flanked them on the way into the living room, each carrying a bin.

"Well, great talk." Gillian hopped up quickly. "I think I've taken up enough of your time. Let's be in touch."

Maura rolled her eyes, clearly not buying any of it. "I assume you got what you came for?"

"And then some." Sawyer cast a crooked smile at Robin. "Thanks for letting us barge in."

"Sawyer, you know you're welcome here anytime, with or without the entourage."

They weren't sure they agreed with that assessment, or maybe with their mother's definition of welcome, but they were so close to the exit, they didn't dare argue now. "I appreciate the offer."

"And I appreciate you bringing your friends by. I'm glad you have them." Maura looked at each of them before settling on Robin. "And I'm so glad I finally got to meet you."

"Likewise," Robin said, seeming genuine enough.

Then they headed for the door with Maura following them out, but just as they reached the hallway, she placed a hand on Sawyer's shoulder. "I'm sorry for the observation that made you uncomfortable last time. I'm happy you're back, and I'm pleased to see you've added another therapist to your close circle."

Every muscle in Sawyer's body clenched. "I've added another friend to my inner circle."

Maura glanced at Robin. "Good. One can never have too many friends who are also mental health professionals. Perhaps this one might even be better at holding professional boundaries than the others."

Gillian turned, a flash of fire in her green eyes, but before she had the chance to set anyone else ablaze, Robin laughed. The rich sound reverberated off the concrete floors and exposed ductwork, causing every one of them to turn toward her.

"I've actually been talking about that boundary with Sawyer ever since I met them." Robin nudged them all further out the door until only she stood level with Maura. "They seem to fear that I might try to analyze or diagnose them during social interactions, which would be so inappropriate, right?"

A small muscle in Maura's jaw twitched, but Robin plowed on, her voice full of amusement and a type of confidence few people managed to keep in the face of this woman. "I keep explaining over and over that I am *a* therapist, but I'm not *their* therapist. For some reason, they have a hard time separating the two. Don't worry, though. I take my work seriously, and my friendships even more so, and that's one boundary I absolutely intend to hold."

Nineteen

"Holy shit." Tegan stared at Robin with the same sort of mystified wonder the others had the whole way home, and she didn't know whether to bask in the warmth of their admiration or squirm under the assessment that she'd done something radical. She'd never minded being the wild card of the group, but she hadn't really seen her comments to Maura as anything revolutionary.

Sure, she'd been terse, firm even, but she hadn't said anything that didn't get discussed openly in even the most basic intro to psychology class. Therapists can't run around diagnosing randos in their life. The prospect got even more off-limits when it came to people you couldn't keep a healthy clinical neutrality about.

She shrugged. "I simply said what we were all thinking."

"What we've all been thinking for years," Brooke said.

"Okay, but that was the first time she directly attacked my professionalism." Gillian seethed as she aggressively cut into her pancakes. "Better at holding professional boundaries? Robin? Sorry, I mean you're a brilliant therapist, maybe even better than I thought, given how deftly you handled her little dig, but can we all agree boundaries are not exactly what you're known for?"

"Whatever do you mean?" She chuckled. "I'm so good at holding boundaries."

"You tried to high-five me when you found out I accidentally slept with a junior colleague," Brooke said.

Sawyer laughed and they all turned to them. Robin's heart kicked her ribs. They'd been quiet. Aside from quick comments or affirmations that they were okay, they'd mostly allowed the conversation to flow around them rather than wading in, which honestly bothered Robin more than anything Maura had implied, or even said outright.

The family dynamics struck Robin as super weird and, by extension, fascinating. She had no idea why a woman like Maura, smart, accomplished, and so well respected in her field, would choose to nitpick her queer child, or why a person of Sawyer's grace, experience, or adventurous spirit would let such a petty thing shake their well-earned confidence. She also didn't have a full read on why Brooke and Gillian would act so skittish in the middle of those firing lines. Still, Robin didn't hate the bump in her friends and colleagues' estimation. She wasn't the type of person who needed to fully understand something in order to enjoy it.

"Gilly's right, though," Brooke said softly. "Sawyer, Maura's getting worse since you came back, or maybe she's merely more blatant, and ever since our conversation last weekend about why you had to go away to have top surgery, I can't stop thinking that if I'd been able to say something sooner, maybe—"

"No, no, no. Don't do that," Sawyer said, then turned to Gillian. "You either."

"Okay, but being brilliant at work or in a classroom doesn't excuse treating your kid like that. If I'd seen the full scope of it before you left, maybe I couldn't have stopped it, but I would've understood more or maybe offered you better support."

"I didn't want to put you in the middle. She's been kind of your boss ever since I met you, and still you've chosen me so many times. She mostly keeps things in check in public, or at least couches her issues under more academic concerns around colleagues. I never expected you to blow up your professional relationships over a couple of snide comments. There's too much at stake with too little upside for anyone," Sawyer said, then smiled. "I didn't expect Robin to go in swinging, though."

Robin protested. "I didn't say anything that woman hasn't told thousands of first-year students over the course of her career, right?"

"Right," Tegan answered emphatically. "We all know the rules."

"Besides, I don't even know what she's talking about half the time anyway," Robin went on, "and to Brooke and Gillian of all people. What is she even accusing you of?"

"Of not handling me in the way she thinks a mental health professional should," Sawyer said flatly. "Of not holding some line she's trying to draw, of allowing me to be fluid instead of forcing me to pick a well-defined condition she can treat or cure."

"Treat or cure what?" Robin shook her head.

"My fluidity. She sees it as a kind of inconsistency, and there's nothing a researcher like her hates more than random data points. Only static identities are valid identities."

"Oh, fuck that. Static identities are boring identities." Robin pretended to snore. "Unless there's some memo I didn't get, which, honestly, happens to me a lot, there's never any harm in rolling with people's fullness, which is what I did today."

Sawyer nodded. "You rolled with a lot, on more than one front."

The two of them exchanged a heavy look, and a rush of memories predating the exchange their friends were hung up on rushed back. Sawyer buckling, Sawyer with their eyes closed, Sawyer with their hand against the evidence of Robin's desire.

Her heart rate picked up. God, what had she been thinking? Surely, Maura wouldn't approve of Robin's methods of grounding her only offspring. Probably none of the other therapists in the room would either, but she wasn't acting as a therapist then. Plus, it had worked … and not just for Sawyer.

"I didn't even ask." Tegan pulled her back to the moment. "How did the sorting of personal items go?"

"Fine," Sawyer said quickly. "I think we got it all. Bonfire date and time are TBD."

Everyone seemed to wait for more, eventually turning to Robin to fill in the gaps, making her remember Brooke and Gillian still had no idea what had transpired during the time they were distracting Maura. While she didn't think anything

211

needed to be kept in confidence, she also saw the exhaustion in Sawyer's glazed eyes and the way they slouched on the couch. "We found an inordinate amount of rugby shirts, and I stole a few items for my personal collection."

"Shocking." Gillian polished off her pancake before turning back to Sawyer. "Did you find anything worth the effort and angst?"

They seemed to think about it for a second until their lips turned up at the corners. "Actually, yeah."

"Anything we'll see you wear soon?" Brooke asked.

"Oh, I could take or leave the clothes," Sawyer said, then turning more fully toward Robin, added, "but I did pick up a few new concepts I'm going to try on and maybe wear around for a while."

She grinned at them. "I bet they'll be super sexy on you."

Robin closed the door behind the others, not even pretending she planned to leave as well. Thankfully, everyone was either too worn out or too impressed with how she'd handled the morning to question her now. Not that she had any wicked plans, or even regular plans. There was no reason for her to stick around other than she merely wanted to. And that logic had always served her well, so she turned to Sawyer with a little grin. "I'm already bored."

Sawyer chuckled. "Of course you are. You're still buzzing from your triumph."

"Hardly." Robin dismissed the comment. "That was a run-of-the-mill conversation in my line of work."

"Another reason for me to avoid your line of work." Sawyer didn't quite manage to sound sardonic so much as tired as they walked around to the end of the couch and folded their long frame onto the corner cushion. "What about the conversations before that? Are you and I ... do we need to like, debrief ... or something?"

Robin understood the question, but she also understood Sawyer was in no position to dive back into those waters so soon. "I can't imagine why. I had a good time and got some new clothes. Everything there is winning for me."

"I think you're a sadist."

"I think you're into it, but Sundays are for chilling and vibing."

"Yeah? And what plans do you have to chill and vibe on this glorious Sunday afternoon?" Sawyer asked.

"Probably going home to lie around in my ratty clothes and watch questionable movies."

Sawyer seemed to think about that for a minute. "I have access to movies. I have a television."

Robin smiled at the simple joy in the statement. "Of your very own?"

"Well, I mean, it's Tegan's, but I pay rent, so kind of mine."

"Possession is nine-tenths of the law. Don't think I'm not up on squatter rights."

"I'd never underestimate you on that count, or probably any count."

"I like that in a friend."

Sawyer arched an eyebrow. "Friend, huh? The kind of friend who sticks around after gender dysphoric meltdowns and mommy issues?"

"Duh. Trauma bonding is still bonding."

Sawyer snorted softly. "True. What about the kind of friend who hangs around when you're crashing from the comedown."

"The kind of friend who's hoping to watch movies on your squatter TV and comfy couch."

Sawyer's shoulders relaxed. "The kind of friend who puts your hand in her pants at random moments?"

She laughed. "Yes, but you've met your inappropriate trip to third base quota for today."

Sawyer sighed and settled a little deeper into the couch. "It's honestly several bases farther than I expected, but just so you know, if I'd been better prepared, I could better … well, you know."

Robin came around and curled up on the other corner of the couch. "Your reputation is safe, and so I'm safe. I'm going to sit all the way over here while we watch a buddy comedy or something."

"As opposed to some sexy sapphic romp?"

"Exactly," Robin agreed. "*Carol* is off the table."

"*Carol*?" Sawyer laughed. "That's not a romp. It's way too depressing for a sleepy summer afternoon."

"What? You don't find closeted, sneaking-around custody battles to be super fun?"

"Sadist." Sawyer shook their head. "If I wanted that kind of tension, I could've stayed at my mother's."

Robin grinned. "Your mom has similar vibes, but she's got nothing on Cate Blanchett's icy exterior."

"Thank God. I don't think I could survive if she did."

"I think you've survived a lot."

Sawyer arched an eyebrow. "Oh, are you moving into phase two?"

Robin stared at them, waiting for more.

"My mother tends to inspire a real pattern of reactions in people," they finally explained. "She starts by impressing the hell out of them, either by reputation or demonstration. She's always impressive, and while you didn't get to see it today, she can be rather charming in situations that suit her."

"What, like lecture halls, board meetings, exorcisms?"

Sawyer grinned. "Nailed it. Also, from what I've seen in interviews and with her favored students, I suspect she's probably very good in therapy sessions that hold her interest, though I've steered clear of those for at least a decade, because eventually phase two always kicks in, which involves scaring the hell out of anyone who doesn't fall into line."

"Huh," Robin said, not finding it hard to believe Maura had the capabilities, but more interested in hearing Sawyer's unfiltered take.

"What about your father?"

"He was of a similar ilk. A psych senior professor when she was still untenured. I always suspected their relationship held its own hint of scandal in their world, but of course Maura would never cop to such details, and my father was quite a bit older. He died when I was eight."

"I'm so sorry."

"Don't be. I never had much of a relationship with him. They never married, and he didn't live with us. I mean, he was around, and I guess as involved as he knew how to be. He'd take me to the lab and let me draw on his chalkboard, but I always felt like I was being observed rather than enjoyed. If you're feeling sorry for me and my ultra clinical childhood, or perhaps projecting some of your own clinical observation—"

"Whoa." Robin held up her hand. "That escalated quickly."

Sawyer shrugged. "Not in my world. I've had a lot of conversations like this over the years. Maura often leaves people trying to make sense of their own reactions to pointed encounters. You can process with me. I'm used to it."

"Okay." Robin took in a deep breath. "This topic sounds like a lot for someone who found *Carol* too serious for a summer afternoon, but if you want to know the truth, I found your mother low-key fascinating. She seems very good at her job when it comes to everyone but you. It's super interesting that she chose to take a potshot at Brooke and Gillian's professional boundaries when she's clearly struggling to hold her own. You wanna talk about projecting?"

"Oh, she's going to hate you," Sawyer said as if they found the idea delicious.

"Maybe, but I get it. Everyone tries to apply what they know best about the world to situations they can't control. People are weird and wonderful and complex and completely enthralling. It's sad that she does such supercool work around all those characteristics without seeming to revel in them at all in her own life, but I can't say that I'm any more impressed or afraid of her than I would be of any other professional who does interesting stuff. Honestly, I'm way less interested in her than I am in you."

Sawyer seemed to ponder that for a moment. "Are you more interested in me after meeting her?"

"No," Robin said. "I might be curious about different things, but that's par for the course with you. Every time I see you in a new situation, you spark some new curiosity in me, like for instance, how do you not find the movie *Carol* to be sexy AF?"

Sawyer cracked a smile. "You're not like anyone I've ever met before either."

"Good." Robin extended her legs so they slid along Sawyer's. "I'd hate to think you're infinitely interesting while I'm over here rocking my basic bitchness."

"You could never be a basic bitch. You and I are not capable of such a thing. And for what it's worth, I didn't say *Carol* wasn't sexy. I said it was depressing, and then you somehow connected it to my mom, so now I've got one more thing not to ever work on in therapy, which fuck you, by the way."

Robin laughed again. "Okay, no *Carol*, both for the tone and the sex appeal and the unexamined Freudian bullshittery. But you have to admit, that scene when Rooney Mara wakes up to find Cate Blanchett gone and Sarah Paulson watching her sleep is peak lesbian culture."

Sawyer laughed. "True. Cate's like, 'sorry to sneak out in the middle of the night, but here's my butchy, '50s wingwoman to drive you back across the country.'"

"Don't pretend we've haven't all been there."

"I mean, I have snuck out of women's hotel rooms before," Sawyer admitted, "but I've never left Sarah Paulson in my wake."

"Rude." Robin practically cackled. "Fair trade, though."

"Now that you mention it"—Sawyer stretched out a little more—"if I nod off during the movie and wake up to find you bolted, and Sarah Paulson is here, I'd forgive you."

"Noted. Same goes for me. If you decide to leave town or stand me up again, I expect you to send Sarah in your stead."

Sawyer yawned. "Sorry, Charlie, you might be stuck with me for a bit. We all went through the trouble of getting my stuff back, and you leveled the sickest burn anyone has ever landed on my mom. I can't let all that be for nothing, so I'll probably hang around for a bit."

They made the comment with the same casualness as their previous jokes, but Robin couldn't help but hear it differently, and she didn't hate that.

Robin let her eyes wander down the length of Sawyer's body, languid and relaxed, one arm hooked rakishly behind their head on the couch cushion and the other on the flat plane of their stomach. The attraction that had colored her vision around them hadn't waned since the first night in the bar, but here, casually crashed out after running an emotional gauntlet, other feelings began to bleed in like a spark flickering into a flame. "Cool."

"Cool," Sawyer repeated sleepily. "I'm glad you approve."

They stared at each other for a long, lazy minute, almost as if daring each other to say some of the quiet parts out loud, but every time Robin thought about making something more out of the moment, her heart kicked her ribs uncomfortably.

"So ..." She finally drew out the word to make sure the new emotions didn't bleed through into her voice. "Wanna watch *Booksmart*?"

Sawyer sighed. "Now you're talking."

Twenty

Sawyer leaned against the brick wall of Gillian's office building, soaking up the fading sun. They probably could've worn shorts tonight, as summer had begun to tease Buffalo in earnest. Mid-June could go either way around here, but, given that they'd spent the last two summers gadding about Scandinavia, an early evening in the upper seventies felt downright balmy. Still, they'd chosen a pair of jeans when they'd left their apartment, knowing that on a day like this, Robin had likely ridden the motorcycle to work.

As they stood there waiting for her, they tried not to think too hard about the fact that they had actually visualized a good deal about how they'd like the evening to go. Doing so didn't really mesh with their go-with-the-flow philosophy, neither did standing around waiting for one woman in a city full of them. But then again, they'd seen Robin four or five times over the last week, and they'd never failed to have fun. Sawyer didn't really feel the need to put in the extra work of finding someone cooler when they had a pretty sure bet just on the other side of the wall, so they closed their eyes and relaxed in the orange glow of a low sun and rising anticipation.

"Hey, Creeper," a familiar voice called.

Sawyer slowly turned their head and opened their eyes to take her in. Robin stood a few feet away, still holding open the door to the office, sunglasses perched atop her head, hand up to shade her vision. Her dark eyes squinted as she took them in.

Sawyer allowed her the same kind of unapologetic appraisal they were currently enjoying.

Robin wore a white Oxford shirt open over a navy-blue tank top and gray cargo pants that rested easily on the curve of her hips. Sawyer's fingers twitched with the urge to let their palms rest right there or maybe splay one against her stomach while she drove, because sure enough, she had on a pair of motorcycle boots, in brown this time.

"You planning to loiter out here like a juvenile delinquent all night?"

Sawyer shrugged. "Don't know. Feeling cute, might fuck around and find out later."

Robin's grin spread. "Sounds like my kind of Thursday evening. Want to come in and say hello to the crew?"

They shook their head. "I'm not feeling like going in. I want to go out."

"What are you about to drag me into?"

"No, no," they said. "You misunderstand. I want to be taken out. I'm here to be amused."

Robin laughed. "Thank you for clearing that up, Your Highness."

Sawyer flashed their most practiced smile. "What, you don't think I'm pretty enough to be shown a good time?"

Robin gave them another solid once-over, letting her eyes trace their body like a caress, then pressed her lips together as if the jury was still out for a moment before cracking a smile. "No, you totally are."

"I thought so."

"Yeah yeah." She stepped close enough to touch them without actually doing so. "That's part of the appeal, isn't it? Someone who knows their worth?"

"I'm not sure I'd go that far." Sawyer leaned in slightly. "I said I was pretty, but knowing the total of my whole worth is harder to do when such a number might be unquantifiable."

Robin rolled her eyes playfully, but she didn't argue, one of the many qualities Sawyer liked about her.

That's how they'd taken to couching those moments when their mind wandered to Robin, as it did so often these days. Sawyer didn't overthink it, a skill they'd honed to near perfection, though they'd rarely had such a compelling reason to practice. They didn't need to read any deeper into their own desires or analyze any hidden yearning to accept the obvious fact that there was simply so much to like about this woman.

Her looks obviously came to mind first, her dark features, tempting figure, and, of course, kissable lips, but her quick wit, sense of humor, and ability to roll with whatever Sawyer threw her way upped the attraction way past pure physicality. Robin oozed a "yes and" kind of energy, and people with that quality always ended up being Sawyer's favorite kind of people, so it only made sense that they'd practically memorized her work schedule and nights off in case they wanted to show up at exactly those moments, toeing right up to the stalker line. That wasn't like Sawyer at all ... it was just Robin who inspired such behavior with her whimsy and colorful antics.

No, Sawyer wasn't playing their usual games or trying to sweep her off her feet. They weren't asking her out or trying to pick her up, and they certainly weren't getting in over their head. They merely wanted to be entertained, and Robin was nothing if not entertaining.

"Okay, I have an idea," Robin finally said.

Sawyer grinned. "Of course you do."

Within ten minutes they were on the bike, gliding down the skyway with Lake Erie stretching off to the right in a glorious expanse of azure. Robin leaned into the curve of an exit ramp, and Sawyer bent with her as they veered toward the Outer Harbor. Sawyer hadn't been here in years, and the city seemed to have spruced up the place with some new playgrounds and picnic areas, in stark contrast to the concrete grain silos, creating a particularly Buffalo kind of clash. They loved it.

Robin slowed to a stop in a parking spot closest to the old grain elevators and the last of the newer floating docks.

Swinging off the bike, she unclipped her helmet. "You're CPR certified, right?"

Sawyer arched an eyebrow. "Yes. Am I going to need those skills on this outing?"

Robin's expression turned coy. "One never knows."

She was joking, Sawyer felt mostly certain, but they followed her down the dock anyway. They passed a slew of boats and a few people along the way, but Sawyer only saw them in their periphery as they couldn't focus on anything else with Robin's hips swaying seductively as they sauntered on ahead. They might've walked right off the end of the pier in pursuit if Robin hadn't stopped at the second-to-last slip. Without explanation or pause, she hopped nimbly onto the bow of a boat, then extended her hand. Sawyer had zero inclination to question the invitation.

"She's a beauty, right?" Robin shed her jacket as she headed right for the steering wheel.

"Yes." Sawyer said, still looking at her. "Gorgeous."

"You know boats?"

"I've met a few over the years."

"Life jackets are under the benches," Robin said casually as she ran her hand under the dash as if feeling for something.

"Am I going to need one?"

She chuckled.

"Let me guess," Sawyer implored. "One never knows?"

"Quick learner." Robin kept searching for something, working her fingers up underneath the panel holding all the instruments until she pulled a wire loose.

"Are you about to hot-wire this boat?" Sawyer asked. "You want me to play lookout?"

"I've always wanted to learn to hot-wire an engine, but I've never gotten around to it." Robin gave one more tug, and a key came into view. She slipped it free of its fastener and held it up for Sawyer to see. "Wanna go for a ride?"

"Literally or figuratively?" Sawyer grinned. "Never mind, doesn't matter. The answer is 'yes.'"

"Wanna know something blasphemous?" Sawyer asked as Robin slowed the boat to a low drone and a gentle rock on light waves.

"Always."

"I think Buffalo is every bit as pretty from this angle as any city I've ever seen from the water."

"Yeah?" Robin turned to glance at the Buffalo skyline rising up from the shore. "How many have you seen?"

Sawyer gave it some brief thought before realizing the day was too nice to do math. "Quite a few."

"What's the next closest?"

"Probably Palma de Mallorca."

Robin laughed. "Oh yeah, sure, an island in the Mediterranean, absolute rubbish compared to Buffalo. Did you look at it and yawn?"

"Not quite. The two are very different. I didn't exactly consider it a hardship to look at it from the bow of the sailboat we were diving off, but I do remember making the comparison in my mind at the time."

"How'd that shake out?"

Sawyer sighed. "Well, Mallorca's warmer. And Buffalo doesn't have a massive cathedral or palm trees, or mountains in the backdrop."

"But"—Robin pointed back to the shore—"I bet Palma doesn't have an art deco city hall as its centerpiece."

"Exactly," Sawyer said emphatically without adding it also didn't have Robin either, which in this moment felt like a serious detractor.

"I dig it." Robin nodded. "Beauty's all around and in the eye of the beholder."

They nodded, not wanting to ruminate too hard on the latter part of that statement.

"I'm super envious of your travels though," Robin said. "I love this city, but I think I'd also love to be able to draw the kinds of comparisons you toss out casually."

"You haven't traveled at all?"

"Oh, the usual. Conferences in various U.S. cities, one weekend in Cabo in college, occasional trips to Toronto to see a show or gorge myself on poutine and potstickers, a cruise with my grandma that sounds tame, but ended up wilder than Cabo."

Sawyer smiled. "I love that."

"Me too," Robin admitted.

"I never knew my grandparents. I would've liked to have some rabble-rouser I could point to in my gene pool to explain how their DNA can skip a generation or something. Honestly, I think my mother might actually be doing that research, now that you mention it."

"You mentioned it," Robin said, tongue planted firmly in cheek. "Care to step into my office and say more?"

"Ah, trickery." Sawyer shook their head. "Trap me half a mile offshore, then tell me this is your remote work location."

Robin made a big show of glancing around. "You gotta admit, it beats a corner suite on the thirty-second floor, but I'm not your therapist. Remember? Just like I told your mom."

"I love how you make that sound like a 'your mom' joke."

"Kind of is," Robin admitted. "And 'your mom' jokes are evergreen, but we don't need to go back there. I provided the entertainment. You choose the topics of conversation."

"Me?" Sawyer blew out a heavy breath. "No pressure or anything?"

"None." Robin relaxed back in her captain's chair. "I've got at least until sundown before I start to worry about how to drive a boat in the dark."

"Don't they teach you that when you get your boating license?"

"I don't have a boating license."

Sawyer stared at her for a second, trying to figure out if she was joking again, but saw no signs of it. "Okay."

"It's not my boat," Robin offered, as if that were an explanation. "I borrowed it."

"Borrowed or stole?"

She laughed. "You really are getting to know me. But, borrowed. It's my uncle's. We're cool. He's an artist and a playboy and a rake. He used to let me drive his big old Cadillac when I was fifteen. We'd go for rides, and he'd smoke cigars in the passenger seat and look at women."

"So, he saw you as a sort of protégée?"

"Hardly. I was a nerdy little punk back then."

"Right, hanging out with the art teacher and your uncle." Sawyer sighed, having a hard time picturing such a thing. "I guess you couldn't take either of them to homecoming with you."

"I mean, my uncle probably would've gone, but it wouldn't have exactly helped my social status to show up with a forty-year-old man in a fedora."

"You would've had more fun than I had at mine," Sawyer admitted. "I never enjoyed a single school formal."

"Why keep going?"

"I don't know … I mean, I do, but I hate the reasons now. Trying to conform, trying to be something, anything for sure, anything static, anything stable, anything that would let me jam myself into any of those tight high school boxes … that's what she said."

Robin laughed lightly. "You beat me to the 'tight boxes' joke. For real though, those old pictures of you suggest you had some mad chameleon skills. I'm glad you don't need them anymore, but for what it's worth, I don't even have that tool in my box … which is also what she said."

Sawyer grinned, endlessly appreciative of her ability to keep a conversation like this irreverent. "I'm surprised. I feel like you could be anything you wanted to be."

"Maybe now, but I was such a late bloomer. Or maybe an uneven bloomer. I figured out I was queer too soon, and I was artsy too soon, but I got slutty too late to be popular in high school. I never quite fit in."

"Or maybe high school didn't fit you. Sounds like a shoe that's too small."

"Yeah, I never got good at making myself small. This might surprise you, but I had opinions and a bit of a mouth on me."

"You?" Sawyer feigned surprise. "Shocking."

"I know. I made good grades, but I didn't make a lot of friends, as I fought against the confines of teenage hierarchies. I got so sick of always bumping up against social norms. My mom says I blossomed the moment I graduated, but, honestly, I think I just had more space to get as big as I always should've been. And once I felt what it was like to take up space, I couldn't stop. I got defiantly self-secure and self-aware. I became almost militant about defining who I was based on my own terms. I may have gone overboard at times, but I prefer overboard to being boxed in by anyone else's opinions or expectations."

"Agreed," Sawyer said, but as a slightly bigger wave rocked them side to side, they added, "so long as you don't go overboard in the literal sense on this trip."

"You said you knew CPR."

"Much like my chameleon skills, just because I know how to do something doesn't mean I want to."

Robin glanced over the side of the boat. "The lake is still too cold for my taste this time of year anyway."

"Good. And for what it's worth, I do prefer the going overboard in the figurative to the literal sense. You're good at it," Sawyer said with genuine admiration. "I like that quality in you."

"Not sure I had any other choice. I think part of me would've liked to be one of those girls who wore cute dresses to dances, but I never got the hang of conformity enough to get invited."

"Good for you," they said, then realized they might sound insensitive. "I'm sorry people didn't accept you. But, take it from someone who became way too good at playing the game, you got the better end of a shitty equation. I spent the first ten years of my adult life trying to figure out how to take up space, and even now, the urge to conform is so freaking insidious.

Going with the flow turns into agreeing to get along, which becomes swallowing shit to keep the peace, and before you know it ..." They shook their head, realizing they'd gotten dark again.

"What?" Robin asked. "You'll look up one day to realize you own a house in the suburbs and drive a minivan?"

Sawyer laughed. "It could happen. It *does* happen in smaller doses. Then I freak out and bounce back with some overreaction that sends me spinning off in some wildly different direction."

"Like you ditch the van at the airport and fly off to Singapore to spend a season fishing on a shrimp trawler?"

Sawyer stared at her. "Did you just think of that off the top of your head?"

Robin shrugged. "We all have those urges. I love my job, my colleagues, and the vast majority of my clients, but sometimes I dream about burning it all down."

Sawyer had heard plenty of people say similar things and rarely believed them, but with Robin, they could sense the wild edge under her soft surface. "Why don't you?"

"I do, in my own ways. Just because I don't want to actually burn everything down doesn't mean I don't occasionally enjoy playing with matches."

Sawyer leaned against the side of the boat. "Tell me more."

"Cutting loose is relative. Looking at your life makes me feel mild-mannered and restrained, but looking at Gillian, I'm a rebel wild child. Brooke, too, except for a few months last year. I ride motorcycles too fast and jump out of planes and end up in compromising positions with sexual partners."

Sawyer's grin spread. "I could offer a little assistance on the latter."

Robin eyed them as if considering it, then glanced around the open expanse of lake. Sawyer's heart beat faster with each second that ticked away. The two of them had come close a couple of times, and Robin had very clearly demonstrated her physical desire for them, but they'd also slipped into a stage of amiability that lessened some of the tension. Jeopardizing that probably wasn't a good idea, but they weren't talking about making reasonable or well-measured decisions. Robin was literally waxing poetic about her need to bend or break rules. Wasn't she?

Honestly, they weren't sure what decision Robin was trying to make at all as her gaze had grown hazy and she worried her lower lip with her teeth. Sawyer had only been joking, unless Robin was up for something. They'd always been up for something where this woman was concerned. Robin had been the one to set the hard boundary around friendship, but then again, they'd both been pretty hard when Sawyer'd had their hand in her pants last weekend.

Finally, Robin sighed. "Things have been going really well."

Sawyer nodded slowly. "They have."

"Seems like a stupid time to fuck things up."

"Undoubtedly," they agreed, without adding that that's exactly when they tended to fuck things up. Instead, they stood still and self-assured as they watched Robin's eyes wander lower and basked in the heat rising between them.

Heat. The corners of their mouth twitched up as an idea sparked.

"What?" Robin asked warily.

"I was noticing how warm it felt out here with the sun reflecting off the waves." They clutched the hem of their shirt. "Do you mind if I ..."

The brown of Robin's irises disappeared almost completely around her expanding pupils. "Go ahead."

Sawyer slipped off the shirt, taking their time to enjoy a hint of teasing before shedding it completely and tossing it on the bench seat behind them. Then they leaned back and stretched an arm along the smooth wooden side of the boat, comfortable both in their own skin and their ability to make the most of an opportunity that may come their way.

By the time they made eye contact with Robin again, there were no more questions about what she was considering.

"Fuck you," Robin whispered as she stared at them.

"You can if you'd like." Sawyer drew out the words as a sense of power grew in them. There was still plenty of uncertainty in their world, but here, half-naked on a beautiful day so close to an even more beautiful woman, there was little worth questioning. Robin had been the one to bring up burning things down. Sawyer was only there to pour a little fuel on the fire. "Or I could take the lead if you need to focus on steering."

Robin tore her eyes away from Sawyer's body only long enough to nod toward the Peace Bridge towering in the distance. "Do you know what's looming in the middle of that river up ahead? Spoiler alert: Niagara Falls."

Sawyer laughed and stood, stretching their arms over their head, elongating the muscles in their torso and basking in the glow of Robin's lustful gaze every bit as much as the setting sun. "Well then, we better not waste our time. Thankfully, if memory serves, you've got a quick trigger, and last weekend you already seemed locked and loaded."

"You're awfully sure of yourself," Robin said, which wasn't quite a disagreement.

Sawyer took the two steps needed to hook an arm around her waist and eased her out of the chair, so they both stood mere inches apart and largely shielded by the dashboard. "You like that in me as much as I like it in you."

Robin made a little growling noise in the back of her throat.

It could be so easy, it would be so quick, and it would most definitely be satisfying. Still, Sawyer wouldn't close the distance.

Robin had been the one to make the rules. She had to be the one who decided to break them, so Sawyer waited, the space between them charged with the type of electricity that probably shouldn't be allowed this close to water.

Robin reached out, tentatively at first, pressing her palm flat against Sawyer's bare chest before whispering, "This really isn't a smart idea."

"Playing with matches rarely is."

Robin's fingers twitched, but instead of pushing them away, she slid up until her grasp tightened around the tense knot of Sawyer's shoulder, and then she pulled them forward into a kiss.

Twenty-One

Robin stared down at Sawyer as she straddled their hips. They looked like some sort of demigod, transcendent in their androgyny, golden in the light of a nearby streetlamp shining through the open blinds. They'd been at this for hours, and still, she couldn't get enough.

She rocked her hips forward, sinking a little lower onto their strap-on and relishing the stretch of fullness she hadn't even let herself realize she ached for. Wanting was one thing, needing was another, but somehow, she'd edged dangerously close to the latter when it came to Sawyer.

"Oh God." Robin gasped as the hips beneath her rose a little higher off the bed. It had started innocently enough on the boat, or as innocently as the two of them were capable of. Casual mischief, light conversation, a little innuendo like always, but the moment Sawyer slipped out of that shirt, Robin's mind had gone blank. Except not completely because her senses had stayed on high alert as Sawyer had taken her, rough and fast, rocking on the waves and a raw kind of hunger.

Still, whatever part of her brain carried the burden of responsibility for restraint had clearly broken, because she didn't even remember returning to shore or driving the bike back into the city. Those kinds of lapses in short-term recall should've been scary, but she clung to the fact that she had a very clear recollection of stripping Sawyer's magnificent body bare and pinning it to the door of their apartment mere seconds after arriving there.

They'd both come so fast and hard, she'd barely managed to stumble to the bed, but when she'd rolled over and seen

Sawyer stepping into the black leather harness, something else flickered to life in her. Not the good decision-making part, obviously, but at this point, what did it matter? What did anything matter in the face of this magnificent human sprawled out beneath her doing the most glorious things to her body.

Robin fell forward, sliding skin against slick skin as she nipped at Sawyer's earlobe. "This escalated quickly."

Sawyer's laugh was low as it shook the place where their chests pressed together. "You didn't take much convincing, and you know if you give me an inch, I'm going to take a, well, eight inches."

She wanted to laugh, but Sawyer emphasized their point by arching up, pressing deeper, and suddenly Robin was too close again. Maybe she'd been too close all along, but what would it take to resist this kind of perfection long-term? Certainly, no skill or character trait she'd ever possessed.

Pushing up on her arms, she stared down at them. They were a portrait of perfection with eyelids heavy, chestnut hair tousled, muscles glistening with sweat. Robin ran her tongue in a slow swipe along their neck before sucking the hint of salt.

Sawyer wrapped an arm around her waist, and pinning them together, expertly rolled them both over in a tangle of sheets and sexiness. Using their body weight to spread her knees further apart, they pushed all the way in before pulling out and starting again. The move was controlled and deliciously deliberate but managed to inspire the opposite impulse in Robin. She started to unravel, every nerve ending sizzling, and Sawyer worked in an undulating rhythm designed to hold her on the edge.

She clawed at them, need building in her with each frantic beat of her pulse. She clutched their shoulders, nails digging into tight muscle. "Faster."

Sawyer's voice was low and full of their own power. "What's your rush?"

She gritted her teeth.

"Don't you want to make it last?" Sawyer teased.

She might've said this had already lasted longer than she should've let it, or maybe explained that she didn't know if she was capable of holding herself together if it went on much longer, but she possessed neither the skill nor the inclination for conversation when all she wanted was to have this human deeper inside her.

"I'll let you come as soon as you're ready." Sawyer continued with their long, slow strokes. "You just have to ask me nicely."

Robin would've laughed if she'd been capable of drawing enough air to do so. Instead, she moved her hands down their back to cup that perfect ass with both hands and pull them closer.

Sawyer accepted the encouragement, driving all the way in this time and holding themself there as they lowered their mouth to her ear. "Robin."

She tried to wiggle her way back, but they'd pinned her to the bed.

"I'm going to give you everything you want," they continued slowly. "I'm going to give you more than you ask for. But, you have to ask."

She opened her mouth, but the words wouldn't come out with both her body and her brain on fire. She'd seen Sawyer confident and cocky, but never exerting this kind of command, and while she normally bucked up against authority, she'd never had someone earn the right to wield it with such complete competence.

"Now." Sawyer worked a hand up behind her head and curled their fingers in her hair before tugging just hard enough to expose her neck. They sucked sharply there for a second before returning to her ear. "Do you have something you'd like to ask me?"

"Yes." Robin finally managed to hiss.

"Yes what?" They punctuated the question with another quick tug.

"Fuck me," Robin forced out. Then, as her natural defiance cracked, she added a raspy "please."

"There you go." Sawyer released her hair and slid a hand all the way down her side, hooking it behind Robin's thigh, and pulled her leg up. They eased back only enough to drive forward with more force. Picking up speed and power, they angled themself to hit every spot that mattered, and true to their promise, gave more than Robin had dared to ask for, and in doing so, obliterated everything other than the sweetness of total submission.

She didn't even know how long she shook and shuddered, or if she'd had the strength to call out. Her mind flashed an array of colors through the back of her eyelids, while breath seethed through tightly clenched teeth. Still, at the end of it all was Sawyer, slick and sticky and spent on top of her, kissing her slowly and deeply as she sank back into herself.

Robin drifted even more so than she had on the boat as the rush of orgasm faded, creating space for something she couldn't fight. New feeling seeped in through the cracks of her shattered resolve as she relished the weight of Sawyer to keep from floating away on the new tide building inside of her.

"Boy, when you break a rule, you really break a rule," Sawyer mumbled sleepily, still inside her.

"Rules are made to be broken." She'd delivered the line often enough, and lying there with such flawlessness pressed against her, she was surprised she hadn't broken this one sooner. Then again, it was always easier to justify pushing back on rules other people tried to make for her, rather than ones she set for herself.

As Sawyer slowly eased back and slipped out, she got a stark reminder of why she'd made this one in the first place. She was never going to sate this hunger for them, and she didn't like the empty feeling that accompanied the thought of them not always being there to feed it. She hated not having control of at least her own impulses. She didn't like who she'd become when Sawyer'd cut her off the first time, but clearly, trying to cut herself off hadn't worked any better.

"Uh-oh." Sawyer grabbed the sheet and pulled it over both of them. "I feel like the postcoital cocoon is already shredding. Are you about to fly away?"

"No." Robin sighed. "Sort of the opposite. I don't think what we've been doing is sustainable."

"Which part, the sex or the not having sex?"

"Both, maybe, but for sure the rule about just friends. You and I were never going to be able to keep our hands off each other if left unsupervised."

Sawyer yawned. "You are eminently touchable."

"Likewise, but just because we can't follow a rule doesn't mean it was completely without merit. The last time we started down this path, it got super weird, and I don't want to go back to that to keep having mind-blowing sex."

"Fair." Sawyer seemed even more agreeable when sated. "I'll take responsibility for the lion's share of the awkwardness. I should've handled things better."

Robin felt no inclination to rebut that assessment. "I'll take whatever's left after the lion's share, though, because I kind of went off, which scared me. I do not get weird or hung up about sex."

"I think you got hung up about respect and communication." Sawyer snuggled a little closer. "But you made rules about sex, because sex is easier to control."

"Such bullshit." Robin snuggled in, too. "What if we tried again, though, and instead of forced celibacy, we banned the weirdness."

"I like it," Sawyer said quickly. "And for what it's worth, I think it'll be easier now."

"How so?"

"We've pushed up against our limits. It's not just raw physical compulsions driving us. We've got lives that are more intertwined. I understand how you fought to build your life on your own terms, and you've met my mother. We're not going to accidentally trip those triggers anymore. Besides, I understand the consequences better."

She arched her eyebrows. "The consequences?"

Sawyer propped themself up on one elbow. "Yes, and if the cost of weirdness is not getting to fuck you, I promise to never be weird about anything again."

Robin laughed. "I'm done making promises I can't keep, so I'll make no such vows. I'm inherently weird, and if we have to lie to our friends or sneak around, or worse, if you ghost me again, I'm highly likely to lose my shit. Even that's weird for us. Hell, the fact that we're even having this conversation is weird for me."

"Me too." Sawyer threw an arm around her midriff and pulled her closer. "But we're having it in mutual weirdness. That's how much I want to keep doing what we just did, along with all the other stuff we've been doing. Can't we be like completely normal out in the world and completely freaky in here?"

She shrugged. "That's the question, right? I'm worried we can't, which is why I made the rule in the first place. Ugh, now do you see why no one took me to prom?"

Sawyer kissed her temple. "This is new for me, too. I really hate having conversations like this, but not as much as I hated not getting to see you naked, so for the first time ever, I'm open to figuring things out. Maybe we could lay some new ground rules for going forward."

Robin groaned. "Seeing how good we both are with rules in the first place?"

"Okay, no rules." Sawyer tried again, and their willingness to keep doing so softened Robin's resolve. "How about we keep doing what we've been doing, except now without guardrails?"

"I'm listening."

"Look, we're friends now," Sawyer went on. "We weren't really before. We can talk and joke, hang out, and juggle friendships with other people in our social circle now. We did benefits first, and then we did friendship. It's not the order most folks go with, but when you put them together, we might still have something viable this time."

She nodded. "Instead of friends with benefits, we've got benefits with friendship. Same basic components put together differently. Still chill, fun, relaxed ..."

"Sexy." Sawyer offered as they started to run their hands upward toward Robin's breasts before drawing a lazy circle around one and dipping lower once more. "It's very nonbinary of us, and you know I excel in that arena."

Robin's brain began to settle. "You really do."

"And you're pretty cool on the fluidity acceptance scale, too."

"So into it." Robin liked where this was going. She also liked the way Sawyer's hands felt on her body. "I guess being fluid together couldn't be any harder than what we've been doing."

"Easier, really." Sawyer nuzzled her neck. "If the rules are the problem, why not chuck 'em and see where it leads us?"

It made sense. Then again, with their hands on each other's bodies, everything made sense, but she wasn't at all certain whether that was an argument for more or less touching. She ran her fingernails down the center of Sawyer's chest, watching the skin pebble in anticipation.

More. Definitely an argument for more touching.

"Okay," she whispered.

Sawyer looked up at her, ice-gray eyes regarding her through thick lashes. "Okay?"

"No weirdness, no rules." She ran a hand through their thick hair and pulled them close. She'd always done her best to meet people right where they were, and right now, both she and Sawyer were right here.

There wasn't any place she would rather be.

"Good morning," Gillian said as Robin wandered into the waiting room at work.

"Yeah," she replied as if that were an appropriate or full response. Who needed sleep? She was high on life, or maybe not high so much as pleasantly achy and still floating on an internal sea of postcoital hormones.

She headed straight for the coffee pot and filled her favorite "chaos coordinator" mug, then took her first sip before adding anything or allowing it to cool. It wasn't that she didn't feel the burn so much as she enjoyed the way it drop-kicked her senses. Squeezing her eyes shut for a second, she breathed through the quick flash of pain, then smiled before turning to the others. "Oh, hello."

They stared at her with a mix of concern and amusement. Gillian, the former, and Tegan, the latter, with Brooke, as usual, falling somewhere in between.

"How's everyone doing?" she asked, starting to feel a little … not guilty, but maybe exposed under their inspection.

"I'm great." Tegan grinned. "Care to tell us how you're doing?"

"Or more importantly, if those are the same clothes you left here in yesterday?" Gillian jumped right to the point.

"Oh, are they?" Robin glanced down, not because she didn't know the answer, but because she hadn't given any thought to that particular tell. She shrugged and added it to the long list of things she hadn't given sufficient consideration over the last twelve hours.

"Aren't they?" Gillian turned to the others for confirmation, but Tegan did a poor job of pretending she didn't know.

Brooke held up her hands. "Don't look at me. I wasn't here yesterday."

"And why are you here today?" Robin dodged the original question. "Everything okay?"

"She was dropping me off," Tegan explained, "but since I'm barely going to see her next week when her big conference starts, I dragged her in to steal a few extra minutes."

"Oh yeah, big week?"

"The first of several," Brooke said. "Honestly, I think everything's good. My grad students are fantastic, and all the presenters seem self-sufficient. Aside from managing a bit of conversational awkwardness, I think I'll just have to show up and be present."

"If that's true, it's because of the work you've already put in for weeks to make sure everything runs smoothly." Tegan wrapped her arms around Brooke's waist and pulled her close. "I'll be glad to have you around the house more, either way."

"Not getting tired of the cohabitation then?" Robin figured the longer she kept them talking, the less time they'd have to focus on her.

"Not at all," Tegan said at the same time Brooke said, "Absolutely not."

Then they both smiled at each other, so deeply in love that Robin felt a little voyeuristic watching them, but neither could she look away, or dismiss the pull in the pit of her own stomach toward something familiar and dangerously close to the surface. When Tegan turned back to her, Robin worried she might see it, too.

"What about you?" Brooke asked, as if she'd picked up on something as well.

"What about me?" She tried to choke back a hint of defensiveness.

The others exchanged a quick glance, suggesting she hadn't quite succeeded.

Tegan gave her a polite work smile. "I think we're all trying to be respectful but also dying to ask you the thing."

Her gut clenched, afraid she already knew the answer before asking, "What thing?"

Tegan grinned. "How are you and Sawyer enjoying my old bed?"

Robin groaned.

"What?" Tegan laughed. "Too blunt?"

Brooke held up her thumb and index finger about an inch apart. "Li'l bit, Babe."

"It's Robin. She likes blunt."

"True." Gillian nodded. "Not how I would've phrased it, but you have to admit, it's not uncommon discourse for you."

She couldn't argue.

"Wouldn't you rather have it out there so we can all razz you openly?" Tegan asked.

She would prefer openness, and she'd said as much to Sawyer last night. No more weirdness, that was the rule, the only rule. There was freedom in telling the truth. She just wished she had a better grasp on what the truth was before she explained it to the people she loved most in the world. Instead, she took a deep breath and answered the question she'd been asked rather than the ones she feared might come. "The bed is magnificent. Five stars, totally recommend."

"I knew it!" Tegan turned to Brooke. "I told you they were back at it."

"Back at it?" Gillian asked. "Did I miss a first time?"

Robin grimaced. "There was a thing when Sawyer first got here. Then there wasn't."

"But now there is again?" Brooke asked.

"I mean, there's stuff, but like, not a thing."

"Thanks for clearing that up," Gillian deadpanned.

"You're dating again, though?" Tegan pressed.

"We've never dated, and we still aren't."

Brooke nodded solemnly. "What terms would you use to define the relationship?"

"We're not in a relationship. We just hang out and do stuff together. Sometimes we watch movies or go check out hot spots around town, get dinner together, or hike. Last night, we took the boat out on the lake."

"Right." Gillian looked like she was trying extra hard to control her facial muscles. "Those don't sound like dates at all. So, you're not physically attracted to each other?"

"Of course we are," Robin said in the same tone she would've used if Gillian had asked her if she supported a woman's right to choose. "Have you seen us?"

"Okay." Gillian drew out the word. "Someone else want to take this?"

239

Brooke stepped forward. "So, you and Sawyer go out together and do things just for the two of you to spend time together, and you're attracted to each other, and you've been sleeping together—"

"We didn't sleep together for like, a month."

"You haven't had any sexual contact with them since the first time?" Brooke pressed.

Robin blew out a heavy, steady breath. "It's a gray area."

They all stared at her, clearly waiting for more.

"There was one time I sort of encouraged them to cop a feel at their mom's place, and then last night we did some things, or, you know … all the things."

"Hence yesterday's clothes." Tegan bit her lip as if trying to hold in a smile. "Not so much a gray area as much as, what?"

"A clusterfuck," Gillian mumbled.

"No, it's fine." Robin's voice went up a few octaves as her palms began to sweat. "Everything's totally chill. I promise it's not going to get weird."

"Can we go back to the month where you two didn't sleep together?" Brooke asked calmly. "Did you sleep with anyone else?"

"No," she said quickly, then paused. The realization surprised her. She hadn't purposely held herself back, but she hadn't exactly gone looking either. She could have, but she hadn't. She couldn't even remember the last time someone other than Sawyer had caught her interest.

"Because you didn't have the opportunity to, or because you didn't want to?"

"I always have the opportunity. I make my own opportunities." She shot back before letting the truth of the words settle over her. She could've slept with anyone else, technically, she still could, but she hadn't even thought about doing so.

"And how would you feel if Sawyer slept with someone else?" Brooke continued gently.

She bristled immediately as her brain rebelled at even the question. "I have no right to tell Sawyer what they can or can't—"

"I didn't ask about rights." Brooke kept her tone even in the perfect way that would've been so freaking annoying if it weren't also totally disarming. "I asked how you'd *feel*."

Robin ground her teeth, not wanting to answer, not wanting to consider what her answer would be, but the tension vibrating through her at the process of examining the prospects told her enough to remind her how unhinged she'd felt when Sawyer'd ghosted her the first time. "I would have … feelings."

"Okay, so not neutral?"

Brooke sounded sympathetic enough to make Robin want to scream. "No. Not neutral." Nothing about Sawyer had ever been neutral where she was concerned. "Shit."

"Yeah." Gillian pinched the bridge of her nose. "I can't believe I have to explain this to someone with an advanced degree in marriage and family therapy, but if you regularly go out with someone over the course of several months, and you sleep with them, and you don't sleep with anyone else, and don't want them to either, you are in a relationship."

The skin on the back of her arms and neck stood on end, and a chill worked its way up her spine.

"It could be an unconventional relationship," Tegan offered, as if to soften the blow. "You and Sawyer get to define it, and it sounds like you are, in your own way."

She nodded, trying to push down her rising nausea. "We did talk a bit last night."

"Good," Brooke said with a little too much enthusiasm. "That's something. And you know we'll get on board with whatever you communicate to us. We love you. We'll honor any boundaries you set or rules you'd like followed or terms you feel most comfortable with."

They would. Of course they would, because her friends were perfect, but the fact that any of them had to dance around her relationship preferences freaked her right out. Her relationship preference was not to get into relationships in the first place. Still, nothing they'd said was wrong. She and Sawyer were going out and sleeping together and not with other people, and like it or not, she didn't want to stop feeling what she felt with them. "We decided that neither of us is great with rules or labels or guardrails."

"Great start," Gillian said flatly.

"It is," Brooke said. "You both know yourselves well and respect each other's free spirit."

"Exactly. So, we agreed that we aren't going to do rules anymore." She realized that sounded considerably more shady and less logical than it had in bed last night, so she quickly added, "I mean, we did make one rule though."

"What's that?" Tegan asked.

"We both agreed we aren't going to be weird about it this time. Not with each other, and not with our friends. So, yeah, whatever we do or don't do, or label it or not, we're going to have fun and have sex, and not let any of us make it awkward."

Gillian blew out a breath and stared at the ceiling for a second before saying, "How's that working out so far?"

Everyone burst out laughing.

Robin smiled at her friends as some of the tension slipped away. If any group of people could do this, whatever "this" was, these were the people, her people. "We're getting there."

Tegan threw an arm around Robin's waist and pulled her in. "Talking about it is at least less weird than tiptoeing around it, right?"

She leaned her head on Tegan's shoulder. "Probably."

"Good. Because there's something I've wanted to do for a while now."

"Yeah?" She glanced up at her. "What?"

Tegan grinned and lifted her hand. "High five?"

Robin slapped it as Brooke groaned and Gillian rolled her eyes before saying, "Okay, everybody back to work."

Twenty-Two

Sawyer rang the bell on Brooke's front door, then stepped back and leaned against the porch railing, listening to the muffled voices inside. At just past eleven on a Saturday morning, they didn't have much concern about waking the women inside, more likely they were too introverted to answer the door for fear of having to socially engage with a stranger or salesperson. Sawyer thought about texting to let them off the hook, but since their reason for visiting still felt mildly unsettling, it seemed only fitting for the others to start slightly off-balance, too.

They rang the bell again and smiled at a rustling that suggested someone was at the peephole. A second later, Tegan swung open the door in faded sweats a size too big for her. "Sawyer, what a pleasant eventuality."

They arched an eyebrow at the unusual welcome.

"Normally, I'd say it's a nice surprise," Tegan explained, "but after Robin showed up at work yesterday looking like something the cat dragged in, I figured you'd be around to chat sooner or later."

"Ah." They rubbed a hand on the back of their neck and managed an expression they hoped was more sheepish than pleased with themself. "I hate to be a foregone conclusion."

"Never." Tegan opened the door wider. "After this point, I have no idea what to expect."

"Me either." They stepped inside. "I'm more of the wild ideas and whims kind of person, which is why I came here hoping Brooke, my hopeless planner, might be home."

"Honey," Tegan called down the hallway, "Sawyer's here, and I think they're up to something."

Brooke chuckled and came out of the back in bare feet and carrying a book, as if Sawyer had interrupted the most perfect picture of weekend domestic bliss. Their chest tightened at the memory of Robin snuggled up on their couch a couple of weeks ago. Did some people really live that way all the time?

"Hey you." Brooke gave them a quick hug before turning back to Tegan. "And if Sawyer's here before noon on a Saturday, they're definitely up to something."

"Fun." Tegan headed for the open kitchen. "I'll make more coffee. Talk loud, so I don't miss anything."

Brooke gave them a little nudge, and they headed for the couch. Where Gillian's house was sleek and chic, Brooke's oozed comfort with plenty of pillows, photos, and books around a central fireplace. Sawyer wasted no time sprawling sideways in an overstuffed chair, so their head rested on one arm and their legs dangled over the other.

"To what do we owe this honor?" Brooke took a more conventional position with her hands folded in her lap.

"Not to jump right in or anything, but you know Robin and I have been hanging out?"

Brooke nodded without even the slightest change in her facial expression.

"And we've gotten close over some shared experiences."

Brooke waited patiently, neutrally, and too fucking calmly for Sawyer's tastes.

"Don't do that."

She arched an eyebrow.

"Don't give me your therapist face."

Brooke cracked a smile. "Then don't play games with me. You're sleeping with Robin. You're also going on dates with her even if you don't want to call them that. You're both playing with fire, which is completely consistent with your personalities and part of the reason we love you so much. It's also part of the reason I can't decide if I'm thrilled or terrified about this development, but I don't get a vote, and, honestly,

I'm not sure how I'd vote, or which of you I'd warn about the other because you're both equally amazing and chaotic."

Sawyer stared at her for a minute. "Wow."

"You asked for it."

"I guess." They rubbed their face with their hands, not at all sure they'd wanted what they'd got. It wasn't like they hadn't given a few thoughts to Brooke's points, but hearing them stated so concisely and bluntly didn't do anything to settle their unease.

"We don't have to be careful with each other, Sawyer."

"Okay, sure. I guess if you can have a one-night stand turned workplace affair turned age-gap epic romance, then there's nothing I can do to create shock and awe anymore."

Brooke laughed. "What was I supposed to do? You disappeared. Someone had to be the wild one, and with no one here to play instigator to drama, I had to learn those skills for myself."

"What about Robin?" Sawyer asked. "Isn't she the kind to shake things up?"

"You tell me. How much has she shaken you?"

"We're having a good time together." Sawyer tried to sound casual. "But no one has endangered their professional credentials if that's your new standard."

Brooke shook her head but didn't hide a smile. "You don't have any professional credentials to endanger, but that's not an endorsement for throwing all caution to the wind when it comes to anyone's heart."

"Who said anything about hearts, Brookesy? You know me."

"I do. I know you have more heart than you willingly let people see. I know it's big and closer to the surface and more tender than you'd like. For what it's worth, so is Robin's."

"Yeah." They sighed and stared at the ceiling. "I'm realizing that."

"Is that what you came to talk about?" Brooke asked.

"Not really, but I guess adjacent."

"Adjacent how?" Tegan came back into the room and handed them a mug of coffee with the perfect hint of cream and sugar, just like they liked it. God, these women were detail people, which was why Sawyer had turned to them in the first place.

"Well, you're right, Brookesy, as usual. I'm in a little deeper with Robin than I generally let myself get with women, and I think it's partially because we're all friends. You and Gilly had this preexisting relationship with her, and with me, so all that affection got swept up with a whole lot of attraction and chemistry, and I've dated women before, a lot of women. The woman in Iceland and I worked together for a couple months, and we had fun, but with Robin … I don't know, this sounds stupid—"

"It doesn't," Brooke said calmly. "It sounds really nice."

"It is, and I want to be nice back to her, and not just in bed."

Tegan pressed her lips together as if trying to smother a grin.

"Anyway, I had an idea I'm afraid is kind of sappy, maybe too sappy, but in my head it also feels like it could be quirky, which is more on-brand for Robin and me, but this is all new and I'm feeling … I don't know …"

"Vulnerable?" Brooke asked at the same time Tegan offered, "Exposed?"

"Among other things," Sawyer admitted. "I'm good with women. I kind of know what to do with them even when I don't know anything else. I'm good at wooing. I'm good at extravagant, charming, sexy, appealing vibes. I know what they want and how to give it to them."

Tegan leaned toward Brooke. "Coming out of almost any other person, that statement would've sounded horribly conceited or off-putting, but when they say it, it sounds true."

Then Tegan turned back to Sawyer before continuing, "But, Robin has it, too. I've seen her in action. Which leaves me wondering how either of you can possibly impress someone who plays the game as well as you do. Fascinating. Let's dive in."

Sawyer stared at her for a second before smiling at Brooke, "Okay, I see how this one rocked you out of your professional whatever long enough to remember you're a woman."

Brooke's cheeks colored beautifully. "Way to point those uncomfortable feelings right back at me. I can handle them, though. You're right. Tegan shook me out of some incredibly well-established patterns, and I fought her very hard, but I'm much better for having opened myself up in the end. Are you dancing around a similar experience?"

"Oh no. No. Not the same," Sawyer protested quickly, "nothing quite like that."

And yet, as the three of them sat in a few seconds of silence, Sawyer realized that what they were doing and feeling with Robin might actually be the closest they'd ever come to having that legitimate kind of romantic experience. "I want to do something nice for her."

"Sounds like you've already done some pretty nice things for her," Brooke said.

Sawyer burst out laughing. "High five."

"No," Brooke scolded even though she did crack a smile. "I meant you and Robin have gone out on dates. You've taken her out for ice cream and to dinner."

"Right, but those are small things. Robin and I aren't small people. And, honestly, the things we've shared with each other aren't small things. I want something bigger, something more."

"More than what?"

"More than we do with other people." The words were out before Sawyer fully understood all their implications, and they rushed to say something else so they wouldn't have to examine that impulse any further. "Robin never went to prom."

"What?" Brooke asked.

"Or homecoming, or anything really. She missed out on all those experiences because she was too queer, too soon. And I went through them all, but not as queer. I went with a guy in a dress. I mean, the guy wasn't in a dress, I was." The thought overwhelmed them for a moment, and they clenched their jaw against the memories threatening to overtake them. "Anyway, Robin suggested that maybe I hadn't really gone to homecoming or prom either. Maybe someone else posing as me had. She said it better, but she helped me think about things differently."

"Sounds like an amazing reframe," Brooke said, her voice and her eyes both full of sympathy.

"Yeah, well she's done that a few times, helped me view an old thing in a whole new way, and I'd really like to do the same for her if I can."

Tegan leaned forward. "You have ideas?"

"A few." They shrugged. "I'm kind of a big idea person, but pretty much everyone I know will tell you I'm not as great with the follow-through."

"Which is why you came here." Brooke smiled. "I'm so glad."

"Me too," Tegan said. "Are we all about to rewrite some narratives?"

Sawyer laughed lightly. "I just wanted to ask a girl to prom, but if we can do both, I'm in."

"Summer might be short around here, but it sure is glorious." Sawyer lifted their sunglasses from the bridge of their nose and slid them up to the top of their head to get an unfiltered view of Delaware Park. A jewel in the crown of Buffalo's glory days, the park and its extensive parkways sprawled through the city like lush, green tentacles shaping the flow of traffic and the tenor of neighborhoods. Today they'd chosen a spot in the shade not far from the zoo. Every now and then, amid the sounds of birdsong and playing children, they could make out the bark of sea lions in the distance.

Robin rolled over on one of the picnic blankets Brooke and Gillian had brought, looking up at them through the lattice of sun and shade cast from the trees overhead. "Your hair is glorious like that, all pushed back and cool."

They shrugged. "What can I say? I'm doomed to perfection."

"You bear your burden with grace and poise."

They laughed, but Tegan said, "She's not wrong. The picnic, the spot, the company, you just wished the perfect afternoon into existence."

"My manifestation game is strong," Sawyer said, "but I had help. I didn't even know anyone made legit picnic baskets anymore, much less had them sitting around already filled with red-and-white checkered blankets."

Now it was Brooke's turn to shrug. "I like cute things."

"Lucky me." Tegan gave her a quick kiss on the cheek. "Why have we never done this before if we had all the stuff waiting to be called into service?"

"Because Sawyer wasn't here," Gillian said matter-of-factly as she stretched her long legs across the grass. "We've been all work and no play."

"Speak for yourself," Robin said. "I play a lot, and I always invite you."

"No, you invite us to adventure, and we love you for that, but it's much easier to say 'no' to a leap out of an airplane than it is a relaxing day in the shade."

"That has not been my lived experience," Sawyer said. "I love skydiving, but y'all are like frogs. Robin, if you just drop them into a pot of boiling water, they'll hop right out. You have to ease them into a nice, warm bath and then slowly turn up the heat."

"Gilly, are we getting cooked in this rather unflattering analogy?" Brooke asked.

"I think we are, and now I'm nervous. What are you buttering us up for, Sawyer?"

They laughed. "Nothing too dastardly, I promise. Actually, I think you, in particular, will be inclined to enjoy my next escalation."

They grabbed a small backpack from the ground behind them and emptied a football into the space between. "What do you say, Ivy League? You got any game left in you?"

Gillian's smile spread slowly, confirming Sawyer had pushed exactly the right button. "Enough game to flatten you."

"No tackling," Brooke said quickly.

"Two-hand touch," Sawyer offered, then with a suggestive grin added, "and I plan to touch Robin a lot."

"Of course you do." Gillian rolled her eyes as she hopped up. "You and Tegan against me and Robin. Brooke can be referee and cheerleader."

"God bless you." Brooke relaxed. "I do not want to play sportsball of any kind."

"We all know this." Sawyer stood and extended a hand to Robin to pull her up. By the time Tegan joined them, Gillian was already marking out the boundaries of their makeshift field and shouting out random rules, like a five-second audible count before rushing the passer, and four downs to cover the length of the field.

Tegan leaned a little closer. "Do either of you know the language she's speaking, or is this just an excuse to get sweaty and roll around in public?"

"Little bit of both," Robin said evenly. "She's going to throw the ball four times. I'm going to try to catch it. You two will try to fuck things up. Then we'll switch sides."

"Works for me."

They lined up right where Gillian told them, and she whispered a few things to Robin.

Tegan glanced at Sawyer. "They're making plans. We don't have plans. Shouldn't you tell me a plan?"

Sawyer winked at her. "You know the main plan, but for right now, count to five out loud and then charge your boss."

"What?" Tegan asked. "Hitting my boss was not part of the main plan."

"Think of it as a bonus."

"Break!" Gillian called.

"Not a bonus," Tegan complained. "Why don't you take Gillian, and I'll cover Robin?"

Sawyer shook their head. "Robin's mine."

Then everything sprang into motion. Robin snapped the ball to Gillian, then took off running. She was fast, so fast it caught Sawyer off guard, or maybe they were merely caught flat-footed by the sight of her, strong, powerful, and so freaking sexy as she moved. Either way, she put plenty of distance between them before Sawyer found it in themself to sprint after her while Tegan counted loudly behind them. She didn't make it to five before Gillian launched the ball with predictable zing and accuracy. Robin caught it neatly and pulled it to her chest while she streaked into the makeshift end zone.

"Shit," Sawyer mumbled.

"How's that for game?" Gillian called as Robin did a victory dance.

"Was that bad?" Tegan laughed. "I think that was bad for us."

Sawyer nodded but couldn't manage any frustration with Robin still laughing as she walked back toward midfield.

"Beat that, you bums." She tossed the ball lightly to Sawyer.

"You got one," Sawyer said. "Don't get cocky."

Robin waggled her eyebrows. "That's not what you said last night."

They snickered as everyone lined up again.

"Do we have a plan this time?" Tegan asked.

"I don't know. Can you catch like that?"

"Doubt it," Tegan admitted.

Sawyer leaned over and whispered, "Hand me the ball, then run to the right. I'll toss it gently, then try to block for you."

"Deal."

To her credit, Tegan was no slouch in the speed department either. She took off, and Sawyer did their best to get between

251

her and the other team, but Gillian took every bit of their attention, and Robin darted after the ball, landing both hands on Tegan's back after about ten yards of forward progress.

"Good job, T-Bone." Robin patted her on the back as they lined up again.

"Same play?" Tegan asked.

"No, they're expecting that. This time, run straight out for ten steps, then turn around and come right back toward me."

Tegan nodded, and they broke forward once more. This time, Robin caught up with Tegan, but blew past her when she reversed course, and Sawyer managed to get a soft toss to her the second before Gillian rushed at them. Tegan made it past midfield before Robin got back to her.

"That was fun," Tegan called, then turned to Brooke. "This is fun, Babe. You should try."

"No, thank you," Brooke called, "but I do enjoy watching you."

Tegan blew her a kiss, then turned back to Sawyer. "Third down?"

"Sneak play," they whispered. "You hand the ball to me, then run straight at them, but pretend like you're stuck while I run around you."

Tegan nodded. "Love it."

The play started well enough. Tegan snapped the ball then charged right at Gillian, who did seem caught off guard enough for Sawyer to take off around her, but Robin wasn't fooled and chased quickly on their heels. They made it only a few yards before strong hands caught them on the waist.

"Two hands," Brooke called.

Sawyer shook their head. "I do love a fast woman."

Robin slapped their backside. "And I love chasing that ass of yours."

The others joined them, either oblivious to the foreplay or choosing to ignore it.

"They still have a long way to go," Gillian called to Robin. "They'll need a long ball."

Robin nodded. "Switch."

Gillian arched an eyebrow.

"Trust me," Robin said emphatically. "I've got the QB this time, you take T-Rex."

Gillian shrugged and looked at Tegan. "I will flatten you."

"Weirdly aggressive." Tegan grimaced, then turned to Sawyer. "I'm going to run really fast away from her."

Sawyer laughed. "Works for me."

The ball snap went smoothly enough, and Tegan did, in fact, take off with a new jolt of speed, but Robin stayed close at the line, "Hey, SSB."

Sawyer made eye contact with her, which was a mistake. She looked like a lion about to absolutely devour its prey, but instead of making them nervous, it made them hot.

"One. Two, I'm about to top you. Three ..."

Sawyer glanced up to see Tegan already in the end zone, but Gillian all over her. They'd waited too long. The only chance they had to score was to run for it.

"Four, wanna bottom for me ..."

They laughed, concentration fully broken now. Besides, they'd had worse offers.

"Five." Robin charged, but not with two hands. They launched their whole body into the blow, hitting Sawyer and wrapping her arms around them as they both stumbled back, then down. Sawyer landed with a thud, immediately followed by the weight of Robin's amazing body atop them.

"Foul," Brooke called in the distance. "Roughing the passer, or something like that."

"The passer likes it rough," Robin called as she straddled Sawyer's hips. "Don't you, Boo?"

Sawyer stared up at her, very much liking whatever was happening.

"It's still a penalty," Gillian called with a mix of annoyance and amusement.

"A penalty?" Robin bit her lower lip as if she didn't mind the idea at all. "Does that mean you have to punish me now?"

"Probably." Sawyer's voice sounded a little breathy from both the weight of their arousal and the woman on top of them. "Do I get to choose the method? Because I have an idea."

"Seems only fitting." Robin ground down a little harder, and their brain started to short-circuit. The only thing keeping Sawyer from blanking completely was the sound of their friends approaching. If they were going to do this, now was as good a moment as any. Then with the question on the tip of their tongue, they got hit with a wave of nervousness, so silly and juvenile, but for some reason, it mattered, and they wanted to do it right. They needed it not to be a joke or made light by the situation or played off as a penalty. Their palms started to sweat, which hadn't happened to them around women in years, or maybe ever.

"What's wrong?" Robin asked, clearly reading the change in their expression.

"Nothing." They said the word, and it hit them how true it felt. "Nothing's wrong, and that's awesome. It's kind of been a long time for me since nothing was wrong, and I owe a lot of that to you."

Robin's whole body softened, but she made no move to get off them.

"And since you've helped me rewrite a lot of things, or at least look at them differently, I think the natural conclusion for this football game is for you to go to prom with the quarterback."

Robin stared at them for a minute, confusion clouding her features. "What?"

"Go to a school dance with me. I'm asking you." They blew out a breath. "Not smoothly, but here, in front of our friends, at the sportiest event I could summon, would you like to go to a school dance with me?"

Robin laughed, but clearly not at them, a sound of real joy that shook Sawyer's core, both literally and figuratively. "Sounds weirdly wonderful, and I don't know how, but, um ... yeah."

"Yeah?" Sawyer's hopes and voice rose.

"Yes." Robin folded down and kissed them. "Yes. I would very much like to go to a school dance with you."

Twenty-Three

"Damn, girl." Tegan froze mid hair-pinning to stare at Robin as she stepped into the living room of her apartment.

"Yeah?" she asked, but she already knew the answer. The dress fit her like a glove, a very sexy glove. Black and slinky like a shimmery second skin, its velvet trim cut low enough in the bust to show a hint of cleavage without giving too much away. Hugging her hips and flaring ever so slightly, it cut off abruptly around midthigh. High school Sawyer might not have known what they wanted back then, but this dress showed they'd always had an instinct for the stylish, a quality that transcended gender and identity every bit as much as the person who'd clearly put a great deal of thought into making this evening everything their younger selves had been denied.

Everything had been planned down to who would get ready together, when and where, with Robin and Tegan paired up at her place, and with Gillian at her condo. Brooke was already at work, which apparently was where they'd meet her later, though many of the finer details had been held close to the vest.

Tegan took Robin's hand and gave her a little twirl. "That dress is pure fire. Did you buy it for the occasion?"

"No." She smoothed it over her body just to enjoy the feel. "Sawyer bought it for me a long time ago."

Tegan's eyebrows shot up, as if trying to make sense of the statement.

Robin waved her off. "Don't try to do the math."

"Fine, math and I have a tenuous relationship anyway. Should I chalk it up to the rewriting of history we're all doing tonight?"

"Very much part of those revisions."

"Then I'm glad you're getting that chance, and I know Sawyer is, too."

Robin smiled at the memory of them asking her out last weekend. She'd replayed it in her mind at least a hundred times, from the cocky grin to the hesitation and the sweetness that had edged in at the last second. It was almost as though Sawyer had been nervous, or maybe just intent on doing this right, and the hint of something so earnest had caught her off guard in the most wonderful way. Robin had always been one to seek her thrills on the physical end of the spectrum, but seeing Sawyer search and strive and open themselves up produced a rush in her, similar to a free fall.

"So," Tegan said tentatively as she went back to pinning her hair. "Things are getting serious this time around?"

"No," Robin said quickly, then caught herself. "I mean, we're still having tons of fun together."

"I didn't mean 'serious' as in 'solemn.' I meant 'serious' as in 'significant.' Meaningful relationships can be fun, should be fun, and, honestly, with you and Sawyer, I can't imagine anything not being fun."

"So much fun. And yeah, meaningful, too. We really get each other, but I haven't had time to dwell on that because we're having a blast like, several times a week, and not only in bed, though no complaints there either."

"And you two have been seeing each other exclusively, either by design or desire, for a couple of months now?"

Had they? Her chest tightened, suggesting she'd known that deep down. "Everything kind of snuck up on me. We see each other a lot, but it doesn't feel like too much. Two months? Shit, that's a new record for me."

"Really?" Tegan inserted the last strand into place. "How do I look?"

"Sheer perfection." Robin scanned the light pink dress with a shimmery overlay, down to Tegan's toes, painted to match, peeking out from strappy sandals. "Brooke's going to melt when you walk in."

"That's the goal. She's been working on this conference for weeks. I know she's tired, but I'm hoping to pep her up a bit when we crash this after-party. Hey, wait though." She tilted her head to the side. "Is this thing with Sawyer really your longest relationship, or just the longest in recent years?"

Robin sighed, not sure she wanted to focus on the question, but it wasn't exactly a hard one to figure. "Ever."

Tegan's hazel eyes widened. "Even when you were young? There was never a high school or college sweetheart who made you all angsty, writing names together on notebooks or shattering your tiny heart when they sat with some other girl at lunch?"

Robin laughed. "Doesn't the prom night redo tell you that there was never a high school sweetheart? And in college, I went right from nerdom to glow-up. I was not about to settle too soon when I finally had the option to play the field, which segued right into the wild woman you know and love today."

"Okay. I wouldn't change anything about the journey that made you into your current awesomeness. I want you to be happy. You deserve all of that, in all the ways."

Robin tried to brush off the sincerity. "I am happy, and, honestly, I've always enjoyed my life. It's not like I've been sitting around pining for a relationship."

"I know, but I'm wondering how it feels to realize you've ended up in one anyway, and you're kind of loving it."

She laughed again, this time a hint of nervousness kicking in. "Honestly, Teegs, I haven't felt any sort of way, because I haven't been thinking about it nearly as much as you clearly have."

"Fine." Tegan shook her head. "Then go with the flow. Your accept-things-exactly-how-they-are vibe is totally on-brand. I'm just super impressed, because I couldn't do it. I was right where you are at this time last year, at least emotionally, and I overthought every damn detail to the point of obsession."

"What's to overthink?" Robin grinned. "It's not like I'm one of Sawyer's supervising clinicians or anything."

Tegan rolled her eyes. "Even when we took that out of the mix, I still did a ton of back-and-forth about whether Brooke really liked me enough to take risks. Then again, I guess you don't have to worry about that either, what with Sawyer asking you to prom, then creating a prom specifically for you, then getting you that dress all those years ago somehow and …" Tegan's voice trailed off as she glanced out the big bay window in the front of the apartment. "Oh my God, did they just pull up in a limo?"

Robin walked to the front of the house and stared down at the street below to confirm a sleek, black limousine had, in fact, pulled up out front, drawing the attention of several of her neighbors. She covered her mouth. Normally, something so ostentatious and formal would instantly earn her ire, but the queerest of nonbinary princes rolling up on the west side of Buffalo like some *Pretty Woman* cosplay held enough irony to offset the over-the-top display. Of course, Sawyer wouldn't know how to do it any other way.

Tegan clutched Robin's shoulder. "Did you know this was happening?"

She shook her head and bit her lower lip to hold her smile in check.

"Okay," Tegan said with a hint of the forced calm she usually reserved for work. "I think we can strike questions about how much Sawyer likes you off the list of things to worry about."

Robin's grin finally broke through. "See, nothing to obsess about."

Tegan made a little noise she couldn't decipher, nor could she tear her gaze from the window as Sawyer climbed out of the limo wearing a black tuxedo, vest, and tie with their hair pushed back into feathery waves. They headed toward the house with the confidence that had to come from knowing they looked like a sapphic wet dream.

Robin swallowed her arousal and took an extra-long inhale to get oxygen to her brain as all the blood in her body headed south. She felt a little lightheaded when she heard footsteps on the stairs. Was she in danger of swooning?

"Breathe," Tegan encouraged. "Everyone has to keep their pretty clothes on for a few hours, okay?"

"That obvious?"

"Totally," Tegan said, "and good for you."

She laughed, the sound more natural as she came back to herself. "I'm fine. No overthinking, even with naughty thoughts. We're cool."

Tegan gave a low whistle. "Then you're a superior human, truly the best among us."

Footsteps fell on the landing, and Robin moved toward the door. "I don't know what you're talking about."

"You're a pillar of strength, because with someone as good-looking and smooth as Sawyer, the only thing I'd have left to worry about is getting my heart broken."

Robin faltered.

They were having fun. They were getting close. They were just getting started, even if they'd already gone further together than she ever had with anyone else. Why would someone worry about getting hurt at a time like this? Except now that Tegan had mentioned it, her heart was beating awfully fast, and maybe, as if to prove a point, it skipped a beat when Sawyer knocked.

And damned if it didn't expand enough to press on her ribs as she opened the door to this perfect human, sexy, cool, confident, and sweetly holding out a corsage like some sort of offering.

Sawyer smiled broadly, unguarded and unreserved, and yeah, okay, the sight of them, so open, hopeful, and handsome, did all sorts of things to her heart.

If Sawyer had the power to alter it, did that mean they also had the power to break it?

Sawyer opened the door to the limo and then held it for everyone else to exit before extending a hand to Robin, who slipped hers into it, enjoying even the most casual of touches. "You ready for your first school dance?"

Robin glanced around the college campus and up to the academic building ahead of them. "When you said school, you weren't kidding. Are we breaking in again?"

They pulled her close, wrapping an arm around her waist. "I know how much that turns you on, but no. Brooke has us on the up-and-up ... mostly."

"I'm not sure I appreciate being legitimized against my will, but after that dinner, I can hardly doubt your judgment."

They'd had an amazing meal at Cornelia inside Buffalo's most prestigious art gallery, where everything on their plates had rivaled the masterpieces on the wall.

"I'm not sure how I can dance after a meal like that," Tegan agreed. "You outdid yourself, Sawyer."

"Nah. We're only getting started. Right, Gilly?"

Gillian shrugged. "You know I'm inclined to be suspicious, but dinner impressed me."

"The dinner or the waitress?" Robin teased. "She practically tripped all over herself trying to give you extra-special attention."

Gillian rolled her eyes, but her lips quirked up.

"Would you blame her?" Tegan bumped Gillian's shoulder with her own. "You look hot in that suit."

"Rawr." Robin gave a little growl and ran her fingernails down the sleeve of their boss's ruby-and-gold jacket, barely resisting the urge to muss the copper hair she'd pulled into a sweeping updo for the evening. "Cougar on the prowl."

"I'm trying to be a good sport tonight," Gillian warned, "but don't forget who signs the paychecks."

Sawyer laughed. "Not mine, Gilly Bean. And therefore, I fully expect you to start the grind pit at this soiree."

Gillian's eyes narrowed. "The what?"

"Oh look, there's our sign." Tegan pointed to a placard with the words "Closing Ceremonies – University Conference on Modern Research in Family Systems."

"So sexy." Robin laughed. "Everything I always wanted in a prom theme."

Sawyer opened the door with a flourish. "Our theme for tonight is 'Revisionist History.'"

"Love it." Robin kissed them quickly as she passed and stepped into the conference room. At first glance, it looked like any other professional event she'd attended, full of round tables and middle-aged professionals sporting business attire under fluorescent lights, but it didn't take much of a second glance to notice several discordant details. Balloons and streamers hung in almost every corner, and a silver, selfie backdrop dominated one wall near a refreshment table featuring a tray of sweets alongside a large punch bowl. In the middle of the room, several tables had been removed, creating an open space except for one large speaker and a small spotlight, presumably to serve as a dance floor, though no one was using it. Scattered around the room were tabletop centerpieces and decorations made from the same lilies in Robin's corsage. Her heart swelled, pushing on her rib cage in the disconcerting way she'd started to associate with Sawyer.

"I couldn't get them to put up a flowery archway for us." Sawyer leaned close enough for their lips to almost brush Robin's ear, then opened the flap of their tuxedo coat to reveal a silver flask. "I am about to spike the punch though."

"Just like every prom movie I've ever seen. You're playing on all my high school fantasies."

"Don't worry. The fantasies won't stop at PG-13 tonight." They winked at her and made a beeline for the refreshments.

She turned to find Brooke making a fuss over Tegan before expanding her attention to include Robin. "What do you think?"

"I can't believe you did all this."

"I didn't. I merely let Sawyer crash the tail end of the conference."

"That's still awfully rule-breaky for your tastes."

"A little bit, but, honestly, anyone who's still at an official function at 8:00 on a Saturday night could probably use a little pick-me-up, which is why I let Sawyer add the speaker and event lighting."

As if on cue, the overhead lights dimmed and the music switched from a low instrumental piece to The Black Eyed Peas' "I Gotta Feeling."

Everyone glanced up to see Sawyer wielding an iPhone playlist with a wicked grin. Brooke seemed to hold her breath for a second as the last of her conference attendees processed the tone switch, but when most of them began to smile or nod along to the beat, she exhaled. "See, it's fine. Everything's fine. I'm not worried at all."

Gillian laughed. "How many times did you tell yourself that this week?"

"So many, but if Maura crashes in demanding to know what's going on, I already have a mental speech prepared about how we're doing reexposure exercises centered on healing adolescent trauma."

Tegan wrapped an arm around her waist. "Babe, you're so sexy when you use work talk to bolster the rebellion."

Gillian pinched the bridge of her nose. "I'm going to need more than one flask in that punch bowl to get through tonight."

"Sorry, my rebellion didn't carry that far, but …" Brooke pointed to a lone university employee standing behind a drinks cart in the opposite corner. "I did keep the cash bar for the initial mixer open an extra half hour for you."

"That's why you're my favorite," Gillian said before heading that way with new purpose in her step.

The evening took off from there.

Several conference attendees stayed and a few even joined in as Sawyer and Robin warmed up the dance floor, but for the most part, their group stayed close and light, laughing and joking easily with one another, loose and comfortable.

It wasn't too long before everyone ended up dancing together, as even Gillian couldn't resist a little bit of Britney Spears' "Womanizer."

"What a fun song to play in a room full of marriage and family therapists," Sawyer noted.

Robin snorted softly. "Not that we don't share multiple spheres of experience when it comes to women."

Tegan gave Brooke a little twirl. "Some of us are infinitely more experienced than others."

Robin shook her head playfully. "I'd take you more seriously if your girl wasn't currently organizing conferences to escape the ethics conflict you induced with your hotness."

Gillian laughed outright. "I mean, it's not funny, but it's kind of funny."

Sawyer waggled their eyebrows. "And Ivy League's tipsy … just like prom night."

"Hey, you're rewriting yours, I'm reliving mine." Gillian grinned lazily. "Some of us came out early."

"That's why you're the boss of us," Brooke said. "Always one step ahead of the crowd."

The song came to a close, shifting to something softer and slower, as Gillian eased back. "Exactly, which is why I'm stepping away from this sappy song."

Robin inclined her ear to make out the opening strains of a Bruno Mars ballad as Sawyer turned to her. "Ready for your first prom-style slow dance?"

A little flutter flitted through her stomach. "I would say I was born ready, but given that I'm over thirty years old, I guess it's better-late-than-never territory."

"I'll be a gentle teacher … at first." Sawyer pulled her close, bringing their bodies flush and instantly increasing the temperature in the room by a solid ten degrees. The two of them moved beautifully together, which wasn't exactly breaking news, but Robin still let herself enjoy confirming that the trait extended outside of the bedroom, or boat deck.

Sawyer held her close and breathed deeply. "God, you even smell amazing. Are you irresistible in every single way?"

"I do what I can."

Sawyer's hands dropped lower to the small of her back. "It's working."

A smile tugged at her lips. "Is this how you danced at prom?"

They took a step back and guided her arms around their neck before placing their own lightly on her hips. "This is how I danced at prom. Gotta leave enough room for the Holy Spirit to move between you."

"Did you go to a religious school?"

"With my mother, the psychologist?" They laughed. "No, thankfully. That's one trauma she didn't pass down. I just liked to keep a healthy distance between me and boys. I may've looked the part, but I was not about to touch any parts, if you know what I mean."

"Good to have boundaries, Boo, but we don't have to do everything exactly like high school."

Sawyer's eyes smoldered as their fingers tightened on her waist and drew her close once more. "Absolutely not. We're here to do it all differently."

They were all over and against each other at once, slow, sexy, sensual, moving in time together with the same unspoken intuition that'd guided them to each other from the beginning. There was something effortless about the magnetic pull of their bodies, but Robin never lost track of the fact that Sawyer had put a lot of effort into making this moment possible. "This means a lot to me."

"This?" Sawyer rolled their hips and nuzzled her neck, filling her senses with sandalwood and the memory of sex.

"Yeah," she mumbled, then shook her head. "I mean, obviously, but also everything else. No one's ever done anything like create a prom for me. I'd never even thought to want something like this evening, or any of the evenings that preceded it. You've raised the bar by a lot. I don't even know what meaning to attach to that realization, but I'm enjoying every bit of it."

"I'm so glad you're having a good time."

"I am, but it's more than just fun. It matters, you matter, and you make me feel like I matter, which of course I do. I never doubted that, but you're making me feel those things in new ways. You're making me feel a whole lot of new things, honestly."

Sawyer kissed her temple, the tenderness combining with the sensuality of their physical connection proving the point she was trying, somewhat inarticulately, to make. "I know what you mean."

She arched back enough to search their gray eyes. "Do you?"

They nodded. "I swear. I may've pulled tonight together, but it was really your idea, or at least your inspiration."

"Say more."

Their muscles tightened slightly against her body, and for a second, Robin worried she'd triggered something, but Sawyer forged on. "That day at my mother's, you took a memory that had haunted me for more than a decade and seamlessly rewrote it, and not just by letting me get straight to third base without a preamble."

"That was a bonus."

"The cherry on top of an ingenious reworking of how I viewed myself or a version of myself in the world. You took something that felt shameful and made it your special blend of sweet and sexy and smart. You made me think it could be done with other memories, too, or maybe even in the present."

She nodded, brushing her cheek against their shoulder. "I think that's happening here. We're rewriting the past, but it's changing the way I think about myself right now, too."

"Just now?" Sawyer asked softly, "or maybe, if changing the way we look at the past changes the way we live in the moment, does that, by all terrifying and exhilarating logic, suggest we might look differently at the …"

"Future." Robin managed to say the word with a little shiver.

"It's not a thing I talk about with women," Sawyer said. "The future is always a fluid concept, a grand hypothetical amid a whole slew of other fluid concepts in my life and identity."

"Good," Robin whispered. "I like fluid. I like evolving. I like, well, you."

Sawyer leaned back enough to stare into her eyes once more. "I like you too, Robin, so much that the word 'like' feels insufficient, but I don't want to ever make you any promises I'm not sure I know how to keep."

She stared back at them, hoping Sawyer could see the deep understanding and all those same emotions mirrored in her eyes. "I've never asked you to make promises. I've never offered any of my own."

"I know," Sawyer whispered, "but I want you to know I think you deserve them, and that's made me want to figure out if I'm the kind of person who could make them. I guess tonight was my first step."

Her heart gave her ribs a little kick. "How's it working out for you?"

Sawyer smiled. "Pretty sure I nailed it."

"God, I do love it when you get cocky." She laughed and ran her hand up into the back of their hair before giving it a little tug. "But the night's not over yet. If you really want to fulfill all my prom fantasies, you've got one more thing you have to nail."

Sawyer's grin turned sly. "What's that?"

"Me."

Twenty-Four

"Oh my God, Sawyer." Robin tugged on their hair and reached fruitlessly for their shoulder before grasping their tie and giving it a weak pull.

"Yes?" They grinned up at her wickedly.

Robin slouched down on the seat of the limo, wrecked and sexy, with her hips tilted forward and her dress pushed up around her waist. Her dark hair was down, and several strands stuck to the beads of sweat on her neck. "You know."

"I know what?"

She laughed lightly. "Everything."

Sawyer's heart, head, and several other places swelled at the assertion, not because they believed it, but because they loved that Robin did. Smart, quick, gorgeous, adventurous Robin, who met every moment and person with the same zest and passion and openness. She'd been perfect all night, and well into the morning. They'd dropped the others off around 1 a.m., then rolled up the window separating them from the limo driver, and Sawyer had been ravishing her ever since. They'd lost track of time, and the number of times they'd pulled back like this, sitting on their knees only far enough that Robin couldn't thrust up to meet their mouth on her own. Not that she seemed to have the energy anymore.

Sawyer hadn't intended to bring such a relentless edging game to their little prom play, but they couldn't control the urge to drag this out. They didn't want anything about this night to end. They'd withheld Robin's orgasm, not on some power trip, but out of sheer greed to keep living between her splayed knees. They wanted this woman shattered, wet, and panting against them always. They wanted to get drunk on her taste and delirious on her scent and never sober up. Not letting her climax was just the beginning. They wanted more, they wanted everything, from wrecking her tonight to waking up with her tomorrow morning, to going out for breakfast and a slow walk along the lakeshore, then catching a flight only to jump from the plane in tandem. Sawyer wanted to ride roller coasters of their own making, then crash right back into bed with her.

"Please." Robin tugged on their tie again. "I'm no good to you if I pass out."

The logic was as flawless as the woman herself, and Sawyer's desire to do this all night clashed against the compulsion to give Robin everything she wanted.

Leaning forward once more, they buried themself between trembling thighs and followed the cues of her body as it climbed one more time. When every part of her vibrated against them, Sawyer stifled the urge to pull back and, instead, allowed them both to press forward.

Robin cried out, gasped, shook, and released a string of incoherent words. Still, Sawyer continued, varying pace and pressure, but not resistance, until Robin crashed, so limp she nearly slid off the seat completely.

Sawyer caught her around the waist and lifted her gently before turning them both sideways, so they lay, spent and sweaty, against each other. Sawyer relished the weight of Robin sprawled half on top of them in a rumpled dress that had always been meant for her. Maybe Sawyer had been meant for her, too.

Something in their brain tried to rebel at the idea, but then again, their brain felt so far away and hard to hear amid all the amazing things happening in their body. The thought rolled through like the road beneath the wheels of the limo and passed as quickly as the faint glow of streetlamps outside deeply tinted windows.

"You cannot tell me what you did there was anything like a real prom night," Robin finally said.

They smiled up at the ceiling. "I mean, probably not the details. I doubt any high school students ever had the skill or the willpower to do the job so thoroughly, but at least conceptually, it works, because every guy I know tried to get laid on prom night."

"You more than tried there, Champ." Robin kissed their neck. "I'm completely wasted, and not from whatever you put in the punch."

"I wanted to do things right tonight. Your first prom is a big deal. Opportunities like this don't come around often."

"Once," Robin said sleepily. "A girl loses her promginity only once."

"Promginity." Sawyer snorted softly. "Thanks for trusting me with yours."

"Thanks for wanting the honor enough to work for it."

Sawyer pulled her tightly to their chest. "You're worth it, Robin, and so much more."

"More from you? I like the sound of that." Robin yawned.

"But can the next round be in a real bed? This back seat business is for teenagers."

Robin laughed. "Fair, even with a back seat this big."

Sawyer pressed the call button, then asked the driver to head back to their apartment. "You'll stay with me tonight?"

She nodded against their chest. "As if I have the strength to go anywhere else."

"Don't worry. I'll help you right out of that dress and into my bed."

The limo slowed, and Sawyer helped them both sit up. Thankfully, their clothes were askew but not missing, and there was little left to collect when they pulled to a stop in the sleepy streets of predawn Buffalo.

Sawyer helped Robin out and kept one arm around her while thanking and tipping the driver, both to help her stay upright, and because they simply didn't want to let go yet. Then the two of them staggered to the door and up the stairs. They laughed as they bumped into each other and the wall. "No one's going to believe we're not drunk."

"We're kind of drunk." Robin pulled them close enough to kiss. "Not on the booze so much as the intoxicants of us."

"Poetic." Sawyer fished in the pocket of their tuxedo pants for the keys, but as they reached the landing, Brooke opened the door.

They froze, trying to make that make sense. This was still their apartment, right? Had Tegan decided to take it back? Had they missed a surprise party? So many questions. Instead, they simply said, "Hey."

Brooke smiled, but the expression held no joy, only sadness, maybe pity, and plenty of concern.

"What's wrong?" Robin snapped upright. "Where's Tegan?"

"She's at your house. We weren't sure where you two would go. We've been trying to call for hours."

"My phone's dead." Sawyer said the last word with dread. "Where's Gillian?"

"She's fine. Well, she's safe, but she's at the hospital with your mother."

"My mother?" Sawyer ran a hand over their face, trying to scrub away the haze, but only caught the scent of Robin on their fingers and stifled the urge to fall back into her.

"They think it was a heart attack," Brooke continued. "She's going to need surgery soon. Maybe now. Sawyer, it's not great."

They nodded, slowly, trying to buy time, hoping that it would make sense in a minute, but it didn't. They stood there on the landing, Brooke in front of them, eyes full of compassion, Robin with a gentle hand on their back, Sawyer completely unable to figure out how they'd got here. For the first time ever, they'd just wanted to stay where they were, how they were, with the woman they'd clung to. How had that all been taken so quickly, replaced by a twitchingly familiar compulsion? It ran up every limb and along their spine, like ants or an electrical current. They clenched their jaw, willing it to subside, but the tighter they wound their muscles, the deeper the feeling worked, coiling around their throat.

271

They had to say something, now, before they lost the ability to do so. They spit out the only words, the only thought they could process. "I have to go."

"I'll drive you to the hospital," Brooke said quickly.

That hadn't been what they'd meant. They hadn't even for a second considered running toward the problem, but somehow the steady certainty Brooke always brought seemed worth borrowing.

"Okay." Their voice sounded far away to their own ears.

"Do you want me to go?" Robin asked softly.

They shook their head.

They didn't want Robin to go anywhere, ever. It was one of the few things they knew for sure, and it gave them the strength to say as much, to ask her to do the one thing they'd never been able to do for themself.

"Please, just stay."

Sawyer scanned the room numbers along the walls of Buffalo General Medical Center, partially hoping they never found the right one. Then maybe none of this would be real, and they'd wake up to find they'd merely dozed off in the back of the limo with Robin. Instead, the bustle got busier as they entered the cardiac wing. Brooke caught their arm and guided them around a corner. Sawyer didn't know if they felt more grateful or annoyed. Maybe they didn't want to go the right way, maybe they wanted to run. No, not maybe. They did, but they couldn't. Or they could, but leaving town wouldn't mean just getting away from the familiar aches and insufficiencies this time, it would mean leaving Robin behind when the scent of her still filled their senses.

"Hey." Gillian stepped out of an open door and pulled Sawyer into a hug. "How're you doing?"

They shook their head, not able to fully process the question. "Robin's back at my apartment."

"Good," Gillian whispered.

"How's Maura?" Brooke asked as Gillian stepped back.

"Lucid, calm, but there's a tremor to her I've never seen before. She's still got opinions, though. She's already asked the surgeon to cite his studies twice. Physically, she seems small and frail, but cognitively, she's taking up as much space as ever."

"Good." Brooke grimaced. "I mean, you know, not great, but …"

"I know," Sawyer said. "If she's still smart, she's still sharp."

As if on cue, Maura called, "Sawyer, are you loitering in the hall with your friends at a moment like this?"

They closed their eyes and took a slow breath before stepping through the door. "Good morning, Mother."

Maura lay in a hospital bed, an IV in her right arm and wires extending from under her hospital gown. She seemed especially pale beneath the fluorescent lights and white blankets pulled up to her chest. Adjusting her glasses, she scanned them with a flicker of something akin to relief before narrowing her eyes. "Are you wearing a tuxedo?"

"Parts of one. I didn't know the dress code for attending an open-heart surgery, and you always told me one couldn't overdress for a serious occasion."

The corners of Maura's mouth twitched up. "I'd be honored, if I believed you. Out all night with a woman I presume?"

"Oh, it'd be uncouth to brag about my prowess when you clearly had a more exciting evening. How does it feel to be the more dramatic member of the family for once?"

"I'd hardly call it drama," Maura said flatly. "My left main coronary artery is blocked due to damage of the arterial wall, likely stemming from chronic hypertension and perhaps a family history of heart disease."

Sawyer tried to parse out all the words. They understood each of them on their own, but somehow putting them all together and applying them to their mother, of all people, made their brain spin. "Do we have a family history?"

"The correlation is mild for me, but I suppose it's just gotten stronger for your genetic predisposition."

"No kidding." They rubbed their face. "What do you need?"

"The odds of survival are around 80% for a person of my age with a slight dip due to my sex and the location of the rupture." Maura recited the facts in the same tone she used to lecture her graduate students, equal parts gravity and boredom. "There's no need to be maudlin. However, in the interest of due diligence, I'd like to speak with you about a few things."

They nodded. "Sure."

Maura's eyes flicked past them. "Alone."

Sawyer glanced over their shoulder to see Brooke and Gillian still standing in the doorway, then smiled, feeling better for knowing they wanted to stay. At least two out of three of them had that capacity. "I'm okay."

Brooke started to step back, but Gillian stood her ground. "Boundaries still matter even when things get complicated … especially when things get complicated."

Sawyer laughed. "When are things ever not complicated?"

Gillian sighed.

"Go get some rest. I've got this."

"You do," Brooke affirmed, then looped an arm through Gillian's and eased her away from the door. "And we've got you. We're only a text or call away."

Sawyer feigned casualness and blew them a little kiss before closing the door, steeling themself for what was about to happen.

Maura launched in without preamble the second Sawyer turned back to her. "You'll find all my essential documents inside the locked drawer of my office desk. The key, along with those for my home and car, are in the pocket of the jacket I wore in the ambulance. Also, the code to my personal computer is your birthday backwards."

"Aw, that's unexpectedly sweet of you," Sawyer said.

"Please, they'll take me down to surgery in a matter of minutes. We don't have time for sentimentality," she said curtly, then seemed to catch herself. "Though I suppose what I have to say next is born from a similar set of emotions, and I'd appreciate the chance to get through them without interruption."

Sawyer's chest tightened, and they hoped Maura didn't feel the same way given her current condition. "I'm listening."

"I'm aware enough to realize this isn't fair to do in such a loaded situation, one where you may feel trapped by a sense of obligation, but I'm not in a position to offer the grace of time or proper mediation."

They moved closer to the bed but couldn't bring themself to sit down for the nervous energy coursing through their veins. "I understand."

"I suspect you don't," Maura said with a slight tremble to her voice. "I suspect there's a great many things I've done or choices I've made as a parent that make no sense to you, and I'm relatively certain you have little concept of how much I love you, how much I've always loved you."

They blinked a few times, not sure where they'd expected this to go, but not here.

"I see from your expression I'm correct, and I'm sorry for that. I'm not a woman who shows her feelings well, perhaps a hazard of my work or remnants of my own upbringing, but I realize the ways in which I've tried to show my affection to you haven't been particularly well received. I gather you've felt as though you were raised under a microscope, and you were."

They held their breath, not sure what to do with such a concession.

"I study things that interest me," Maura continued. "I study things I care about. I don't know any other way to approach something of import, so it's what I've always done with you. From the moment I found out I was pregnant, I read every book, every journal, every theory. I became an expert in developmental milestones and identity formation to collect, and sometimes create, the knowledge I felt would help me serve you or shape the world you inhabited for the better. I desperately wanted to consume every piece of research that could assure you lived a healthy, safe, fulfilling life."

"Mom." Sawyer finally sank into the chair next to her, all the fight draining out of them at such a vulnerable admission. "That makes all the sense in the world, honestly. We all do what we know how to do best, and you're the best in your field. It's only logical that you'd do your things unceasingly."

"Thank you." Relief flooded Maura's voice. "I appreciate your acknowledging that."

"And, if it offers you any kind of peace," Sawyer forged on cautiously, "I am living a fulfilling life. I know I've acted out a lot, but tonight was the happiest I've been in … maybe ever."

"I do enjoy hearing that. Personally, a parent will always find those revelations gratifying, and professionally, it also gives me hope to hear you're capable of such experiences. You've been so distant and aloof with me, I'd honestly developed concerns your bifurcation may've undermined your emotional capacities."

Sawyer gritted their teeth. "My bifurcation?"

"As I've explained in the past, you live in a suspended state of being faced with a choice between two outcomes, and you've refused the work necessary to make the choice, which leaves you split between the two halves."

"Mother—"

She held up a hand. "You promised to let me speak. You can do what you will as soon as they take me away."

They sat back, not granting consent so much as resignation. Maura was apparently in the mood to accept either.

"I want you to be able to experience a more integrated sense of well-being, which would require you to develop skills and identities that foster stability. I cannot fathom why you seem dead set on doing the opposite, almost defiantly eschewing even basic benchmarks like a permanent address."

"Okay, I have." They conceded the point with a hint of shame. "I've made a habit out of running away when things get uncomfortable, but not out of some oppositional defiance to you. I'm capable of staying in places where I'm happy, and again, I'm very happy with my life, at the moment."

"I'm not talking about moments, Sawyer." More of her usual edge returned. "And I'm not merely referencing your penchant for gallivanting across the globe. I see the habit as a mere symptom of deeper inner turmoil, and until you do the work necessary to firm up your sense of self, you'll always be a servant of your impulses and whims."

They sighed. None of this was news, but the fact that their mother chose to spend what could possibly be her last breaths rehashing it stung.

"You're thirty-five years old, and your identity development is woefully underformed, stunted even. While I understand fluidity might be all the rage among people whose frontal lobes are still developing, nothing can be trusted long term if it can't be repeated."

"Like the studies you produce?"

"Yes. Studies that explain life and relationships, cognitive and emotional best practices to order a life in meaningful ways. You need consistent data points to form meaningful patterns, Sawyer, but you're scattered and split in two. When things like your gender fluctuate daily, it prevents you from ever knowing who you are well enough to share yourself consistently with anyone else."

Their mind flashed back to Robin in their arms, the things they'd admitted to each other, the things they'd reconstructed together, the way the two of them could exist exactly as they were in situations ranging from risqué to ridiculous.

"It's why you've failed to hold down a job or a home or a relationship." Maura picked up speed, which probably wasn't good for her heart, but if Sawyer had the ability to control such outbursts, they would've done so by now. "Even the people you claim to be closest to, your friends who enable you at every turn, didn't know where you were for two years."

They winced as the barb landed. It was much harder to rebut her central arguments when so much of her evidence held up.

"I know you don't want to hurt them." Maura's voice softened. "But you let them down, repeatedly. You can't help it. You cannot be true to anyone else until you know yourself. You simply don't have those skills, but you do have every resource, every opportunity to accept help, to accept a sound diagnosis and treatment."

"Treatment." They repeated the word, tasting its bitterness against the recitation of their many shortcomings. "Like my surgery?"

"No. Accurate treatment, not simply the one you find most compelling. I know you claim to suffer from persistent gender dysphoria, but the clinical definition of that condition requires a consistent desire to live fully as a member of the opposite sex, which you refuse to do."

"I'm living in opposition to the idea of one clearly defined gender." Sawyer finally pushed back. "I cannot live as an *opposite* gender, because gender is a spectrum. Men and women are not opposites. We are all humans. Mom, please, I'm not trying to argue with you. You're brilliant. Surely, you see there's more to this socially constructed system of gender and sexuality."

"I'm not a bigot or an idiot, Sawyer. Of course I understand people express themselves in a myriad of ways. Dye your hair, get an earring, tattoo your arms, and, honestly, when you told me you preferred the company of women, I was thrilled. It's always seemed a logical impulse. At times, I wish I shared the inclination." She squeezed her eyes shut as if in pain.

Sawyer started forward again. "Mom."

"Let me finish." She stared at them once more. "I support your sexual orientation because it's static, reasonable, reliable. Be trans, be a man, be a woman. I can support either choice. I have the knowledge to fix this, and I want to. I care about you so deeply, and I stand ready to give every ounce of research that has served me so well over the years, but I cannot support something you can't consistently quantify."

"Like my gender identity."

"You don't have a gender identity. You have confusion, chaos, and no, I cannot support something you will not even convey clearly from one day to the next. I cannot support the fact that my child, so smart, so charismatic, so full of potential, and graced with so many gifts, has chosen to squander all of them on a half life."

"Okay then." Sawyer stood on wobbly knees, fighting the pulsing urge to bolt. "Anything else?"

"Sawyer, I knew you'd be upset, which is never my intention. I want only for you to be a whole person. I want to see you settle down and settle into everything you can become instead of constantly settling for being half of yourself."

"I am a whole person," they said, but they could barely hear their own voice through the cacophony of her assessments and their own screaming urge to run.

"You're only half in your body no matter how you carve it up, half present in friendships, half relationships with women if you can offer them even that, because, honestly, you're not living up to anywhere near half of your potential."

A knock at the door interrupted her speech, or maybe she'd finished. Where else could one go after telling your only child they were half of a person, or maybe less.

A nurse stuck her head in. "Miss Stroud, we're ready for you now."

Maura peered over the rim of her glasses. "It's Dr. Stroud." Then turning back to Sawyer, she said, "I don't expect you to stay."

They blinked a few times, wondering if she'd read their mind.

"During the surgery," Maura clarified, "you don't have to be here. It'll take at least six hours, likely longer. Don't feel obligated to pace about."

They didn't. They didn't even feel obligated to stand here any longer, but they didn't know what else to do, so they watched a series of strangers enter the room and begin disconnecting cords or adjusting the bed. Sawyer even stood stock-still as they checked vitals, then began to roll their mother toward the door.

As she was about to leave the room completely, Maura called back. "Sawyer?"

They raised their eyebrows with a hint of silly, stupid hope. "Yes?"

"Do think about what I've said."

Swallowing the bile rising in their throat, they managed to say, "Of course."

They'd likely be able to think of little else as they ran.

Twenty-Five

Robin rolled over, struggling to make sense of the discordant sounds without opening her eyes. However long she'd been asleep didn't seem long enough. Grabbing the pillow with the intention of pulling it over her head, she noticed the texture wasn't right, which allowed further awareness that she wasn't in her own bed, or in a bed at all.

Details drifted back in a jumbled mess. The limo, the dress, Sawyer's mouth. She may've drifted back into the makings of an amazing dream if not for the sound of something rummaging around like an animal. Slowly, she opened her eyes, bracing against the onslaught of daylight, until Tegan's apartment came into focus. No, not Tegan's, Sawyer's. She'd fallen asleep on the couch waiting for—

She sat up as the memory snapped into focus. Glancing around frantically, she spotted Sawyer crouched in the corner, stuffing clothes and their laptop into an olive-green duffel bag. They reached for their passport on the bedside table, and her heart seized. "Hey!"

"Shit!" Sawyer startled, eyes wide, body tense.

"Sorry. I didn't mean to scare you."

"I didn't know you were here." Sawyer glanced around as if something else might jump out at them.

"You asked me to stay."

That gave them pause. "Did I?"

She nodded, but they weren't quite looking at her. Robin moved toward them slowly, like one might a frightened animal. "What's happening?"

"My mother ... the doctors took her to surgery. It'll be a while."

"Okay. What time is it?"

"Afternoon. I've been ... I don't know, wandering."

"Want to lay down with me for a bit?"

They shook their head quickly. "I don't think sitting still is the right call."

"Sure," she said softly, even though her heart pounded louder as she tried to control her own fear. "Want to go for a walk?"

Sawyer glanced guiltily toward the bag near their feet. "I'm not a good person to be around right now."

Her chest constricted for a myriad of reasons from the pain and shame radiating off them to her own increasing panic. "I don't need you to be anything other than who you are."

"Yeah, well." Sawyer's beautiful features twisted like they'd tasted something bitter. "I need to be something else. Maybe I need to be somewhere else."

"We can bust outta this joint."

"Not we," Sawyer said flatly. "Me. It's me. I'm not a good person."

She sighed. "Pretty huge statement there. Wanna break it down a bit?"

"No!" Sawyer exploded. "I don't want to break anything down. I am breaking down. Or maybe I'm just broken. I'm in pieces you can't jam together, and you can't process through them or force the puzzle into a whole, so stop trying. Do not fucking counsel me."

She held up her hands as she fought a losing battle to control her own breath. "Fair enough."

"No." This time it came out more like a whimper. "It's not. I'm not being fair to you. I hear it, but I can't stop, and the calmer you stay, the clearer it becomes that you deserve better than I'm capable of giving."

"You don't like me calm?"

They clenched their jaw.

"You'd prefer I scream? Yell? Throw things?" Robin waited without an answer before grabbing a lamp off the end table. Clutching its glass stand in her fist tightly hurt enough to draw her senses away from her emotional pain. "I will throw things, Sawyer, starting with this ugly-ass lamp. I bet it shatters like ice when it hits the wall."

Sawyer stared at her for a long second as if daring her to do it, so she reared back.

"Wait," they finally said.

"What? I thought you wanted to see me desperate. Here I am."

"I don't." They sounded less than convincing. "I can't be managed right now, or ever. I cannot be centered, and … whole."

"What do you mean?"

They scrunched their face up again and set their jaw.

Anger surged through her at their ability to pull away when she felt only an animal instinct to cling to them. "I'm gonna throw the lamp."

"I thought therapists had to be distant and neutral and detached," they blurted.

She lowered her fist to her side. "Why are we back to this? I am *a* therapist. I'm not *your* therapist."

"Neither is my mother." Sawyer's voice cracked. "Doesn't keep her from being clinical as fuck every time she hurts me."

Her stomach turned over. "What did she say?"

"Nothing she hasn't said over and over and over. Except that she loves me, which is a new justification for dragging me back into her clutches. She usually couches it in her work, which allows her to remain calculating and neutral while cutting me open."

"She's wrong." Robin set the lamp back on the table and moved toward them, but they backed up.

"She's not wrong about everything. She made a few heartbreaking points about all the people I've let down, how I'm incapable of doing anything else, and the only thing that's kept me sane is believing that's who she has to be for her job.

I've always thought her brilliance and drive and the importance of her work required her to maintain that kind of objective distance with everyone. But if that's not true, if psychologists can be open and caring and close and still see people clearly, that's worse."

"Why?"

"Because then I'm the problem. If her reaction to me isn't some occupational hazard, it means I've never been good enough or worthy enough or interesting enough to overcome her need to diagnose."

"Absolutely not. It's all her. Not her job, not her intelligence, not you."

They looked away, and Robin took another step forward. "Listen. You are good enough to overcome Brooke's professional instincts, and Gillian's, and Tegan's, but most of all, mine. Your mother is not the only therapist who knows you, but she's the only one who treats you like a case study or a lab rat instead of a real person."

"It doesn't add up." Sawyer started to pace, just out of reach. "I'm sure you've had plenty of clients with well-deserved mommy issues, but my mom, she sees everyone but me. She's so fucking smart, so fucking accomplished. She's worked out so many problems for the entire field of psychology, but she can't even see me as whole."

"I see you," Robin whispered.

"What if you only see the parts I want you to see? The fun and adventure and cute prom role-plays, but here's the thing: maybe it's all a role I play. Deep down, I'm not the kind of person people can count on. Ask your friends, they'll tell you."

Robin came closer, shaking her head. "I don't need our friends to tell me anything. I hear you, I feel you, I know you."

"You don't," they snapped. "Remember how mad you got the first time I ghosted you? That's nothing compared to what I'm capable of."

"You're not going to do it again."

They pointed to the duffel at their feet. "I'm doing it right now, Robin!"

She lunged, catching them by both shoulders as her own restraint snapped. "You're not."

"I am," they shouted. "I'm running. It's all I'm good for. Running out on my mother while her chest is cracked open in an operating room. Running out on my friends, who only want to be here for me. Running out on you while you slept on my couch. And it's not because you don't deserve better. It's because this is my best, and you're too good to live a half life."

She stared at them trying to make sense of the last part amid her own horror at everything that came before. "I'm not living a half life."

"I am." Sawyer hung their head. "I'm half in my body, half in this room, half in this relationship."

"Did she tell you that?"

"It's true. I'm half a person, and you deserve someone whole. Can't you see you are wholly, genuinely all the things I only pretend to be?"

Robin caught their face in her hands and lifted it enough for their eyes to meet. "I see you."

Sawyer's breath came shallow and ragged as they tried to turn away, but Robin held their chin steady.

"I see you struggling. I see you trying to protect me even in your anguish. I see you doing tremendous emotional lifting. I see you holding back all the pain until you get someplace where it won't splash on the people you care about, which makes you fundamentally better than your mother."

"I don't want to hurt you the way she hurts me."

"You're not. I understand now. You're ready to run only because if you don't, you're afraid you'll explode. But you're a volcano, Baby. You have to explode. You're the one who told me that's how new ground gets made. Stay here and blow your top so we can build something new."

They stood there, chest heaving, their pulse beating under the spot where Robin's hands cupped their jaw.

"Come on, Sawyer," she pleaded. "I can take the heat."

"You don't know that."

"Let's find out together. Let's try to stand somewhere no one else has ever stood before." She ran her fingers down their neck and into the little hollow at the base of their throat. "I see you. I'm standing right here. Please see me, too."

Their eyes dropped to her body, and something darker, more present flickered through their eyes.

She caught hold of the connection like a life preserver. "Do you want to see more?"

They exhaled slowly.

"I want to show you what I see." She touched the first closed button of their tuxedo shirt. "I'll stop if you tell me."

Sawyer pressed their lips together and nodded.

She flicked open the button and those below before tugging the hem free of Sawyer's slacks. "I love to look at your body. All of it. So much more than two halves. The fluid perfection of you drives me wild. Masculine on top, and feminine below the waist, but only an idiot would try to separate the two when the artistry that blends them together is so damn appealing."

Sawyer glanced down, and Robin accentuated her point by running her hands along the V-shape of their torso, then out along the curve of their hips. "I'm mesmerized by the way you take everything good about the human form and bend it to fit your totality. You're not half of anything, Sawyer. You are everything."

She unclasped their belt and the button of their pants, allowing them to fall. Then, easing Sawyer back to the edge of the bed, she nudged them to sit. Sinking to her knees, she untied their shoes and slipped them off, along with their socks. Sawyer's hips rocked forward as instinct or habit took hold, but as Robin rose again, she placed a palm squarely in the middle of their chest. "I'm not going to fuck you right now."

They squinted up at her, gray eyes confused under a haze of attraction.

"Look at me," she commanded gently.

Their eyes swept over her body.

"No." She caught their chin once more and guided it up. "Watch me look at you."

She pushed them fully back on the bed, then shed her own dress, and together they scooted up to the pillows, Sawyer on their back, Robin crawling over them without breaking eye contact.

"What do you see in my eyes?"

They shook their head.

"See me, Sawyer."

They ran their tongue along dry lips. "Um, attraction?"

"Absolutely. From the moment you stepped into the bar the very first night, I spotted the most perfect human I've ever seen. What else?"

They stared at her for a few seconds. "Affection?"

She smiled and ran her hand from their chin down over their collarbone. "Very much so, probably from the minute you tried to keep me from going overboard in the whitewater raft."

The corners of their mouth twitched. "You took me with you."

"We've been in over our heads with each other ever since, and I still can't get enough. What else?"

Sawyer stared at her for another long minute before saying, "I don't know."

"What about awe or adoration, or even admiration?"

"Don't."

"Don't what? Don't admire you? Adore you?" Robin laughed lightly and placed a kiss in the middle of their chest. "How about don't tell me what to do?"

"Robin." They sighed and sank a little deeper into the mattress.

"You made a prom for me. That's the nicest thing anyone's ever done *ever*, and I have very nice friends. You make me feel cared for and interesting and heard. I admire you, appreciate you. Hell, I'm in awe of you, even more so now that I understand what you've fought against. All this pain and doubt and undercutting of yourself, but still you dream and create and explore and thrill."

"I don't."

"You do. You tell me about places I haven't even thought to imagine, and you challenge me when I'm used to being the challenging one, and you turn me on and egg me on and never try to rein me in and, sorry, not sorry, but I admire all the 'ands' I had to put in that sentence without even exhausting them all. Someone living a half life doesn't inspire so many 'ands.'"

"And I'm also a mess." The last bits of fight in them tried to rebound, but the exhaustion bled through in their voice. "And my mother—"

"Your mother's not here, and even if she were, she couldn't see what I do. She doesn't know you. She could only accuse you of a half life because she sees only half of you. She sees the block of marble, I see the masterpiece. She sees you as a problem. I see you as pure poetry. She hasn't earned anything more, but I have," Robin said gently. "You're with me, and I know you. Stay with me. Be fully with me."

"What if I can't ever be fully one thing or another?"

"Then I'll be even more drawn to you than I already am."

They rolled their eyes, and she gritted her teeth at the thought of losing them to whatever echoes were trying to drown her out.

"Have I ever blown smoke with you?" she asked sharply.

"What?"

"Have I ever lied or flattered or played games or danced around anything I wanted from you?"

Sawyer seemed to consider the question, but their focus wavered as she brought her knee up between their legs.

"Do I strike you as someone who gets clingy or needy with partners?"

"No," they finally admitted.

"Do you think I don't have other options? Do you think I couldn't go down to Ambush and find ten people willing to share this bed right now?"

They drew a shaky breath.

"I could. I have," she said, no longer sure which one of them she was reminding of that fact. "I've run through prospective partners as quickly as you have. I've played the part and accepted the easy outs. We both have, and that's worked for us our whole lives. I could keep on doing it, and so could you. There's no shame in taking what we want, but we're like, ten weeks in, and I'm still with you because I keep choosing you."

"Why?" Sawyer asked, the jagged edge in their voice now so close to breaking.

"Because you intrigue and inspire and excite me more than the rest of the world combined. Because I have an authenticity kink, and you feed it with your fullness. You're more than half a person, more than any other whole person. You're more than all of them together, Sawyer." Robin let the weight of her body settle more completely across theirs. "Your fluidity doesn't scare me. It enthralls me. I don't need you to pick or choose or settle for some static identity. I want you to be every stop along every continuum that's ever mattered, and I want you to do so with me."

"What if it's not enough?"

"Then we'll sleep and rest with each other, knowing we'll get up tomorrow and do it all again."

"Why?" they asked again, this time sleepily.

"Because I'm selfish and gluttonous and as over-the-top as you are." She ran a hand through their hair tenderly as the truth of it all settled over her the same way she tried to smother the body below her. "I want every bit of you, every wild and radical and chill and thoughtful part of your essence, and I want it completely for myself."

Sawyer curled into her. "What if I don't know how to give you all the parts I can't even sort out for myself?"

"You don't have to know anything else right now." She kissed their temple, and felt their body soften before whispering, "All you have to do is stay."

Robin woke from the deepest sleep of her life and squinted at the clock beside Sawyer's bed. For a second, she couldn't tell if it was six in the morning or six at night, and she sure as hell didn't know what day it was. What she did know with heartbreaking clarity was that Sawyer was gone. She felt their absence even before the awareness of what that meant sank in.

She'd lain awake holding them for hours, fear and hope warring inside her, unsure if Sawyer had succumbed to her blend of logic and begging, or if they'd merely crashed from physical and emotional exhaustion.

Now she had her answer.

Pulling the covers to her chest to fight the raw chill coursing through her, she sat up and glanced at the empty spot where the duffel bag had been. Maybe if she focused on the missing bag, she wouldn't have to think about the person who'd carried it out the door.

No, she couldn't hide from this. Her breath came in tight bursts. Her own crash was coming, and for the first time in her life, she felt afraid of facing something alone. She forced herself to rummage through a pile of half-folded clothes on the floor, another remnant of Sawyer's hasty escape, until she found a pair of sweatpants and one of the rugby shirts they'd rescued from oblivion. Pulling them on, she grabbed her dress from the floor.

It was still hers. It had always been hers. Even in her pain, she wouldn't deny Sawyer theirs. She wouldn't have denied them anything, but even her everything hadn't been enough.

Was this how they felt all the time?

Was this why the accusation of a half life had ripped at their confidence? Had they always known the crush of giving everything they had and still coming up short? She hadn't known, and she desperately wished she still didn't.

A scream built inside her, or maybe a howl, something plaintive and animalistic.

She had to get out of here. She couldn't feel their absence while still breathing in the hint of their cologne.

Collecting her shoes from the floor by the couch, she fumbled with the stupid straps and dainty buckle, preventing herself from ripping them to shreds only with her last fraying strands of reason. She had to go somewhere, anywhere, and she couldn't walk through downtown Buffalo barefoot.

Finally pulling herself together enough to take a few wobbly steps, she passed the lamp she'd threatened to throw earlier and almost reached for it again, but the move that had felt so dramatically satisfying earlier now seemed petty in the face of her own shattering.

She staggered down the stairs and started walking without realizing where. Careening through the early morning awakenings around her, she probably looked drunk or walk-of-shamey to early commuters, but she didn't care about anything other than the fact that she'd begged another person not to leave her. She'd held them and opened up to them and showed herself so completely, and she didn't even get to see Sawyer walk out the door.

"Robin?"

She turned to see Gillian climbing out of her car.

Glancing around, she realized she'd wandered toward work. It made sense as the office was her closest safe space, but the fact that she hadn't made any conscious decision to do so still ratcheted up her sense of being out of control.

Then there was Gilly in a business suit, her hair flawless and makeup perfect as her eyes scanned over Robin in Sawyer's too-big clothes and her own dress shoes.

"They're gone." Robin's voice shook, and then the rest of her body joined in.

Gillian opened her arms.

Robin practically collapsed into her.

"It's going to be okay," she whispered. "We're all going to get you through this. Then I'm going to murder someone, and then you're going to get me off on justifiable homicide."

"It's not their fault."

"It never is." Gillian steered her into the office and toward the waiting room couch.

Robin sank onto the couch and curled into a ball.

Gillian moved away only far enough to start a pot of coffee. Robin didn't watch, but she could hear Gillian as she called someone and whispered a few things. Then hanging up, she returned to the couch. "Reinforcements are on the way, along with a pair of tennis shoes."

She shrugged. The footwear didn't rank high on her list of concerns, and Gillian must've realized as much, because she settled in beside her. "It's not about you, you know?"

"I do. I didn't see them walk out, but I watched them disappear. I fought so hard, and I know I can't save someone. I know all the things. I, of all freaking people, preach a gospel about having to let individuals make their own choices, and meeting people where they are ... Fuck." Her stomach hurt so bad, she clutched at it fruitlessly. "I guess for the first time in my life, I wanted it to be about me. I wanted it so badly, I thought maybe it would be enough, like maybe I'd be enough to overcome all the rest."

Gillian sighed. "You were never going to entirely undo thirty-five years of conditioning in a couple of months, and that doesn't mean you didn't do anything worth doing. I've known Sawyer a long time, and I've never seen them with anyone the way they were with you. For that matter, I've never seen you with anyone the way you were with them. Honestly, it scared the hell out of me."

"Because you saw this coming?"

"The odds heavily favored this outcome."

"Why didn't you say something?"

"What, because the two of you are so prone to logic and accepting personal advice?"

She snorted softly.

"Besides"—Gillian leaned into her—"which one of you would I have warned? You were both just as likely to break a heart as the other was."

"I wasn't ... I didn't ... it's not my heart."

Gillian eased back enough to stare at her for a second, but before either of them could respond, Tegan and Brooke bustled through the door. Robin didn't even have to speak. They wrapped around her in an instant, a pile of therapists, friends, and confidantes. She let herself be enveloped, even as Gillian's assessment rattled through her brain.

Had Sawyer broken her heart? Did that mean she'd given it to them? "I think ..."

They all sat back and waited patiently. "Gillian thinks Sawyer might've broken ... well, my heart."

They all stared at her, confusion and concern filling their expressions.

"They left." She said the words like a sob. "I asked them not to, more than asked, maybe begged."

Tegan reached for her hand and gave it a squeeze.

"I'm embarrassed, and I feel ... not good enough. Intellectually, I know someone else shouldn't have the power to change how I feel about myself, but I don't feel intellectual. I feel like someone carved out a piece of my chest, and I'm numb, but also in pain, which shouldn't be possible. I'm so angry, but not exactly at them, kind of around them, like I might want to rip their head off, but also want them to come back and kiss me one more time before I shake them senseless." She dissolved, shaking and struggling to get air all the way into her lungs. "Make it make sense."

Brooke shook her head. "I'm not sure this part of being in love ever makes sense."

She shook her head. She couldn't bring herself to deny the charge, which also sounded a bit like a sentence to be served. "Love? Fuck."

"Yep," Gillian said. "The first time's a kick in the teeth. It's kind of hard to believe you've avoided it this long."

"First time?" she practically shouted. "You people have done this more than once? Why?"

Gillian laughed softly. "No one ever falls in love expecting it to happen."

"But you knew it could." Robin's incredulity took over as she pointed between Brooke and Tegan. "You two had felt this way before, and you still signed up again? That's bullshit!

You're two smart people who understood what was happening. You looked at each other and said, 'I'm falling in love right now,' then didn't stop it?"

"We tried." Brooke gave Tegan a sweetly subdued smile. "We tried not to fall. We tried not to hurt each other, and we failed on both counts. We broke each other's hearts and our own along the way. Then we rebuilt ourselves knowing full well it could happen again."

Robin sagged back. "I didn't feel myself slipping, much less falling, or maybe I did at times, but I sure as hell didn't know it could hurt this bad."

"Maybe that's a blessing," Tegan offered. "Sometimes the pain of losing something is a wake-up call, that you've strayed from the path of something good and important."

"I didn't stray from anything, and I definitely didn't choose to fall in love," she shot back. "I was deliriously happy, cruising along, being awesome together, having fun, having sex, having great conversations and adventures. I was having so much fun I didn't notice anything but Sawyer. I didn't even think about it ending. They saw me and I saw them, and we got it, so deeply." She noticed all three of them biting back smiles. "What?"

"Hate to break it to you, Babe," Tegan said, "but you're describing being in love. You found someone who set your world on fire and rearranged what you were willing to consider for yourself, and you dove in headfirst, because that's who you are."

Her vision swam. "This is terrible."

"The worst," Gillian agreed. "It's horrible to have someone see you so completely, and to be vulnerable and raw and have all those big emotions dangling by a thread that another person can cut at any moment."

"Surely, that's not normal. I refuse to believe regular humans are out there feeling this way or risking feeling this way all the time."

"You get used to it," Brooke said sympathetically.

"I don't want to get used to it," she exploded, hopping off the couch. "I don't want to feel like this a minute more, and I refuse to give anyone the chance to make me feel like this again."

"But you will," Tegan said matter-of-factly.

She gritted her teeth against the idea. "Why would anyone knowingly sign up for this? Not only allow it, but write songs about it and go see movies about it and write books or poetry about falling in love?"

"Because the other side is so good," Brooke said. "You're crawling out of your skin right now at the thought of missing it. That's all grief is, love with nowhere to go."

She held her fists to her chest, trying to press against the pain. She did miss them. Even amid the ache and anger and inability to breathe normally, she wanted Sawyer back, wanted to forgive, wanted there to be nothing to forgive, wanted to keep careening blindly together. She would never have that again. Maybe that hurt worst of all. As long as she lived, and no matter what happened, she'd always know how she felt in this moment. Even with nothing to forgive, she could never forget. Sawyer had taken that kind of blissful oblivion with them, slipped away with it while she slept.

She swallowed another sob trying to push up in her. "Now that I know how it feels to hand another person the power to hurt me this way, I can't imagine why anyone would risk this ever again."

"The same reason you jump out of planes."

She turned to see Gillian still sitting on the couch, perfectly put together, one leg crossed over the other, her expression neutral except for the compassion in her eyes. "What?"

"I'm not here to tell you to love Sawyer or not. I'm also tremendously hurt and angry they're choosing to walk out on all of us." Gillian spoke calmly and evenly. "But let's not pretend you aren't the queen of risk-taking. You seek risks, you chase risks, you inject risk into normal outings. You go whitewater rafting, bull riding, bungee jumping, and you've gone home with strangers. I'm pretty sure you've had sex in at least semipublic places, and God knows what else. For what? A thrill? Because danger turns you on? Or because it makes you feel alive and whole?"

She froze. "Whole?"

Gillian shrugged. "I don't share the compulsion. You tell me."

"I don't know," she said slowly, not totally sure that was correct. "I've never risked anything like this."

"Seriously?" Tegan pushed gently. "Given Gilly's woefully incomplete list of your exploits, it sounds like you've risked catastrophic injury, public exposure, your professional reputation, and even your life."

"It never felt this way."

"Why?" Brooke asked gently. "Because you didn't let yourself fully consider the outcome, or because the reward outweighed the danger?"

She recognized they were tag-teaming like some kind of empathic group project, but the question remained. "There's a moment whenever I skydive where the plane door opens and it hits, really deeply physically and emotionally hits you, that the chance of splatting into the pavement might be low, but it's never zero."

"And you keep jumping anyway." Gillian sounded completely mystified, and Robin couldn't blame her anymore. It's the same way she felt when looking at Brooke and Tegan. They'd assessed every possible outcome and still chosen to step out of the plane door together. Robin had only ever done it alone.

"I think I choose the chance to fly over the fear of falling."

Gillian raised one finger. "Point of clarity: When you step out of a plane, you are falling. You manage to do it with style and the illusion of control, but you're flying while you're in the relative safety of a plane, you're falling anytime you leave it before it lands."

She laughed, a short scoff of a sound.

"Am I wrong?"

"You're never wrong, Gilly." She rubbed her face, trying to make all the discordant concepts fit together.

"Sometimes she's wrong," Brooke mumbled, then grudgingly added, "but not now. You choose to fall."

"That's it." She pointed at Brooke. "I choose to *fall*. I *choose* to fall. *I* choose to fall. Ever since I graduated high school, I've been choosing for myself. I spent years building a world and a life based around my choices. I defined every parameter and every boundary, the ones I set, the ones I kept, the ones I broke. My career, my friends, my partners, I looked every one of them in the eye clearly and made the choice for myself."

"And you feel like Sawyer made this choice for you, or you feel like with Sawyer you didn't see the choice clearly?" Brooke asked.

Her brain hurt nearly as much as her heart now. "I'm not sure."

"Does it matter?" Tegan asked softly.

They all turned to her.

"Sawyer made the choice to leave," she continued, "but you made every other choice. You chose to be with them, to share adventures with them, to share parts of yourself you didn't share with anyone else. You chose to sleep with them, to open up to them, to rewrite your history with them. You chose to see them, stand with them, buck up against their mother with them. And you chose to love them even after you saw what they were up against."

"I didn't choose to fall in love. It just happened."

"Fine," Gillian said calmly, "let's say for a second you'd been given the choice. Say you could wave a magic wand and then be standing at the open door of this particular metaphorical plane. Below you is every single thing you chose to experience with Sawyer, every minute of joy and connection and vulnerability and whatever the two of you did together in bed or any other number of mildly exposed places. Imagine you're standing in view of it all, and I say, 'You can fall into that, but you might also fall in love on the way down.' Would you have chosen to jump, or would you have told me to land the plane safely and quietly somewhere else?"

She thought for a moment, opened her mouth and closed it again, unable to speak through the blur of emotion and memories assaulting her senses.

She didn't want to choose, even now, even in the hypothetical. She wasn't sure she could. Despite the demons that had driven Sawyer away, they couldn't be compartmentalized. There was no halfway or half life. Wasn't that what she'd begged them to believe? She would always have to assume the risk of falling if she wanted even the illusion of flying.

She sagged. "I don't know."

Twenty-Six

Sawyer's phone buzzed, but they didn't reach for it. They hadn't been able to bring themself to disconnect completely or swap out the SIM card for one of the international ones they'd need when they crossed the border. Still, they couldn't look at the messages either. They'd seen enough of the notifications over the last hour to know Brooke, Gillian, and even Tegan were trying to reach them. It didn't surprise them that the one person they most wanted to hear from hadn't called.

They steeled themself against the cold edge of loneliness starting to set in. Robin had spoken her piece yesterday, and it had been a rather compelling speech. For a few blissful hours in her arms, Sawyer let themself believe the things she'd said. A part of them still believed. There was no way to doubt the depth of emotion in Robin's eyes, but Sawyer couldn't go through their entire life staring at just one woman or sleeping in her arms or letting her make a full-time job of propping them up. There would always be a morning like this when the real world crashed back in.

Across the sterile room of the hospital, their mother slept, so small, frail, and weak she seemed almost far away, though only a few feet separated them. The doctors said she came through the surgery well and had been awake and alert in the recovery room, but by the time Sawyer arrived in the middle of the night, she was sleeping soundly, likely the product of physical exhaustion and heavy painkillers. Sawyer certainly understood the former but couldn't relate to the latter. Their pain over the last several hours had been as strong as ever before. What right did Maura have to dull hers after inflicting so much of theirs?

Sawyer shook their head. They didn't want her to suffer. They may've wanted her to wake up and do a little reckoning. Now that she'd survived, it seemed only fair that Sawyer should have the same opportunity, but they'd stopped expecting fairness from Maura ages ago. They'd get a chance to rebut her arguments eventually if they wanted to, but what good could it do now? They'd done the one thing they promised they wouldn't. They'd run, panicked and blind, from the place they'd felt safest, straight back into the lion's den. Didn't that at least lend some credence to Maura's assertions of their maladjustment? Why couldn't they take their hand off this particular stove?

They stood and stared down at the woman who'd raised them, seeing her in her moment of frailty instead of as the formidable figure who'd towered over so many, only the more Sawyer examined her, the clearer it became that Maura's size hadn't changed. She was identical in height to the woman who'd gone into surgery, and she likely weighed roughly the same. Her hair was the same length and brassy blonde, her cheekbones and manicured nails the same as they'd been yesterday. Aside from the wires and IVs, there was no discernible difference in her. Outside the medical context, there would be no outward sign of trauma.

Then again, Sawyer's trauma couldn't be seen from the outside either. Perhaps that was something the two of them had always had in common. Neither of them ever fully understood what haunted the other. At least now they'd both carry scars across their chests, matching medical tattoos, to hint at what they'd both survived.

The thought struck them as poignant. No one would ever judge their mother for her scar. No one would accuse her of existing half in her body or criticize the choices she'd made. Then again, she hadn't had much choice if she did want to keep living. Sawyer had that in their favor. Their scars, at least the physical ones, were there by their choice, a choice they'd also made not only to stay alive, but also to live more fully.

"Hmm." Why did Maura, a woman who'd always done what she needed to survive, get to have a say in what Sawyer had done to thrive? Because she was smart? Because she had experience as a researcher? As a professor? As a practitioner? Surely, all of those things carried weight, but more weight than lived experience?

What had Robin said about Maura treating Sawyer as a case study or lab rat?

Maura had studied Sawyer only as a problem to be solved, not as a person to be known.

The phone buzzed again, and their fingers twitched with the urge to pick it up. There were people looking for them, people reaching out, people offering concern and maybe even comfort if they weren't totally pissed at them.

No, their friends could be both. They'd always offered both to Sawyer. Gillian had been angry enough to choke them, and still she'd loved them. Brooke's heart had been broken, and still she'd welcomed them back as a beloved prodigal. Sawyer had absolutely been a problem in their lives more than once, and still both women had nearly climbed over tables to get to them on their first night back in town.

They smiled at the memory. Had Maura ever received such an exuberant welcome? They walked around the bed to where their mother's phone rested on a table. Tapping the screen lightly confirmed what they'd already known. No one had called. Even after forty-eight hours in the hospital, there were no cards or flowers. No one else had come to visit all morning. Gillian had been there the day before, only while waiting for Sawyer.

Sawyer turned back to their mother, seeing her differently for the first time. She had the respect of everyone in her field, and more professional admiration than most people could imagine. Sawyer had known how much respect their mother commanded ever since they were a child. They'd known it so deeply they'd failed to internalize the depth of the affection some of those same people held for them until Robin forced them to see it in her eyes.

Maura was respected, undoubtedly. Sawyer didn't have to take anything away from that to also acknowledge that they were adored in ways she wasn't. The two ideas didn't exist in conflict. What other false associations had they left unexamined?

Maura was brilliant but also brutal, and for the longest time, Sawyer believed the two went together, but Robin had muddied those waters. Maybe they'd always been muddy. Gillian was smart enough to run intellectual circles around anyone. Even Maura regarded her as a prized pupil for her dry wit and sharp humor, but Gilly had never used either to hurt anyone. And Brooke, who had the capacity to hold so much space for others and her own boundaries, seemed almost infinite in her ability to offer insights without ever weaponizing any of them. And Tegan, who'd been so easily open and accepting, had the ability to dive right to the heart of any matter while still managing to be endlessly affable.

And Robin.

"Robin." They whispered her name aloud to feel the brush of it on their own lips. The others may've tried to show them a series of truths, but Robin made Sawyer feel that truth, made them live it. Robin saw everything, welcomed everything, accepted everything about them. She'd seen them cocky and crashing, sexy and sinking, scared and soaring, and still she'd wanted more. Her expansiveness gave her the capacity to recognize the same in Sawyer even when they couldn't see it in themself.

Maybe that's what had ultimately caused them to run away. Sawyer'd spent so much time claiming they were afraid Robin would be like their mother, when, in reality, she terrified them by being Maura's opposite.

What if Robin's great threat to their sense of self wasn't that she'd see Sawyer fully and find them lacking, but that she'd see them so fully it would force them to see themself the same way? Robin's danger lay not in seeing Sawyer as too little, but in her ability to show them a wildly new vision of what they could be, what they already were.

The tightness in their chest suggested they were circling close to the truth now, and they glanced at the duffel bag on the floor across the room. They could still run. They'd always run when this feeling clawed its way up, carrying the sense of something too big to be contained or even faced, as though whatever knowledge it carried might rip them in two the way their mother had warned. Wasn't that why she'd told them they had to decide, to choose, to trade exploration for certainty, fluidity for a firm foundation, freedom for stability?

They closed their eyes against the familiar pressure.

"I can take the heat." Robin's whisper wafted back through their memory, and they stood still as the whirlwind kicked up inside them. "Stay here and blow your top so we can build something new."

They opened their eyes and stared down at their mother again, and for the first time, it felt like looking into a mirror. How many trades had Maura made in her own life? How many choices had she let herself be trapped into making out of some sense of obligation or professional responsibility? Had looking at Sawyer stirred the same fears in Maura that Sawyer felt when staring into Robin's eyes? Did facing their expansiveness threaten the foundation upon which Maura had made so many of her own sacrifices?

As Sawyer examined her features, the lines etched in worry or restraint, they finally saw their mother not as some monolithic authority, but as the woman she'd always been. Human, flawed, complex.

Sawyer had missed out on so much by running. What had Maura given up in her quest to remain unmoved? Surely, she'd faced her own slew of hard choices over the years. She must have. Had she tried to force Sawyer into the same ones because she felt secure in hers, or because she didn't know any other way? Had she been fighting to make Sawyer into someone she could make sense of, or did she fear they'd lived a half life because she'd lived one of her own?

They glanced back at the dark screen of her phone. Maura had accused Sawyer of being half in relationships, but she didn't seem to have a single significant one of her own. She'd accused Sawyer of being half in a job when she'd let her career take away her wholeness in other areas of her life. She'd accused Sawyer of being half-present, even as she admitted she chose quantifiable metrics over emotional connections with her only child.

Had Maura settled down, or had she merely settled for less?

Did it matter? Sawyer didn't need to look at their mother's life with the same kind of harsh judgment she'd applied to theirs in order to realize they didn't want to emulate it. If nothing else, that line of questions confirmed they didn't know Maura any better than she knew them. Perhaps that was the most salient point Robin had made. They could see each other as living only a half life, because they only showed each other half of their lives. Even the most stringent researcher would draw flawed conclusions if they could examine only half the variables.

The corners of their mouth lifted as they landed on an explanation they could both understand. Still, as new awareness flooded past old barriers, now was not the time to make arguments or score points. Doing so suddenly mattered less than it ever had.

"We can build something new." Robin filled the back of their brain once more, so full of the grace she'd nearly smothered them in.

"Mom," they started, their voice shaky, throat dry. "I, uh, I see you doing the best you can, the best you know how, and I want you to know I don't blame you. I don't condemn you for making the choices you did, even though they hurt me at times, the same way things I've done hurt you without meaning to."

They sighed. Maura wasn't hearing any of this, maybe she never would, but maybe they weren't saying them for her. Maybe Sawyer wasn't doing anything for or in opposition to her anymore, but rather stepping into the fullness they needed for themself.

"You see me living a half life because you can only recognize half my life. Maybe that's all I've allowed, or maybe it's all your own choices have allowed, but I haven't been standing on some precipice unable to choose. I simply don't want to choose. I shouldn't have to choose between halves of myself. I want it all. I deserve it all, and I met someone who helped me understand I can have it all." Their smile finally broke through as the final piece of the puzzle slid into place. "I met someone who made me realize I already *do* have it all."

They stared down at her, waiting for some kind of response or recognition, but when none came, nothing changed.

Maura knew a lot of things, but she didn't know what Sawyer did, and now that they'd spoken their truth aloud, they also knew what they needed to do.

The ride across Buffalo had never felt so interminable, and Sawyer hopped out of the cab a block from their destination certain they could run faster. They practically sprinted up to the therapy office, then skidded to a stop just outside the door. They'd been this far before, but to take the next step would require a level of vulnerability and fortitude they'd never yet possessed. The sense of purpose inside them wavered as their fingers brushed the door handle, then shrank back.

Apparently, old habits die hard.

They could pull out their phone and call Robin or sit out here for hours waiting for her. It might be a good use of time to think about how they could adequately convey the awakening they'd experienced, but Sawyer wasn't sure mere words could prove sufficient to such a task. Still, they may've tried if not for the twist in their gut at the prospect of letting Robin continue to think whatever horrible things she must be thinking a minute longer. She deserved better, she always had, and yet Robin had repeatedly come more than halfway to meet them. The next steps were Sawyer's to make, and for the first time, they desperately wanted to take them.

Everything good and loving, comfortable and thrilling, was on the other side of that door, and they were done letting whatever half-informed assessment their mother had handed down under the guise of therapy keep them from accepting that fullness any longer.

With a deep breath, they swung the door wide and stepped inside. As their eyes adjusted to the dim light, they took some easy solace in the fact that they'd stepped across the threshold of a therapy practice and no lightning bolts had struck them down. Taking a few more steps, they passed a door to the left with a "vacant" sign. Across from it, an open door revealed a waiting room. Warm and inviting, the place held a cozy couch, some overstuffed chairs, a desk, and a coffee machine next to a mini fridge. A few potted plants occupied each corner, and little touches like ceramic mugs, coasters, books, and a lone pair of dress shoes discarded in the middle of the floor told Sawyer they'd found the right place, if not the people who'd cultivated the space.

Inching further down the hall, they treaded lightly, partly out of respect for the fact that their friends might be working, and also because Sawyer might not be completely welcome at the moment.

Still, the low mumble of voices at the end of the hall drew them forward and instilled more hope than fear. Sawyer had always claimed a desire to experience everything life had to offer, and it now occurred to them that maybe they should've specified to the universe that they didn't need every single emotion to hit at the same time. Even so, a cacophony of sensations overwhelmed them as they stood on the outside of the circle they still so deeply wanted to be a part of.

What if they were too late? What if their friends were mad at them? What if Robin had decided what they'd put her through wasn't worth it anymore? They could still choose to run. They were so good at it. They weren't at all sure they could be good at whatever they were doing here.

Then Robin laughed.

It wasn't exuberant. She sounded tired, weary even, but the pull of her eclipsed everything else pushing them away.

They stepped into the doorway and cleared their throat.

Everyone around the big conference table froze, then turned slowly.

Sawyer shifted under their combined gaze without meeting anyone's eyes, as no one ran to them this time. Everyone seemed to hold their breath waiting to see who would make the first move.

It needed to be them. They knew it, and yet they were learning that knowing and doing required two separate skill sets. "Nice place you've got here."

The dam broke.

It had taken so little and so much all at once, but their friends sprang forward.

Brooke had them in a hug and Tegan clasped their arm, pulling them toward the table.

"You came inside," Gillian marveled, as if they'd turned water into wine.

Brooke stepped back. "I didn't even think about that. I was just so happy you're not gone again. I worried you could be anywhere in the world by now, but instead you came here."

"Yeah, well, I thought about going a lot of places. I even had the first cab take me to the border."

"The first cab?" Tegan asked.

"There've been several today. The second one took me back across town to the hospital."

"Oh God," Gillian mumbled. "She finally drove you into a therapist's office."

"She doesn't have that power over me anymore." Sawyer saw the horrified look on all their faces and rushed to clarify. "No, she's not dead. Shit. Let me start over. My mother is out of surgery. It went well. I was with her much of the night and all morning, but she just slept."

Brooke let out a sigh of relief. "Probably the best outcome anyone could hope for."

They nodded, still hating that their mother's lack of consciousness constituted a win, but they didn't want to linger there, because they couldn't help noticing Robin hadn't gotten up from her chair when the others did. Sawyer's need overwhelmed their fear, and they finally let themself look at her.

Robin sat in an office chair, knees pulled up to her chest, and her arms wrapped around them. They recognized their own hoodie and sweatpants hanging loosely from her frame, along with the dark circles under her red-rimmed eyes. Still, Robin managed a weak smile and a tentative shrug. Both her appearance and demeanor were such a drastic departure from the woman who'd shaken them from their own trauma last night. Sawyer suffered a staggering pang of regret, and their resolve faltered again.

If this was the legacy of their lack of fortitude, it might've been more merciful to make a clean break.

They shook their head. Robin didn't need mercy. She needed them to show up. "I, um, I'm sorry for so much. Maybe being here isn't the right thing. It's your place of work, and I probably broke a rule by invading a safe place, but the only other thing I know how to do is run, and I'm trying not to do that."

Brooke opened her mouth, but Gillian placed a hand on her arm, and she closed it again.

Sawyer got the message. This was their time to sink or swim, so they jumped in. "Robin, you told me once that you very often don't understand why people act the way they do or make the choices they make or value the things they value." They tried to smile but suspected it came out lopsided. "You also said you find humans wildly unpredictable and illogical, and that they regularly work against their own best interests, so I'm here to say I'm guilty as charged on all counts."

Robin continued to watch them, very still and alert, like an animal who'd been hurt but remained curious.

"I'm a mess. I know you see that, and have probably always seen it, because you see me better than any person ever has. I found you impossible to believe because it didn't make sense that anyone who ever saw me fully could still want to move toward me. I've always been taught I had to choose between being myself and being accepted. I'm sorry it took so much scratching and clawing and fighting to make me see that's who you are, what you do. I hope I didn't wait too long or break too much along the way, because I'm asking you to do it one more time, to meet me right here and right now … in the middle of all this mess, which I made, in case that wasn't abundantly clear to everyone."

Robin seemed to steel herself, lifting her chin and exhaling a long, slow breath before nodding. Extending her legs and leaning forward with great effort, she folded her arms on the table. "What do you need?"

Sawyer wanted to weep. It wasn't exactly a warm welcome, but it wasn't a rejection either. "As much as I know I probably need to say something to everyone here at some point, I'd like to talk to you first, alone."

Robin lifted one shoulder and one eyebrow, part question, part challenge. "I mean, you can if you'd like to step into my office."

"Yeah, I deserve that." Sawyer laughed lightly. "And okay, sure. I think I'm finally ready."

Robin cracked a wry smile and turned to Gillian. "This is it, right? The plane door?"

Gillian folded her hands and steepled her fingers in front of her lips. "You're looking at it. Want me to land safely, or do you want to pull the cord?"

Robin seemed to consider the question while Sawyer waited without fully understanding until she finally pushed herself up from the table. "Maybe keep it running while I take a peek at what's outside?"

Gillian nodded, and Robin walked out of the room, leaving Sawyer to trail after her, holding their heart in their hands.

Twenty-Seven

Robin held open the door to her office and closed her eyes against the onslaught of emotions as Sawyer walked through it. They looked like shit, gray eyes sunken and their normal, perfectly feathered hair disheveled. They clearly hadn't slept or showered since Saturday, but they still smelled faintly of sandalwood, and she had to gird herself against the most sensual of sensory reactions. Thankfully, all she had to do was picture the empty spot where their bag had been on the floor to summon something equally strong and raw.

She shut the door behind them and spun toward Sawyer. "I could throttle you."

"I'm sorry."

"I know." She gritted her teeth. "And even that pisses me off, because you walked in here today all contrite and willing to do the work, and I have to respect that. You know I respect that."

"I mean, it's a lot of work. I still have a high probability of fucking things up."

"Yeah." She felt no inclination to argue or sugarcoat anything. "And I can forgive you for making honest mistakes. I can forgive you for all of it, except …"

They hung their head. "You can't forgive me for leaving."

"No." She sighed. "I can't forgive you for making such a fool out of me."

"You're not a fool."

"I didn't think so, but apparently, I am. Do you know how hard I've worked?" She shook her head. "I grew up and studied and learned to demand better for myself. I built this whole world, and it was perfect. I had everything I wanted, and I had it all on my terms, my choice, my boundaries, all me. Damn it, Sawyer, the minute that I got free of all that adolescent bullshit, I promised I'd never again let anyone else define me or make me question my worth or limit my potential or make me feel like I wasn't enough."

"You are more than enough." Sawyer stepped forward, then caught themself. "You're everything I wanted to be, pretended to be, and it scared me, but it hurts even worse to know I made you feel the way I've always felt, especially since you're the person who gave me the tools to see myself differently."

"Well, you did. You made me feel small and insignificant, and don't for a second think I don't also want to know about what you're seeing differently, because I do. I still do, and that makes me so mad I could scream. I don't want to be drawn to you to the point where I give you the power to hurt me, and I was, and then you did. Now I feel like a stupid jackass for letting you have that power over me. I have never, as an adult, allowed any other person to have that kind of control in my life."

"I'm sorry," they repeated.

"I believe you, but ultimately, half of this anger is at myself, because I have this level of self-awareness that can really suck at times. You didn't force me into any of this. I blew past all the warning signs because I wanted you that bad. Maybe a part of me wanted you because I understood the ratio of risk to reward was so high, and if so, I'll take the responsibility for my share, but I was always honest. I always met you where you were, and all I asked was for you to talk to me. No matter how I spin my own culpability, I cannot make it add up that I risked the life and the sense of self I'd built on someone who didn't think I was worthy of basic communication."

"That's not true," Sawyer said quickly. "You deserved everything I couldn't give. In fact, in my own messed up way, I left because I'm painfully aware you deserve a level of communication I'm not capable of … yet."

"Yet?" Damn them and the one little word that could keep her hanging on.

Sawyer sighed. "Communication has never not been weaponized for me."

"Never?" She pushed. "There's a room full of therapists down the hall who might disagree."

"Touché." Sawyer shook their head. "I've been entirely too thickheaded about that. I love them, but I also held them at a safe distance. In every conversation where the stakes really mattered, communication was something to be won or lost. I accumulated so many examples of why I'd never measure up that, when you tried to show me otherwise, it seemed like a speck of sand next to a mountain of contrary evidence."

"So that's it? Quantity over quality?"

"No," Sawyer said. "I realized that this morning. Standing over my mother in that hospital bed, for the first time, I really understood the contrast you worked so hard to show me. All her research and metrics and assessments over the last thirty-odd years couldn't compare to what you'd proven in two and a half months. You were right."

She folded her arms across her chest, not wanting to soften to flattery, but still wanting to hear it. "About what?"

"Everything." They laughed lightly. "However, I'm specifically referencing your assertion that you knew me better in the short span of time we've spent together than my mother has in my entire life. You see more clearly than she ever has, and you're not the only one who handed over control, because you couldn't have seen me this clearly unless I let you, and I did."

"Why?"

"Maybe deep down I saw you, too. I recognized the ways we're the same, and I craved the ways you're different. I know you're scared to trust me. I've spent decades being afraid to trust myself, but while we're here weighing the quality of evidence, experience, and intuition, could I please make one more point?"

Robin wasn't quite sure when she'd lost the steam in this argument, or when Sawyer had picked it up, but she did want, hopelessly, to believe something, anything, they could say would have the power to undo the knowledge she'd acquired this morning and the way shame still burned like lava in her chest. "What?"

"I could walk away from anyone I ever knew, Robin. My mother, for all the barbs and claws she landed in me, could never hold me here. Brooke and Gillian, two of the best people to ever live, for all their patience and acceptance, could not tether me. Every other woman who ever caught my attention faded from my memory the moment they asked for more. I've run from every single person who's ever mattered, but I'm here right now because I could not walk away from you."

"You did. You walked out this morning. You left me."

"I *tried*. I gave it my best shot, and I'm sorry for that, but now we both know. I don't have any other choice, and I don't want it any other way."

Her heart ached in a new way, not tightening or shrinking, but expanding to press against the guards she'd started to build around it. "What do you want?"

"I want to believe in you. I want to believe in us. I want to believe everything you said could be true, that we can withstand the heat, because I'm melting under it right now. I want to believe that, even though neither of us has ever been anything close to relationship material, what we're feeling for each other is enough to erupt and form new ground."

She sighed. "It's really unfair of you to take my words and use them in equally meaningful ways."

Sawyer stepped close and reached for her hand.

She let them take it.

"I tried running. It didn't work. Maybe it never has, or maybe we already made new ground. Maybe it started the minute we melted into each other the first time, but I'm here now because I have to be, and because I want to be. I want to

313

stand in this thing we're making and plant seeds in it, and when we get too big or too fluid or too scared or out of control, I want to blow our tops again and keep making more."

"What if we're bad at it?" Robin asked. "What if we try and we get burned?"

Sawyer pulled her close. "Then we'll crumble and start stoking another fire from the embers. You told me I don't have to be any one thing. We can keep being all the things until we figure out how to build something that works for us."

She rested her head on their shoulder. "Do you think relationships can really work that way?"

"Hell if I know. Don't you have a degree in this stuff?"

She rolled her eyes. "It's more Brooke's area of specialty, and even if it were, I'm not your therapist."

They smiled. "I think you may've mentioned that before."

"It's a pretty good point. I'm not neutral, and I've never been able to keep my distance, but even if I could, I'd say it would be terrible for you to try to be only one thing. Your whole, your extravagance, your fluidity, your expansiveness, they aren't problems to be feared or managed. They're the good stuff, they're the appeal, they're the everything."

Sawyer nuzzled into her neck, and their bodies molded together. "Please, let me stay."

"Ugh." She afforded herself the comfort of being held. "Fine, you can stay. I want you to. Gillian got to me. Well, all of them did."

"'Got to you' how?"

"We have to sit down for this part." Robin backed them toward her office couch. "I have some terrible news."

Sawyer's gray eyes clouded over, and they clutched both her hands in theirs as they sat together. "What's wrong?"

"Apparently, I'm normal."

Sawyer's brow furrowed.

"Okay, maybe not normal, but what I'm experiencing is normal. I ignored the signs because I didn't think it could happen to me. I'm strong, I'm healthy, I'm self-sufficient and

I'm self-aware. I thought I knew what I was doing. I thought I was special, but come to find out, I actually am a basic bitch."

Sawyer pressed their lips together as if trying hard not to smile.

"It's true," Robin said seriously. "I'm a basic bitch who's not immune to your considerable charms and heart and all your other charisma, because I've fallen head over heels in love with you."

"Oh. Wow."

"Yeah. I didn't see it coming either."

Sawyer didn't manage to hide their smile anymore. It radiated the kind of joy and exuberant self-assurance that had drawn her to them from the beginning. "Is the condition contagious?"

"Who knows? This is my first time."

"I ask only because I've been going through some stuff recently, too. Feels kind of like my heart is getting too big for my chest, and my pulse gets erratic. I sort of wrote it off as a run-of-the-mill case of attraction veering into lust."

Robin went along, grateful for the chance to regain some of their playfulness. "That's how mine started too, but it grew into erratic behavior and over-the-top emotional dysregulation."

"Uh-oh." Sawyer leaned a little closer. "Was it followed by an utter disinterest in doing things you'd previously done before ending in an almost chemical dependency on being with someone, even when the logical part of your brain reasoned you'd be better off on your own?"

Robin placed a hand on their forehead. "I don't know why I'm doing this. You don't feel any more feverish than I am, and even if you did, I'm not qualified to diagnose anything."

"You are," Sawyer said, "because it takes a basic bitch to recognize one. We're both suffering from the same affliction. I don't know who gave it to who, but we're both in this love boat together now."

"Yeah?"

"Pretty sure I've fallen in love with you, too," Sawyer said, and damned if Robin's heart didn't soar. "What's the treatment?"

"I don't know. Sounds like it might be terminal, or at least chronic. I fear we may have to muddle through it with everyday magic, like every other sad sack who ever lost their heart to another imperfect human."

Sawyer brushed their lips against hers. "What about kissing? Does that make it better?"

"I don't know, could risk making it worse." She reached up and ran her hand through Sawyer's hair. "Good thing we're both prone to risky behavior."

Twenty-Eight

"Don't you people ever work around here?" Sawyer stood in the doorway of the conference room once more, this time feeling like an entirely different person from the one who'd tiptoed in an hour earlier.

Tegan, Brooke, and Gillian all turned to them, expectantly.

"I tried not to think too much about what y'all did at work," Sawyer continued, "but I sort of imagined there'd be clients involved."

Gillian rolled her eyes. "We called them all off for the morning. Even therapists need a mental health day when the people they love most in the world put them through the wringer."

"Yeah, about that …" They rubbed a hand over the back of their neck for a minute, trying to massage away the tension they didn't want to rebound despite having one more hard thing to do.

"Where's Robin?" Tegan asked.

"She needed a minute," Sawyer said, then noting the stricken look on all their faces, rushed to add, "she said to tell you, 'go ahead and land the plane wherever you want, she already jumped.'"

Gillian sighed in relief. "Could've led with that."

"I'm still not sure what it means, but I have a feeling it's a metaphor about me. She said you got to her earlier today. Thank you."

"I didn't do it for you," Gillian said. "I take no responsibility for anything the two of you decide to do with each other, or separately."

"Good." Sawyer nodded to Robin's empty place at the table. "Can I join you for a second?"

Gillian pursed her lips together, but Brooke said, "Of course."

"Look." Sawyer took the seat and leaned forward. "I owe all of you an apology for what I put everyone through this morning, and Brooke, Gilly, I'm especially sorry for what I put you through in the years leading up to it."

"It's okay." Brooke let them off the hook too quickly.

"It's not. It was a lot of things for a lot of reasons, but nothing was okay, and there wasn't anything you could do about any of it because I wasn't in a place to let you. You two have never been anything but loving and accepting, and I hate that I couldn't accept you the same way in return. My leaving had everything to do with me and my own insecurities."

"We know." Gillian softened. "We saw what it cost you to be here."

"It shouldn't have, though. If I'd been stronger or more thoughtful or, I don't know, less defiant, I would've been able to separate you all from what I needed to fight against. I didn't know how, though. I couldn't extract who you were as people from what you did as professionals."

"You didn't have great examples on that front," Brooke offered.

"I did. I had you two, and I loved you both so much, it scared me. I'd built all these protective mechanisms against my mother, but I could never be anything but open and unguarded with you. I got scared when I started trying to really, deeply figure out who I needed to be on my own. I didn't trust myself or my own judgment. I had to go away in order to hear myself without worrying if anyone else's voice would drown out my own, the same way my mother tries to. However, the way I did it …" They shook their head and swallowed a swell of emotion. "I could've told you. I disappeared and left you worrying and wondering and thinking God knows what. I know now how unfair my choices were to you, and I'm sorry."

Gillian blew out a heavy breath. "Thank you. And you're forgiven. You were forgiven the minute you walked back through the door, but I won't lie, the explanation helps. We missed you every day."

"Every single day," Brooke affirmed, "and we talked about you. We asked each other where we thought you were. We looked for you online and asked your mother."

Sawyer grimaced. "I can't imagine how fun those conversations were."

"So bad," Brooke admitted. "We understood the need to go. We'd seen you slipping away, but you're right, we worried we could've done more, should've done more. We worried we'd gotten so caught up in starting this practice that we neglected you or grew too boring for you to stomach."

"Never," Sawyer said emphatically. "You never left me out or made me feel like an afterthought. I'm the one who put up the walls. I should've known better, or at least seen it sooner, because so many people acted like I was this whole other person when I came out, first as queer, then as nonbinary. The whole world treated me differently when I had surgery, everyone but you. The two of you just accepted me as the same person I'd always been, only now that was visible on the outside too."

"I still wish we could've been there," Gillian said. "I would've loved to have seen the moment you woke up looking like the real you."

Tears shimmered over their eyes at the depth of caring in the sentiment. "I'm sorry I robbed us of that experience. It's on me, but I'm the same me inside the body I had to fight for, and you're the same women inside careers you worked hard for. Just because you ended up in the same job as my mother doesn't mean you aren't still the people who pretended to be backup singers when the Indigo Girls played at Six Flags so we could all get backstage."

"What?" Tegan laughed. "Did you really?"

Brooke groaned.

"We're a little different now." Gillian pulled them back on track. "I don't even go to Six Flags anymore, but growing up and getting real jobs never changed the way we loved you."

"And neither did you disappearing for two years," Brooke added.

"And neither did you sleeping with Robin," Gillian said grudgingly.

"There's my cue." Robin came back in and managed to grin sheepishly for only a few seconds before letting her eyes land on Sawyer and starting to smolder again. "Who's going to Six Flags?"

"No one," Gillian said at the same time Tegan said, "Everyone."

Robin laughed, her real laugh, the one full of mischief, and another little piece of Sawyer's heart healed.

"Are we through with the emotional upheaval and metaphorical bloodletting?" Robin asked.

Everyone glanced around at each other tentatively.

"Are we going to see you tomorrow?" Gillian finally asked. "Both of you?"

"I'll be here," Robin said, then turned to Sawyer.

They pushed back from the table. "I think twice in one week is a lot of therapy office for me, but if I can go sleep for like, twelve hours, I might swing by. I'd love to see your faces a lot more regularly."

"Take-out Tuesday?" Tegan asked.

"I don't know what that is, but I'm in."

"It's a big honor," Robin explained. "You'll be our first non-therapist, but Brooke comes, so you don't have to work here. I guess we can make it a thing where we bring our ..."

"What?" Sawyer asked, standing up.

"Um, our ... Brooke is Tegan's girlfriend. You are my ..." Her cheeks flushed pink, and Sawyer got the hang-up.

"Oh, we need a label. I'm your ... let's see ... lover?"

"No," Gillian said flatly.

"You're my partner?" Robin tried, and wrinkled her nose. "Boring."

"And businesslike," Sawyer agreed as they walked around the table to join her. "I'm not a colleague or an investor. Do we need a title, or can I just be the person who fell in love with you?"

"I like that." Robin smiled. "You don't have to be anything other than exactly who you are. You're a person. My person."

Their own grin stretched so far it made their cheeks ache. "Your person. Yeah. I've tried to be a lot of things over the years, but I think becoming the person you see when you look at me might be my favorite."

Epilogue

"Surprise!"

Gillian had no more walked through the door to the waiting room before jumping right back out into the hallway.

Robin tossed a handful of confetti after her and then laughed.

"Babe, let her in." Sawyer chuckled and pulled Robin out of the way. "It's her party."

"My party?" Gillian stepped into the waiting room, looking less than thrilled with the announcement. "It's my office."

"Also, your birthday," Brooke said. "We knew you were too smart to be tricked into going out someplace tonight, so we brought the celebration to work with us."

"*My* birthday, *my* place of work. Shouldn't I get to decide to celebrate it how I want, or not at all?"

"Sorry, not sorry, boss." Tegan stepped forward, holding a cake alight with candles. "You're too lovable not to celebrate."

"Then I resolve to be less lovable in the year ahead," Gillian grumbled.

"Good luck with that," Sawyer said. "I tried awfully hard last year, kind of backfired."

Gillian looked at them, her eyes homing in on Robin's arm around their waist, and her expression softened. "Whatever's kept you here for three months could serve as a cautionary tale as easily as a ringing endorsement."

Sawyer laughed and pulled Robin closer. "You know what's kept me here, all these amazing women."

"Three months? A new record for stability!" Robin hardly found it possible that three months had flown by since she and Sawyer had officially decided to stand on the new ground they'd forged together. She would've thought she'd be bored by now, but the opposite had turned out to be true. Every day felt like a fresh adventure, though she didn't want to derail the evening by banging on about it now. "Come on, G-Money, put your lips together and blow. We all need dessert."

Gillian rolled her eyes but obliged. Once the flames were out, she squinted at the writing in the icing. "'Happy Cougar Era, Ivy League?' Let me guess who placed this order."

"Technically, I did," Sawyer admitted, "but Robin dictated the inscription."

"Shocking."

"She said I had to sign the receipt because you can't fire me," they explained. "I said you could banish me, though."

Gillian caught them tightly by the arm as Tegan whisked the cake away to cut. "If I have to stay and endure this chaos, you do, too."

"It's my pleasure." Sawyer pulled Robin closer. "Robin's, too."

"So much pleasure." Robin kissed them for emphasis and started to fall into the sensuality of that amazing mouth once more.

"Okay, okay," Brooke said quickly. "How about the presents now?"

"Brookesy," Gillian warned in a low tone, "you know how I feel about gifts."

"We do, and also your feelings on late-stage capitalism, which is why we all agreed to go with nonmaterialistic offerings to your awesomeness," Robin cut back in. "Sawyer and I decided on a choose-your-own-adventure option."

She regarded her with suspicion. Still, she eased into a chair as Tegan passed her a plate loaded with thickly frosted goodness.

"Option number one, we would like to pay for and accompany you on your first skydiving excursion."

"Absolutely not."

"Told you," Sawyer said. "You can't just jump into things like this. You gotta crank up the temperature slowly."

Robin folded her arms across her chest. She hadn't really expected her to go through with it, but she thought the boss might at least appreciate the connection to what they'd all gone through a few months ago and how far everyone had come since then. "Gillian and I like jumping metaphors. Skydiving is a guided imagery exercise come to life. It could be a real milestone moment."

"Every minute with you is a real moment," Gillian deadpanned.

"Aw thanks, boss." Robin accepted the comment as a compliment. Even if it hadn't been delivered that way, the statement still felt true. "We do have a plan B. We'd like to get tickets for the whole crew to go to a Cornell women's basketball game and let you show us the site of your former glory."

"Now you're talking, except for the 'former glory' part. I'm not that far removed from triumph. Thank you. That would give me something to really look forward to."

"Good, and you can bring a date if you want," Sawyer added.

"Very funny." She took another bite of cake.

"If you're looking for options, we have ideas," Robin piled on.

"The waitress from Cornelia looked like she'd like to serve you on a plate," Tegan suggested.

"Or the woman who delivers packages from UPS and always lingers to get your signature?" Brooke offered.

Gillian rolled her eyes. "That is literally her job."

"What about the woman from the gym who waits until you pick your treadmill every morning, then chooses the one right next to you?" Brooke prodded.

"So annoying." Exasperation crept back into her tone. "It's 6 a.m. There are plenty of open treadmills. Spread out. What is wrong with people?"

"Not really the point." Sawyer tried to pull her back. "Aren't you ready to finally lean into your fabulous forties? Play the field, knock some boots—"

"Stop." Gillian held up a hand. "Not everyone needs to pair up, and I can't believe I have to explain that to Sawyer and Robin of all people."

Robin conceded the point. Hell, she'd practically made the point for years. Just because she was deliriously happy didn't mean the shift had to make sense for everyone. "It's still super weird to me, too."

"So weird," Sawyer agreed, then locked eyes with Robin and smiled like they might be marveling at the same thought, either that or a sexy thought as they started to lean in.

Tegan cleared her throat, reminding them they weren't alone in the room just because they had eyes only for each other.

"Sorry," Robin said quickly. "We're not trying to get you wifed up. I'd just enjoy seeing you go out and rock those cougar vibes."

"Yeah," Sawyer piled on. "Maybe pounce on some hot young thing looking to learn the ropes. Brookesy, wanna give her the pointers in that department?"

Brooke shook her head as her cheeks flushed and she steadfastly refused to look at Tegan. "Not even a little bit, but I do want to give her a birthday present that I hope everyone's happy about."

Gillian's interest seemed to pique. "What's that?"

"With the new semester underway and Maura easing away from teaching and Tegan settled in, I think it might be time for me to return to the practice, slowly."

Gillian about jumped out of her chair. "Are you serious?"

"There are still details to work out," Brooke continued as Tegan beamed at her. "I'm teaching two classes, and I want to stay connected to the program going forward, but I've really missed working one-on-one with clients. I thought I might build my base back up over the next couple of months and return full-time in January, if that's okay."

Gillian hugged her. "Of course. More than okay!"

Robin's own excitement at the news bubbled over, and she wrapped her arms around them both. "We're getting the band back together."

"Damn," Sawyer said. "Now I'm extra glad I stuck around."

Gillian sighed. "I'm glad we're going to have our crew all together. It feels like a real righting of the ship."

"I agree." Tegan reached for Brooke's hand. "We're ready to get back to the good stuff."

Gillian finally took a bite of her cake and sighed happily. No sooner had she swallowed than her phone buzzed. Glancing at the screen, she frowned, handed her plate to Brooke, and headed for the door. "I have to take this."

Everyone watched her step out into the hallway, and Robin wondered if she wasn't just looking for an excuse to abandon her own party. Just because Sawyer had gotten good about staying around didn't mean Gilly wasn't still a flight risk in social situations.

"It's cool that you're coming back to work here, Brookesy," Sawyer said. "I'm glad my mother letting up her vise grip at the university freed you up to make the best decision for you."

Brooke smiled softly. "The end of an era. She's making it known to everyone who will listen that she still intends to keep up her full research load, though."

"I know. She's belabored the point to me every time I've seen her."

"I've gotten the talk, too, as well as an invitation to collaborate," Robin added. "Still not sure if that's a compliment, or a suggestion I need to up my academic rigor to be found acceptable."

"Good luck figuring that one out," Brooke said, continuing to eat her cake. "It's still weird to me that the two of you see Maura together."

"It's not like we have her over for movie nights or anything." Sawyer gave a little shiver. "But she keeps me updated and sends Robin articles she thinks she might find interesting from time to time."

"Maybe she's trying to connect the only way she knows how," Tegan offered. "Does she seem to have mellowed at all since her surgery?"

Sawyer shrugged. "Maybe she's let up a bit, or maybe I just care less now. If nothing else, she's learned she can't get away with giving me shit in front of Robin."

"What do you mean?" Robin feigned confusion even though she did suspect her presence helped keep Maura in check, though Sawyer had also gotten much stronger in their own boundaries as well, another area where they made a great team. "I give you shit all the time. It's like, my favorite hobby."

"Yeah, but I deserve what you give me. Hey, did I tell you all Robin shot me last weekend?"

Brooke and Tegan both froze, staring from Sawyer to Robin and back again.

"Not with a real gun, obviously. Paintball," Robin explained. She laughed at the memory of hitting them squarely between the shoulder blades. "You're supposed to shoot people in paintball."

"She hit me in the back at close range … and I was on her team," Sawyer said, sounding equal parts incredulous and amused.

"Uh-oh." Tegan stiffened, and Robin followed her gaze to the doorway of the waiting room where Gillian wore an expression that made her stomach tighten.

"More changes ahead." Gillian delivered the verdict as if it very much signified bad news. "The landlord rented out the office across the hall. The only detail I got was that the business is called 'Healing Touch,' and we'll have to share the waiting room with them."

Robin released her tension and smiled. In the grand scheme of things that had happened to them, new neighbors hardly ranked as a big-ticket concern. "That could be cool."

Gillian stared at her, doubt and a bit of exasperation on her face.

"Hey now." Sawyer stepped in gently. "I know it's your birthday, and you can cry if you want to, or pout, or be pissy, but change can be awesome. Look at me. I'm practically domesticated. No one ever thought I'd settle down."

"I'm not sure we share a definition of 'settle down.' You two went bungee jumping last week," Gillian said flatly. "I wanted this year to be able to settle into a routine, into a groove, into our tight-knit little group, but I get your point. If you'd told me six months ago you and Robin would both be in a steady, committed relationship, I would've asked if I should also expect to see pigs fly."

"No one's more surprised than we are." Robin wrapped her arms around Sawyer's waist, marveling for the millionth time at how well they still managed to fit together. "But that's what makes it radical. The steadiness is still new and unexpected. We're breaking the old molds every day, and that's wild. You just never know what's going to blow your mind in the best way."

"Besides," Tegan added, "'Healing Touch' has potential. Maybe it's a masseur."

"Oh, that'd get me back here faster if a massage therapist worked across the hall," Brooke mused.

"Faster than me working here?" Tegan teased.

Brooke blushed. "You also give a good massage."

"So do I." Sawyer grinned mischievously.

"It's true." Robin stared at them as all kinds of specific memories and wicked ideas rushed into her head. "The kinds one can give in a respectable office and the ones you can't … legally."

"Great," Gillian mumbled, "now we're talking about a sex worker across the hall."

"Hey, we're a shame-free office," Robin popped back. "Besides, you're single, Birthday Girl. Maybe the services Healing Touch offers could get you—"

"Could be a physical therapist," Brooke cut her off. "Or acupuncture."

"Lots of options," Tegan agreed in a placating tone.

"And does it even matter?" Sawyer asked. "There's someone new across the hall. Who cares?"

"Says the one person who doesn't work here," Gillian pointed out.

"But I'm here all the time, and so is Brooke. Clients come and go, but *you* set the tone, Gilly," they continued soothingly. "If there's anything I've learned over the last few months, it's that there's nothing more affirming than accepting people exactly as they are, right where they are, all authenticity welcome."

"Aw, baby." Robin grabbed them and kissed them hard, running her hands down their back until she cupped their ass. "You're so freaking hot when you appropriate the healthy therapist vernacular."

"Oh yeah?" Sawyer leaned close to her ear and whispered, "Boundaries, coping mechanisms, self-care."

Robin fanned herself. "Will you all excuse us please? Carry on with the party. We'll be back in twenty minutes."

Brooke scrunched up her face. "Am I going to have to get used to them having sex in Robin's office all the time when I come back?"

"Not all the time," Robin said coyly. "Sometimes we use your office."

Tegan laughed. "It's not like we haven't all done it."

"No," Gillian shot back. "I've never had sex in any of your offices."

"But be honest." Sawyer nudged her. "Have you ever had sex in yours?"

She opened her mouth to deny the charge, then stopped as her cheeks flushed. "It's my birthday. I'm allowed to plead the Fifth."

Everyone lost their minds en masse.

Laughing, yelling, talking all at once, they bombarded her.

"Wait? When? Who? Why haven't we heard the story?" Brooke seemed particularly scandalized, but Gillian held her ground.

"Sorry, but after everything you four have put me through over the last year and a half, and with the prospect of more change on the horizon, I feel more convinced than ever that my primary function in this office and this friend group is to be the last woman standing with a healthy sense of boundaries and the ability to hold them no matter what."

The conversation turned to chaos once more, but Robin found herself calm in the heart of it. Shaking her hair from her eyes, she stared at Sawyer as they laughed, bold and bright and unencumbered.

"What?" Sawyer asked when they finally caught her watching.

"Nothing," she said, then shaking her head, realized that wasn't the right answer at all. "Actually, nothing with you is ever nothing, and I love it."

Sawyer arched an eyebrow. "Love what?"

Robin pulled them close once more. "That every minute we're together is always full of everything."

Acknowledgements

Those of us who write, either for a living or from a deeper compulsion to create, often quip that doing so is cheaper than therapy. To be clear, no one I know argues that writing is more effective than therapy, so much as most of us see the two processes as being deeply related. I'm not sure that's ever been truer than it was with this book. To my mind, the human desire to be seen and valued in our wholeness is central to both good mental health practices and good sapphic fiction. It seemed only natural for me to use this genre I love to explore those deepest of human desires, so that is what I tried to do with Sawyer and Robin's romance, and I hope you take a little of the same from reading their story. I'd never be so bold as to call this work therapeutic for anyone other than myself, but if you've ever struggled to accept your everything as being worthy of acceptance, love, or the right to live your truth in fullness, I want you to know you are as entitled to your own happiness as these characters are to theirs. I believe in you every much as I believe in them. I believe in all of us.

A big reason I can hold that belief so securely is that so many people have modeled it for me, and I am deeply grateful for every one of them. Because I'm here using fictional therapists as my imaginary friends, it seems like a good idea to start by thanking a couple of real therapists who've never once made me feel bad about talking to them about the aforementioned imaginary friends. Leah Eagan has done a beautiful job of affirming both my own sense of self and my sense of connection to these characters as well as detangling the places where my insecurities on both counts got conflated. I'm not sure there'd be a finished product without those sessions, so thank you. Ashera Derosa not only served as expert reader again on this one to lend authenticity to my characters' voices and vernacular, she also spent hours wandering around Elmwood Village and ducking down every rabbit hole our brains could find. Thank you for all your "Hell yes" energy.

I'm also grateful for the faith my amazing production team of professionals continues to offer me. My beta readers, Barb and Toni, continue to be my earliest and most enthusiastic readers. Without them I'm not sure where I'd get the confidence to keep putting my characters out there. Thank you to Lynda Sandoval, who is so into this series she's ready for the two of us to go to co-therapy together, partially so we can better support these characters, and partially because she thinks it would be hilarious to edit me with an audience…she is correct on both counts. Thank you for being one of the only people I'd feel safe enough to even consider something like this with. Avery Brooks continues to be a steady and affirming hand at the copy edit stage of the process. I am grateful for her ability to focus on the details of the trees I so often miss when looking at the proverbial forest…and also loving motorcycles. Thank you Ann McMan, who not only gave me a beautiful cover, but also sat with me in some moments of real vulnerability as I processed through way more than she probably bargained for. My proofers, Victoria Black, Jules Revel, Diane Nixon, Monna Herring, and Lyn Cathony-Rork, are the last line of defense, and I cannot thank them enough for catching the entire page-worth of things that somehow manages to sneak past a full battalion of professionals.

With this book I have some familiar names to thank in new ways. As you may or may not have noticed, *Relationship Material* is the first book I've ever published fully under my own imprint, Bigger Table Books. In that sense it would be appropriate to say this is my first attempt at self-publishing, but thanks to Caroyln and Susan at Brisk Press, I didn't actually have to do any of this by myself. Their kindness, generosity and patience in teaching me this business over the last seven years is impossible to quantify, and I will spend the rest of my career trying to thank them adequately.

So too have my friends and colleagues supported this wild attempt to learn, grow, and take responsibility for my own work both in the arena of craft and on the business side of publishing. Marcie Lukach sat at my table and helped me file all the paperwork to form an LLC. It's not an exaggeration to say there would be no Bigger Table Books without her willingness to share her expertise. Writing friends Jenn, Virginia, Susan, Georgia, Mila, and Nikki have all acted as sounding boards, cheerleaders and trusted confidants. Anna Burke has taken several wandering and emotional phone calls from me curled up in my hammock, and Melissa Brayden graciously shared both her excitement and research when I was entirely too overwhelmed to process on my own. My Patreon members have given both their money and their enthusiasm at every step along the way, as I often turn to them first and most fully when standing on the brink of something new or looking for the courage to take that leap. And Will Banks is ever the best Big Papi. He got up early to take Jackson to school just this morning so I could sit in a wifi-free zone and knock this out.

And while there would be no book without everyone listed above, there would be no stories worth telling if not for the two people who make all the adventures worth having. Thank you, Jackson, for continuing to serve as my model for people who manage to be everything all at once. Sports, theater, school, and music (welcome to the Renaissance), you do it all, but please never forget that while I stand in awe of your many talents, it is your kindness I am most proud of. To Susie, the heart of every project worth pursuing, the work you continue to do every day inspires me to do my own. Your steady quest to learn and grow has pulled me forward through some of the hardest conversations and soul-searching I've ever done. I know I'm supposed to believe in me because I'm worthy all on my own, but I still don't know how I'd ever do it without your willingness to meet me right where I am, in the midst of our everything, every day. The version of myself I like best is the one I see reflected in your eyes.

To my creator, redeemer, sanctifier, and giver of everything I am grateful for, *soli deo gloria.*

ALSO BY RACHEL SPANGLER

Learning Curve
Trails Merge
LoveLife
Spanish Heart
Does She Love You
Heart of the Game
Perfect Pairing
Edge of Glory
In Development
Love All
Spanish Surrender
Fire & Ice
Straight Up
Thrust
Heartstrings
Christmas Mouse
Seeking Approval
Quiver
Informed Consent

THE ENGLISH ROMANCES
Full English
Modern English
Plain English

THE DARLINGTON ROMANCES
The Long Way Home
Timeless
Close to Home

About the Author

Rachel Spangler never set out to be a *New York Times*-reviewed author. They were just so poor during seven years of college that they had to come up with creative forms of cheap entertainment. Their debut novel, *Learning Curve,* was born out of one such attempt. Since writing is more fun than a real job and so much cheaper than therapy, they continued to type away, leading to the publication of twenty-six sapphic romance novels. Now a four-time Lambda Literary Award finalist, an IPPY, Goldie, and Rainbow Award winner, and the 2018 Alice B. Reader recipient, Rachel plans to continue writing as long as anyone, anywhere, will keep reading.

In 2018 Spangler joined the Bywater Books substantive editing team and worked their way up to the rank of senior romance editor. They now proudly offer substantive editing services for private clients and love having the opportunity to mentor young authors. In 2025 they founded their own publishing LLC called Bigger Table Books to further embody their commitment to creating safe and inclusive spaces to tell queer stories.

Known to friends as Rey, Spangler lives in Western New York with wife, Susan and son, Jackson. Their family spends the long winters curling and skiing. In the summer, they love to travel and watching their beloved St. Louis Cardinals. Regardless of the season, Rachel always makes time for a good romance, whether reading it, writing it, or living it.

For more information, visit Rachel online at www.rachelspangler.com or on Instagram, Facebook, Twitter, or Patreon.

www.ingramcontent.com/pod-product-compliance
Lightning Source LLC
Chambersburg PA
CBHW030243120726
47903CB00005B/1597